MIDNIGHT DELUXE

Stories
by
Michael Subjack

Table of Contents

Rerouted

Too fucking broke to fly. The bitter mantra repeated in Callie's head as she drove through the empty Western New York landscape. The day was gloomy and overcast. One could assume based on her sour demeanor that this suited Callie's mood perfectly, but it didn't.

"It would have to be fucking black outside for that to happen," she said to no one in particular. Too fucking broke to fly. There it was again. Callie did her best to refocus her thoughts. This was supposed to be a joyous occasion.

She went to the memories of college with the girls (now women) she had spent those formative years with. When she had arrived as a freshman, Callie had a head full of frizzy hair and an army of stuffed animals on her bed. Her new roommate Sandy was quick to point out that boys wouldn't find the site of pink teddy bears very becoming. Sandy knew how to act, dress, and speak in a way Callie, a certified band geek and Disney aficionado, didn't.

Despite them being polar opposites, the two became inseparable and Sandy began schooling her in the ways of proper college girl behavior. By Thanksgiving, Callie's stuffed animal army had been retired to a storage container under her bed and her formerly frizzy hair was now a flowing mane that made her look like Jennifer Aniston (or so Sandy said). The pair fell in with four other girls in their dorm and by sophomore year, they were all living together. The rest of Callie's time there was a blur of exams, textbooks, and papers but the real focus was on the "finer things." That was Sandy's term for the non-academic aspects of college life.

The finer things included weekends (and some weeknights) of make-up, tube tops, dollar shots, and mini-pitchers at the various homes and establishments on and around campus. These activities came to define the Sass Squad's (Sandy's suggestion) collegiate experience. Callie was frankly shocked when she managed to pull a GPA of 3.4 when all was said and done. There were boys but they mainly went with Sandy. Pretty Sandy. Fun Sandy. Sandy who would get a high-paying advertising job right out of school, allowing the good times to continue. Cuervo shots became Martinis and her current crop of brief conquests now wore Armani instead of Gap. And she had the stream of social media posts to prove it, at least until four months ago when Sandy met Steve, the handsome day trader. The romance was brief and the engagement happened quickly. And why not? Callie and Sandy, the only holdouts in the group, were on the wrong side of thirty now. You had to settle down eventually. At least that's how Sandy rationalized it in an email, followed by the all-too-polite and dutiful "So how are things with you?" inquiry.

How was Callie doing? Unemployed? Check. Unable to make payment on two maxed-out credit cards, in addition to her outstanding student loans? Check. She had learned to shut her phone off during business hours to avoid the persistent calls from her lenders and creditors. And how about her living situation? Were things so bad she had to move back in with her parents? You bet.

"I'm doing just peachy, thanks for asking," she said again to no one in particular. Sandy wanted to know if Callie would be a bridesmaid. Could she be a bridesmaid? After her parents lent her money for the dress and the shoes, she could absolutely be a bridesmaid. If she came to Chicago for the weekend and stayed at the Hilton where Sandy and Steve had a block of rooms set aside, she'd get a discount by mentioning their name. That was possible as well, but only after withdrawing from the ATM at The Mommy and Daddy Bank of America. Now it was just an issue of actually getting there. After careful calculation (something her Dad knew very well), he found that driving, even with exorbitant gas prices, would be cheaper than flying by thirty-five dollars. A penny saved, indeed.

So here she was, driving to Chicago to face old friends happier and more successful than her. It didn't seem unfair (they were all hardworking and intelligent) but that didn't stop it from being any less painful. Callie had debt she could no longer handle and her dreams of library science were no more or at least severely on hold. Jesus, had library science truly become her dream? She didn't know but it paid well enough and had an enjoyable atmosphere. When it came to an unceremonious end eight months ago, Callie took it in stride. She'd find something else.

Yet here she was with no job and seven hours to go before she reached Chicago. Aside from her phone in GPS mode, her only company was the mantra that repeated in her head, ad nauseam. Too fucking broke to fly. This was going to be a fun weekend.

The hours and miles passed with numb efficiency and Callie was now in Ohio. She thought of something her friend Hal had said during the 2004 election.

"Can we just pave over that fucking state and start over?" he had exclaimed with a Keystone Light clutched in his hand.

It made her laugh then but now it was just a mildly pleasant memory. She looked at the waning daylight before examining her surroundings. She wouldn't be missing much once it got dark. It would be after midnight before she got to Chicago. Her parents would call it bad planning and Callie would agree. It was bad planning. And it seemed like she had a lifetime of practice with it.

As day continued its crawl into night, she entered Indiana and noticed she was down to two bars on her fuel gauge. This was hardly a cause for concern for most people but Callie didn't like her car being anywhere near empty, especially on long trips. She saw a sign for a Mobile station up ahead and decided that would do. As she pulled into the rest stop, she noticed most of the other vehicles were trucks and that was to be expected, especially at night. Sharing the highway with trucks always gave Callie comfort. Those guys were in their own world and that allowed Callie to be alone in hers. It was a luxury few others would give you.

Callie looked at her phone, which still had the directions to Chicago on it. She wondered if she should text her mother and Sandy with an update but that would entail clicking out of the map, sending the text, and then bringing the map back up. That seemed like an awful lot of work at this point, so she let it go. As she swiped her debit card at the pump, she was startled by a voice behind her.

"Can I help you?"

Callie turned to see an unassuming-looking young man in a gray, oil-stained work shirt. The name "Dustin" was embroidered in red on the left breast. He kept a respectful distance as he waited for her answer. Normally, her answer would immediately be "No" but swiping her debit card had seemingly triggered something else: Callie had to pee. Badly. Welcome back, Coke Zero.

"Hello?" Dustin asked, interrupting her thoughts.

"I think I've got it," she said as she went for the pump. Could she really leave her car alone with this guy? The better question was could she keep what seemed like a gallon of urine in her bladder from exploding everywhere in the next thirty seconds.

She scanned the gas station and saw an older man pulling up in a pickup truck, as well as a younger couple in a hatchback wearing matching vests (adorable). She wasn't alone, which was good news, as the urge to pee was quickly giving way to desperation.

She decided he couldn't do much damage with an audience present, so she called out to him as he walked away.

"Actually, if you don't mind," she said. Dustin turned around and came back. Thank God. Her teeth were floating now.

"Sure thing. Unleaded?" he asked, reaching for the pump.

"Please," Callie answered. "And do you have a bathroom?"

"Head into the store and take a right. Can't miss it." Dustin replied, pointing inside the station.

Callie nodded and hurried inside, not realizing this seemingly innocuous young man had just selected her. Dustin admired his choice as she disappeared into the store. Not too shabby. And to think it almost didn't come to pass. If she hadn't called him back over, her evening would be ending very differently.

He peered inside her car and took note of the phone stuck to the windshield in a plastic holder. Her GPS was up and running. She'd be perfect.

As Dustin was finishing up, Callie came back outside. He had already deposited the chlorine tablets into her gas tank but it wouldn't have mattered if she were there or not. He was discreet.

"Long trip?" he asked as he replaced the pump.

"Not too bad, just headed to Chicago for a friend's wedding," she replied.

"Well, drive safe," he told her with a broad smile. Callie reached into her pocket to tip him but Dustin gave her a dismissive wave.

"Not necessary. Have yourself a good night," he said as he headed back to the store. Callie got back in her car and started it up. Had he even bothered with the other customers? She supposed Dustin only went full service for the ladies. How sweet. No tip, though? That seemed strange to her but maybe it was company policy. Shitty policy, she decided as she pulled back onto the highway.

Dustin looked out the window as she drove off. He took out his phone and sent a quick text to the necessary parties: "Black Chevy Caprice, going to Chicago, topped off the tank." And that was it. "Topped off the tank" was their code for the chlorine tablets that would dissolve in her gas tank and ruin her engine within the hour.

The timing wasn't the best, as his shitheel boss was making him work late tonight but you had to take advantage of an opportunity when it presented itself, especially with that ass. He just hoped the fun wasn't over before he had a chance to get there. He hated when that happened.

As she got a few miles down the road, Callie's GPS decided to speak up. It startled her, as she hadn't heard a peep out of it since Pennsylvania. Using her GPS was mainly something she did to appease her mother (and admittedly herself) but she hadn't expected to need it until she got outside the city. Getting to Chicago was a straight shot on I-90 West until then. What could it possibly want now?

"Recalculating," it stated. Callie looked at the screen and saw it bringing up new directions.

"In a tenth of a mile, take Exit 35 and turn right," it clarified. Callie didn't get it. Was there construction up ahead? An accident? Callie couldn't see any lights but she supposed the GPS knew something she didn't. Exit 35 loomed closer and she had only a few seconds to make her decision. All things considered, it was an easy one to make.

"Don't you dare lead me astray, you bitch!" she exclaimed before taking Exit 35. Life had a way of presenting you with the unexpected. For months Callie had hoped and prayed for a job to present itself. Would doing that really make it unexpected? Callie supposed not but she had more pressing matters to attend to right now.

"God help you if we end up anywhere but Chi-town," she told her phone. It glowed back at her, promising a route that was not only new but also three minutes shorter. Maybe her luck was turning around after all. She was quick to scoff at this idea, though. Fat fucking chance something like that would happen.

Exit 35 brought her to a road the GPS reminded her to take a right at. When she did that, she saw only an inky black void ahead of her. Did she still want to do this? Then she remembered Sandy telling her on a Skype session that part of Callie's problem was that she wasn't much of a risk-taker.

"Don't be afraid to show up to places without an appointment. Demand an interview!" Sandy had said, stopping to sip wine that probably cost more than Callie's shoes.

"Does that really work?" Callie asked. Sandy gave her an incredulous look in response. "Going places I'm not invited to is like ninety percent of my job, babe!"

And with that memory, Callie pressed on the gas and drove into the darkness. It was pathetic that this qualified as an adventure but it had been a rough few months. Callie was going to take what she could get.

After fifteen minutes of twists and turns, Callie started to think this might actually qualify as an adventure, even by normal people's standards. Should she turn around and head back to the highway? She would lose half an hour at this point. Although slightly worried, Callie pressed on.

"El riesgo siempre vive!" she exclaimed. Luck favors the bold and Callie was feeling bolder than she had in years. This was uncharted territory and she'd have an anecdote to at least temporarily deflect all the inevitable "So how are things going right now?" questions that would plague her throughout the weekend. She'd make Dustin a lonely creep who had awkwardly flirted with her. What would the harm in that be? Everybody exaggerates. Did Sandy really spend the majority of her time negotiating with people who didn't want to deal with her? With those legs and that smile, Callie seriously doubted it.

Callie thought it best not to dwell on Sandy's good fortune during the weekend of her wedding. Bad feelings had a way of eking out, especially in the presence of alcohol.

Suddenly, her engine seized up and her dashboard was filled with symbols she didn't recognize. Panic swept over her as she realized her car had completely shut down. She pulled it over and turned the key but the car wouldn't respond. It was dead. Callie angrily ripped the phone from its holder. Somebody was at fault for this and it certainly wasn't her.

"You cunt!" she spat at it. Her phone flashed her "Signal Lost" in response. At this moment, it was the worst thing she could imagine.

"No!" Callie screamed, her eyes widening.

She went to her home screen but the signal was indeed lost. The wave of panic that hit her was coming very close to consuming her completely. No car and no phone? What was she going to do?

And that was when she saw the headlights in the distance. She needed help but was this it? A million horror movie scenarios ran through her mind as the headlights came closer. She expected it to be a hulking, rusty pick-up truck. Should she flag it down if it was? Would that mean ending up in a ditch somewhere? She presented herself with countless hypotheticals as the vehicle (an older Jeep. That at least beat a rusty pick-up truck) passed her. It slowed down and pulled off to the side of the road about twenty feet behind her. She was soaked in sweat and her heart was racing so fast she could feel it pulsing in the back of her throat.

She looked in her rearview mirror and saw the door swing open. Thick, stubby legs clad in well-worn denim emerged and work boots hit the ground as her potential rescuer exited the Jeep. Callie could only see the silhouette of this (hopefully) Good Samaritan as they slowly ambled toward her car. Her mom had offered to get her pepper spray years ago and Callie deemed it unnecessary. Now she felt stupid and helpless in what was becoming a marathon of it.

Callie tried to keep it together but she only imagined the worst until a meaty fist knocked on her window. She opened it a crack and her prospective savior knelt down so she could see his face. It was weathered with red-rimmed eyes. And was that booze she smelled? Perfect.

"Trouble?" he inquired, raising an eyebrow as he said it. He also had some teeth missing. Her new friend was just full of surprises.

"It just stopped," Callie replied.

"Any idea what's going on?" he asked her. "Not out of gas or anything?"

"I just filled up," she said. "And my dad checked it before I left, so there shouldn't be anything wrong with it!"

"Well, this in an older car, so good intentions don't always guarantee good performance. I'd tell you to pop the hood but I actually don't know a whole hell of a lot about cars," he said. "Gonna call for a tow?"

"Probably," she answered a little too quickly.

"So you've got reception? I never get any out here. This is God's country," he said with a knowing look.

"Yeah, this is a really good phone," she said, knowing full well it didn't sound even remotely convincing.

"Well, if you don't feel like waiting, I can give you a lift to a service station on the highway. Probably set you back an hour or two," he offered.

She wondered if the service station on the highway he was referring to was the Mobile she filled up at. That meant seeing Dustin again or possibly his Sunoco equivalent. For some reason, this made her laugh.

"Something funny?" he asked.

"No, I'm sorry, it's just been a long night," Callie said. It was as good an explanation as any.

"So what's it going to be? I can give you a ride or I can make a call when I get home and send somebody out here for you. Don't know when they'll get here, though. You might be in for an even longer night," he warned, blasting a snot rocket as he finished.

Seeing this made Callie nauseous. She didn't handle bodily functions of any kind very well but she needed to make a decision. Staying out here alone meant she wouldn't just lose a couple of hours; she'd lose damn near the entire next day. Good-bye, rehearsal dinner. Did she really want to take a ride with this guy, though? He boorishly scratched his crotch and she decided she did not.

"It's okay," she said, trying to keep the conversation amiable.

"It's okay you want a ride with me or okay you don't?" he asked, narrowing his eyes.

"Okay I don't. No offense intended," she replied.

"Well, I'd feel awful bad leavin' you behind. The name's Clem. I ain't such a bad guy," he said with a friendly smile. No, this wasn't a smile at all. It was a leer.

"You can just go, I'll be fine. My friends texted me and said they're on their way to pick me up!" she responded, her voice going up a few octaves. She wasn't freaking out yet but she was close.

"You ain't even looked at your phone. Why are you bein' strange? I'm tryin' to help you!" Clem shot back, shoving her car. This was not going well.

"Please don't do that!" she said in an attempt to sound assertive. Why didn't she say yes to that pepper spray?

"My old lady's got dinner waitin' for me and you got the fuckin' nerve to jerk me around when I offer to give you a hand?"

He was yelling now and Callie was running out of things to say. How aggressive would this guy get? Callie didn't want to find out and when another set of headlights appeared in the distance, she thought it was one of the most beautiful sights she had ever seen.

Although still angry, Clem backed off as the car pulled up. It was a slick, new BMW. Relief fell over Callie as it pulled up next to them. The window opened with a soft whirring sound, revealing a face that was young and pleasant.

"Everything okay?" Pleasant Face inquired.

"Car just stopped working," Callie sputtered. Pleasant Face looked at her with blue eyes (nice ones) behind glasses that belonged to either a lawyer or a computer programmer. Callie was almost sure of it.

"Do you have help coming?" he asked her.

"I don't have any reception right now," Callie replied.

Pleasant Face checked his phone. "Me neither. Do you want a ride to a gas station?"

Was that a serious question? Callie wanted to be anywhere but here. She cast a look at Clem, who hadn't said a word since her new rescuer had arrived.

"That would be great. Thank you!" she announced. Pleasant Face smiled and motioned for her to get in. Callie got out of her car and walked as far away from Clem as she could. He stayed quiet until she opened the door to get into Pleasant Face's car.

"Yeah, you can take a ride with him but not me. Fat guy in the old Jeep's nothing but trouble, right?" Clem asked, adjusting his grimy overalls at the crotch.

Callie said nothing and got in the BMW. Pleasant Face pulled forward, leaving the baleful-looking Clem behind in a wash of red lights.

As they drove away, Callie wondered if he would do anything to her car. It was a possibility but one she let sit distant in her mind. She was just grateful to be alive as she rode along in Pleasant Face's warm BMW.

She discreetly ran her hands over the leather seat. This could have ended much worse. Oh yes, this could have been a fucking disaster. She looked at Pleasant Face gratefully.

"Callie," she said.

"Matt," he offered in return. "So what was going on back there?"

Callie groaned. "He was the first person to stop. He seemed okay at first but then he got really creepy really fast!"

"The heavyset redneck was creepy?" Matt said, feigning surprise. "I never!" Callie laughed at this. It was the perfect icebreaker.

"Water?" he inquired. "I've got some in a cooler in the back seat." Water sounded perfect. Her mouth was dry and tasted sour.

"Please," she answered.

"Help yourself," he said and Callie reached into the backseat, popping open the small blue cooler and removing a bottle of water.

"So what are you doing out this way?" she asked Matt as she cracked open the water and took a big sip.

"I do computer repair work," he answered. "So I'm on the road all the time." Callie took another look at the BMW. She figured something like that paid well but not this well.

"So I was close then," she offered.

"I'm sorry?"

"I took you for a computer programmer," she finished as she downed some more water.

"Well, I do a little bit of that, too. That's where the real money is," he said. And that explained the BMW.

"So have you done anything I'd be familiar with?" she asked. Clem's leer was still fresh in her mind and this conversation, even if it was cliché and banal, was a welcomed alternative.

"Maybe, but you don't want to hear about any of it."

"Why not?"

"Because it's really fucking boring!" he exclaimed and there was more laughter. As it subsided, Callie started to feel a little dizzy. She decided this had been a pretty exhausting affair. She'd just have to load up on caffeine and sugar before she hit the road again.

"Let's talk about you," Matt said. Here it was. This wasn't a topic Callie wanted to discuss at all but what could she say to the man who had rescued her from certain roadside doom? Still, she wished the conversation would go anywhere else. How many people needed to know she was unemployed and living with her parents at her age? Luckily, Matt seemed to pick up on that. Thank you, not-so-internal monologue.

"Is getting accosted by greasy men after breaking down in the middle of nowhere a common occurrence for you?" he asked. Odd question but it beat where the conversation was headed.

"First time," Callie answered back with a forced smile that she partially concealed with another sip of water.

"Well, it's tough to get a pretty girl in your car," he said, his tone becoming cryptic. "There's no coercion that works these days."

Panic started to creep up her spine. Why did this have to get weird? He drove a nice car and had equally nice eyes. Why couldn't he just be normal? Then the panic gave way to more dizziness and a heavy feeling of fatigue.

"Because getting them to your car isn't the problem. You wouldn't believe how easy it is to hijack a GPS signal," he said.

"What are you talking about?" Callie slurred. She sounded drunk. She wished she were drunk. This felt so much worse.

"I told you I'm a computer programmer. Did you really think your GPS changed directions on its own?" he asked with a smile. No, it wasn't a smile. It was a leer, just like the one Clem gave her. Callie struggled to stay awake but it was a losing battle. Matt pressed a switch on the steering wheel and her seat started to recline.

"Yeah, it's real tough to get a pretty girl in your car without forcing her," he continued. "Because if you force her, you risk leaving behind all kinds of evidence. That's why you need someone completely gauche like Clem to make the first pass. Compared to him, I'm Channing fucking Tatum!"

Callie wanted to jump out but her muscles went limp and her head felt like it weighed a hundred pounds. Her seat was completely reclined now. Matt held up a hypodermic needle and waved it in front of her face.

"I'm just glad you took the water. Sticking you girls with this is always such a chore!" She tried to open her mouth to respond but it was too late. Darkness overtook her and she was out.

When Callie came to, she found herself handcuffed to a large pipe. To make matters worse, her pants were missing. The floor consisted of cold concrete and when she looked around, she saw the entire space looked just as cold and almost barren. Fluorescent lights buzzed above her. Was this a warehouse?

"Welcome back, bright eyes," a familiar voice said. She turned to her left and saw Matt seated at a scuffed metal table and he wasn't alone. Clem sat across from him; giving her the same leer he had earlier.

"I hope you don't mind us taking your pants off but you pissed in them while you were asleep," Matt stated matter-of-factly. "Don't be embarrassed, others have done much worse."

The location of her pants was the last thing on her mind at this point. Matt stood up and scrapped his chair across the floor to get closer to her. He held up a medium-sized black box with an LCD screen on it.

"My own invention," he announced holding it in front of her. On the screen were numerous maps, divided into rows. The movement on each map confirmed these were live GPS signals. "I just push a few buttons and I've got you going wherever I want. Another push of a button and you don't have a cell phone signal. Pretty cool, right?" he said, sounding like a kid on Christmas morning. "I hope you don't mind me showing it off but it's not exactly something I can patent, so you're pretty much my only audience for it. Lucky you," he finished with a laugh before setting it down.

Then he just stared at her. The still-groggy Callie did her best to look small by tucking her legs back and looking away from him but it was no use. He reached out and slowly turned her head around until she faced him.

"That phone I dumped a few miles back was old and beat-to-shit. Are you going through a little bit of a rough patch right now?" he asked with mock sympathy.

"Not to mention that fuckin' car," Clem piped up. "What junk sale did you get that heap from?" Like she'd give him an answer. Like he wanted an answer. And he didn't but Matt was a different story. He leaned in and gave her a hard look with those blue eyes she thought had seemed so nice at first.

"My friend asked you a question, bitch. Are you going to answer him?" he asked, leaning in even closer. Callie answered him but it was quiet. Matt was so close now she could feel his hot breath against her face.

"I didn't catch that?" he whispered to her.

"I said fuck you," she finally managed, clenching her jaw as she said it. Matt let this soak in before grinning at her. It was almost disarming. But then he brought his fist in, prompting a fresh wave of blinding pain. She looked down to see blood dripping on the concrete from her newly broken nose.

"Look at me," he commanded but Callie could only shiver in response. "I said look at me, bitch!" Callie stayed still. She knew another punch was coming. And she was right, only this time it was a blow to her jaw, causing her teeth to crunch together. She decided maybe it was best to look up and when she did, she saw Matt undoing his pants.

"This is fucking pointless. It's always fucking pointless! You try to talk to these bitches and they look at you like you're some fucking dog that pissed all over the floor!" he ranted. Callie thought he might be addressing Clem but the maniacal look in his eyes suggested otherwise. His pants were off and he was sliding down his underwear. Callie turned away again. It was only going to get worse from here. He grabbed her legs and tried to straighten them. She fought as best she could, knowing full well it was a futile gesture.

The next step was ripping off her urine-stained panties and with that, he was inside her. Clem followed after Matt was finished. It seemed to go on forever. When it was over, they had either drugged her again or she had just passed out. Either way, it was a relief. That used to be a cigarette or a shot of Vodka. As she went unconscious, Callie had a feeling those days were long gone.

As Callie drifted in and out, she caught bits and pieces of their subsequent activities. At one point she smelled something that brought her back to countless 4th of Julys and Labor Days past. The bastards were fucking barbecuing. As she descended into deep sleep again, Callie's only thought was that if they were barbecuing, then this place must be ventilated. It wasn't an important thought but it at least offered her a mild distraction from the immense pain that coursed through her entire body. She had wondered yesterday how her life could get worse. Maybe she should emphasize she was being rhetorical. Like it mattered now. She was out again.

Some time later, Matt zipped up his jacket and cast a meaningful look at the unconscious Callie.

"Nothing better happen to her while I'm gone!" he told Clem, who was finishing the remnants of his T-bone.

"You ain't gotta worry about me but what if Dustin gets here before you get back?" Clem whined at him.

"Then you tell him to fucking wait! I don't want him doing any of that weird shit just yet," Matt said. "Especially after what he did to the last one!" He shook his head in disgust at the memory of Dustin's unspoken but horrific deed.

Clem took another bite of his T-bone and nodded. "I was here, remember?"

Matt climbed the ladder leading out of the room. "Good. Keep that fucking dog on a leash and I'll be back," he said as he went up. Clem stood up and went over to the ladder, looking up at Matt.

"Domestic this time! No more of that microbrew craft shit!" he hollered.

Matt looked down at him with disdain. "You'll drink what I bring you, hillbilly!"

And then he slammed the door closed and was gone. A resigned Clem went back to his T-bone, giving Callie an appreciative glance. She wasn't the prettiest one they had gotten but she had proven to be quite a little crackerjack, regardless. If nothing else, Dustin had good taste.

Clem smiled, meat juice dripping down his chin. He gave a loud belch and continued eating.

It was the belch that brought Callie back to the land of the living. She remembered how grossed out she was when he fired the snot rocket next to her car. The memory was faint now and after everything that had happened, not nearly as revolting. How the times had changed.

She carefully looked around and saw Clem was alone, though she doubted Matt was far. She watched Clem eat his steak. He looked so much like an animal it was almost uncanny. That this thing would have the ambition and brainpower to execute such an evil act confounded her. What happened to people using their abilities for good, like Callie, who had studied hard in graduate school and came out with a perfect four-oh. The same Callie who was the life of every Christmas party. The same Callie who was promised a hefty pay raise for her excellent work, only to be let go two months later because of budget cuts. And now that same Callie, jobless and broke, who would end her all-too-brief life in a basement or warehouse somewhere as a sex toy for these demented monsters.

Callie began to tug on the handcuffs at the thought of this injustice. Life wasn't fair but there was only so much a human being should be asked to take. The handcuffs gave a faint clang and scrape as she pulled on them but Clem was too wrapped up in his meal to notice. Callie watched his knife and fork work, almost mesmerized by the expertise he moved them with. These steak dinners were obviously a common occurrence for Clem.

She began to pull her left hand through the cuff. The pain was slight at first but then it blossomed as Callie mustered up all her strength and rage. She decided there would be no more good eating for this piggy as she continued to pull her hand free.

Tears of pain squirted from her eyes as she applied more pressure. Slow wasn't going to work. There was only one option and with every bit of strength she had left, Callie ripped her hand through the cuff. There was a sickening crunch followed by an immediate blast of pain but she jerked forward with a newfound freedom. She lifted her shaking hand to see it scraped, misshapen, and swollen but free. Free! She couldn't believe it.

She felt renewed energy as she brought her still-cuffed right hand away from the pipe. As she stood up, she saw Clem's eyes were finally on her. The surprise and panic in them made her smile. Or at least she thought it was a smile. Maybe it was a leer. Clem shot to his feet, surprisingly fast for such a large guy.

"Hey!" he screamed as he lumbered toward her. Even with this blast of adrenaline, Callie was still a little dizzy (and one-handed, to boot). As Clem got closer, Callie knew she had only one chance. She swung her right arm around and cracked him across the bridge of his nose with the loose handcuffs. It was a brilliant shot and one she couldn't replicate again if she tried.

Clem shrieked and fell back, covering his face with both hands as blood squirted from his nose.

"You fucking bitch!" came the muffled exclamation from behind his hands. Clem was slightly incapacitated but he was also furious now, meaning Callie had to move. Her eyes shifted to the juice-stained steak knife that was glinting in the fluorescent light.

Callie ran for it. It was her only chance. As she got close, she reached out for it, allowing Clem to grab her by her broken hand. The pain was excruciating but Callie lunged forward even further, dragging the surprised Clem with her. She got a hold of the knife and spun around with it, burying it in his throat.

Clem let out a sound that fell somewhere between a grunt and a wheeze. He stumbled back, blindly groping for the knife sticking out of his throat. A picture formed in Callie's head of Yosemite Sam dancing around as he tried to pull an arrow out of his backside and it made her laugh. That was twice she had laughed at an inappropriate moment with Clem around. Callie decided he just had that kind of face.

At the moment, said face was contorted in a combination of fear and rage as he struggled with the knife. He finally managed to rip it out, causing an immediate spray of blood that splashed her legs and feet. Clem continued to stumble around before finally hitting the ground dead, a pool of bright, red blood forming underneath him.

Callie heaved and vomited, making the laughter she had experienced mere seconds before seem impossible. She collapsed, breathing heavily. She only moved once Clem's warm blood touched her feet. She dragged herself away and let the darkness swallow her up again. She wasn't out of the woods yet but she could rest for a few minutes, right?

Her answer came in the form of a car pulling into the unseen space above her. It idled for a few seconds before turning off. She sat up as she heard someone get out. Matt was back. Footsteps approached the door. It swung open and she saw a pair of dirty jeans descend the ladder. The dirty jeans disappeared into a familiar work shirt and she saw it wasn't Matt but her old buddy Dustin, the patron saint of full service (no tip necessary). And his role made sense. Matt's little device tapped into GPS signals but he wouldn't know if those signals belonged to women traveling alone without help from this gutless bastard, she thought as he continued down the ladder. And whistling. The son of a bitch was whistling.

Callie looked around the room and saw her salvation hanging on a wall that was covered with it. She had missed this before and given she was handcuffed and helpless at the time, that was a good thing. The site of all this would have only made things worse. She walked over and grabbed what she needed, realizing that if all had gone to plan, this wall of torture devices was the next step. Not today, boys.

"Yo, Matt! Yo Clem!" Dustin called out as he jumped off the last step of the ladder. His eyes widened when he saw Clem. "Oh, Jesus!"

And then Callie fired. The nail pierced through the air and caught Dustin in the back of his left leg. He screamed and dropped to one knee. Callie began firing the nail gun as fast as she could (no easy task with one good hand), mostly missing but some of them managed to hit the mark on his hand, shoulder, and even his cheek. The baffled look on his face was almost humorous. Callie decided it was time to for him to find out what was going on, so she ceased fire.

"What the fuck?" Dustin gasped as pulled the nails from his body.

"Remember me, asshole?" she asked. Dazed, he looked up at her. She was caked with blood and almost naked. To her shock, he smiled.

"Yeah, I remember you. You were looking a little better at the gas station. Guess you didn't make it to Chicago after all!" And then the smile turned into laughter. She couldn't believe it. Dustin didn't stop there, though.

"It's too bad, I've been thinking about that ass and your tight little pussy…"

31

He didn't get to finish. Callie shot him dead center in the forehead with the nail gun. Her dad was a gun nut who liked to go to the shooting range every Saturday. She supposed under different circumstances, he'd be proud of her accuracy. Actually, given the circumstances, she decided he'd still be proud of her. Dustin looked up at her as blood began to trickle down his face.

"Cobbler," he sputtered before falling back dead. The only sound now was the buzzing of the fluorescent lights. She dropped the nail gun and stumbled over to where they had handcuffed her and recovered her panties. In addition to the urine soaking them, they were now ripped and bloody but they'd have to do. She put them on as best as she could, wincing as pain shot through her broken hand. She noticed that when she was killing Clem and Dustin, she didn't feel anything. Would she get her chance with Matt? She decided she didn't want to find out. She dropped to her knees next to Dustin and dug his keys out of his pocket.

She walked over to the ladder and began the Herculean task of climbing up. Each step meant agony shooting through every part her body but each step was also one step closer to freedom. So she climbed.

She breathed a sigh of relief when she finally reached the top, allowing herself to get that much-needed moment of rest. When she was ready to move again, she saw she was in a barn, empty except for Clem's

Jeep and Dustin's car, a Hyundai roughly the same age as her now long-lost Caprice.

She thought of a world where years of schooling and hard work gave her the same economic status as a gas station attendant (probably less so) but there were more important things to deal with right now. She wouldn't make Sandy's wedding. She wondered if Clem had left the dress in her car when he dumped it. Probably not, but it no longer mattered.

"Sorry I couldn't make it, babe, but something came up," she said out loud. Would Sandy understand? Would anyone understand? This seemed impossible to explain. Callie slid behind the wheel of Dustin's Hyundai. It smelled of fast food grease and cigarettes but now was not the time to nitpick affronts to her olfactory system.

She looked in the rearview mirror and saw Dustin had parked directly in front of the barn door. Did she have the strength to open it? No, she did not.

"Fuck it!" she said, throwing it in reverse and slamming on the gas. She drove through the doors, which splintered and broke easily as she went through them. The victory was short-lived, as she smashed directly into Matt's BMW. He was back. Talk about timing.

Matt honked his horn in short, fast bursts. He wasn't happy and his mood wasn't going to improve when he saw who was behind the wheel of Dustin's car.

His door opened and Callie began to look around for anything to defend herself with. Dustin looked like a "conceal and carry" guy. Surely there was a gun around, right? She saw there wasn't and Matt was getting closer.

"What the fuck, asshole?" he screamed, kicking Dustin's car as he approached. Time was running out and Callie found a can of WD-40 on the floor. It wasn't a gun or even pepper spray but it would have to do. She grabbed it and pointed it toward the door, which Matt was now standing next to.

"Get the fuck out of there, dick head!" Matt hollered. He still failed to realize she wasn't Dustin.

"Did you hear me, mother fucker?" Matt said slamming the roof of Dustin's car. Callie heard him all right and she knew her next move meant life or death. Would she be able to open the door and blast him? She didn't know but once Matt took a closer look and saw it was Callie and not Dustin, the choice was no longer hers to make.

"Bitch!" he screamed. In a panic, he groped for the door, finally getting it open and haphazardly grabbing for her. Now was Callie's chance. She raised the can of WD-40 and hit the nozzle. It hissed out in a silver mist, coating his glasses (those fucking glasses!) and his face. He dropped back, screaming and covering his face with his hands. It had worked! Callie rolled out of the car, gripping the WD-40 as she hit the ground. She crawled a few feet before gathering enough strength to stand up and run to Matt's car.

"You fucking slut!" he yelled at her. How close was he? Callie opened the door and got her answer as he grabbed her from behind. She dropped the WD-40 and watched it roll helplessly under the BMW.

He shoved her into his car, causing her to bang her head on the gearshift. His face was shiny from the WD-40 and he wasn't just enraged now, he was crazed. He wrapped his hands around her throat and began to squeeze. Callie gasped as her throat closed. She tried to ward him off but it was useless. Matt wouldn't stop until she was dead.

A length of white saliva dripped from his mouth as he applied more pressure. Callie did her best to look away. She couldn't face him. And that was when she saw the hypodermic needle in a compartment below the dash. The needle he had taunted her with earlier. The needle he would have used if she hadn't drunk the water. She grabbed it and stuck it in his arm, pressing the plunger down as hard as she could.

Almost immediately, his grip loosened. With her good hand, she shoved him away and started coughing profusely as he fell away from the car. She sat up, still coughing, and saw him staring up at her with a look of bewilderment. The needle was still stuck in his arm but he made no effort to remove it. He didn't have the strength. Callie managed to smile at this. How the tables had turned.

"Money," he finally managed.

"What?" Callie croaked. She didn't sound like herself anymore. Would she ever?

"Take my wallet and go to the address on my license. I've got lots of money in a safe. Take it and leave me alone. Please?" he slurred at her with a pleading look that was quickly giving way to sleep. He had no choice in the matter and he knew it.

So he offered her money. After everything that happened, he intended to fix it with money. And he probably had lots of it but money would never fix this.

When Callie didn't speak, he made eye contact with her to get his answer and her look told him everything. Tears filled his eyes before the drugs fully took hold and knocked him out.

Alone now (more or less), Callie tried to process everything but couldn't. Her entire body throbbed with pain and her head was still swimming. She needed a hospital and there was no time like the present.

She turned the key that was still in the ignition and the car started immediately. She began to shut the door when she gave Matt's unconscious body another look. She could see the tears drying on his cheeks. He knew he wasn't coming out of this alive. He had seen it in her eyes, which meant Callie had unfinished business. She turned off the car and limped toward the basement, where there was an entire wall of justice waiting to be put to good use. And she intended to do just that.

Callie began to climb down the ladder, which hurt like hell but she knew it was going to be worth it. Once she was down there, it didn't take her very long to make her choice. She just needed something sharp and the bone saw she selected would do nicely.

After it was all over, Callie was driving down the road to an unknown destination. Matt had a GPS built into his dashboard but Callie knew she'd never use one again. Along the way, she stopped to dispose of something Matt would never use again. She figured he had taken enough from her, so she might as well take something from him (or at least what was left of him). As she looked at it, she remembered how painful it felt but now she marveled at how small and insignificant it was.

Callie tossed it into a brook and within seconds, it had disappeared downstream. Good fucking riddance.

She looked ahead and saw the sun starting to poke its way over the horizon. Although her future was uncertain, something else was stirring inside of her.

Was it hope? Callie didn't know, but she continued driving out of the darkness and into the clear dawn. If nothing else, it was at least going to be a nice day.

Who Delivers the Blue Sheets?

Robert was reading Holes when he heard the familiar light slapping sound of the blue sheet being dropped into the basket. Normally he paid this action no mind. The blue sheets were as much a part of the school's schedule as lunch or recess, so why should he? Today was different, though. Maybe he had finally grown bored of reading Holes. It was one of his favorite books but after having read it a dozen or so times, it had started to lose its luster.

Robert needed something new to stimulate him and learning who delivered the blue sheets was as good a thing as any. He looked up and although it had only been a few seconds, the door was already closed and the crisp blue attendance sheet rested complacently in its basket. Robert glanced around the room and saw the other children were either reading their own books or sitting quietly with their heads on their desk. Robert turned to Miss Collins, who was busy grading papers.

"Miss Collins?" Robert called out.

"Yes, Robert?"

"Who delivers the blue sheets?"

Miss Collins looked down at the tests she was grading but Robert had seen something flicker in her eyes, which were magnified by the large glasses she always wore.

"Oh, I don't know, Robert. I think it's whoever's available during Quiet Time. I don't think it's the same person every day," she answered. Her voice sounded convincing but the fearful look he had seen in her eyes, however brief, let Robert know something was going on. And while Robert was ordinarily a well-behaved child, his overly curious nature had gotten him a trouble more than a few times. Now was probably going to be one of them.

"So how come we never see them?" he pressed on.

"Well, Quiet Time is only an hour, Robert," Miss Collins replied, her voice growing impatient. "They have a lot of classrooms to go to. Now go back to reading your book."

"But Miss Collins..."

"Robert!" came the curt reply.

Miss Collins was nice but you didn't want to cross her. And Robert knew if he continued to push the issue, she'd likely make him sit in the hallway and subject him to the judgmental eyes of the entire school. He instead looked out the window and saw a perfect spring day waiting for him when school let out. If his curiosity was going to get the best of him, it wasn't going to be today.

School let out a couple of hours later and Robert was walking home with his best friend Kenny. He could tell Kenny anything. Kenny even knew that until second grade, Robert had to wear diapers to bed. Such a thing going public would have meant certain doom for Robert's reputation but Kenny had never laughed or told anybody. If that didn't make somebody your best friend, Robert didn't know what did.

"Who do you think drops off the blue attendance sheets?" he asked as Kenny ran a stick along a wrought-iron fence they were walking past.

"I don't know," Kenny said, throwing the stick away. "A janitor or one of those ladies who sits in the back of the classrooms, I guess."

"So how come we never see them?"

"Because it's like Miss Collins said. They have the whole school to take care of and Quiet Time is only like an hour."

They walked in silence for almost an entire block before Robert spoke again.

"You don't care, do you?"

Kenny shook his head.

"Not really. It's just a list of the kids who were absent," he said, his eyes trained on two fat squirrels that were busy chasing each other around a tree. "It's not that interesting."

Robert knew that on the surface, Kenny was right. The attendance sheets weren't interesting but he also kept picturing Miss Collins' frightened expression. She was a small woman but she had a reputation for being tougher than most of the male teachers at their school. Robert had seen her break up a fight between two boys who were at least twice her size. If something like that didn't scare her, what could?

From the time he got home until he went to bed that night, the blue sheets were all Robert could think about.

He decided the next day he was ready to find out who delivered the blue sheets. He hadn't told Kenny about it because Kenny wasn't interested and if he kept pressing the issue, he was afraid Kenny would start to think he was weird. Robert couldn't help but wonder if he would be right in that assessment.

Quiet Time always took place right after lunch, which seemed like forever. Robert was antsy the entire morning and had a hard time concentrating on his schoolwork. Lunch was even worse. Robert was so distracted he didn't even bother to eat most of his lunch and his mother had included a baggie of Chips Ahoy, which were his absolute favorite.

After what seemed like a million hours, it was finally Quiet Time. Robert had made sure to use the bathroom after lunch. He didn't want to miss anything. He had Holes open in front of him but he wasn't actually reading it. He kept his eyes on the door and he was convinced he was being discreet about it until he heard Miss Collins' voice call out to him.

"Robert?"

He slowly turned around to face her, putting on his best "Who, Me?" face but he could tell she wasn't fooled. The stern look on her face confirmed Robert was treading on dangerous ground.

"Do you need anything?" she asked him, arching her carefully plucked eyebrows in a manner that reminded him of Dolores Umbridge.

"No, I'm okay," he said, his face growing hot enough to fry an egg on.

"So why don't you go back reading your book?"

"Okay," he said, looking down at Holes. Out of the corner of his eye, he saw Kenny smirk at him from two rows over. It was quick but Miss Collins was on her A-game that day.

"Kenny!" she said sharply and Kenny returned to his math homework, his ears turning a scarlet red.

Robert looked up from the book and saw Miss Collins staring at him from behind her large glasses. There was no fear in those eyes today.

Robert dropped his head back down and as if on cue, he heard the door creak open and the blue sheet get dropped into the basket. He wanted to look up but he also knew it was too late. The whole thing seemed to take place in less than a second. Robert told himself that if and when he finally did learn who it was, he would just see the sweater-clad arm of a teacher's aide but he still wanted to know.

He needed to know.

Robert waited until after dinner to bring up the blue sheets to his parents. He wasn't expecting much but maybe they knew something.

"Who delivers the blue sheets?"

"What's a blue sheet?" his father asked without much interest.

"The blue sheets they drop off during Quiet Time. They say who's absent and stuff," Robert answered, taking careful note of their facial expressions but unlike Miss Collins', their expressions remained blank and indifferent.

"What about them?" his mother asked.

"Who brings them?" Robert asked, growing somewhat impatient.

"Oh, I don't know, I suppose a teacher's aide or something," his mother said, turning her attention back to the Big Bang Theory rerun that was playing on the television.

"Yeah, that's what Kenny said," Robert said. The reality that this whole thing was going to be a huge disappointment was looking more and more likely.

"Why do you care? Seems like pretty boring stuff to me, pal," his father said, as if confirming the idea.

"I don't know. I've just never seen them. They drop them off so fast you can never get a look," Robert explained. "And it's always during Quiet Time, when we have to stay in our classroom."

"If that were my job, I'd probably be in a hurry to get it done, too," his father said with a chuckle.

Knowing he wasn't going to get any more out of his parents, Robert looked down at the action figures he had spread out in front of him. They were the same action figures as always. They only did anything when Robert made them. In a couple of hours, he'd go up to the same bedroom and sleep in the same bed. The next day he'd wake up, eat the same cereal and then take the same walk to the same school.

Had he been a little bit older, the word "ennui" might have crossed his mind but a vocabulary like that was still well out of his reach. The alluring mystery of who delivered the blue sheets, however, was well within his reach. And even if it was just disappointment waiting for him at the end of it; he was more determined than ever to figure it out.

When it came time for school the next morning, Robert carefully placed his digital camera into his backpack. Robert knew he was taking a big risk because electronics were strictly forbidden at school and if you were caught using one, it was promptly taken away and you wouldn't see it again until the end of the day.

If you were bold or foolish enough to bring in said device a second time, it was gone until the end of the week. If you were unlucky enough to get caught three times, it would be sent to the principal's office and your parents would have to come in with you to retrieve it. The system worked, as Robert had only seen a handful kids be stupid enough to take their phone or Nintendo 3DS out when a teacher was nearby. Robert knew he wasn't stupid but he was also dealing with special circumstances. Although it probably was foolish, he didn't have many options.

It was right before lunch when he carefully removed the camera from his backpack and showed it to Kenny, whose eyes widened at the sight of it.

"Why did you bring that?"

"So I can get video of the person who delivers the blue sheets," Robert answered, no longer worried about Kenny judging him. His tragically curious nature had superseded that.

"You're so weird," Kenny said. "If Miss Collins sees that, she's taking it away."

Kenny walked away from him and joined two other boys, tacitly confirming to Robert that they wouldn't be eating lunch together. That stung a little but if there was something interesting behind the blue sheets, Kenny would move past it and want to be friends again. Lunch came and went, with Robert eating by himself and waiting for Quiet Time to arrive. Robert felt a pang of doubt as lunch came to a close but then he reminded himself of Miss Collins' frightened expression. It had to mean something.

Lunch ended and the students returned to their classrooms. Miss Collins was grading papers but looked up when she saw Robert enter. She kept her eyes trained on him as he sat down. Fortunately he had hidden his camera in his desk before going to lunch. He waited for her to return to her papers before bringing his camera out and setting it out on his lap with the lens pointed toward the door. Once the camera was in place, Robert brought out his Social Studies textbook and pretended to do his homework.

The bell gave a final, ominous ring. Quiet Time was officially underway. The clock hanging above the door sounded off with loud, rhythmic ticks that Robert found unusually abrasive. His palms were sweating as he held onto the camera, which he half-expected to fall off his lap and break on the floor. Robert knew the blue sheets always arrived at exactly fifteen minutes into Quiet Hour. He had a long way to go.

The minutes pounded away at an unbearably slow rate. Robert tried to focus on a chapter about Columbus but couldn't quite pull it off.

He didn't like Columbus, even if he had discovered America. He was an ugly guy who dressed like a girl.

The fifteen minutes crept closer and Robert turned on the camera. It made a tiny dinging sound as it turned on, which Robert had forgotten all about. Under normal circumstances, it would have barely been audible but on that day, it may as well have been a dump truck starting up. A few kids looked over, as did Miss Collins.

"What is that?" she asked sharply.

Robert tried to hold his ground and focus on his Social Studies book but it was no use. She had him.

"Robert, what do you have?"

Blood began rushing to Robert's face but he kept his head down.

"Robert!"

He heard her chair creak and her jewelry jangle as she stood up. In a few seconds, she'd be standing over him, her intense gaze cutting through him like a knife. With no other recourse, he slowly looked up and faced her.

"Show me what you're hiding!" she exclaimed, her eyes ablaze with anger.

Robert's face was on fire now. His curious nature sometimes required a rebuke from his parents and teachers but it was never this severe. He probably was going to the principal's office this time and they would call his parents, which meant he'd be grounded for at least two weeks. Angry with himself and also embarrassed for having such an odd fixation, Robert held his camera up.

With a swish of her nylons and a series of harried, impatient footsteps, Miss Collins was standing in front of his desk with her hand out. As Robert gave her the camera, he heard the sound of the door opening and the blue attendance sheet being dropped into the basket. It was like they had actually waited for him to be distracted.

"You'll see this at the end of the week!" she said, stomping back to her desk with his camera held tightly in her right hand. "Now everybody go back to what you were doing!"

Robert returned to his book and heard a few quiet giggles and titters behind him. He had never felt so humiliated. After school ended, Miss Collins quietly asked Robert to stay behind. Robert sat down in the chair Miss Collins had put next to her desk. He assumed the worst. Maybe a note to his mother or perhaps extra homework that would take all night and leave his fingers sore from the endless writing it would require. To Robert's relief, Miss Collins didn't look angry. She looked concerned.

"Do you understand why I had to take your camera?" she asked him.

Robert nodded and focused his gaze on a stain on the carpet. He started to wonder how it had gotten there and how long it had been there but then stopped himself. Curiosity had gotten him into enough trouble already.

"Is something wrong, Robert?" Miss Collins asked.

She gave him a minute to reply but he didn't say anything, so she continued.

"You've just been very distracted this week. Quiet Time is for all of us to catch up on work, read a book, or relax. You're usually so good about it. What's changed?"

"I don't know," Robert said, knowing full well it sounded bogus but saying the real reason out loud felt roughly equivalent to peeing his pants in front of her.

"Quiet Time is the same as it ever was, Robert," Miss Collins said. "I've been teaching here for twenty years and I can assure you, there's nothing exciting about it. Okay?"

"Okay," Robert replied, understanding that despite Miss Collins' patient reasoning with him, he had just been handed a major defeat.

"How about I make a deal with you?" Miss Collins offered, seemingly picking up on how disappointed he was. "If I give you back your camera now, do you promise to just read or do homework like before?"

"Sure," Robert said, accepting terms that would only get worse and never better.

Miss Collins reached into her desk and pulled out Robert's camera, setting it in his hand. It was warm, prompting Robert to wonder how it had gotten that way. Shouldn't it have felt cold? Shouldn't it...

"Go on home, Robert," Miss Collins said, mercifully interrupting another train of thought that would have just served to get him into more trouble. He stood up and started to leave when Miss Collins called out to him one final time.

"And remember, things go back to normal tomorrow."

Robert's stomach began to flutter as he looked back at Miss Collins. Although her face was still open and friendly, her tone had shifted slightly. It was as subtle as when he had seen her facial expression change the other day but it had definitely happened.

Miss Collins wasn't just asserting her authority over Robert.

She was warning him.

Robert was so wired that night he couldn't fall asleep. There was something behind the blue sheets. His boring life finally had the same excitement and danger that was usually reserved for his favorite books and movies. Robert had an actual mission now, just like Harry Potter and Indiana Jones.

And nobody could take that away from him. Not even Miss Collins.

The next morning, Robert and Kenny were walking to school when Kenny got mad at him.

"Slow down!" he yelled.

Robert stopped and realized he was no longer walking next to Kenny but ten feet in front of him. He struggled to stand still as he waited for Kenny to catch up with him.

"Why are in such a hurry to get to school" Kenny asked him. "Is getting in trouble with Miss Collins that much fun for you?"

"I didn't get in trouble!" Robert protested as they resumed walking again.

"Yes, you did! She made you stay after school!"

"Just for five minutes," Robert replied. "My mom didn't even notice."

"So what, you're planning on doing it again until she does notice?" Kenny asked.

"Nope," Robert said, not wanting to discuss the matter with Kenny any further. Not even Kenny could know what he had planned. Even the slightest risk could potentially unravel everything, so Robert looked up and stared up the sky.

He marveled at how blue it was.

School began and the children of Miss Collins' third grade class, Robert included, took their seats.

The day slogged along but as Quiet Time got closer, Robert's heart began to race. He was too anxious to eat his lunch and even gave his chips to Derrick, the annoying kid who stole your food whenever you turned away.

Quiet Time finally arrived and Robert realized it was now or never. He was risking weeks of detention as well as looking like a weirdo to the entire class but he had to see. Too much had happened for him to just forget it.

Robert drew in a notebook to look occupied. He wasn't much of an artist but it seemed to be doing the trick. Miss Collins had only looked at him a couple of times in the ten minutes since Quiet Time had been underway. As the moment of truth arrived, Robert ceased drawing and prepared himself. When he looked up from the notebook, he saw Miss Collins staring at him. Did she know? How was that possible?

A thin layer of sweat broke out on Robert's forehead. This was going to be harder than he expected. He decided to play it safe and resume drawing again. He continued to sweat and his mouth was dry and tasted sour. He had Miss Collins' full attention now. There was no way he was going to be able to pull this off.

"Robert?" she asked him, her voice measured and patient.

He swallowed hard and faced her again, his face flush and peppered with beads of sweat.

"Yes, Miss Collins?"

"Are you all right?"

"I'm okay."

"Good, then why don't you keep working?" she suggested, only it wasn't a suggestion. It was a command, perhaps even a plea.

Just as Robert returned to the series of scribbles in his notebook, he heard the door creak open. Suddenly, everything was in slow motion and Robert no longer felt like he was in control of himself.

He stood up and saw Miss Collins' friendly demeanor transform into panic. He turned to the door just as the blue sheet dropped into the basket. The door closed before Robert could get a good look at whoever it was.

There was no turning back. He was already in trouble, so he decided to make the most of it. He ran for the door and opened it with Miss Collins hot on his trail.

"Robert!" she screamed at him, reaching for him as he ran into the hallway. He felt her fingertips brush the back of his shirt but there was no stopping him. All the events from the previous week, maybe even his entire life, had lead up to this monumental moment.

As he entered the hallway, he was immediately thrown off by how dark it was. Usually the fluorescent lights that ran along the ceiling supplied adequate if not especially appealing illumination but this was like entering a cave. He looked to his right and saw the outline of something take a sharp turn down the next corridor. He froze when he saw it. This was no custodian or teacher's aide. It didn't even look human. And it was big.

For reasons he'd never be able to explain, he ran after it. Miss Collins was right behind him, trying desperately to grab hold of him. He could hear her high heels clacking on the tiled floor as they both ran to Robert's destiny.

"Stop!" she shrieked at him but Robert continued running. It wouldn't be long now. He was almost to the corridor when he felt Miss Collins' cold, slender fingers grip his left arm. Despite her small frame, he felt himself yanked back with surprising force.

"You can't see them!" Miss Collins said, her hair wild and her face filled with terror.

"But what is it?" he asked, the adrenaline running through him at full blast. He was ready to tear away from her and start running again but her grip remained firm.

"Please, we have to get back inside the room!" she said as she started to lead him away. At first, Robert planted his feet but then his legs turned to Jell-O. Something came up behind Miss Collins and Robert had been wrong before about the size of it. It wasn't just big. It was massive

Before Miss Collins had a chance to realize what was going on, it reached out and grabbed her with paws the size of truck tires. She let out an ear-shattering scream as it lifted her off the ground like a rag doll. Miss Collins let another scream but it was drowned out by a guttural growl that rattled Robert to the bone. It was followed by a vile crunching sound and Miss Collins suddenly had rivulets of blood running down the entire length of her quivering body.

Robert's next memory was running out of the school while screaming at the top of his lungs. Even as he ran under the bright sunlight of the radiant spring day, he could hear the ghastly sounds of the awful thing chewing on poor Miss Collins.

Delirious with panic and insanity, the only coherent thought Robert was able to muster was that he would never set foot in that school ever again.

And as he blindly ran as far away from that horrid place as he could, maybe that was all he needed.

Pressure

Brenda was on her way to an empty house. As she pulled out of the grocery store, she wondered why it still bothered her. She had broken up with Jason two months earlier and spending time alone was nothing new for her. It was how she spent most of her college and grad school years. She had been so wrapped up in her studies that save for the occasional beer with her classmates; the fun part of college had completely passed her by.

She sometimes contemplated why she had fallen so hard for Jason but she supposed his lackadaisical approach to life (a sharp contrast from her own) was part of it. While ambition and steady employment weren't his strong suits, making her laugh and knowing how to have a good time were. The break-up had mostly been her doing. She had leaned too much on those aspects of his personality and when she was finally fed up with doing all the heavy lifting (both financially and emotionally), she broke it off. He was confused and she couldn't blame him but still, he was thirty-four. Shouldn't he grow up some time?

She often thought that the break-up would prompt him to do just that and some other lucky woman would reap the benefits of her sacrifice and hard work. Would it be worth getting back together with him? After all, his problems extended well beyond being lazy and irresponsible. Or so she told herself. She decided this inner dialogue was a tired one but unfortunately it came too late. As Brenda absently made a left turn, she almost didn't see the yellow Volkswagen Bug bearing down on her. Fortunately the driver was paying attention and they managed to stop mere inches from her car. They gave her a long and impatient honk. Brenda could only offer a sheepish wave and a smile as she drove past the Bug. Reflecting on her longest relationship ever (four years) was becoming a danger to her physical health as well as her mental. As she drove off, she saw the Bug lingering in the same spot it had stopped at. Horns were honking at it to keep moving but it stayed still. Although Brenda found a bit odd, she dismissed it and kept driving. She had a dinner for one to prepare.

Sadie was waiting for her when she got home. She could always count on Sadie; at least when she needed fed or wanted attention. Like most cats, Sadie's affections were conditional on her mood. Brenda scratched her behind the ears, prompting a quiet "Mew" from the fat Tabby. With that out of the way, Sadie jumped down from the counter and disappeared into the bedroom.

"Thanks for stopping by, Sadie!" Brenda called out as she unloaded the groceries for tonight's single lady gourmet dinner, which consisted of chicken and brown rice. As she prepared it, she thought of Shawn, the other man in her life. Shawn hadn't earned this distinction by choice. Until two weeks ago, he was just another face in the hallway of the school they both worked at. He seemed friendly enough but Brenda had never really bothered to get to know him. Things had suddenly changed, though. As it turned out, Shawn wanted the soon-to-be vacated vice principal job as badly as she did and he had the advantages of being male and also a golfing buddy of the school district's superintendent. Brenda hoped that Frank Yellin, the school's affable principal, wouldn't let either of these factors affect his decision but Brenda knew it was out of her hands. She could only hope her interview Monday would be enough to persuade him that she was the best candidate. She didn't just want this job; she needed it. In her twenties, teaching was her passion but her thirties were proving to be a much different story. The books were the same every year and her dwindling interest in them was starting to reflect on the students. Of course that paled in comparison to the Martin Pike incident from two years ago. Just thinking about it made Brenda shudder. No, between all that and the break-up with Jason, she needed a change and a promotion at work would do nicely.

After a mostly flavorless meal (cooking wasn't one of her strong suits), she graded some papers, watched the latest episode of New Girl, and went to bed. She had come to enjoy the extra space in the Queen-sized bed she had purchased after Jason moved in. He was a restless sleeper who hogged the covers and after their infrequent bouts of lovemaking, he tended to snore. Loudly. With that in mind, Brenda could at least take comfort in having an unabated night's sleep. Considering the countless mornings where she had groggily dragged herself to the bathroom, it was a nice advantage for the time being. As she drifted off to sleep that night, she was startled by the sound of tapping against her window. It was slight but undeniable. It reminded Brenda of the tree outside her bedroom window when she was a child. On windy nights, the branches would scratch against the glass, leading to sleepless nights and crying bouts that finally ended when her father trimmed them away.

There was no tree outside this bedroom window, though. Brenda cautiously got out of bed and approached the window. She stared at the tan blinds and wondered what horror was waiting beyond them. A drooling maniac with a straight razor? A hungry bear? Brenda suppressed her overacting imagination and peeked through them. There was nothing. The neighbor's house was dark and the anorexic-looking bushes that occupied the side of her house sat perfectly still. Brenda looked around for another few seconds and decided whatever it was had moved on.

As Brenda climbed back into bed, she thought of her interview on Monday. This meant surviving Friday, Saturday, and Sunday. She already decided to give her students a free day tomorrow, citing it as a reward for their hard work (what a joke) and as for the weekend, maybe she'd go hiking at the state park nearby. That always put her mind at ease. Just the thought of exercise and fresh air was already doing that. It was so effective she allowed herself to fall asleep, even after the mysterious scratching had resumed.

By the time morning came along, she had mostly forgotten about the strange noises. She dressed in an old pink top and tan slacks. Her outfits had been more conservative the last two weeks, as her plan was to wear something dazzling for her interview. She didn't know if it would make a difference with Frank but it certainly didn't hurt to try.

As she walked outside to get in her car, something caught her eye. It was a cigarette butt at the top of her driveway. She wasn't a smoker and she certainly wouldn't allow one inside her house or even near it. Curious, she walked over to it and noticed another one. She followed the trail and found two more residing at the bottom of her bedroom window. This was too much, even for her overactive imagination. Somebody had been here and they had been scratching at her window. She considered calling the police but checked the time and saw she needed to get to school. After double-checking her locks, she was on her way. Once she was on the road, she shut the radio off. The cheerful pop music she normally favored sounded distracting and abrasive today. Whatever had gone on outside her house last night, she didn't need it. She had too much on her plate as it was.

The free day she promised her students was one of her best ideas in a long time. She was in no condition to teach. As her students chattered and laughed, Brenda could only absently stare out the window.

"Miss Franklin?"

Brenda snapped out of her trance to see Julie, one of the few students who actually deserved a free day, standing at her desk.

"What is it, Julie"

"Are you okay?" Julie asked. Her face was filled with concern.

"I'm fine. Just a little tired." Brenda responded. "But thank you for asking. Any big plans for the weekend?"

"I'm going to visit my brother at his college," Julie said.

"Well, have fun and watch out for those college boys!" Brenda followed up with a wink. Julie gave her a cynical smile in return.

"I don't think that's going to be a problem," she said before returning to her seat. The awareness on Julie's face made Brenda feel guilty for making that statement. Julie was a brilliant student with a warm and generous personality but she was overweight and had a bad complexion. Kids could eventually grow out of such unfortunate afflictions but it did them no favors now. Brenda thought of her own high school days. She was blessed with perfect skin, flowing hair, and a trim figure. The affections of boys had never been an issue, though she had dissuaded most of them. Boys at that age seemed crude and immature to her (making her attraction to Jason all the more inexplicable). Relaying this observation to Julie probably wouldn't help matters so Brenda feigned grading papers for the rest of the period.

The school day finally ended and Brenda couldn't leave fast enough. As she headed for the exit, a familiar voice called out to her.

"Miss Franklin!" Principal Yellin called out in the crowded hallway. Shit. Did it look like she was rushing out the door? She turned to him.

"Yes, Principal Yellin?" she asked, donning the same fake smile she had for Julie. He was slightly out-of-breath as he caught up to her. He was balding and overweight but she'd be hard-pressed to find a nicer man to work for. It was one of the only reasons she was still at this school.

"I just wanted to tell you how much I'm looking forward to our talk on Monday!" he exclaimed with a friendly smile. Their talk. For her it was the interview that would determine her fate at this place but for him, it was the talk. Still, his earnest face told her he was being genuine.

"Me, too!" Brenda said. "I've been listening to the Rocky theme all week in preparation." It was a lame joke but he laughed like it was the funniest thing he had ever heard.

"Good to hear, Miss Franklin. I'll see you on Monday. Have a great weekend!" And with a loud puff, he was gone, stopping once to tell a student to remove their hat.

As Brenda watched him shamble down the hallway, she decided that despite a growing indifference to her a job, a messy break-up, and a potential stalker, things might still turn out all right. That optimism lasted until she reached the parking lot.

Brenda was almost to her car when she saw Shawn talking to Todd Harrison, the superintendent. For Shawn, this was kismet but for Brenda, it was a reminder that the deck was stacked against her. Todd was a tall, handsome man who towered over the diminutive Shawn. They were an odd pair but Shawn said something and Todd laughed uproariously. That kind of rapport meant bad news for Brenda. She watched as they shook hands before Todd drove off in his gray Saab. Brenda quickly fished around in her purse for her keys but it was too late. Shawn had seen her.

"Brenda!" he called over to her. Brenda. The few times they did speak it was always "Miss Franklin" but suddenly they were on a first name basis. He walked over.

"You know Todd, right?" he asked her, knowing full well what her answer was going to be.

"We've spoken a few times. He seems like a nice man," Brenda responded, hoping she sounded relaxed. She certainly didn't feel that way.

"Definitely. And a hell of a golfer, too," Shawn said. He was smiling like he had the job in the bag and Brenda feared that he probably did.

"I'm not much of a golfer, Mr. Erickson," she said, allowing her tone to have just a little bit of ice in it.

"Please, call me Shawn," he responded. "Your interview is Monday, right?"

"That's right."

"Well, I hope it goes well for you!" he said. "Have a great weekend!" And with one final slimy grin, he was headed toward his car, which was much nicer than hers.

Brenda found her hands shaking as she unlocked her car. She sat down inside and took several deep breaths before starting it up and driving away. She expected teaching to have its ups and downs but facing stiff competition from a co-worker with several distinct advantages over her wasn't something she ever would have expected. She always assumed it wouldn't go beyond banal conversations in the faculty lounge.

"Wrong again, dear," she said as she pulled out of the parking lot.

When she got home, she pulled a tissue out of her purse to pick up the cigarette butts that littered her property. Just the sight of them made her feel a little nauseous. Her father had smoked and when she used to kiss him goodnight, the pleasant feeling of his beard stubble was always marred by the smell of stale smoke and nicotine.

She got to the front door and her nausea increased tenfold when she saw what was waiting for her on the welcome mat. It was a dead rat, its black fur matted and its glassy black eyes staring vaguely into the distance. She gagged as she went inside, slamming the door closed so hard it rattled the mirror she had hanging in the front hallway. Sadie stared at her, looking slightly alarmed by Brenda's distressed demeanor.

"Hungry, Sadie girl?" she asked, trying to suppress the gags that were coming in quick succession. "There's something out there…"

Unable to finish, Brenda ran into the bathroom and vomited the tomato basil soup she had for lunch. It wasn't just the sight of the rat that did it. It was the idea she had somehow earned such hateful ire from another human being. She had always done her best to show kindness to other people. What could she have possibly done to deserve this?

She changed into her old Chicago Bears t-shirt (actually Jason's) and yoga pants. Yoga always calmed her nerves and made her feel better. As she started to stretch, she realized she wouldn't be able to get anything done with the dead rat still out in the open. Mustering all her strength, she put on dishwashing gloves, fetched a plastic bag, and headed for her cluttered garage.

She hadn't been able to park in it since she had bought the house five years ago, as it was filled with dusty boxes she still hadn't bothered to unpack. Given her new admirer, maybe it was time to empty them and make room in the garage for her car but first she needed to deal with the unpleasant business lying on her welcome mat. She grabbed a shovel and went outside.

Fortunately for Brenda, the gagging managed to subside after she got the rat onto the shovel. As carefully as she could, she aimed it over the bag and dropped the rat inside. Looking away, Brenda tied the bag closed and dropped it into the large blue garbage can that would get emptied Monday morning. The rat was only going to be a temporary guest but even a weekend seemed way too long. She replaced the shovel and went back inside, throwing the dishwashing gloves into the garbage.

She attempted to resume doing yoga but it was no good. Her mind was too pre-occupied with a job that already seemed like a lost cause, as well as cigarette butts and dead rodents. She skipped dinner and went to bed early. Fortunately for her, nobody scratched on her window that night. Thank God for small favors.

The next day she woke up early to go hiking with her friend Katie. It was the first time she had spoken to somebody about everything that had gone on and for Brenda it was a huge relief. Katie, normally something of a blabbermouth who loved to interrupt, listened with uncharacteristically rapt attention. When Brenda finished, "Wow" was the only word Katie could manage. They walked in silence for a few moments.

"Are you going to call the police?" Katie finally asked her.

"And say what? I found cigarette butts and a dead rat outside my house? I don't think that's enough for them to get involved," Brenda said.

"You know, on those true crime shows, whenever these cases happen and the woman hesitates to call the police or the police don't listen to her, she always disappears or ends up dead," Katie offered. Tact was not something she was blessed with.

"Thanks, Katie," Brenda said.

"I'm not trying to scare you but you should at least file a report or something," Katie followed up. That actually wasn't a bad idea. Maybe she could even convince them to have a police car drive by her house every couple of hours.

"And you have no idea who it is?" Katie asked. "You don't think Jason would do something like this, do you?"

"Jason doesn't smoke and leaving me a dead rat would take effort," Brenda said. "It's not Jason."

As they continue down the path, Brenda's heart skipped a beat when she thought she saw Shawn approaching them. As they got closer, she saw it wasn't Shawn at all. In fact, the guy didn't look anything like him. That didn't stop him from giving Brenda and Katie an appreciative wink as he walked by, which Brenda ignored. Katie was far more intrigued.

"He's cute! You should go talk to him!" Katie offered.

"No thanks. He's all yours," Brenda responded, a headache beginning to form. Playing matchmaker for Brenda had become one of Katie's favorite pastimes of late and Brenda was not in the mood.

"Why not?" Katie persisted. Her headache was becoming more insistent now. Brenda carefully counted down from ten before answering her.

"Honestly?" she said, making sure her voice was level and patient. "He looks like Shawn, that creep I'm competing against for the job." Katie's eyes widened at this reveal.

"You don't think it's him doing all this stuff, do you?"

"Shawn? I mean, he clearly seems me as a threat but I don't think he'd go that far," Brenda answered but the idea didn't exactly leave her head, either. It would at least make some sense. Before she could think about it any further, Katie cut in.

"Whoever's behind it, I don't care," Katie said. "I don't want you alone in that house tonight. You're staying at my place until you get all of this sorted out."

"I couldn't do that, Katie. That's too much," Brenda said, although the offer didn't sound half bad, given her circumstances.

"Come on, True Blood on Blu Ray and all the wine you can drink! What do you say?"

Brenda hated True Blood but a drink (or several) sounded fantastic. Katie could see Brenda was considering it, so she made her final offer.

"You can even bring your stinky kitty."

Brenda let her jaw drop in mock surprise.

"My kitty is not stinky!"

"That's not what Jason told me!" Katie said, laughing. The shrill sound echoed in the valley below. Katie could be inconsiderate and obnoxious but Brenda knew at that moment there wasn't going to be a better way to spend her weekend.

She gave Katie a playful smack on the arm and they continued walking. Brenda couldn't think of the last time she had a girls' night. It was well before Jason at the very least. Brenda knew she wasn't old but realizations like these made her feel like she lived a life that was largely wasted. It was painful to think about but at least tonight would be fun. Or so she thought.

The hike ended two hours later. Brenda and Katie finalized their plans in the parking lot and went their separate ways. It rained on the drive home and as Brenda turned down her street, her heart began to race. What would be waiting for her this time? Another dead rat? Perhaps a severed eyeball? Brenda cursed her overactive imagination as she pulled into her driveway. At first glance, everything appeared normal. She got out of the car and other than the goose bumps on her arms and legs from the cold rain, there was nothing out of the ordinary. No surprises by her front door, nothing littering her driveway, and best of all, the area below her bedroom window was clean. Brenda entered her house and allowed tiniest bit of optimism to creep into her brain. A little could go a long way come Monday morning.

Sadie was waiting and gave Brenda an indifferent "Meow" as she walked over to scratch the cat's head.

"We're going to spend the weekend with Aunt Katie," she told Sadie. "How does that sound?"

Sadie meowed again and jumped to the floor. As long as Sadie had a window ledge, litter box and food, she was good to go. Brenda sometimes envied that simplicity.

Brenda packed quickly, remembering all of Sadie's things, as well as her outfit for the interview Monday. Everything, from the skirt to the shoes, came from Nordstrom. It was a little out of her price range but Brenda foolishly rationalized that it would even out once she got the job and the raise that came with it. That was a week before Shawn threw his name into the hat, making the purchase seem even more unnecessary and ridiculous but it was too late to back out now.

Brenda was almost finished packing when the strange sensation fell over her. Was there was someone in the house with her? She heard Sadie meow again, which was her standard greeting for all visitors (not that Brenda had many of those). Brenda listened for footsteps but didn't hear anything. It was her imagination. It had to be. Nonetheless, she finished gathering her things and went out the door, scooping up Sadie as she went. She locked the front door and obsessively yanked on the door handle several times to make sure it was locked. Would it matter if somebody was already inside the house? Brenda dismissed the thought and loaded everything into her car and drove off. Had she taken a minute and looked down on her way out of the house, she would have seen the fresh wet footprints that lead into her darkened kitchen.

The evening at Katie's started out promising enough. Katie had made a fresh pitcher of margaritas and Brenda relaxed as soon as the first sip touched her lips. She sat back and even made an effort to watch the episode of True Blood Katie had playing. They watched in silence for a few moments before Katie spoke up and that was okay. The show just didn't interest Brenda.

"So hypothetically, what's going to happen if you don't get this job?" Katie asked. As tactless as she could be, Brenda couldn't deny this was a fair question and one she had thought about many times. Katie was the first one to ask her, though, and Brenda decided saying her answer out loud was probably a good thing.

"I don't know. Stick with my current job and maybe poke around some other school districts to see if any similar posts open up," she answered and it sounded sensible. It just wasn't true. Brenda was going to quit. She'd likely stick the school year out on autopilot but once fall came around, Brenda Franklin would be a distant memory at Fall Oaks High School.

The answer seemed to satisfy Katie, who topped off Brenda's margarita. Once that pitcher was gone, they cracked open the wine. A bottle into that and Brenda's head was spinning nicely. She could tell by the sanguine quality of Katie's complexion that the alcohol had worked its magic on her as well.

After the umpteenth True Blood episode had ended, Katie took mercy and put on Bridget Jones's Diary. It was a favorite of Brenda's, even if Renee Zellweger's idea of fat was somewhat removed from reality.

"If Renee wants to see fat, she should have seen me my last year of grad school," Brenda said, her speech somewhat slurred.

"You were a chub?" Katie asked. "I can't picture that."

"I guess it wasn't too bad. Once I took up yoga and stopped eating pizza three times a week it went away."

Katie took a sip of wine and gave Brenda a long look. She had something on her mind and if she was hesitating to say it, it was going to be a doozy. Brenda decided to get it over with.

"Penny for your thoughts, Katie."

Katie poured more wine for Brenda, who had more than her fill but didn't bother to say that to Katie. She had a feeling she might need another drink.

"Why do you even want to be vice principal?" Katie asked. "It seems like a lot of bureaucratic bull shit for a small pay bump."

"It's not a small pay bump," Brenda shot back. "It's actually pretty significant."

Okay, maybe it wasn't significant but it was an improvement.

"Plus, I don't know, you'll have to do detentions and all that shit," Katie pointed out. "You never give your students detention and with the discipline aspect of it...."

She hesitated here but Brenda figured she might as well finish. They had come this far.

"After the Martin Pike incident, I didn't think you'd want to bother with that sort of thing again. You didn't go to work for two weeks after that happened!"

Brenda remembered. She didn't need a reminder of it but Katie continued.

"What if there's another Martin Pike at your school? Or three of them? Or ten? Are you up for that?"

Brenda drank her wine and decided how to process this. Martin Pike was a fluke. Frank confirmed that to her when she finally came back to school. It was traumatic but Brenda had survived. And as the saying goes, what doesn't kill us...

"I think I can handle it," Brenda responded.

"Can you?" Katie asked her. "You just don't strike me as the authoritative type. Jason walked all over you and he never brandished a knife while he did it!"

That pissed Brenda off. Who was this bitch to tell her what she could and couldn't do? Katie was an administrative assistant at a law office. Talk about somebody who didn't know anything about authority. She was just about to tell her good friend where she could stick her advice when Katie reached out and began to soothingly rub Brenda's arm.

"I'm sorry. I shouldn't have said anything. You obviously can do whatever you put your mind to. It's just I've seen how much pressure you've put on yourself for this job and I don't want you to be disappointed if it doesn't work out. You've had enough of that lately."

"I know, sweetie. You're just looking out for me and I appreciate it," Brenda said with a fake smile.

Katie nodded and went back to her side of the couch and resumed watching Bridget Jones. Renee Zellweger was sliding down a fire pole and inadvertently flashing her backside to everyone. It was a fleeting moment in a silly romantic comedy but to Brenda, it was the perfect summation of her life.

As she fell asleep in Katie's spare bedroom that night, she decided to go back home tomorrow. The interview was Monday and she knew another night here meant more wine and more unsolicited advice from Katie. Regardless of what might be waiting for her, Brenda knew her peace of mind was too important to sacrifice this close to the interview. As it was, Brenda could swear she could hear tapping against the window. Was there a tree outside? Brenda didn't know and she was too drunk and scared to get up and find out. Everything in her life suddenly seemed inescapable and that feeling was the worst one of all.

Leaving Katie's house the next morning was no easy feat. Brenda not only had to convince Katie she'd be safe but also let her know it wasn't because Katie had offended her (which was only partly true anyway).

Brenda finally told Katie she'd have her neighbors on alert and that if anything seemed out of the ordinary, she would come right back. Katie begrudgingly accepted this and Brenda was on her way home with Sadie, feeling relieved. She loved Katie but she had a tendency to poke her nose where it didn't belong, as well not knowing when to quit when she got on a certain tangent. She hounded Brenda for thirty minutes one time after Brenda accidentally revealed Jason was rather well endowed (that wasn't one of the reasons Brenda stayed with him but it didn't hurt). Katie had cursed her tendency to end up with "small to medium-sized men" and wanted all the gory details from Brenda, who was frankly horrified somebody would be so intrusive about such a personal thing. That awkward memory aside, Brenda pulled into her driveway and saw that everything still looked normal.

She entered the house with Sadie and everything seemed to be in order. Maybe it was all over. After Brenda put her belongings back in her room (carefully hanging her outfit on the door), she felt the rest of last night's alcohol wanting to make its escape. As she sat down on the toilet and voided into the bowl, she noticed the seat was warm. Paranoia gripped Brenda as this seemingly never-ending pee continued. Would her stalker really get her on the toilet? Brenda finally finished and stood up, yanking up her jeans. She flushed the toilet but instead of going down, the water rose dramatically, spilling onto the tiled floor. Brenda scurried away. Even if it was hers, it was still pee. Muttering words under her breath she generally saved for her drive home after a really bad day at school, she went into the laundry room and grabbed some old towels. She came back into the bathroom and dropped them on the ground, knowing full well they would be joining the rat and going out with tomorrow's garbage. Once the floor was covered, she went over to the toilet with the plunger. Fittingly, this had always been Jason's job, as he was generally the person who clogged it in the first place. Brenda stuck the plunger inside the bowl and began to work it as hard as she could. After several pumps, the toilet freed up and the water was swallowed down with a drawn-out glugging sound.

Brenda wondered what caused the plug when a white rag fell out of the plunger. It landed on the ground with a wet plop. As she looked at it closer, she noticed it had red stains on it. She hoped with every fiber of her being that it wasn't blood but she knew that was too good to be true. Unable to stare at it any longer, she ran out of the room and returned with a plastic bag and another pair of dishwashing gloves that would also be going in the trash once this was over. She took a deep breath and held up the rag. It unrolled in her hand and several small white objects fell out of it.

Brenda peered down at them and whatever strength and resolve she had left was gone. She screamed and with good reason. The small objects were human teeth.

The police arrived twenty minutes after Brenda made the call. There were two of them in neatly pressed uniforms. The white officer's nametag read "Austin" and the black officer's read "Hudson."

Austin had a few years on Hudson, who was quite handsome. Even in in her current situation, Brenda found that hard to deny. He was also much kinder. Austin made it seem like coming here was an inconvenience.

"So cigarette butts and a dead rat?" he asked while writing in his notepad. Brenda half-expected him to be drawing doodles.

"And the bloody rag with human teeth in it," Brenda said trying to maintain her cool. "That's why I called you."

"It's possible your sewer backed up," Austin said.

"People flush teeth?" Brenda asked. "That's a new one."

"People flush all kinds of things, Miss Franklin," Austin replied.

"What about the cigarette butts and the dead rat?" Brenda said, her voice starting to waver. "Those just didn't magically appear!"

"I'm not saying they did, ma'am. It's just we need to eliminate all other possibilities," Austin replied.

Hudson was a softer touch.

"Why don't you tell us if there's anybody you have a reason to suspect might be after you," Hudson said, his voice low and warm. "Think hard. What might feel minor to you may have made someone else very angry."

"Martin Pike," she said after a moment.

"Who's Martin Pike?" Hudson asked.

"Martin Pike was a student I had two years ago. It was the beginning of the school year and I had heard all the stories about him. He was a troublemaker. Disruptive in class, always picking fights. He only lasted three weeks in my class and for the first two he actually wasn't a problem. I was surprised and naively thought maybe I had gotten through to him somehow."

At this point, a weak smile appeared on her face. She remembered how excited she was to tell the rest of the staff that the evil Martin Pike was a complete gentleman in her class. She wasn't just a good teacher; she was the type they'd make a movie about someday. The notion would prove to be completely false soon after but Brenda remembered it as the last moment she had any real passion for her job. After Martin Pike, the canon had gotten stale and the kids seemed scary. It was only after Frank had a long, encouraging talk with her that she decided to come back. None of this was relevant to Hudson, though, so she continued.

"One day I was running a little a bit late. The printer in my classroom had gone on the fritz and I had to use the one in the office. I couldn't have been more than thirty seconds late. As I got closer to my classroom, I could hear screaming. When I came in, Martin had another student on the floor and he was punching him over and over. I ran over to pull him off and that was when he brought out the knife. It was this huge hunting knife and he wasn't using it to threaten me. He was planning on killing that student."

Tears were beginning to form as she relived this terrible memory. The patient look from Hudson kept her going.

"I grabbed Martin's wrist but he was too strong. I screamed for help and shifted my weight and dropped to the floor, which was enough to throw Martin off-balance. I was able to hold on to his wrist and I remember seeing the knife against the floor and thinking that if he got his hand free, he'd probably kill me. Another teacher came in and got the knife away from Martin. Security hauled him away and he was expelled. I never saw him again but before they took him out of the room, he looked right at me and said 'You won't know where and you won't know when but I'm going to get you bitch.' And that was it. I took a leave of absence," she finished. She looked up at Hudson's sympathetic eyes. They really were comforting. Even Austin cold demeanor had softened.

"Nice kid," he scoffed before looking at Hudson. "Guarantee we've got a file on him."

"Anyone else, Miss Franklin? Ex boyfriend, current boyfriend, anything like that?" Hudson asked.

Brenda blushed when he said this. Of course he was only doing his job but the thought that this handsome man was gauging her relationship status was definitely a pleasing one.

"There's Jason but I'm positive it's not him," she said, making sure her tone sounded firm.

"What's Jason's last name?"

"Sheridan but trust me, this sort of thing isn't his style."

"We're going to explore all possibilities, Miss Franklin. Is there anyone else?" Hudson asked.

"If it's not Martin Pike, I honestly have no idea who it could be," Brenda replied. And it was true. She had always been well liked by her co-workers, at least until they saw her as competition. She thought of Shawn again. On the hike, it seemed plausible but now it was wholly unnecessary on his part, especially given his friendship with the superintendent. Brenda decided to dismiss it but Hudson had taken note of her hesitation.

"Are you absolutely sure there isn't anyone else who might want to cause you harm, Ms. Franklin?"

And that was when Brenda had a wicked thought. What if she said Shawn's name? It probably wasn't him but surely being questioned by the police would cast some doubt on him as a candidate, especially if his target was a co-worker (and a woman) applying for the job he wanted. The thought was fleeting, though, and Brenda felt dirty for even having it. Not only was it unethical, it could also backfire on her. She would look paranoid and unstable when Shawn's alibi likely proved to be airtight.

"No, there isn't anyone else," she answered him, making sure her tone sounded confident.

"Is there somewhere you can stay tonight if you don't feel safe at your home?" Hudson followed up.

She briefly entertained the notion that he was making her an offer but like most nice thoughts these days, it was fleeting.

"To be honest, I have a big interview tomorrow and I'd prefer to stay here. If it's possible…" she began, hoping Hudson would get the hint. Luckily, he did.

"We'll send a patrol car past your house every hour," he said. "How's that?"

"That would be wonderful. Thank you so much!" she said flashing him a grateful (and hopefully pretty) smile.

"You're very welcome. Have a good day, ma'am." Hudson said and motioned for Austin to follow.

As they walked away, she blurted out "Brenda."

They turned around.

"Excuse me?"

"You can call me Brenda," she said, hoping to continue the conversation but Hudson just gave her a polite smile in response and continued on. She pictured Austin making a snide comment about her in the car and Hudson laughing at it. As she walked backed into the house, she pictured Renee Zellweger sliding down the fire pole and exposing her backside.

That's me, she thought, slamming the door behind her.

Once Brenda was back inside, she fed Sadie and took a nap, looking around at the outside before closing all the blinds and curtains in the house. It was a beautiful day that was ideal for another hike or a walk downtown to get bagels at her favorite coffee shop. None of that seemed appealing today and all Brenda wanted to do was sleep. She was out as soon as her head hit the pillow. At least one thing was coming easy for her.

It was dark out when Brenda woke up and she cursed herself for sleeping so long. It would prove impossible to go to bed at her usual time. Resigned to possibly having a sleepless night, she went to the kitchen and opened up the refrigerator, settling on some leftover tuna casserole. She set it on the counter and looked outside. Her timing was perfect as a shiny black and white police car rolled past her house slowly. Hudson was holding up his end of the bargain. She wondered if he was driving but decided his shift must have ended in the middle of her prolonged nap. Mourning another missed connection; she ate a little bit of the casserole and made some peppermint tea. She needed to get to sleep tonight. She hadn't pulled any all-nighters since grad school, mainly because she was useless without sleep. She was nervous enough about the interview and the last thing she wanted was to go in there feeling like a zombie. Between the tea and the patrol car putting her mind at ease, it looked like sleep was going to possible after all. She went in a little after midnight, stopping to make sure her outfit was still pressed and wrinkle-free. When she saw it was, she fell back asleep, noting she had spent almost the entire day in bed. She doubted a vice principal would have time for such nonsense.

The next morning, Brenda woke up as soon as her alarm sounded. She went into the bathroom and looked at her reflection in the mirror. The woman staring back at her had puffy eyes and frizzy hair but that didn't stop Brenda from giving her a confident smile.

"You've got this, girl."

Forty-five minutes later, Brenda was dressed and ready to go. As she gave herself one last admiring glance in the mirror, she knew things were going to change for the better. They had to.

When Brenda stepped outside, she noticed a small crowd had gathered at the foot of her driveway. She recognized some neighbors but there were also people she didn't know. Some of them were whispering among themselves and others were taking pictures with their phones.

She walked out to get a better look and when she saw what had everyone's attention, she became light-headed.

"Someone catch her!" one of the onlookers called out. As Brenda started to fall, she felt strong hands grab her.

"You okay?" she heard the person ask.

No, she wasn't okay. Far fucking from it.

When Hudson arrived with Austin in tow, Brenda decided she no longer found him handsome or sympathetic. He was just another meathead cop who had the same indifference for his job as she did for hers. That was not something she wanted to have in common with him.

Mr. Hampton, who lived two doors down, was already painting her garage. The paint he was using wasn't an exact match but anything beat having "Watch it, bitch!" scrawled across it in large, jagged red letters. Mr. Hampton worked fast and now it just read "t, bitch!" though that last word seemed to jump out at her accusingly. But accusing her of what?

Hudson pointed at it. "Did you get pictures?"

"Oh, I've got pictures. And even if I didn't, half my fucking neighborhood did."

"You really should have waited until we got here…"

"I don't care, I want it gone!" Brenda yelled at him. "What the hell happened to the car that was going to keep an eye on my house?"

"We had an emergency and that unit responded to it. I'm sorry about that," he said, with a look that could almost pass for apologetic.

"Yeah, sure you are," Brenda said without looking at him. "I had a really important interview I needed to get to. Do you understand that?"

"You said they also slashed your tires?"

"All four of them!" she said, tapping her wheel with her expensive new shoe that was proving to be a worthless investment. She had made this lovely discovery after almost passing out in front of everyone. Even her tires weren't slashed; she couldn't have gone to the interview, not after this. When she called and explained what happened, Frank was sympathetic and told her they could reschedule for Wednesday.

"I have to strongly suggest you find somewhere else to stay until we clear this up, Miss Franklin," Hudson suggested.

"Yeah, no shit!" she snapped at him. "In the meantime, are you making any progress in finding out who this psycho is? I mean, I call you guys, you make it sound like everything's going to be okay and then…"

Hudson waited patiently for her to calm down. Austin had already checked out and gone over to Mr. Hampton, who was almost finished painting.

"We looked into Martin Pike and he's missing," Hudson said.

"Missing?"

"He was living with his grandmother. She told us he took off a few weeks ago and she hasn't heard from him since. We have several leads we're following up on," Hudson said in his soothing voice.

"Do you think it's him then?" Brenda asked.

"He's our best suspect. I promise you we're doing everything we can to find him."

And Brenda believed him. It just didn't make her feel any better.

After everyone had left, Brenda called her mechanic and ordered a tow. In addition to the tires, she'd have him check the entire car. She wasn't taking any more chances. She changed into jeans and a sweatshirt and went outside to wait for the tow truck. She decided to ride along and wait at the garage. Anywhere was better than her house. As she stood on the sidewalk, Mrs. Anderson walked over. She was Brenda's favorite neighbor.

"How are you doing, sweetheart?" Mrs. Anderson asked her, clutching Brenda's hand in hers. They reminded Brenda of her grandmother's hands, giving her some much-needed comfort.

"I've been better, Mrs. Anderson," Brenda replied.

"I just want you to know if there's anything you need, you call me right away!" Mrs. Anderson said, her tone insistent.

"I will. Thank you so much!" Brenda said and Mrs. Anderson clutched her hand even tighter.

"You're overdue for something good, Brenda. And I'm going to pray you get it," Mrs. Anderson said as the tow truck pulled up.

"Please do. It would mean a lot."

"I'll let you go now but you hang in there, Brenda!" Mrs. Anderson finished. She gave Brenda's hand a final squeeze and headed back to her house. Brenda walked over to greet the tow truck driver.

Mrs. Anderson stood in the doorway of her house and watched the driver load Brenda's car onto the flatbed. Mrs. Anderson thought Brenda was a sweet young woman who held a good job and knew how to carry a conversation but like so many women of her generation, she had no brains.

Mrs. Anderson knew this to be true because of that do-nothing Brenda had been shacked up with. Her husband (gone five years now) was an honorable and hardworking man. When Mrs. Anderson had seen that slug of Brenda's enter that house with more cases of beer than bouquets of flowers, that's when she knew that Brenda had no brains. Why else would she allow herself to be treated like that? Mrs. Anderson grieved over this fact before shutting her door and going into her living room to watch television. She just loved that Michael Symon.

Brenda spent two hours at the garage. Her mechanic changed the tires and gave it a once over and found nothing else wrong with it. Seven hundred dollars later, she was on her way home.

When she got back, there was no evidence of last night's misdeeds. Not that it really mattered. The memory would be forever burned into her brain and she knew reliving it would make her stomach feel like it was filled with rotten fruit. She didn't expect it to ever get better, either. And going inside her house only made it worse.

It was completely trashed. The contents of the kitchen were spread out all the floor and the furniture in her living room had been ripped open with white stuffing spilled everywhere. Worst of all, Sadie was missing. The back door was wide open, which is how her admirer had gotten in. The lock had been jimmied and not by a professional based on the scratches and sloppy appearance of the doorknob. Even if this person hadn't taken Sadie, she had surely run out of the house, leaving Brenda completely alone in a place that was now strange and dangerous. With no other recourse, Brenda fell to her knees and cried.

Brenda was back at Katie's. The mood was solemn. She hugged Brenda and offered to cook her dinner, which Brenda accepted with a nod. She didn't feel like talking right now. In the interest of preserving her sanity and keeping her mind busy, she decided she was going back to school tomorrow. There might be some whispers but as long as she did her job and kept it together, school was what she needed. Katie had called animal control and told them about Sadie. They said they would keep their eyes open and while Brenda was sure they would, she thought Sadie was lost forever. Hopefully she could find some kind of peace, which was beginning to feel impossible for Brenda. The police had come again, only it wasn't Austin and Hudson. They promised to step up their search for Martin Pike and to keep a careful eye on the house, which was a fool's errand at this point. How much worse could it get?

Brenda went to bed early that night and fell into a restless sleep. When she woke up the next morning, she felt like she had been beaten with a sack full of hammers. She powered through, knowing her peace of mind for the interview rested on her ability to maintain her normal schedule.

She dressed in gray slacks and a navy top and went to work. As expected, there were stares and whispers, as well as some sympathetic well wishing from her co-workers. She took it all in stride and went to her first class and taught Jane Eyre.

Jane didn't have it easy but at least she had a Mr. Rochester waiting for her at the end. Despite his troubled past and missing extremities, Brenda didn't think that sounded bad at all. The kids were bored, of course, and she couldn't blame them. It was frustrating that the school system introduced such wonderful literature to children at an age where they weren't ready to properly process or appreciate it. A couple of her female students seemed to enjoy it and Brenda chalked that up as a minor win. Teaching provided her little else these days.

As she left school that day, she saw Shawn standing at the end of the hallway talking to a couple of other teachers.

"Brenda!"

She looked over at him.

"Good luck with your rescheduled interview!" he said with a thumbs up.

"Thanks, dick," she muttered as she went out the door.

Shawn turned back to the teachers he was talking to.

"What did she say?"

Brenda got back to Katie's a little after four; knowing Katie wouldn't be back until five. She had driven around looking for Sadie but after the tears started to flow, she was in no condition to drive. She thought the time alone would be good for her but it proved be the opposite, as the crying continued. Brenda was exhausted when it finally ended. She poured herself a glass of wine and flopped down in front of Katie's television. The first channel she stopped at had Full House reruns on. There was probably something better but Brenda didn't have the energy or interest to find it. When Katie came home a short time later, she looked at Brenda with an eager expression on her face.

"Half-priced appetizers and drinks at Applebee's on me?"

She noticed Brenda's morose expression and rolled it back.

"Order in?"

Brenda gave her a weak smile in response. "I thought you'd never ask."

Brenda went to bed extra early that night. Just as she started to drift off, her phone started buzzing. The sound was jarring on top of the nightstand and Brenda only assumed the worst. When she mustered up the strength to look at the display, she saw it was Jason. She couldn't believe it. A million thoughts raced through her head, ranging from annoyance that he'd be calling on her a school night to excitement and curiosity. What could he possibly want? Taking a deep breath, she answered.

"What is it?"

"Bren?" the voice on the other end slurred at her.

"Who else would it be? Now what do you want? I have a big day tomorrow?"

"Can you come and get me? I need a ride and I'm too drunk to drive."

"Then call a cab, Jason."

"Brenda, please," he bleated at her. "I don't have any money and I've had a really bad night!"

"You've had a really bad night? Let me tell you about my life lately!" she shot back at him.

"Pick me up and you can," he said, affecting his little boy voice. It was a cheap trick and worst of all, it was working. Brenda sighed.

"Where are you?"

Ten minutes later she was on the road, fighting against her better judgment, as well as Katie's vehement protests. She had followed Brenda all the way to her car and although she made a lot of sense, Brenda wanted to see him. She needed to see him. Any semblance of her past happiness was welcomed at this point. Maybe Jason had changed. Being drunk on a Tuesday night didn't make that seem very possible but Brenda was willing to risk it.

She arrived at Coyle's, one of his favorite bars. She could never figure out why. She had accompanied him here twice and thought the place was a pit. The men looked ready to fight and the women wore trashy clothes and had poorly-inked tattoos covering their arms and legs. One of these women was standing with Jason and screaming at him as she pulled up. This was definitely a bad idea but Jason saw her and gave her a grateful wave. He ran over to the car and desperately yanked at the door handle, which Brenda unlocked for him. As he got in, the woman threw her shoe at Jason, striking him in the head.

"Watch it, bitch!" he yelled at her before getting in the car. Brenda's grip tightened on the steering wheel when he said this. She looked at Jason, who reeked of cheap whiskey.

"Brenda, go!"

She hit the gas while the woman continued screaming at Jason. Within seconds, she was just a speck of white trash in Brenda's rear view mirror. She just hoped she stayed that way for Jason.

They drove in silence for a few moments before he spoke up.

"Thanks for coming to get me."

"Oh, no problem. I have an interview for the vice principal job at my school but you're drunk on a Tuesday night. It warms my heart to see you doing so well."

"Don't you want to know who that was?"

"Why would I want to know who that was, Jason?"

"Fair enough. So you have an interview to be vice principal?"

"Yes, and I should be in bed right now," Brenda said.

"They'd be stupid not to go with you," Jason offered.

"Thanks, I'll tell them to take that into consideration."

"So I've been thinking lately," Jason started and Brenda decided this was as good a time as any to ask him the question that was burning into her brain at the moment. Jason thinking could often prove dangerous.

"Have you been coming by my house, Jason?"

There was an awkward pause. Jesus, was it him? And what did she do if it was? Throw him out of the car? Take him to the police? She knew he didn't take the break-up well but she never thought in a million years he'd be dangerous.

"Did you see me?" he finally managed.

"Jason, if I saw you, you'd be in jail right now!"

"Jail? What the hell are you talking about?" he asked and she looked at him. His bewilderment was genuine. She let him continue.

"I drove past the other night but I didn't stop after what I saw."

Brenda's blood froze.

"What did you see?"

"Well, there was a car in your driveway that I didn't recognize. I figured you had met somebody else."

The ride back to Katie's seemed to go on forever even though Jason's parents lived only a few miles away. Of course Jason didn't get a good look at the car, he had only seen enough to know it didn't belong to anybody he knew. He claimed it was so painful he just kept driving. Although she didn't owe him an explanation, Brenda informed him it was also somebody she didn't know and refused to divulge further details. The rest of the drive was uncomfortable. When they arrived at his Mom's house, he told her how much he missed her. If that wasn't enough, he actually leaned in to kiss her but his breath was a rank combination of booze and the corn chips they served at the bar. She turned her head away and refused to look at him until he got out of the car.

Whatever happiness he had brought her was completely gone.

She felt numb when she woke up the next morning. It was an improvement from the crying jags but the absence of the nervousness she should be feeling was unsettling.

She dressed in an outfit that was different from the one she had purchased for the interview. She had sweat clean through it and doubted she'd ever wear it again. She ate a small container of yogurt for breakfast and said goodbye to Katie. It was the only words they had spoken since Brenda had taken off in the night to affirm her connection to Jason was actually long dead and not worth the trouble in the first place. The pain of this realization had diminished as well. She knew Jason would simply be some guy she mentioned in passing if there was ever a proper context to bring it up. Otherwise, he was history. A distant memory that would fall somewhere between the summer camp she attended in eighth grade and her twenty-first birthday, which consisted of a few margaritas, kissing some random guy, and falling asleep on her friend's couch. And yet dating her was probably Jason's greatest accomplishment. Talk about pathetic.

She arrived at Frank's office and was greeted by Janet, his pigeon-breasted secretary. Janet rarely smiled and never engaged in small talk. At this point, she was one of Brenda's favorite people.

"I'll let him know you're here," she said as she reached for her phone. Brenda nodded in response and that was when she noticed the rip in her tights. It extended from the top of her left knee down to her ankle. She couldn't believe it. She had only worn them one other time. Alarms began to immediately fire off in her head. She was screwing up now at a fundamental level. Dressing well was something her overbearing mother had imparted on her from a young age. If there was a frayed hem or rip that couldn't be fixed with a sewing machine, to the garbage or Goodwill it went. Her mother's motto had been "Dress well, test well," which Brenda had utilized through college and grad school. It worked, too. She had maintained a perfect four-oh. Brenda making sure her hair, clothing, and make-up were immaculate didn't just provide a good first impression with employers; it made her feel confident and put-together.

She stared at the white skin visible through the long tear in her tights and recognized this wasn't just an oversight; the events of the past week had completely thrown her game off. Frank came out as she continued gaping at the rip. She tossed her skirt over it as best she could and stood up to greet him with a handshake and a smile that made her feel like The Joker. She was doomed but Frank motioned for her to follow him into his office. It was now or never.

Frank sat down in his threadbare chair. It made a long creaking sound as he sat back. At first, Brenda let her eyes dart all over his office. She started at the picture of him with his family, all of them grinning vacantly in front of a bland blue backdrop. She moved next to his bowling trophies, then on to his degrees, which had adopted a yellowish tint. Frank had been in school a long time ago. He had been Principal since she had started nine years ago. This meant they had a rapport, right? Frank seemed to think so.

"My bowling trophies," he announced, pointing at them. "My wife thinks I should engage in sports that emphasize fitness a little more."

He patted his gut and smiled.

"But stick to what you're good at, right?"

"That's my motto," Brenda said in an effort to match his congenial tone.

"As a younger man, I enjoyed basketball but I was never very good at it," he continued. "Took up bowling fifteen years ago. With four league championships, I like to think it's justified."

"Sounds like it. I don't have any bowling trophies." Sweet Jesus, those words had actually left her mouth but Frank didn't seem to care. His demeanor also suggested they'd be moving on to business now, so hopefully she was done putting her foot in her mouth.

"Why don't you tell me why you think you'd make a good vice principal?"

Brenda had rehearsed this speech in her head, ad nauseam. It sounded good saying it out loud. So far, so good. Frank seemed impressed as he moved on to the next question.

"You've been at this school for awhile. What kind of changes do you think we could be making?"

She also knew this question was coming and in a lot of ways, it would be the hardest one. It would require some gentle wording. Like any underfunded public school there were a myriad of problems that needed fixing but pointing out the most obvious ones would only remind Frank of the things he couldn't change. That wouldn't exactly put her candidacy in a positive light, so she gave another rehearsed answer and named ideas that were just ambitious enough to sound impressive but also the kind that would easily be forgotten and swept under the rug in a year. It worked. She could tell Frank was hooked by the way he leaned forward and nodded at each of her suggestions. Optimism began to swell in her chest. This might work out after all.

That was when Frank's eyes left hers. He sat back, looking slightly ashamed. She knew what was coming next.

"Now if you'll forgive me, Miss Franklin, I have to ask you a question about a past incident that I know isn't a pleasant memory for you but since a similar incident could arise in this position, it needs to be addressed. Martin Pike."

"What about him?" she said, trying her best to sound steady.

"The incident with Martin Pike was one of the worst we've ever had at this school. Given its effect on you, how equipped do you feel to deal with a situation like that now?"

Brenda fingered the rip in her tights and took a long time to answer. She thought of the cigarette butts below her bedroom window, the dead rat on her patio, the bloody rag, the teeth in her toilet, the slashed tires, and the vandalism to her garage. And of course Sadie. Poor Sadie.

"Miss Franklin?"

Her eyes started to blur with tears. This wasn't happening. Not now.

Frank was concerned.

"Miss Franklin, is everything all right?"

No, everything was not all right but she owed him an answer.

"I just need this job."

"Excuse me?" Frank asked.

"After Martin Pike, teaching wasn't the same for me anymore but I stuck with it because I had loved it so much and it's the only thing I know how to do."

Frank stared at her, unsure how to respond.

"You probably heard I broke up with my boyfriend. And now all these terrible things have been happening to me and the one thing I held onto was getting this job. And I know I must look like the worst candidate right now but I promise you, I'll do an amazing job. I'll be the best..."

And that was it. She was sobbing. Frank's silence told her everything. It was over.

Frank thanked for her coming in and gave her the rest of the day off. As she walked out of the office, she pictured him rolling his eyes and shaking his head to Janet. This would spread like wildfire. She doubted she could ever set foot in this school again.

When she got back to Katie's, she flopped down on the couch and kicked her shoes off. Sleep seemed like the best possible option and just as she drifted off, she heard her phone vibrate on the coffee table next to her. She slowly lifted her head up and checked the display. It was a number she didn't recognize. She answered it. Maybe somebody had found Sadie.

"Hello?"

"Miss Franklin?" The voice was familiar but she couldn't place it.

"Yes?"

"This is Officer Hudson, how are you?"

She sat up. "I'm fine, thank you."

"I'm just calling to let you know we've tracked down Martin Pike."

Now she stood up. "Really?"

"He's been living with a cousin in Wisconsin, he just didn't bother to tell his Grandma. He's been there two weeks, which was confirmed by multiple people. It wasn't him."

"So what does that mean?" she asked, knowing full well what it meant.

"It means the person harassing you is still out there. But we'll find them."

He said this last part firmly, as if it should put her mind at ease but it didn't.

"That's just great. Thank you," she said, hanging up on him. He had started to say something else but she didn't care. Defeated, she fell back on the couch and let herself sleep.

When she woke up, Katie was unloading groceries in the kitchen. She turned around when she saw Brenda stir.

"Hey you!" Katie called out. "How'd your interview go?"

A headache began to throb in Brenda's head.

"Don't ask."

Katie's face wrinkled in concern. "Really?"

"Really."

Katie walked over and sat down next to her. "What happened?"

"I don't want to talk about it. And in more good news, it's not Martin Pike."

"Well, that is good news, though, right?"

"No, it means the person is still out there, although I'm not sure what else is left in my life for them to fuck up."

Katie didn't respond and that was fine. What could she say?

"How was your day?" Brenda asked, expecting a long-winded rant about Katie's co-worker Gwen but Katie mercifully spared her that.

"It was work. I thought I'd make us stir-fry for dinner. How does that sound?" Katie asked.

Brenda had a feeling all food would taste like cardboard for the near future but she told Katie it sounded fine. Katie patted her leg and stood up.

"Great, I'll get started right now."

She looked at Brenda closer.

"And I don't know if you noticed but your pantyhose are ripped."

The headache in Brenda's head surged as she watched Katie skip to the kitchen. She began slicing vegetable and singing an off-key rendition of Selena Gomez. From out of nowhere, Brenda had a vivid picture in her head of Katie slicing her finger off and screaming in pain. It was a horrible thought and one she pushed out of her head as quickly as it had arrived.

Still, for the first time that day, she smiled.

By the time dinner was ready, Brenda had changed into jeans and a black crew neck. The food was as flavorless as she expected but she complimented it when Katie asked her about it. And it turned out being spared from hearing about Gwen was only temporary, as Katie spent the entire dinner complaining about her. Brenda had never met Gwen but guessed she was hardly the horror show Katie made her out to be.

After they finished eating, Katie sat down to catch up on Scandal, giving Brenda some more peace and quiet. She was about to head to bed when her phone rang. The display told her it was Mrs. Anderson. Great. Had Brenda's house been burned down, too? Assuming the worst, she answered.

"Hello?"

"Hi, Brenda. I have good news for you."

Brenda froze. It couldn't be.

"Are you there, dear?" Mrs. Anderson asked.

"Yes, I'm here," she finally said

"Good, because I found Sadie!"

Mrs. Anderson kept talking but Brenda didn't hear it. She had dropped her phone. This unexpected good news had halted all her motor functions. It was just too good to be true.

Ten minutes later, she was on her way to Mrs. Anderson's house. It was true. After she gathered herself and picked up the phone, Mrs. Anderson had held her phone out to Sadie and at the sound of Brenda's voice, Sadie gave her an all-too familiar "Meow." It was Sadie and that meow sounded like music to Brenda.

She pulled into Mrs. Anderson's driveway without even giving a passing glance to her own house. She just wanted to see her cat, which had sadly become the lone ray of sunshine in her life.

She walked quickly to Mrs. Anderson's front door and saw her behind the storm door holding Sadie and stroking her head.

"Look, Sadie, it's your Mama!" Mrs. Anderson said as Brenda came inside.

"Sadie!" Brenda said as Mrs. Anderson handed her the cat, which merely regarded her with casual indifference. That didn't stop her from planting kisses all over the cat. She probably looked foolish but she didn't care. She needed one thing to go right and finding Sadie would do nicely.

"Would you like some iced tea, sweetie?" Mrs. Anderson asked.

"Yes, please."

"Have a seat and I'll be right back," Mrs. Anderson said before heading for the kitchen. Brenda sat down in on the couch, setting her purse and Sadie down on the floor next to her. Mrs. Anderson returned with ice tea that had freshly-cut lemon wedges on the rims of the glasses.

Brenda took hers and sipped it gratefully. It tasted wonderful.

"So any news?" Mrs. Anderson asked.

"No, they ruled out the person I thought it was but they still don't have a clue who it is," Brenda said, sounding glum.

Mrs. Anderson looked at her with sympathetic eyes.

"I've been keeping my eye on your house and I have noticed police cars come by on a fairly regular basis."

"Yeah, too bad they didn't come by when I needed them to," Brenda said.

"Well, I'm sure it's just a matter of time," Mrs. Anderson said.

"I suppose," Brenda said, wishing she had Mrs. Anderson's optimism.

"Are you staying with your friend in the meantime?"

"Yeah. I have to stop in to get Sadie's things after I leave here but otherwise, I don't think I'll be back until it's all sorted out," Brenda replied.

"Just remember that when you do come back, my eyes and ears are wide open," Mrs. Anderson said before leaning in close, as if to divulge a huge secret.

"I still have my husband's pistol. And it's loaded," she whispered to Brenda, her eyes widening. Brenda didn't take Mrs. Anderson for a gun owner but given everything that had happened, it was hardly surprising.

They chatted for another fifteen minutes and then Brenda gathered up Sadie, who had disappeared into one of the spare bedrooms. She pulled out of Mrs. Anderson's driveway and parked in her own, which now belonged to a home that looked dark and foreboding. She took a deep breath, reminding herself she would be in and out in no time. She turned to Sadie, who was asleep in the backseat.

"Back in a minute, Sadie."

She got out and entered her house, oblivious to the car idling in the shadows three houses down.

Brenda unlocked the door and went in, practically tripping over herself to turn on as many lights as she could. She worked as fast as she could, grabbing Sadie's food, bed, and litter box. She would need more clothes but she decided to come back during the day with Katie in tow. She had already spent too much time here. Balancing Sadie's things in her right arm, she flipped off all the lights and went out the front door. As soon as her foot hit the porch, the hit to her head came quickly, prompting a brief blast of agonizing pain and then nothing. She was unconscious before she hit the ground.

When Brenda came to, she was on her kitchen floor with her arms and legs tightly bound with duct tape. There were footsteps behind her and she craned her neck around, only to get a glimpse of dark loafers and black pants. As the mysterious figure moved closer, Brenda could see they were carrying a red container. The person began spilling the liquid contents out and a pungent and familiar smell filled her nose. It was gasoline. She was going to be burned alive. She tried to talk but the gasoline fumes were too strong. Her throat constricted and she could only cough. Her attacker finished pouring the gasoline and stood by her front door, pulling out a pack of matches.

"You should have watched it, bitch!" the voice rasped at her.

Next door, Mrs. Anderson was watching an old episode of Law and Order. Repetitive show but she always found it addicting and comforting. When the commercial came on, she stood up to use the bathroom and noticed Brenda had left her purse behind. Mrs. Anderson shook her head at the sight of it.

No brains, indeed.

The person lit the match, dropped it, and the flames immediately sprang to life. Brenda croaked out a scream and did her best to wiggle to safety, the flames moving closer to her. She dragged herself into the living room but knew it would only be a matter of time before the fire worked its way through the entire house.

"Oh my God! Brenda!" she heard Mrs. Anderson scream from the front of the house.

"I'm back here!"

"Hold on, dear!"

The flames grew higher and the smoke was getting black and thick, causing Brenda to choke and feel light-headed. In the back of the house, she heard glass shatter.

"Brenda! I'm coming in!" It was Mrs. Anderson. She entered the room, covering her face with her shirt. She tried to undo duct tape that was tied around Brenda's feet and hands.

"Brenda, I can't do this! You need to help me!"

Mrs. Anderson's words faded as Brenda finally passed out, the smoke and heat overwhelming her.

When she came to, she was in a hospital bed. Her throat and chest felt like they were filled with ground-up glass.

A doctor and a police detective were standing near her bed. After the doctor checked her over, the detective introduced himself as Sergeant Matthews.

After Brenda regained her bearings, she spoke, which proved to be a Herculean task given how sore her throat was.

"How's Mrs. Anderson?" she asked Sergeant Matthews.

"She's okay. After you passed out, another neighbor came in and helped her get you out. You're both very lucky," he replied.

"And my cat?"

"Your friend Ms. Fields took it back to her house. She'll be back in a few minutes. We notified your parents and they're also on their way. They should be here tomorrow," Matthews said.

"Did you find out who did this?"

"No," Matthews said. "But we will."

"Yeah, I've heard that one before," Brenda said, her tone bitter.

"Witnesses saw a yellow Volkswagen Bug leaving the scene. They didn't get a license plate but we're already looking into every owner of that model and color. We'll get them," Matthews finished.

Yellow Volkswagen Bug? It seemed familiar but Brenda couldn't place why. Whatever it was, it would have to wait until later. She needed sleep.

Her parents arrived the next day and after admonishing her for not telling them about all this in the first place, her mother tearfully begged her to come and stay with them. Although Brenda loved her mother, it would take roughly a day and half for her to get on Brenda's nerves. Still, without many options, Brenda relented.

Brenda was released from the hospital two days later. Her parents went home but only after Brenda made a firm promise to be at their place no later than Sunday. It was already Friday. No rest for the wicked. She had Katie drive her past her house, which was a black shell now. The first real home of her own and there it sat, a sad relic of her now former life.

Katie convinced her that night to finally go to Applebee's for half-priced appetizers and drinks. The alcohol burned her still-sensitive throat and the appetizers were mostly cold but she was alive, such as it was. As she pretended to listen to Katie go on about Gwen, Brenda made a mental checklist of things to do before heading to her parents. She had already taken care of work. Frank, along with two other teachers and Julie, had visited her and told her to take all the time she needed. Brenda thanked them but didn't have the heart to say she wouldn't be coming back. It wasn't just Fall Oaks, either. Brenda didn't think she'd ever teach again. She also didn't bother to ask who got the job. She supposed it was Shawn but did it really matter now?

She also made a mental note to go and see Mrs. Anderson. There would be hugs, tears, and likely some more iced tea. There could be worse notes to leave town on.

Just as they were finishing their food, Brenda got a phone call from Sergeant Matthews.

"Miss Franklin? We've found your attacker."

Twenty minutes later, Brenda and Katie were at the police station with Matthews.

"We picked her up an hour ago going the wrong way on a one-way street," he said.

"Her?" Brenda asked, bewildered.

"And it gets weirder. Follow me," Matthews said.

He led them into a room with a two-way mirror. The person seated on the other side looked like a woman, though "shell" might be a more accurate term. She was thin and emaciated with a shawl wrapped around her head, likely to mask baldness. There were dark circles under her eyes. She didn't look crazy or weird to Brenda. She looked angry.

"Her name is Alice Connors," Matthews asked. "Do you know this woman?"

Brenda could only shake her head, unable to take her eyes off Alice.

"Well, she claims she knows you. Said you had an altercation in the parking lot of a grocery store last week. You cut in front of her..."

Matthews continued and realization hit Brenda. The yellow Volkswagen Bug she had cut off. That's what all this was about? It was a fleeting moment a week ago (though it seemed like decades). That's what made this woman homicidal?

"So she must have followed you back to your place," Matthews continued. "She was diagnosed with terminal brain cancer six months ago. The teeth you found in your bathroom are hers. We noticed she was missing some, probably from the chemo treatment she's been going through."

"Didn't anybody notice or care she was running around so much when she's that sick?" Katie asked.

"Her husband's dead and she has two kids who don't visit very often. She has a neighbor that helps her from time to time but she's mostly on her own," Matthews replied.

Brenda watched as Alice began yanking on her handcuffs. When the officer watching her went over to calm her down, she started shrieking and screaming incoherently. It was an awful sight but Brenda still couldn't look away.

"We could charge her but given her physical and mental state, she's likely going to end up at a full-time medical facility," Matthews told Brenda. "Brain cancer can make you behave erratically. It's safe to say she wasn't herself when she went after you."

Brenda continued to watch Alice, who had calmed down but was still clearly agitated. Brenda thought about what Matthews just said and looked into Alice's eyes. What she saw confirmed Matthews assessment was completely wrong. This woman knew exactly what she was doing.

When they got back to Katie's, Brenda tried to keep her thoughts trained on Alice, which wasn't easy, as Katie had been talking non-stop.

"I can't fucking believe it. So you just pulled out in front of her? That's it?" she asked Brenda.

"That's it," Brenda said.

"Jesus, the fucking nuts out there. I mean, I know she has cancer and everything but to go to those lengths because somebody pulled in front of you. It's absurd!"

Katie stopped to reflect on this before turning back to Brenda.

"How about I make us some margaritas?"

It was a bad idea but Brenda was leaving soon and likely never returning, so she agreed. Katie ran into the kitchen and fired up her blender. If that wasn't grating enough, she also started singing an atonal rendition of an Adele song.

The abrasive noise provided the perfect soundtrack as Brenda thought about a future that wasn't looking particularly bright. She was quitting her job and while she could get her house fixed, it would be full of nothing but bad memories. Feeling like her life was devoid of any real goodness or meaning, she turned her thoughts back to Alice. Here was a woman facing a painful death sentence with almost no friends and children who barely made time for her. Brenda knew life could deal you an unfair hand and that was about as unfair as it got. When you had everything stacked against you with no hope for a positive outcome, was it really that hard to believe something trivial could put you over the edge? As Brenda listened to Katie loudly butcher Adele while grinding margaritas in her equally obnoxious blender, it wasn't hard to believe at all. Despite the vicious things Alice had done to her, Brenda not only found her actions understandable but also strangely relatable. Everybody has a breaking point. How much shit should you be expected to take in this life?

Brenda suddenly had another horrible thought about Katie. Only this time she didn't push it away. She let it linger as Katie returned with the margaritas.

"What are you grinning about?" Katie asked her.

Brenda let the smile stay but decided to keep her thoughts to herself, at least for now.

She imagined what might happen when her mother inevitably rolled out her first backhanded compliment in a few days. It was even worse than what she pictured for Katie but it made her smile grow even wider. Katie looked confused.

"Brenda? You're starting to freak me out a little bit," she said.

"Katie, my dear," Brenda said with her grin firmly intact. "You don't know the half of it."

And with that, she took a sip of her margarita.

It was delicious.

A Fool's Errand

In a few minutes, Freddy Wingate would be dead and nobody would care. Why should they? Most of the other residents in his building were polite enough but save for Percy, Freddy didn't have many friends. And that was fair. Freddy knew his limits. He had an eighth-grade education. It wasn't like he could offer much in the way of stimulating conversation.

"You're keeping the world clean!" his mother used to tell him with a warm smile. And that was enough to give Freddy purpose each day. He was keeping the world clean. He remembered the immense sense of pride he got from looking at a freshly mopped floor. Even if the well-dressed people who walked over it the next day didn't notice, it was still a huge task that he had completed all by himself.

As he continued his painful hike up the stairs, he was saddened by the fact it had been such a long time since he had done anything productive. Once he threw his back out, Freddy's days of working were over. He went on disability and that meant days in front of the television with his mother. That was okay, though. Freddy was almost able to keep up with the soap operas she watched but he got more enjoyment from watching her "Ooh!" and "Aah!" at the various reveals that somebody's brother was sleeping with somebody else's wife. However, those slight but pleasant times ended once obesity and emphysema took Freddy's mother from him. Not only was Freddy alone now, he was unable to keep the house he had spent his whole life in. He settled for a one-bedroom Section 8 apartment in the middle of downtown and that's where he had spent the last twelve pointless years.

After what seemed like an eternity, Freddy finally reached the roof. His knees were screaming but the pain in his back was merely a dull roar tonight. At least things weren't all bad. Freddy opened the door and stepped onto the roof. He could hear the lively sounds of the city buzzing below him. That had taken some getting used to. When he lived with his mother, Freddy only had to contend with her snoring (and farting) at night, coupled with the rickety air conditioner unit she had in her window. Those familiar sounds from the next room brought Freddy comfort, allowing him to fall asleep with ease, even on the nights when his back was acting up.

The sounds of the city, however, were hectic and unforgiving. Every honking horn and shout seemed like a direct threat to him, even though he lived five floors up. He wore a sleep mask and earmuffs but even those scared him, as it prevented him from knowing what was going on in his apartment. Anyone or anything could come in and he wouldn't know it. Freddy eventually came to terms with these intrusive noises and was able to get a decent night's sleep but it was a far cry from the nights of warmth and peace at his mother's house.

Freddy stared at the edge of the roof. He had thought a lot about it and decided it was best to jump from the other side of the building, away from the rec room where the other residents liked to watch television and play pool. He knew some of them would find his body and that made him sad, particularly for the ladies. They shouldn't see something so horrible but Freddy didn't have a gun, so jumping seemed like his best option. Even if nobody cared about him, he hoped they could at least forgive him.

Freddy took a deep breath and walked toward the edge of the roof. It wouldn't be long now. He got about halfway before he stopped dead in his tracks. It turned out Freddy had company up here, although this person wouldn't be able to provide much in the way of conversation. They were seated in a lawn chair with a plastic bag over their head that was tied in place with a black leather belt. The bag wasn't moving. Freddy didn't know how many stars were on the American flag but he knew this person was dead. Freddy stared at the figure, unsure how to proceed. After a minute, he decided this was a sign from God and he should probably at least see who the person was. At least that's what his mother would say and that was good enough for him. Although he was nervous, Freddy walked over to get a closer look.

He reached out and poked the body. He had heard dead bodies were stiff like wooden boards but this one felt pretty loose. For one harrowing moment, Freddy wondered if the person was still alive somehow. Shouldn't he rip the bag off? But what if it was a trick? What if it was somebody waiting for a fool like Freddy to do just that so they could do something horrible to him?

Freddy decided that didn't make sense. He stared at the body for a little while longer before finally building up the strength to remove the bag.

With a quick snatch, Freddy tore the bag away and gasped at what he saw.

It was Percy. Sweet, wonderful Percy. The only friend Freddy had left in the world. The same Percy who treated everybody like they were royalty. The same Percy who would sing and dance like Gene Kelly to the delight of everybody (particularly the women). And the same Percy who dressed up as Santa Claus and handed out gifts on Christmas Day for as long as Freddy could remember. He still had the scarf Percy had gifted him three years ago.

Somebody so joyful would never die in a manner that was so horrible and isolated. Freddy knew that Percy had been murdered and he knew who the culprit was.

Carl.

As Freddy went down the stairs, there was almost no pain in his knees or his back. The perpetual sadness that had clouded his existence for so long was also gone. It was replaced with a steely resolve and determination that invigorated Freddy.

Before he left the roof, Freddy had replaced the bag on Percy's head. He didn't look like the Percy Freddy had grown to love and he never would again. He hoped that once the undertaker got a hold of him, Percy would at least look peaceful. That's how his mother had looked and though it had pained Freddy to see her dead, he was grateful for that.

Freddy had to change gears, though. Peace wasn't in the cards right now, at least not until he had taken care of Carl. Just thinking about him made Freddy angry. He had only lived in Freddy's building for six months but he was already infamous among the other residents. Carl had no time or patience for anybody, often shoving past people and spewing profanity at them as he went. Freddy knew that Carl was a war veteran and while he respected soldiers, that didn't excuse Carl's rude behavior.

He had called Freddy a retard on several occasions. It was a hateful word that Freddy hadn't heard since he was a child. His mother used to tell him that the only people who used that word were people who didn't like themselves very much. Freddy had always taken that as gospel but meeting Carl changed that slightly. Carl seemed to like himself quite a bit. He wore boots that jangled when he walked and he would throw his cigarette butts into the garden that the other residents had worked so hard on maintaining.

There were complaints about Carl but somehow he always cheated eviction. Freddy wondered if it was because he was a soldier. He didn't like that people abused that power. When Freddy was little, he remembered seeing some soldiers march in a parade and he was so impressed with their neatly pressed uniforms and shiny shoes. The men seemed so strong and capable to Freddy. For a long time, he wanted to be a soldier but his mother finally sat him down and explained that Freddy was special and that the Lord had other things in mind for him.

As Freddy entered his hallway, he thought maybe this was the special thing his mother was talking about. He went into his apartment, which he had left unlocked. It seemed pointless to lock it if he was going to be dead and he didn't have anything good to steal, save for his Matchbox cars. He intended for those to go to Mrs. Murphy's grandson Peter. Mrs. Murphy was mean but Peter was a sweet kid who was always nice to Freddy. Even though Freddy was still alive, he decided Peter could still have his Matchbox cars. Freddy decided he wouldn't need them again, even if he lived through this.

Freddy went to his closet and dug around on the top shelf, sliding over an old pair of shoes and a flashlight before he found what he was looking for: His daddy's old hammer.

He brought it down and swung it around a few times. The handle was worn down and there were some flecks of rust on it but Freddy thought it would do the job just fine.

As Freddy went back into the hallway with the hammer tucked carefully into the waistband of his sweatpants, he doubted his daddy ever intended it to be used for something like this. His mother had given him the hammer a few months before she died. She said it was special because Freddy's daddy had used to it to build Freddy's crib, along with the shelf that held all his toys and stuffed animals. Freddy had barely known his father but he knew he'd want Freddy to use the hammer for good things. Freddy intended to follow through with that tonight.

As he made his way to Carl's apartment, he thought of the Valentine's Day where Percy had jokingly offered Carl a carnation. Percy and two of the ladies sold them every year and although Freddy had never received one, he thought it was sweet to see how much people cared about each other.

Carl was the exception to that rule. He had slapped the carnation out of Percy's hand and called him a faggot. That was another word Freddy didn't like. His mother had said that although she didn't agree with homosexuality, she knew God loved all his children and that Freddy should never use that word.

Seeing the frightened look on Percy's face had upset Freddy. It got even worse when Carl got in Percy's face and said he'd kill him if he did something like that again. Witnessing that only made Freddy feel sadder about life. He didn't understand how anyone could hate Percy but Carl did. And it looked like Carl had stayed true to his word when he said he'd kill poor Percy. Freddy stopped and touched the hammer that was tucked away in his waistband. Before he left the roof, Freddy told Percy he was going to kill Carl. And unfortunately for Carl, Freddy was also somebody who stayed true to his word. His mother wouldn't have it any other way.

Freddy arrived at the apartment and looked at the sign Carl had taped to the front of the door. "Do Not Disturb At Any Time" was scrawled across the paper in accusatory red letters. When the sign first went up, it took Freddy a few moments to figure out what it said and by the time he did, Carl came out and asked him what the hell he was doing. Freddy got scared and quickly walked away. Carl shouted something at him but Freddy was too frightened to hear what it was. Carl was a bad man. He wasn't the first one Freddy had met but he was definitely the worst. He prepared to knock when Eve Harris from across the hall stepped out of her apartment with her dog Gadget. Freddy liked dogs but Gadget didn't like him. It immediately started barking, causing Freddy to flinch. For a brief moment, he wondered if he could go through with killing Carl. If a yappy dog scared him, what would a man like Carl do to him?

"Hush, Gadget!" Eve said. Gadget's barking was replaced with a low growl. "What are you doing here, Freddy?"

"I was just taking a walk," Freddy said. It was all he could muster.

"Well, you should probably take a walk somewhere else," Eve replied. "You know what's going to happen if that nasty man comes out and sees you standing by his door."

"I have to ask him a question," Freddy said.

"Whatever your question is, Freddy, I'm sure there's someone else who can answer it for you," Eve said with a curt raise of her right eyebrow. "Now come on, shoo!"

She waved her hand at Freddy and with no other recourse he walked down the hallway. Eve was definitely somebody Freddy wasn't friends with. She was a busybody and she talked to everyone like they were children, especially Freddy.

As he shuffled down the hallway, he looked back to see Eve following him with a suspicious look on her face. He wondered if she knew what he was up to or if she could see the outline of the hammer in his clothes. Freddy decided not to risk it, so he got on the elevator as Eve took the stairs.

Freddy took it all the way to the laundry room in the basement. Freddy hadn't done much since he had moved in here but he had learned to do his own laundry. There were mistakes, of course. Some of the colors ran together and some shirts had shrunk but overall, Freddy had done all right. The other thing he had learned about the laundry room was that everybody did their laundry during the day. After nine o'clock, the place was almost always empty. When Freddy needed a change of scenery, he would come here and sit amidst the whirring of the soda machine and the occasional clank that came from the ancient washer and dryer units that took quarters to operate. Freddy wasn't used to spending money on laundry, so he restricted his use to once every three weeks. He knew he didn't smell great by that third week but money was money and Freddy didn't have a lot of it.

Freddy took a seat in the chair next to the soda machine and leaned against the cool white wall. He had sat in this same position when he had decided to kill himself the previous night. His mother had said people who killed themselves went to Hell because it was an affront to God, not to mention the pain you caused your family and friends. Freddy didn't have any family and friends (except for Percy) and he was always told God was merciful. It might be a risk but it was one he was willing to take. Freddy was just tired of feeling sad and useless all the time.

Freddy touched the hammer again and closed his eyes. He thought back to when was eleven years old and didn't have any friends. Some of the meaner kids called him "retard" on a regular basis. Freddy's main aggressor in those days was a stocky boy named Jared. When Freddy used to play in the front yard with his Tonka trucks, Jared and his friends used to ride by and taunt him, often throwing objects at him ranging from water balloons to rocks. Eventually Freddy learned to play in the backyard but that didn't help when he needed to walk home from school. Jared used to steal Freddy's Dukes of Hazzard backpack and drop it in the nearest mud puddle. Cleaning it every day agitated his mother and although she spoke to the school, it did little to deter Jared's behavior. Freddy eventually accepted Jared's cruel actions as a regular part of his day and continued on as best he could.

That all changed when Carrot died.

Carrot was an orange tabby his mother had adopted from the pound three years earlier. Freddy immediately fell in love with the cat and although Carrot didn't pay much attention to him when they were outside, the two proved inseparable indoors. Freddy came home from school one day and he was actually in a good mood for once. Jared was nowhere to be found and as Freddy approached his house, he found his mom and sobbing and standing over Carrot, who was lying motionless in the bushes next to their house.

As Freddy got closer, his mother embraced him and told him that Carrot was dead. Freddy cried even harder than the time he had fallen down the stairs and fractured his left arm. As much as that had hurt, losing Carrot was so much worse. He had been very young when his Daddy had died, so this was Freddy's first encounter with death. He was inconsolable for the first few days. His mother had gotten Mr. Norton from next door to help them bury Carrot in the back yard. Once Freddy had stopped crying, he realized that the reason he hadn't seen Jared that day was because Jared was busy killing Carrot. Freddy's sadness was replaced with anger. How could Jared be so horrible? Carrot hadn't done anything to him. Unwilling to let this injustice slide, Freddy approached Jared in the schoolyard the next day.

Jared and his friends immediately begin to smirk as Freddy walked up to them.

"What do you want, retard?" Jared asked.

Without a word, Freddy reached into his backpack and pulled out the knife he had taken from the kitchen that morning and pointed it at Jared. Freddy could see fear in his eyes. That was almost enough for Freddy but not quite. He lunged at Jared, who easily sidestepped him and responded with a punch to the side of Freddy's face, knocking him off-balance.

"What the fuck?" Jared screamed.

"You killed my cat!" Freddy yelled back, tears streaming down his cheeks.

Jared pushed him down and kicked him in the ribs.

"I didn't kill your cat, retard!"

Jared and his friends ran inside the school after that. A conference was held between the Principal and Freddy's mother. Freddy was expelled and he was bussed to a special needs school, at least until his mother let him drop out in eighth grade. Freddy was never going to be college material.

The night after he attacked Jared, Freddy's mom held him and told him that Jared hadn't killed Carrot. The cat had likely gotten into some rat poison or something similar but Freddy didn't buy it. If Jared wasn't tormenting him that day, it was because he was killing Carrot. It was the only thing that made sense to Freddy but he never saw Jared again.

"Bad things happen, Freddy," his mother said, stroking his head. "Trying to make sense of everything is a fool's errand."

And although it wasn't what his mother intended, Percy thought a fool's errand was a good summation of life in general. He went back to the elevator, feeling like he hadn't done right by Carrot. The elevator doors opened and Freddy got on, determined to make up for that by doing right by Percy.

As the elevator began its noisy journey to Carl's floor, Freddy felt unstoppable. However, since life enjoyed pulling cruel pranks on Freddy, the elevator stopped two floors below his destination. The situation worsened when the doors opened and Bertha and Maggie got on. They were the building gossips. Freddy didn't like either of them and save for each other, he didn't think they liked anybody, either. To them, people just existed so they could have stories and rumors to pass around.

Freddy did his best to hide his disdain as they waddled inside the elevator.

"Going down, Freddy?" Bertha asked.

"Going up," Freddy responded, trying to sound as amiable as possible. "You should probably catch the next one…"

"Oh, we don't mind the ride," Maggie interrupted. Freddy hated people who interrupted. His mother used to say it was one of the rudest things somebody could do and Freddy completely agreed with her on that.

The doors closed and the elevator resumed its climb to Carl's floor. Freddy faced forward and tuned out Bertha and Maggie's conversation as best he could. He heard something about Mrs. Anthony's son being arrested for drugs and he began to hum Kenny Rogers' "The Gambler" in an attempt to further drown them out. Kenny Rogers was his favorite and if that couldn't suppress Bertha and Maggie, there was truly no hope in the world.

After what seemed like years, the elevator reached Carl's floor and Freddy stepped off without another word to Bertha and Maggie. As the doors closed, the pair looked at each other and rolled their eyes.

"Based on the smell, I'd say he's only gone a week this time without taking a shower," Bertha said. "Why did you tell him we didn't mind riding with him?"

"Because that simpleton doesn't own the elevator," Maggie replied. "The nerve of him to tell us to get on the next one."

"I wonder if he knows about his good pal Percy," Bertha said.

"What about him?"

"Pancreatic cancer. Word just came in today," Bertha answered with a shrug. "At his age, he's probably looking at six months."

"Poor dear," Maggie said. "Should I bake him a batch of cookies?"

"Do they cure terminal cancer?"

"They didn't for my husband," Maggie said, a nasty grin forming on her face.

"Then I guess you have your answer."

"This is truly God's waiting room," Maggie mused to no one in particular as the elevator began its descent to the ground floor.

Bertha farted in response and Maggie gave her a dirty look. Although Bertha was likely her closest friend in this place, the woman was devoid of anything resembling couth.

Maggie accepted that her own turn with death was coming sooner than later. She just wished she could have spent her final years with a better class of people.

Freddy crept toward Carl's apartment. Things were going to get ugly and noisy fast, so the longer he stayed quiet, the better. He reached the front door and although Eve wasn't there to distract him, he realized that he didn't have an actual plan. Should he knock and then hit Carl with the hammer as soon as he answered? That could work but what if Carl looked through the peephole and refused to open the door?

Should Freddy kick open the door and come at Carl full speed? No, that wouldn't work. Between his knees and his back, full speed for Freddy was roughly equivalent to that of a one-legged tortoise.

Freddy raised his hand to knock when a voice came from down the hallway.

"What the fuck do you want?"

Freddy turned and there was Carl, dressed in his worn leather jacket and sporting a paper bag with a bottle in it. Freddy wasn't a drinker and didn't understand people who were. He knew enough to know that somebody like Carl shouldn't be drinking at all. His mother used to tell him that alcohol brought out the devil in you and if that was true, Carl had been drinking non-stop since the womb.

"I asked what the fuck you're doing here, asshole," Carl said, beginning to advance on Freddy. Yes, the devil was alive and well in Carl, at least for a few more minutes.

Freddy knew he needed to say something.

"I wanted to know if you had a screwdriver I could borrow," he finally managed. Freddy knew it was lame but Carl seemed to relax. He approached the door and pulled out his keys and unlocked his apartment before turning back to Freddy.

"Yeah, I got a screwdriver but you ain't gettin' it, so fuck off," he said to Freddy. He regarded Freddy with one last baleful expression before going inside his apartment. The air smelled of cheap aftershave and stale cigarettes. The odors made Freddy a little nauseous but he powered through and removed the hammer from his waistband as he followed Carl into his apartment.

Bewildered, Carl turned to him.

"What the fuck do you think you're doing?"

Freddy raised the hammer with shaking hands and Carl's look of bewilderment became one of annoyance.

"What, do you want to trade or something, retard? You're not getting the screwdriver, so do like I said and fuck off!" Carl said, his boots clopping on the threadbare carpet as he made his way to the kitchen. Freddy followed him with the hammer raised over his head. Carl took the booze out of the bag and prepared to pour himself a drink when he saw Freddy coming toward him with the hammer. Carl's eyes narrowed as the reality of the situation finally sunk in.

"I know you're a little slow but don't go making a stupid mistake," Carl said, his tone low and threatening.

"Percy," Freddy rasped as he continued his slow walk to destiny.

Carl regarded him with a weary look of anger and disgust.

"When I was in Vietnam, I had some skinny gook came at me full speed with a bayonet pointed at my heart. How do you think a slow, fat retard compares to that?"

Freddy tightened his grip on the hammer as he got closer to Carl, who opened a drawer next to the ancient and sickly sounding refrigerator.

"Because you know what stopped that gook, retard?" Carl asked Freddy as he reached into the drawer. "This."

He pulled out a pistol and pointed it at Freddy.

"Got one in every room of this place," Carl revealed. "Wife number three said I was paranoid but that bitch never had anybody try to kill her, which was kind of a miracle in retrospect."

Freddy stopped and stared at the cold steel pointed at him.

"Good boy," Carl said. "Last chance to turn around and walk out of here and we can pretend this never happened."

For one terrifying instant, Freddy had every intention of turning and leaving but then he thought of sweet, kind Percy. And Carrot. And his mother. They were the only things on Earth Freddy loved and they were gone, which meant he truly had nothing now. With that in mind, Freddy raised the hammer and charged at Carl, who pulled the trigger without hesitation. The report was loud and made Freddy's ears ring but that was minor compared the force of the blast. It was like a Mack truck had hit him. He staggered back, dropping his daddy's hammer. There was a hot, wet sensation spreading over his torso and legs. As he did his best to regain his balance, he looked up at Carl, who stared at Freddy dumbfounded. He hadn't expected Freddy to come at him. It wasn't much but it at least provided Freddy with a small sense of consolation as he staggered out of the apartment.

Eve and some other residents were already standing in the hallway when Freddy came out. Eve screamed when she saw him and he could hear Gadget barking uncontrollably inside her apartment. Freddy stumbled for the elevator. He knew where needed to go and was relieved when he saw the other terrified residents step away from him, their eyes as wide as dinner plates.

As Freddy reached the elevator, he could hear Carl talking.

"It was self-defense! That mother fucker came at me with a hammer!"

Freddy used one of his bloody hands to call for the elevator. It immediately dinged and the doors opened, allowing Freddy to collapse inside. The doors closed and Freddy hit the button for the top floor. It wouldn't get him exactly where he needed to go but it was a good start.

Moments later, Freddy was climbing the stairs to the roof again. His knees weren't bothering him this time but the trail of blood he was leaving confirmed he didn't have much time. As he got closer to the roof, he could hear the panicked and excited chattering coming from the residents on the other floors. Word had already spread. Bertha and Maggie would have enough material for weeks. The thought of those two old crows gossiping about Freddy's last stand actually made him laugh, although it came out as a lifeless wheeze. Freddy wasn't sure he was going to make it but just a few minutes prior, he also wasn't sure he'd be able to go at Carl with his Daddy's hammer. Deciding he was full of surprises. Freddy continued his long and seemingly endless climb to the roof.

When Freddy finally arrived, he swung the door open and felt the cold night air kiss his face. While it was a pleasant sensation, it did little to alleviate the unbearable heat that was blooming through his entire body. Unable to walk anymore, Freddy collapsed and crawled toward Percy, who was still seated in his lawn chair, the breeze gently rustling the bag wrapped around his head.

Freddy could hear sirens approaching in the distance and decided maybe Carl would get his comeuppance after all. It wouldn't bring back Percy, Carrot, or his mother but something was better than nothing. And nothing was all Freddy had known for a very long time.

As Freddy got close to Percy, he could feel himself drifting away. He couldn't tell if it was sleep or death approaching but it didn't feel bad and he didn't see a bright light, so he decided it was sleep. Or at least he hoped it was sleep. It was amazing how much things had changed in just a couple of hours. Earlier tonight, he had wanted to die.

Now he didn't know what he wanted.

If he survived, maybe he could be the new Santa at Christmas, handing out presents and candy to the other residents. He would have to practice his Santa laugh, though. Even without attempting it, he knew it needed work.

Better yet, maybe he could round up the ladies and watch soap operas every day like he and his mother used to do.

Or maybe he could go to the pound and adopt a cat and name it Apple (calling it Carrot would be unfair to both Carrot and the new cat).

As he finally lost consciousness, Freddy took comfort in knowing the possibilities were endless.

Maybe life wasn't a fool's errand.

Maybe...

Stone Canyon

Good friends were hard to come by. Although he was just nineteen and had only lost his virginity six months ago, Scotty recognized this. You had to hold on to your good friends and for Scotty that meant Rick and Mark.

After graduating from high school, the three of them had gone their separate ways. Scotty attended college a mere forty miles down the road but Rick and Mark saw things differently. They decided distance was the best medicine to cure their small town blues. Rick enrolled at the University of North Carolina and Mark set up shop at the University of Washington in the scenic Pacific Northwest.

Scotty had every intention of visiting them but once school got underway, those plans faded. It didn't help that Scotty was mostly broke his freshman year, even with his work-study gig. Nonetheless, the three stayed in semi-regular contact over email and Snapchat. Although Scott had gotten friendly with some of the guys in his dorm (and several girls who lost interest in him as quickly as they had gained it), he realized that Rick and Mark were still his best friends. He heard friendships came fast and lasted long in college but he had yet to experience that. That's why he decided during finals week that their annual tradition needed to continue.

He emailed them this in a beery haze (Natty Ice only, please and thank you) and felt foolish when he woke up the next morning with a slight headache. Luckily, Rick and Mark agreed and even seemed excited about it.

Ever since eighth grade, camping had been their favorite pastime. It started with overnights in a pup tent in Mark's backyard and evolved into weekend excursions at the state park fifteen miles outside their town. The boys had their introductions to alcohol and marijuana on these trips, as well as some low-grade Molly they stole from Mark's brother one time. They talked about the pretty girls who didn't know they existed, as well as their misguided hopes and dreams for the future. These trips were the highlights of their summer vacations and Scotty assumed since they were a little older and wiser now, they would only get better.

The trips were usually reserved for the end of June after school let out but since school now ended a month and a half earlier with summer jobs waiting for them, those plans were going to have to change. Scotty decided they should go the weekend before Memorial Day to avoid the crowds. Rick and Mark expressed their agreement over text and they were good to go. Scotty was home by that point but they still wouldn't be back for another three days.

Scotty used the time leading up to the camping trip to spend time with his folks and catch up on video games (his studies had mostly prevented this last semester). Two days before they were supposed to head out, Scotty got a text from Mark asking him and Rick to meet him at Denny's. That worked just fine for Scotty, as Denny's was another regular hangout spot in their small town and it might mean running into more old friends.

To his disappointment, the parking lot was mostly empty when he pulled in. The only cars he recognized were Rick's and Mark's, although he supposed no distractions meant they could map out the trip in more detail. As he would soon learn, even the best-laid plans were subject to change and in this case, Mark wanted to change their destination altogether.

It was a little surprising and confusing but nowhere near as surprising or confusing as Mark's appearance. The formerly clean-shaven boy who preferred button-ups and loafers now had shaggy hair down to his shoulders and a thick beard with a puff of lint in it.

Through social media, Scotty had noticed Mark's appearance had changed but not this much. Scotty glanced at Rick, who looked more or less the same save for spacers in both earlobes. He could tell Rick was also surprised by Mark's transformation.

"Why do you want to go somewhere else?" Scotty asked. "Our usual place has the best fishing around."

Mark smiled in response.

"Not quite. Are you guys familiar with Stone Canyon?"

"I drove past it on a family trip a few years back," Rick said. "What about it?"

"Well, if you want good fishing, you're going to get it. This place just happens to have a little something extra," Mark said holding out his phone to them. Scotty took it and examined the contents on the screen.

"Hiker missing?" he asked before handing the phone over to Rick.

"One of four in the last three months!" Mark exclaimed. Considering what a bleak statistic it was, he sounded a little too excited. Rick and Scotty exchanged a bewildered look.

"Happy you're happy that people are going missing, Mark, but what does this have to do with our camping trip?" Rick asked.

Mark leaned in close. "This place is a hotbed for Squatch activity."

Now Scotty and Rick had no idea what to say.

"I don't know what that means, Mark," Rick finally managed.

"It means in addition to the missing hikers, this place has the most Sasquatch sightings in the tri-state area. There's already been six this year and it's not even June yet!" Mark said, the color in his cheeks rising.

"Sasquatch? As in Bigfoot?" Scotty asked. Mark nodded and toned it down a little.

"I know, it sounds ridiculous but I had a professor last semester who's like one of the reigning Squatch experts in the world. This guy is legit. He has evidence and stories that would make your head spin. He hosts expeditions twice a semester. I went on the most recent one and it was amazing!" he exclaimed.

He was right, it did sound ridiculous but Mark was not easily swayed and for him to fall under the spell of something like this so quickly, Scott decided it must have at least a little merit to it. Rick was less convinced.

"Did you see a Bigfoot?" the skeptical Rick asked him.

"No, but we saw rock piles, makeshift shelters, and we even found a few tufts of fur. My professor had it tested and guess what? It was a primate, though the exact species was unknown!" he revealed before looking at Rick and Scotty's faces, hoping they'd have at least a modicum of his enthusiasm. His face fell slightly when he didn't get it.

"You guys didn't hear about it? It was in the news," he said, sounding somewhat deflated.

Scotty hadn't but to be fair, if it didn't make Reddit or Twitter, it would probably slip by him. He stayed silent but Rick was much less charitable.

"Sorry, I turned off my Google alert for unknown monkey fur," he responded.

Scotty could tell Mark was hurt, so he stepped in.

"It sounds pretty cool," he offered. It was lame but he owed his friend at least some kind of positive response.

"So you went us to drive three hours…" Rick began.

"Four," Mark interrupted

"Four hours so you can look at rocks and possibly a few tufts of King Kong's pubic hair?" Rick finished. Scotty laughed at that. He couldn't help it, even if it further dampened Mark's mood.

"Very funny. The trip is the same as always, we're just driving a little longer to get there. My brother will still get us the beer, we can still cook out, and we can still go fishing. I just want to take a few hours to perform my own little expedition. You're welcomed to join me and if not, you can just hang out at the campsite. Business as usual," he said with a shrug.

Scotty could see Rick wasn't having it and truth be told, neither was he. It seemed like an awful lot of driving to try and spot a creature that likely didn't exist. He began to think of gentle ways to refute the offer when Mark said something that changed everything.

"I'll drive and you guys don't have to chip in for gas money or the beer."

"Sold!" Scotty said with a slap to the table. "Let's go to Stone Canyon!" Rick still wasn't convinced but Mark wasn't done. "I'll get an ounce weed from my brother, too," he offered.

Rick's face instantly lit up. "Damn, Mark. I don't know why kind of a Bigfoot hunter you are but your negotiating skills are on point. I'm in!"

Mark stood up and high-fived his friends in celebration of their new plans. Things had just changed. And since they were his oldest and closest friends, Scotty assumed it was for the better. It wouldn't take long for him to see that wasn't the case at all.

When they left two days later, they were only on the road for thirty minutes when Scotty smelled the familiar odor of pungent, burning leaves. The smoke came next and Mark's agitated proclamation immediately followed.

"What the hell, dude? You can't smoke that shit in here!"

Scotty sat up from the backseat to find Rick holding a joint, smoke lazily wafting from the lit tip.

"You can't wait until we get there?" Scotty asked him.

"Why?"

"Because this is my mom's car! I can't have it coming back smelling like Matthew McConaughey's rec room!" Mark shot back.

"So we roll the windows down when we get there and let it air out. It'll be fine," Rick said.

"No, it won't! You fart in here and she's complaining about it three days later!" Mark insisted.

"All right, fine," Rick said, carefully snuffing the joint out and putting it back inside the baggie. "You don't have to be such a baby about it."

Scotty could tell he was agitated and that was unusual for Rick. He was generally the easygoing one but right now; you could cut the tension with a knife. Scotty decided to change the subject.

"So what's going to happen if we see a Bigfoot?" he asked his friends.

"Considering Mark took Natalie Merrill to prom, it'll be nothing we haven't already seen," Rick answered. This was the Rick they knew, always with a well-timed zinger or joke.

"Fuck you, dude!" Mark said, leaning over to punch Rick and causing the car to swerve. "Make-up made all the difference with her!"

"Yeah, instead of looking like the Tasmanian Devil, she looked like his mother!" Scotty said, which elicited laughter from all three boys. Scotty started to relax. Things were back on track.

When they arrived at Stone Canyon, the daylight was waning. They had gotten a late start and stopped three times along the way. There was a stop for gas, another for food, and one for a supposed bathroom break for Rick that set them back another fifteen minutes. When he returned to the car smelling like a Wiz Khalifa concert, neither Scotty nor Mark let on that it was an unnecessary setback. It was better to keep the peace, especially since the weekend was so young.

Not long after they passed the weathered sign welcoming them to the park, they pulled off at the first parking area they saw. That was Scotty's idea. This was uncharted territory and the closer to the highway they were, the safer they (or at least he) felt. It was empty, save for a lone brown garbage can and a crooked trail that wound its way into the deep brush. Scotty noticed they hadn't passed another vehicle on their way up and even if they were at the lowest point of the park, it seemed strange nobody else was here.

Ordinarily the idea of having the whole area to themselves would be an exciting one but considering people had disappeared and this was their first time here, Scotty was less than enthusiastic about it.

"Are you sure we can camp here?" asked Rick. Mark shrugged in response. "I don't see any signs that say otherwise."

That made sense but it also didn't make it any less unnerving. Regardless, they were on their way.

They walked about a quarter of a mile on the trail before finding the perfect spot. There was plenty of room for all three tents and even a fire pit. Satisfied with their discovery, they returned to the car to get their belongings. If there was one thing they did without fail each trip, it was forget an essential item. One year it had been Mark's sleeping bag and another year it was their fishing poles. The honor this year went to that night's dinner.

"Shit, I forgot the hot dogs!" Rick said. It was the one thing he was asked to bring. "We can wing it, right?"

"No, we can't wing it," Mark said, his voice irritated.

"All right, keep your skirt on, I'll go to that store we saw a few miles back," Rick said. "Can I have your keys?"

"Fine, but no smoking in my mom's car. Got it?" Mark told him.

"Yeah, I got it," Rick said with a dismissive wave before heading down the trail. Mark turned to Scotty. "Do you mind going with him?"

"Not at all. Are you good with the tents?" Scotty asked him. Mark nodded and resumed pounding the stakes in. Scotty took off and jogged down the trail to catch up to Rick, who was reaching into his pocket, presumably not for gum.

"Hey man!" Scotty called out, prompting Rick to turn around and remove his hand from his pocket. "Mind if I go with you?"

"Yeah, no problem," Rick said, motioning for Scotty to follow him. Scotty could tell he was unhappy. Maybe the car ride would give him a chance to find out why.

Minutes later they were driving down the curvy road toward the general store they had passed earlier. It was dark now and the dense forest surrounding them allowed only the headlights of the car to provide them with any real light. So far, there wasn't any progress getting Rick to open up.

"Kind of spooky, isn't it?" Scotty finally asked.

"Yeah, a little," Rick said without much interest.

"But overall it's not that different from out usual spot," Scotty said in an attempt to keep the conversation going.

"That's where you're wrong. There's a big difference this time," Rick said, his tone growing ominous.

"What's that?" Scotty asked.

"Mark looks like Charles Manson and he's hunting for mythical creatures," Rick said, sputtering laughter. "What are the odds he skins us in our sleep?"

Scott didn't respond to this. He didn't like it. It was mean and as much as they threw shade at each other, nobody ever said anything this nasty behind anyone else's back. Rick noticed Scott wasn't laughing as they pulled into the well-lit parking lot of the general store.

"Have a sense of humor, dude. I'm kidding," Rick said in a clipped tone.

Scott feigned a smile. "No worries, man," he said, doing his best to stay on Rick's good side. It seemed to work, as Rick feigned his own smile and got out of the car. The only thing now was getting the hot dogs and Scotty intended to make that quick.

The general store had the quaint look of an old log cabin, complete with a stuffed, moth-eaten bear in the corner and two rifles crossed on the wall above the main counter. There was a faded red and white sign that read, "Nothing here is worth dying for." As Scotty scanned the aisles, he could see that truer words had never been spoken. The shelves were mostly lined with junk food and he could see water, juices, and soda behind the smudged glass of the cooler that stood in the back.

The man behind the counter was busy reading the latest issue of Field & Stream and only gave the boys a passing glance as they entered. It was only after they started rummaging through the cooler that he took notice.

"You boys just passin' through or are you here to do some campin'?" he asked, eyeing them over his magazine.

"We're camping. First time here," Scotty told him, prompting the man to drop his magazine on the counter. They had his full attention now.

"Is that right?" he asked. "Why Stone Canyon? You fixin' to see yourself a Squatch?"

"Our friend is. We're just along for the ride," Rick responded. He clearly had no interest in talking with the guy. "Do you have any…"

"Because you're in the right place for that, my friends," their new buddy interrupted. "Just watch yourself."

"What do you mean?" Scotty asked. Out of the corner of his eye, he could see an impatient Rick rolls his eyes. Scotty didn't care. A local was supplying them with need-to-know information. Or at least the same bullshit he scared all the tourists with. Either way, Scotty's attention was rapt.

"Well, I'm sure you heard we've had ourselves a few disappearances as of late," the man said, raising an eyebrow.

"People disappear in the woods all the time. Are you trying to imply they were taken away by a non-existent creature?" Rick asked.

"Non-existent!" this raconteur cried out. "Boy, I've spent my whole life in this area. Squatch are anything but non-existent. I can tell you they used to be a lot more peaceful. They've been gettin' ornery as of late."

"Yeah, they've probably seen the never-ending wave of shitty horror films that have been made about them," Rick said. "I'd be irritated, too."

"You may want to tone that attitude down, boy. They're sensitive creatures. You go out there with bad vibes and they'll feed off of that. And not in a good way," the man warned them.

"If I start to feel grumpy, I'll count down from ten," Rick said, still not having any of it. "Do you have hot dogs?" The man pointed to the back of the store. "All the way in the back. Got Hebrew National and Oscar Mayer. Name your poison," he continued with a smirk. Rick didn't return it; he just marched to the back of the store to get what they needed. It was time to go but Scotty didn't feel ready yet.

"Are we in danger?" Scotty asked. Why mince words?

"That ain't up for me to decide. If I was you, I'd be sleepin' with one eye open," the man answered, raising his eyebrows for effect.

Rick returned and dropped two packages of hot dogs on the counter. The man rang them up on an old-fashioned cash register. Rick paid without another word and he was out the door. Scotty looked at the man, who had already resumed reading his Field & Stream. Story time was over. Scotty reluctantly followed after Rick.

Although the drive back was brief, the silence was uncomfortable. Rick finally broke it.

"Can you believe that happy horse shit?"

"What?" Scotty asked.

"That 'You're all doomed!' crap that guy shoveled at us," Rick said. "Like we're fucking twelve or something."

"I think he was just trying to help us out," Scotty responded.

"No, that's how he gets his rocks off. Most of his business probably comes from hikers and campers who hear a good ghost story, share it with their friends, and drum him up more business. It's a fucking scam," Rick said. "If we hear or see anything tonight, it's going to be Cletus and his friends wearing a store-bought monkey suit after drinking too many shitty Natty Ices."

"We drink Natty Ice," Scotty pointed out.

"Yeah, but we're poor college kids. We have an excuse. Those good ol' boys are partaking in the same shit they did in high school or however far they made it before dropping out. It's sad," Rick said.

Scotty didn't say anything else. Maintaining a tradition for that long didn't seem sad to him. He was beginning to suspect he was alone in that sentiment. What made matters worse was that Scotty was beginning to regret the trip altogether. Rick's constant pot smoking and bad attitude had grown tiresome and Mark's obsession with Bigfoot made him feel like a complete stranger to Scotty. This feeling of regret would only continue to grow with each passing hour. And what came next was a doozy.

When they got back, Scotty and Rick hoped to see the flickering orange light of a campfire as they came up the trail but found only darkness waiting for them instead.

"What the hell?" Rick asked. "I hope he at least finished getting the tents up."

When they arrived at their campsite, they saw Mark hadn't made any progress. He was too busy staring out into the forest.

"Mark?" Scotty called out. Mark turned and found himself caught in both their flashlight beams.

"Turn those off!" he whispered.

"Why?" asked Scotty.

"Because there's something out there. Listen!" Mark said. Rick and Scotty listened. Outside of crickets and wind, they didn't hear anything.

"What are we listening for?" Rick inquired.

"Bigfoot! One of them is out there!" Mark answered without hesitation. "I started to put up the tents and I could hear it moving around behind me. Then I smelled it."

"And what does a Bigfoot smell like, Mark?" Rick asked.

"You'll know it when you smell it," Mark replied.

"Good to know. How about we finish getting the tents up and get a fire going? Is that agreeable to everyone?" Rick said. Scotty and Mark decided it was. It didn't take long once they got going but Scotty noticed Mark almost never took his eyes off of the woods.

Thirty minutes later, the tents were up and a fire was roaring. The boys used sticks to cook the hot dogs over the fire while indulging in the libations Mark brought. After a few beers, Rick fired up a joint and took a big hit. He exhaled loudly and watched the smoke swirl into the night sky.

"Now that's what I'm talking about," Rick said. He finally seemed to be enjoying himself. Scotty decided now was as good a time as any to find out what was going on with him.

"So how have things been, Rick?" Scotty asked.

"What do you mean?" Rick said, sounding defensive. This wasn't going well but Scotty knew there was no turning back now.

"You just seem kind of distracted," Scotty answered.

"What can I say? Things aren't going so well," he revealed, offering the joint to Scotty who took a hit and passed it to Mark.

"What's going on?" Scotty asked. Rick cracked open another beer and took a sip.

"Oh, the usual. Flunking out of school. If that happens, my dad says I have to join the fucking Army," Rick said bitterly. "But nothing much otherwise."

"Jesus, man. Sorry to hear that." Scotty responded. "Is there any way to fix your grades?"

"Probably but I'm already on academic probation. If I get anything less than a B next semester, I'm toast." Rick said glumly.

"What about..." Scotty began before Mark interrupted him.

"Quiet! Do you guys hear that?" he said, looking out into the woods again. Rick glared at him but Mark had no idea what was going on. He had other things on his mind. Rick finished his beer and his joint before standing up.

"I think that's enough fun for me for one evening, I'm going to..."

There was another interruption, only this time it didn't come from Mark. It was a loud and unfamiliar howl that sounded far too close for Scotty's comfort. The three boys froze before exchanging worried glances.

"What the hell was that?" Rick asked. Mark turned to him, looking like a kid on Christmas.

"What do you think it was?"

"Not a Bigfoot!" Rick fired back.

"Then what was it? We've been camping for years. Have you ever heard anything like that before?" Mark asked him.

"No, but..."

And then there was another howl. This one came from farther away. And then there was another that sounded a little closer. Pretty soon there was an entire chorus of them, all from varying distances but still much too close as far as Scotty was concerned.

"Jesus," he finally managed.

"Let's call it a night," Mark said. "We've got a big day ahead of us tomorrow."

"Mark, is this..."

"Safe? As long as we keep the fire going and stay out of their way, we should be fine," Mark answered, sounding way too relaxed for Scotty. "I'll see you boys in the morning." He went into his tent and zipped it closed, leaving Scotty and Rick alone.

"So what do you think?" Scotty asked Rick.

"I think I'm going to stick to my initial plan and go to sleep. I'll see you in the morning," Rick said. Scotty could tell he was upset by Mark's distracted and dismissive attitude.

"I don't think he meant to act like he didn't care. I'm sure if you talk to him tomorrow, everything will be fine," Scotty offered, hoping to maintain peace.

"No, it's cool," Rick replied. "We all went to different schools and now we've got our own shit to worry about. Life moves on." He spit on the ground before disappearing into his tent. Life definitely moved on and Scotty decided as of right now, it wasn't to a very good place.

Scotty wasn't sure what time it was when the rocks began to pelt the sides of their tents. Cell phone reception was generally non-existent in the woods, so his phone was shut off. In his disoriented state, he thought the thuds he heard were Rick and Mark messing with him.

"Knock it off, assholes!" he said. "I'm trying to sleep!"

"That's not us," Mark replied. Now Scotty was wide awake. He sat up and heard more thuds over his head as rocks continued to land on his tent.

"Then what's going on?" Scotty asked, trying to mask the fear in his voice.

"They're throwing rocks at us," Mark answered, his voice completely calm.

"Who's throwing rocks at us?" Rick asked to another succession of small rocks hitting the sides of their tents.

"Who do you think? Them," Mark said.

"Fucking Bigfoot? Bull shit! It's that asshole from the general store and his friends!" Rick shouted. "Didn't I tell you, Scotty?" The next sound Scotty heard was the harried and impatient unzipping of Rick's tent, followed by fast footsteps shuffling through the leaves and dirt. Through the mesh of one of the windows in his tent, Scotty could see Rick outlined by the dwindling fire.

"You're not scaring us off, you mother fuckers!" Rick screamed at their assailants. "We're staying here all weekend, so if you don't like, go find a goat to fuck or something!"

"Rick!" Scotty admonished. Rick turned toward his tent.

"What? Fuck these redneck assholes! Don't they have anything better to do?"

"No, they don't, Rick. They're just defending their territory. And they're not redneck assholes," Mark said.

"You're right, it's a giant seven-foot ape that's existed for hundreds of years but nobody has any concrete evidence of. You're a fucking genius, Mark!"

"Dude, shut the fuck up!" Mark said. "You've been an asshole this whole trip. I'm sorry you're having trouble in school…"

"Yeah, I can tell," Rick said, cutting him off. "You were so attentive when I brought it up earlier."

"I was listening! And I feel bad and if you want to talk about it tomorrow, we can but for right now, you just need to go to bed. Don't agitate them further!" Mark pleaded. And then there was silence. The rocks had stopped.

"Say what you will, dick head, I get results!" Rick said before stomping back to his tent and zipping it up. Scotty listened to his friends shift around as they prepared to go back to sleep. The trip was a disaster. Could they last another two days? His response came in the form of a howl in the distance.

"Didn't think so," he whispered to himself before going back to sleep. As his mother liked to say, tomorrow was a new day.

Breakfast was tense, with Rick refusing to speak to Mark. When Mark attempted to be friendly, Rick was quick to rebuke him. Scotty wasn't just eager to finish breakfast; he was ready to go home. When Rick brought their fishing rods up from the car, he knew he had to grin and bear it. He just hoped Rick's spirits improved once they got to the river.

As Mark packed up his belongings for his own excursion, he continued to try and make conversation but found himself stonewalled by Rick. Finally, he stood up and strapped on his backpack, offering a goodbye to Scotty and a curt nod to Rick.

"I'll be back around five," he told them.

"Don't feel the need to hurry," Rick said without looking at him. Mark bristled like he wanted to say something and Scotty prayed he'd keep it to himself, which fortunately he did. After he disappeared into the forest, Scotty turned to Rick, who was smoking another joint.

"Ready?" Scotty asked. Rick motioned for him to go.

"Lead the way."

"Lead the way? I know this area as well as you do, which is to say not at all," Scotty said.

"Yeah, but I'm high as shit, so having me try to figure out where to go isn't the best idea," Rick said. His bloodshot eyes confirmed he wasn't lying.

"All right then. Let's go," Scotty told him. Rick was being irritating but they grabbed their fishing rods and set out to find the river.

As it turned out, Stone Canyon wasn't much of a canyon and there wasn't a lot of stone but it looked pretty enough. The trees were ancient and overgrown, some of them contorting and bursting through the moss-covered earth as Rick and Scotty worked their way to the river. Scotty found himself enjoying the walk until they made the rather unpleasant discovery of the dead deer.

While dead deer weren't an uncommon site (there was never a shortage of them on the side of the highway), this deer's head was completely turned around, its glassy eyes still locked in a state of terror.

"What do you think happened to it?" Scotty asked, waving away some of the fat black flies that swarmed the deer's carcass.

"I don't know, ran afoul of a bear or something," Rick answered.

"A bear? Seriously? Look at that thing's head! And why didn't the bear eat it?"

Rick's patience was beginning to wear thin again. "Because it decided to go Vegan. What difference does it make now?"

"I've just never seen anything like this," Scotty said.

"Well, then it was definitely Bigfoot," Rick replied sarcastically. Scotty clenched his jaw and started walking again. He was tired of Rick's negativity. He had never suggested it was a Bigfoot that did this. There was no reason to even think that, right? Scotty decided he just wanted to fish. It was good a stress reliever as any.

When they finally reached the river, they were disappointed to see it was rather small but ran clear and calm. They had mostly forgotten about the dead deer and Scotty really hoped the change of scenery would improve Rick's mood.

They cast their lines and set about drinking beers from the small cooler they had brought with them.

"So can you believe that fucking guy?" Rick said.

"Who?" Scotty asked, knowing full well he meant Mark.

"Who do you think? Fucking nature boy," Rick answered. "Talk about having your head up your ass."

"You should really talk to him. I'm sure it's all just a misunderstanding," Scotty replied and a long silence followed. The only sound was the river gently bubbling its way along.

"It isn't just this trip," Rick said. "You were the only one who bothered to reach out to me this year. I didn't hear jack shit from him."

"I know it's not exactly an accurate barometer of friendship but what about all those Snapchats?" Scotty asked.

"That was all you, man," Rick revealed. "I even tried emailing him and texting him a few times and that fucker never got back to me. I get we're busy but no response at all? It just seemed kind of shitty."

Scotty couldn't argue with that. They fished in silence for a few minutes when they heard a loud scream come from the distance. Unlike the howls, it sounded very familiar.

"Was that..." Scotty began, unable to finish.

"I'm sure he's fine. Probably just saw a snake or something," Rick said, trying to sound glib. Scotty could tell he was nervous, though.

"Maybe we should head back," Scotty said. Rick yanked his fishing pool out of the river in response.

"Yeah, fuck it. This place is dead. So much for good fishing."

When they arrived back at the campsite, there was no sign of Mark and they were losing daylight.

"Should we go looking for him?" Scotty asked Rick, who was sharpening a stick with his pocket knife.

"Let's give him a few more minutes," Rick said.

"But it's getting dark!" Scotty pointed out.

"Nothing we can do about that," Rick said, continuing to sharpen the stick.

"What if that was Mark screaming?" Scotty countered. "He could be hurt!"

"Well, then let's speak his language and see if he responds!" Rick said before doing an eerily spot-on impression of the howl they heard the night before. In the distance, someone (or something) responded in kind.

"See?" said Rick with a grin. "He's fine."

"That's not cool, man!" Scotty said as anger bubbled inside of him.

"All right, fine, we'll go look for him," Rick said, resigned. They grabbed their flashlights and headed off in the direction Mark went earlier.

As they started out, Scotty was worried it would get dark before they found him, which would make getting back difficult. As it turned out, those fears were completely unfounded. They found evidence of Mark almost immediately and Scotty knew getting back in the dark was the least of their problems now. Things had just gotten much worse.

"Holy shit," Rick said. All that remained of Mark was his backpack, ripped open with its contents spread carelessly on the ground. While this was unsettling, it was nowhere near as frightening as the bloody shoe they found a few feet away. There were also ragged streaks of blood leading away and as painful as it was, Rick and Scotty followed them, only to have them inexplicably disappear after about twenty feet.

They were speechless. What could be said that would possibly make this situation more bearable? Something terrible had happened and if they couldn't handle miscommunication and petty squabbles in a mature fashion, how could they possibly handle this?

It was Rick who made the first move. It wasn't especially eloquent but it was more than Scotty had managed.

"Mark!" Rick bellowed as loud as he could. Birds could be heard scattering at the sound of his voice. "Where are you?"

The only response he got were the crickets that had emerged as daylight made its gradual exit. If the situation weren't so awful, it would have been a beautiful night, with a large, full moon and stars that shone so vividly they made the sky look almost artificial. Rick pointed his flashlight at the remnants of Mark's belongings, stopping on a huge footprint in the soft earth. It was something Scotty had seen a hundred times on television and online. He had even seen an obvious fake at the state fair a few years back. Seeing one in the wild up close and personal was surreal, though. Scotty found himself too scared to even acknowledge it, so he offered something else instead.

"What do we do now?" he asked.

"I don't know," Rick said, his acidic demeanor reduced to fear as he moved his flashlight beam away from the footprint. "Get help, I guess. Let's just hope he left his keys in his tent."

As luck would have it, Mark had left his keys in the tent but their good fortune ended there. As they hiked down the trail toward the parking area, Scotty heard something rustling in the bushes. And it sounded big. Based on the way Rick subtly stepped up his pace, Scotty knew he wasn't alone in that assumption.

When they reached Mark's car, things went from bad to worse. The front hood had been torn off and the engine was now a mangled mess of wires and jagged metal.

"Oh, you have to be fucking kidding me!" Rick roared, kicking the side of the car so hard he left a dent. "Why would anyone do this?"

"I don't think it's anyone, Rick. I think it's them!" Scotty said.

"Bull shit! Those fucking things aren't real. This is that fucking store owner and his buddies!" Rick continued, flipping out his pocket knife. "And we're going to march down to that fucking store and I'm going to show that asshole a thing or two!"

In the midst of his ranting and frustrated arm waving, the pocket knife flew out of his hands. In what would be the last bit of kismet in his life, Rick ducked just as a rock whistled past his head and cracked the windshield. Scotty screamed and Rick jumped up, staring at the damaged glass with a dumbfounded expression on his face. That was when they heard the low growling coming from the trees. Scotty grabbed his arm.

"Rick, we have to go. Now!" Scotty said, pulling him toward the road. Rick was dead weight at first but the growling grew louder and Rick finally snapped out of it and began to walk with Scotty down the moonlit road.

"You got your cell phone?" Rick asked, already sounding out of breath.

"Left it in the tent," Scotty said.

"Fuck!" Rick spat into the otherwise serene night air.

"Where's yours?"

"Dead. I accidentally left it on last night," Rick responded, desperation starting to creep into his voice.

"For what it's worth, I don't think we would have gotten any reception anyway," Scotty said, trying to give Rick (and himself) some peace of mind.

"Yeah, but I know I'd feel safer if we had working cell phones," Rick said. "Wouldn't you?"

"Forget it, let's get to the store and call for help there," Scotty said.

"Call for help? You realize it's going to be like Deliverance when we get there, right? They've probably got Mark strung up in the back and…"

"Will you shut the fuck up?" Scotty said, ending Rick's gruesome (and likely accurate) scenario. "We'll get to the main highway and flag somebody down."

And it was a good plan. It was just too bad they'd never reach the highway.

The car wasn't even out of sight when they heard the first howl. It sounded close, as did the ones that followed. Scotty and Rick picked up the pace but only slightly. Running might attract whatever was making those noises and Scotty had a feeling they wouldn't be able to outrun it.

The howls diminished but they were replaced by the sounds of branches cracking in the woods surrounding them. They were being followed; there was no doubt about it. Whether they were being followed to ensure they left the area or because something was waiting for just the right time to strike remained to be seen.

"How much further to the highway do you think?" Rick whispered to Scotty.

"I don't know, probably another couple of miles," Scotty responded. Saying it out loud made the distance seem impossibly long. He didn't know if they'd even survive one mile.

After a short distance, the cracking in the woods continued and Scotty heard the sound of a lighter flicking on. He turned around to see Rick lighting a joint.

"What are you doing?" Scotty hissed at him.

"Calming my fucking nerves, man!" Rick said, his voice shaking.

"Put that out, you're just drawing more attention to us!"

"I don't know, man, I'm pretty sure they already know we're here!" Rick said, his voice on the verge of tears.

Scotty knew there was no point in arguing with him, so they continued on. The smell of the marijuana smoke only served to put Scotty further on edge and it didn't seem to be doing much for Rick, who started breathing heavily.

"Rick?" Scotty whispered. Rick continued his heavy, wheezy breathing.

"Come on, man, we're almost there, we just need to keep walking!" Scotty continued.

"It's all his fault!" Rick said.

"What?"

"Fucking Mark, it was his idea to come here! If we had gone to our usual place, we wouldn't be in this fucking mess!"

"That doesn't really matter now," Scotty said, doing his best to calm him down.

"You know what? Fuck it, I'm over this camping shit at this point. I wish I hadn't come at all!"

Given how the weekend had gone, Scotty couldn't help but agree with him. They continued walking, amidst cracking branches, more howls, and sporadic growling. It was enough to drive Scotty crazy. He'd do anything to make these terrible noises stop and when Rick started crying, Scotty found that to be the worst sound of all.

"What the fuck, man?" Rick sobbed. "What the fuck is going on? Why can't they just leave us alone?"

Scotty found it hard to comfort somebody when he was so on edge himself but he did his best.

"They just want us to leave. Once we're out of here, we can call for help," he said. "They may even be able to find Mark."

"Mark's dead, fucking face it," Rick blubbered. "And I was such an asshole to him. He wanted to talk and I blew him off!"

"It's okay, Rick," Scotty said.

"No, it's fucking not!" Rick said, his voice rising. And then he did the worst thing Scotty could imagine at that moment: He started yelling into the woods.

"You mother fuckers! Mark wasn't going to hurt you!" Rick screamed. "Why don't you come out here and try that shit with me?"

"Rick, stop it!" Scotty said, struggling to maintain the final threads of his own sanity.

"I'll kill you fucking bastards!" Rick bellowed. He had his pocket knife out. It looked incredibly inefficient and Scotty fought every urge he had to run. He already lost Mark, he couldn't lose Rick, even if he had finally snapped.

When Rick stopped screaming, there was silence. It was back to just crickets. Scotty couldn't believe it. Had Rick's outburst worked?

"Rick, let's go," Scotty said. Rick turned to him and Scotty could see his face clearly in the moonlight. He was baffled, as if he couldn't make sense of what just happened.

"Jesus," Rick croaked hoarsely. "I'm sorry, Scotty, I don't know what that was."

"Whatever it was, it worked. I think you scared them off," Scotty said, still in a state of disbelief himself. "I think it's like with bear when you…"

And that was all could Scotty say before something jumped out of the forest with a roar. It was at least seven feet tall and covered with fur. The odor wafting from it was a rancid mix of waste, sweat, and rotted earth. Rick and Scotty screamed but the creature turned its full attention to Rick, grabbing him and prompting him to immediately drop his pocket knife, which would have done little to save him anyway.

"Help, Scotty!" Rick begged as the creature continued roaring and manhandling him. Scotty could only stand paralyzed as the awful scene unfolded. Finally, there was a grotesque ripping sound and Rick's screams were silenced. The creature began emitting a low purring sound as Rick's body hit the ground.

Scotty could see the creature was holding something. To his horror, he realized it was Rick's arm. He looked down and saw dark blood pooling around Rick's body. The bone poking out of his shoulder actually seemed to shine in the moonlight, causing Scotty to vomit. He knew Rick was dead and when he saw the creature advancing on him with Rick's arm still clutched in its hand, he knew he had only one option left, so he ran. The creature let out a howl that shook Scotty's entire body. The howl was returned and Scotty could hear the cracking sounds again. To make matters worse, the putrid odor of the creatures filled his nostrils. It was so dense it almost made Scotty vomit again but he continued running. He knew he wasn't going to make it to the highway. He was out in the open, making him easy prey for the creatures.

Although he knew his chances were slim, he ran into the woods to find a hiding spot. Slim certainly beat nil, which is what his chances were if he stayed on the road. To Scotty's relief, he saw a large uprooted tree and knew he wouldn't do any better than that. He quickly ducked under it, burrowing into the soft dirt and covering himself with dead leaves.

He did his best to his best to maintain steady breathing as he saw one of the creatures enter the area. It was only twenty feet from him, which was a good distance compared to the one who appeared only ten feet from him. And then he saw another one, likely a female based on the smaller build and saggy breasts. The moonlight provided Scotty with remarkable clarity. While their feet were indeed big, Scotty was much more taken with their scrunched faces and pronounced brows. They looked almost human but their cold, black eyes displayed nature at its most cruel and indifferent. Scotty knew his fate would be worse than Rick's if they caught him.

The one closest to him began sniffing the air and emitting a low growl. It slowly made its way over to Scotty's hiding spot. Scotty kept himself from screaming but felt a warm, wet sensation spread in his shorts and run down his leg. All things considered, it was far from the worst reaction he could have. As the creature got closer, tears ran down Scotty's cheeks. The creature's hairy legs, roughly the size of tree trunks, were mere inches away from him now. It was over; he just hoped it was quick.

Leaves rustled in the distance and the creature turned around with a grunt. Scotty could see the tail of a fat raccoon disappear into the brush to his right. The creature roared at it. It was a roar of annoyance and frustration but the distraction worked. Soon after, howls could be heard in the distance. The creature responded and ran off. Scotty was safe for now. As he began to consider his next move, he fell into darkness. Fear and exhaustion had finally overtaken him.

When Scotty jerked awake, it was morning. Birds chirped and the wind gently rocked the trees, creating of a symphony of whispering leaves and creaking branches. Scotty had to sit for a moment before the horrible events of the previous night washed over him. His throat was dry and cracked and his head throbbed.

He knew he couldn't stay here forever but he feared moving away from his seemingly perfect hiding spot. It had been day when they had taken Mark but there was also no time like the present. Scotty cautiously poked his head out from under the tree and saw the coast was clear. Now was as good a time as any. He crawled out of his safe place and stood up on stiff, cramped legs. Through the trees, he could see the road and knew the initial plan had to stay the same: Make it to the highway and find help.

He began to head for the road when he saw the Jeep pulled off to the side. He couldn't believe how fast his luck was changing. He could see the ranger was busy hanging a sign up and he walked toward him, raising his hand and trying to speak but his parched throat wouldn't allow it. As he got closer to the ranger, he saw a sudden flash of white. After that, he could only see black and felt intense pain bloom inside his now-shattered skull. It didn't last long, though. Within seconds, Scotty was gone.

The creature made its way toward Scotty's body, doing its best to stay out of the ranger's sight. The rock it had used to throw at Scotty had landed a few feet behind him; with bits of hair and splotches of blood stuck to it. The creature moved closer to Scotty and saw it had completely pulverized the back of his head, revealing soft pink brain in a few sections. It wanted to celebrate this kill but it also didn't want to invite any more attention. With almost supernatural speed, it scooped up Scotty's body and ran off into the deep woods. Once it was far enough away, it let out a victorious howl. It had to celebrate sometime.

Further back, the ranger heard the creature's cry and looked up. Gregory was his name and being a park ranger was his game. He had been at Stone Canyon for a little over a year and at first, it was a dream come true. Sure, he heard the stories about the creatures that inhabited the woods but he had dismissed them. This was his first full-time ranger gig. That's what mattered. There could have been stories of aliens landing and having orgies and Gregory wouldn't have cared. The euphoria quickly wore off, though. The disappearances and the increasing frequency of them put Gregory on edge and prompted him to spend most of his time at the ranger station.

The trouble began not long after Gregory took the job (talk about luck) and seemed to be getting worse by the month. The sign he was hanging up was long overdue. There had been opposition, mainly from the local shops and restaurants that relied on the hikers and campers for most of their business, even if their patronage usually ended up being a one-time occurrence. There was bribery, begging, and even threats but the danger had become too great to ignore. It was decided yesterday the park would have to be closed to the public.

"No Hiking and Camping Permitted. Violators will be fined and arrested!"

It was clear as they could make it. There would be people who would ignore it but the numbers would still go way down. After hearing the creature howl, Gregory decided his work here was done. The sign was hanging a little crooked but it would have to do. He jumped into his Jeep and quickly peeled out.

As he drove back to the ranger station, he reflected on why the creatures had suddenly gotten so aggressive. His co-workers insisted they had mainly stayed out of sight and were peaceful prior to the attacks. Was there something in the air? Had generations of inbreeding made them crazy?

Gregory finally considered the idea that maybe they had just gotten sick of humans. He couldn't blame them. His co-workers had drafted him to hang the signs, still designating him the "new guy" and smirking at him as he loaded the signs into his Jeep. To make matters worse, the assholes probably wouldn't even save him any coffee or donuts. People were pretty terrible sometimes. Gregory also contemplated the more primal issue of territory. After all, they were animals and this land had been their home for hundreds of years. Who was anybody to change that?

Gregory's answer came in the form of another howl that he could hear as clear as a bell, even in his moving Jeep. He figured they'd eventually make their way to the ranger station. It was at that moment he decided he had no plans to be there when they did.

Life was way too short for that shit.

Primal Urges

Mario was sitting next to an asshole. That wasn't surprising, as his chosen profession ensured he met plenty of them but this particular asshole did everything but stand below a neon sign advertising his asshole status. He wore (not ironically) Ed Hardy gear and his red monochrome Yankees hat still had the foil sticker on the upturned bill. The asshole brayed boorish laughter at the video game he was playing and kept asking Mario for more hits of his weed. Mario was generally willing to share his personal stash with his buyers but this asshole was really pushing it.

"I don't mean to be rude but you need to bounce," Mario said to the asshole, whose name was Andy, though he preferred "A-List." Mario thought the only list this clown would ever make was a sex offender registry but he kept his mouth shut. A-List was a first-time customer but he had bought three ounces. The stack of hundreds he paid with was hot and moist but seeing as how some of Mario's less savory buyers had paid him in bills stained with blood and God knows what else, hot and moist was a more than reasonable alternative.

"Did you hear what I said?" Mario asked A-List, who let out another cackle as he blew apart an alien with a rocket launcher.

"Yeah, I heard you, just give me five minutes!" A-List responded. He couldn't even look at Mario when he said this. A-List's small, piggy eyes stayed glued to the screen. Mario could feel annoyance and the tiniest hint of dread creeping over him. If he didn't kick A List out now, five minutes would mean at least two more hours. He often thought about pulling the plug on giving his buyers free rein of his place but his open door policy was one of the reasons he made as much money as he did. If he stopped that, he'd likely lose half his business. That didn't sound like fun to Mario but giving the boot to A-List did. He was tired and he hadn't eaten much today, which meant he was sporting a pretty nasty headache. Three ounces or not, A-List did not want to fuck with him.

"I've got places to be, man," Mario said, trying to keep his tone as genial as possible.

"I'm almost done with this level!" A-List protested.

"And you can finish next time you come back, I promise. I'll have some new bud that will put the shit you're smoking to shame."

This impressed A-List.

"For real?" he asked, his red-rimmed piggy eyes widening. "This shit was tight, though!"

"But I'll have something better soon," Mario offered. "Why do you think I get so much repeat business?"

And that did the trick. A-List killed a few more aliens before pausing the game and setting the controller down.

"Save my place and I'll be back in a week," he said as he stood up.

"No doubt," Mario replied. "I'll see you soon."

A-List hugged Mario, who had to hold his breath. A-List smelled like cigarettes and sweat. There were a few more hundreds in that wad he flashed. Mario sincerely hoped he invested in some deodorant before he came back.

Although he was confident A-List had taken the hint, Mario walked him to the door. He always did. Sitting down or going in another room sometimes acted as an inadvertent invitation for his buyers to stay little longer.

"Next week, m'man," A-List said as he went out the door.

Why not make it three? Mario thought as he shut the door behind him. He watched out the peephole as A-List got into his souped-up Hyundai and peeled out, the engine roaring in a manner that let Mario know A-List had a fondness for The Fast and The Furious films. A lot of his buyers did. Mario had seen a few of them. They were okay, though he had to admit the series picked up once they added The Rock.

Free again and flush with cash, Mario returned to his living room and shut off the PS4. Had he forgotten to save A-List's place? It didn't matter. A-List would forgive and forget as long as the weed was still good. As Mario crossed the room to turn off the television, he looked at the window and noticed his new neighbor getting out of her car. She had moved in about two weeks ago and made no effort to get to know anybody. Under ordinary circumstances, that would be okay. Mario generally avoided his neighbors but this neighbor was somebody he definitely wanted to get to know better. She had creamy skin and long, dark hair that cascaded down her back. Her firm breasts sat pertly beneath her light blue blouse and he could recognize shapely legs, even beneath the knee-length pleated skirt she wore. Mario watched as she struggled with the heavy bags. As far as he could tell, it was just she and her daughter, a skinny little thing with the same dark hair as her mother. Mario wondered if she'd grow up to look like her mother. She'd have nothing to worry about if she did. Mario thought it was a crime the woman was single. Was he the only one in this town with eyes? He hoped that was in the case as she went into the house, shifting her hips and perfect ass to accommodate the groceries that were falling out of the bag. Mario kept his eyes trained on the house as she went inside.

Breaking his own rules was something Mario had always avoided but it was a time to make an exception. He was long overdue.

Later that night, Mario was in his bed and sleep was eluding him. That happened most nights. His mother used to tell him his mind was too busy for him to relax and the older he got, the truer that was. Mario stared up at the all-too-familiar ceiling. It was depressing to think he had spent his whole life in this house, save for the six-month period he lived in New York crashing on a friend's couch.

That was an attempt to go straight. Mario had intended to go to school at Brooklyn College but one visit to the campus confirmed what he had already suspected about himself: He wasn't college material. The students looked like the kind of people he had avoided in high school and none of the majors seemed interesting. He wasn't entirely sure what he wanted to do with his life but it definitely didn't involve accounting or computer programming.

With school nixed, Mario used his remaining funds to buy a moped so he could take a job as a pizza delivery boy. That was okay for about three months. The tips were adequate and he even began to get a feel for the city, which had seemed so vast and overwhelming when he had first arrived. His humble but charmed new life took a turn once he started delivering pies to El Tiburon.

Mario had spent enough years in the drug trade to recognize one of his own. El Tiburon lived in a relatively modest apartment but the obscenely sized television, expensive clothing, and constant flow of people in and out confirmed El Tiburon didn't sell Avon for a living. After a few visits, El Tiburon recognized Mario's familiarity with the disbursement of recreational substances and enlisted his services.

Although Mario had moved to New York to get away from doing just that, he decided this was fine because he still had a steady job and El Tiburon only asked him to make a few deliveries each week. Mario didn't think much of it until El Tiburon asked him to meet Hector, the neighborhood kingpin. By this point, Mario was making more money working for El Tiburon than he was delivering pizzas, so it seemed like a solid step up.

Unlike El Tiburon, Hector flexed his muscle and wealth in an ostentatious fashion. He lived in an expensive penthouse and his Mercedes sported gold rims covered in diamonds. As soon as Mario set foot in Hector's penthouse, it felt wrong. He was a small town boy and Hector was a new breed altogether. The guys Mario knew and worked with back home liked to play video games, hang out in strip clubs, and wear two hundred dollar jeans. Guys like Hector would carve you into pieces if you came up just a few bucks short. Conversely, there were other dealers looking to carve Hector into pieces so they could move into his territory. Mario was slightly less out of place here than he was on a college campus but the major difference was that Mario likely wouldn't be killed on a college campus. His odds were much higher here but he was smart enough to know not to show any fear. He drank the champagne Hector offered, snorted a few lines with him, laughed at his jokes, but told him he needed to think about his offer to come work for him full-time.

"I might be moving back home," Mario said, trying to sound as apologetic as possible.

"Why the fuck do you want to do that?" Hector asked him. "Tiburon tells me you come from some shitty little farm town."

"My mother's not well," Mario replied. And in another year, that would actually be true.

Hector dipped his fingers in the coke he had spread out on his marble table and sniffed them.

"Do what you got to do but I need an answer soon. Trying to find good people in this fucking city is a joke."

Mario promised him he would and ten minutes later, El Tiburon was scolding him as they made their way back to his place.

"What the fuck, man?" El Tiburon asked. "I put in a good word for you. If you back out, I'm going to look like a fucking asshole!"

"Sorry, but I just got the word about my mom today."

"And what are you? A fucking doctor? Ain't there hospitals for that shit?"

Mario didn't appreciate El Tiburon dismissing his mother, so he returned home the next day without any further explanation. Through the grapevine some months later, he had gotten word that El Tiburon was found shot to death in an alley. That seemed about right to Mario. He made some decent money with the guy and even had a few good laughs with him but El Tiburon, like Hector, was an utter wretch living on borrowed time. Mario's instincts had never steered him wrong. It was why he was still alive and free at thirty-two while so many others had fallen.

"To thirty-two more!" he said out loud before rolling over to make another failed attempt at sleep. It took two hours and three shots of Jameson before he finally drifted off. Had he stayed awake just ten minutes longer, he would have seen his neighbor's car pull haphazardly into her driveway. Stranger yet, she had her daughter with her and although they ran into the house quickly, Mario would have noticed the dark stains splattered on their clothing. Had he seen that he wouldn't have needed his instincts to tell him to stay far away from her; plain old common sense would have done the job just fine.

But for now, Mario slept.

The next day Mario was trying to find something on Netflix when Curtis came over. Curtis was one of his regulars and he was also a cop. That would have given Mario pause under ordinary circumstances but he and Curtis had been friends since fifth grade. Like Mario, Curtis also wasn't college material but his parents had given him an ultimatum to find a real job or get out. Curtis becoming a cop didn't make much sense but it also kind of did. Curtis only needed two years of community college (and he barely squeaked through that) and after six months at the police academy, Curtis was a proud boy in blue. He would never be chief of police but Curtis had a steady income and nice a little house a stone's throw away from Mario's place.

Despite having been a cop for seven years, Curtis was still low man on the totem pole and his "weekends" generally fell in the middle of the week. It was on these days he came to get his weekly ounce from Mario and the two had beers and shot the shit. Curtis had the occasional amusing anecdote but their small town didn't allow for a lot of excitement, which meant they usually discussed their wild high school days. Mario found the topic tired but Curtis' presence was a welcomed one. There was no risk and if he needed Curtis to leave, he usually did so without protest. On this day, however, Curtis's face was flush with excitement.

"Did you hear about the homicide?" he asked, his chubby cheeks damp with sweat.

Mario had seen something on Facebook but he didn't really bother with the local news. Bake sales and school plays had never interested him.

"What happened?" Mario asked. He assumed a couple of rednecks had too many Keystones and an argument about whose pick-up truck was better had escalated into somebody pulling a gun and shooting the other.

"A homeless guy was found torn to pieces!" Curtis exclaimed.

"Really? Was he attacked by a bear or something?"

"Fuck no! This was in an alley downtown. There was almost nothing left of him!" Curtis said, the color in his cheeks continuing to rise.

"It was an animal, right?" Mario asked. It sounded gruesome but not as exciting as Curtis was making it out to be.

"There is no fucking animal around here that could do that, bro," Curtis said.

"So you're saying a person got hungry and decided to have roast hobo?"

"We don't know what the fuck it is, dude," Curtis answered. "Chief's already calling in the FBI. He's never seen anything like it."

"Well, I guess this place was due for a little bit of excitement," Mario said, continuing to scroll through Netflix.

"Do you want to hear the weirdest part?" Curtis asked.

"It gets weirder?"

Curtis paused for dramatic effect.

"They measure the bite marks on the dude. Whatever did it had teeth that were six inches long!"

"It had to be an animal then," Mario said, growing weary of this story.

Curtis smiled.

"The traces of saliva we found on him were from a human."

Mario let that sink in. That was pretty weird but it made little difference. The same burnouts and losers would still come to his house day in and day out for their fix. One less bum wouldn't affect that.

"So what's it going to be? Do we continue watching The X-Files?" Mario asked, pointing the remote at the television.

Curtis sat down next to him.

"I'm sick of The X-Files. Can we watch Black Mirror?"

"Sure thing," Mario obliged.

They watched in silence for a few minutes before Curtis spoke up. You could set your watch by him.

"Remember that night when we smoked behind the Burger King and Stevie walked up to the drive-thru window and convinced that girl to give him a free Whopper?"

Mario forced a smile. Some things just didn't change. That prompted him to think of his neighbor again. He really needed something to spice up his life and her moving in was feeling more and more like kismet.

Two hours later, Curtis was on his way with a fresh ounce of Mario's mid-grade bud and his box set of The Wire. Mario knew it would be at least six months before he saw it again but he let it go. His interest in dreary television had subsided as of late and two episodes of Black Mirror hadn't really helped matters.

As Mario stood in the doorway and waved goodbye to Curtis, he saw his neighbor pull up. He watched as she got out with a fresh bag of groceries. How much did she and that kid eat? Mario began to wonder if there wasn't a live-in boyfriend he hadn't seen. It would be a shame if his hopes of getting to know this woman were dashed before he even had a chance to say hello. Fate smiled him on that day, however, as the bag slipped from her hands, spilling the groceries everywhere. Not one to pass up an opportunity, Mario ran over to help her.

By the time he reached her, she had mostly gathered everything up, save for a few canned goods, which Mario picked up and held out to her.

"Do you need help getting everything inside?"

She cast a suspicious glance at him.

"I live right next door," Mario said, trying to keep it casual.

"Just leave it," she replied in breathy, hushed voice. "I'll come back out and get it in a minute."

"Are you sure…"

"I'm sure! Please just leave it!" she said in a clipped and impatient tone. "I don't need your help."

"Sorry," Mario said setting the can back down. Usually a woman who acted this bitchy was easy to walk away from but it had been awhile since he had been with anybody. And there was just something about this woman. He watched mesmerized as her slim, hosed legs worked double time getting the spilled groceries inside her house. If he were still out here when she came back, it would truly be over, so went back to his own house. He watched out the window but it was a good five minutes before she came back and retrieved the rest of the groceries. He watched as she cast a nervous glance around her yard before going back inside.

Part of Mario knew he should let it go but the other part sensed something dangerous. And it had been months since he had experienced that kind of excitement.

Instincts be damned.

Later that evening, Mario smoked a bowl and watched The Dark Crystal. It was one of his favorites and marijuana was always his companion when he watched it. As the creepy puppets did their thing on-screen, he turned his thoughts to the rest of the week. He had somebody lined up who wanted to buy a pound from him. A big order like that ordinarily screamed "Narc!" but Curtis had made the deal and Curtis would never set him up. While that was mostly out of loyalty, it also stemmed from the fact Curtis was too stupid to set him up.

It would be a solid chunk of change and he couldn't decide if he wanted to upgrade his entertainment center or put in a swimming pool. When his parents were alive, they had always wanted to put in a pool but they never had the money. Mario knew they'd disapprove of him using drug money to put one in but drug money was how he paid for the upkeep of the house since inheriting it. Why stop now?

As he stumbled into the bedroom, his head thick and sleepy from the weed, he heard a sound coming from outside. He dismissed it at first but just as he was about to fall into bed, he heard it again. It was a slamming sound, like somebody was opening and closing a door. Intrigued, he went to the window and looked outside. Everything looked still and serene. Then he heard it again. Three more slams and they sounded close. Mario realized they were coming from his neighbor's house. He wondered what was going on. Was she moving furniture around? And why would she be doing something like that so late? He heard something else slam but this time a scream followed it. Something was going on over there. Mario reached into his desk and pulled out a Glock. He had owned the gun for five years but had yet to use it. Just having it seemed like a formality but when he heard more noises coming from his neighbor's house, he was glad he did. Something wasn't right. He tucked the gun into the waistband of his jeans and went outside.

Crickets chirped and he could hear the sounds of the highway a mile away but there was silence otherwise. He wondered if it was all in his head until he heard another scream. He drew the gun out of his waistband and pointed it at her house. He immediately regretted doing that. Being high made him sloppy and the last thing he wanted was some night owl neighbor looking out their window and seeing him swinging a pistol around. Mario quickly tucked the pistol under his shirt and looked around but the lights in the surrounding homes were off.

He crept toward her house and heard something else come crashing down. What was going on in there? He saw a light turn on in the kitchen, prompting Mario to duck down. He cautiously poked his head back up and saw his neighbor enter. She poured herself a glass of wine with shaking hands and took a big sip. She looked completely different. Her hair was wild and frizzy and her skin looked red and blotchy. Mario thought she looked like a witch and not the sexy ones you see on Halloween. He knew most women let themselves go in the comfort of their own homes but it looked this woman had stopped caring altogether and in the span of just a few hours. Mario watched with distaste as she scratched her admittedly still hot ass before adjusting her frayed yoga pants. She poured another glass of wine and Mario noticed her hands were shaking a lot less. Self-medication. Mario certainly couldn't fault her for that. As she downed this glass, her daughter entered, dressed in pink pajamas that looked like they belonged on a much younger girl. They fit okay but they had a smiling cartoon rabbit on the front. Mario pegged the girl for at least thirteen but her pajamas belonged on a six-year-old. The whole thing was odd and despite his neighbor's frightening appearance, Mario was still intrigued by her. And considering how he had spent his evening, he really wasn't in a position to judge anybody.

He watched as the little girl embraced her mother and Mario suddenly thought of The Exorcist. What if the adorable little jellybean was possessed by the Devil? He guffawed at that absurd notion but it came out louder than he intended. Both of them looked in his direction and Mario crouched down, praying they hadn't seen him. He crawled to safety behind some bushes just as the back door opened. His neighbor stepped out, casting a cautious glance around the yard.

"Is anyone there?" she called out.

Yeah, bitch, because I'm definitely going to answer you, he thought.

She looked around a little more before going back inside. He could hear her talking to the little girl but he couldn't make out what they were saying. After a few moments, the lights shut off and he could hear them walking out of the kitchen. Mario waited and stayed in the bushes a little longer. In his line of work, being rash and careless got you thrown in jail or killed. Once he thought the coast was clear, he got up and went back inside his house.

As he finally went to bed that night, he replayed the day's events in his head. He thought about his neighbor's cold behavior, her strange appearance, and the odd sounds that came from her house. All of that should have been reason enough for him to forget the entire thing but he found himself getting hard just thinking about her. As he reached into his shorts, he decided she was just too good to pass up. He hadn't been this infatuated with a woman since high school and it felt great. Curtis' annoying obsession with nostalgia suddenly made sense and as Mario masturbated, he realized dealing drugs was the last thing on his mind. And any distraction from that was a welcomed one.

The next day was business as usual. Mario had three buyers come by and to his relief, they purchased their product and left. No mooching off Mario's stash, no playing video games, no fuss. If all of them were like that (save for Curtis), Mario thought he could grow to like what he did and not just tolerate it because his other options (what other options?) were so scant.

Mario found himself getting hungry around two o'clock. In true single guy fashion, his fridge was empty, save for a container of parmesan cheese and some strawberry jelly. He looked at the stack of pizza boxes and Chinese food containers on his counter and grimaced. Take-out was out of the question. He figured it was time to go to the grocery store. Chances were good he'd just come home with meals that were microwavable but it would at least get him out of the house. It had been a few days since he had really done that.

Mario decided to nix going to the grocery store a few blocks away and went to the Tops across town instead. He drove his father's old Gran Torino. It was his father's pet project for years and he had restored it almost completely from scratch. There was only some minor cosmetic work left when he died and Mario had used his own funds to finish restoring it. He figured he owed his father at least that. The car was loud and smelled of gasoline but driving it always gave Mario a sense of comfort. He had even kept his father's favorite cassette tape in the car: The Eagles' Greatest Hits. Mario popped it in and began singing along with "Take It Easy" as he drove through his depressing town to buy himself an equally depressing dinner.

Mario arrived at Tops halfway through "Lyin' Eyes" and was relieved to see the parking lot was mostly empty. He hated running into his buyers but not as much as he hated running into his parents' old friends or people from high school that had stayed on the straight and the narrow.

He didn't notice any cars he recognized, so he parked the Gran Torino and went inside. Mario walked aimlessly around the flatly lit aisles and took in the various junk and processed crap he'd likely be consuming in an hour.

As he turned the corner and headed for the meat section, lightning inexplicably struck. There was his neighbor, dressed to the nines and as far removed from her frazzled appearance the previous night as you could get. She was loading her cart with packages of chicken and steak. Mario decided this was as good as it was going to get, so he approached her.

"Hello again," he said.

She looked up at him, her eyes wary and untrusting.

"I'm your neighbor," he continued. "We met yesterday, remember?"

"I guess so," she said as she dropped a few more packages of steak inside the cart. Mario had never seen somebody buy so much meat.

"Are you having a barbecue or something?" he asked her.

"Something like that," she answered. "Now if you'll excuse me."

"My name's Mario," he said as she started to push her cart past him.

"Holly," she replied, clearly not interested in continuing the conversation but Mario knew this would be his only chance.

"So it's just you and your daughter there?" he asked.

"Yes," she answered, tightening her grip on the cart.

"She's a cute kid," Mario said. "Reminds me of my little cousin."

"Thank you," Holly said and although it was slight, Mario could see she was starting to soften.

"What's her name?"

"Pat--," Holly began before stopping herself. "I mean Daisy."

"Her name's Daisy?" Mario asked. It came out more incredulously than he intended. And had she started to say another name altogether?

"Well, your name's Mario," Holly shot back. He could see her appraising him with her dark, hypnotic eyes.

"My mother's name was Maria," Mario said, eager for this part of the conversation to be over.

"That's pretty," Holly said. "Now I really need to go. I have a daughter at home who needs her dinner."

She started to move forward again and underneath all the meats, Mario noticed a couple of bottles of wine.

"You know, I don't mean to be nosy but I have trouble sleeping, too."

"What do you mean?" Holly asked him, that wary and untrusting look falling over her face again.

"I just saw the wine and figured you used it for the same reason I did."

"I don't have to drink to fall asleep, thank you. It was nice meeting you," she said and with a quick sweep of her skirt, she was on her way again.

Mario was getting desperate and that meant he would get foolish and make a mistake. It meant...

"Because I've got other things besides alcohol, if you need to sleep or just want to party."

Shit. Talk about careless. Holly turned back to him.

"Are you saying you're a drug dealer?"

She wasn't turned on at all. Why would she be? Girls who got turned on by drug dealers were young and stupid. This woman was neither.

"Not so much a drug dealer but I do have things," Mario said, trying his best to sound relaxed. "You're welcomed to them."

"Is that supposed to impress me?" Holly asked, sounding like a teacher who had just caught a student scribbling a filthy drawing of her.

"No, I was just trying to be a good neighbor," he said finally.

"Do you really want to be a good neighbor, Mario?"

"Yes."

"Then keep your distance. I'm not here to make friends."

And that was it. Holly was on her way. Mario had blown it. He left the store without buying anything. He peeled out of the parking lot, leaving tire marks and a cloud of blue smoke in his wake.

"Fuck that uppity bitch," he yelled over Don Henley's gentle crooning.

He ripped the tape out of the cassette deck and tossed it into the backseat. It was time for a change.

Mario spent the next day on the couch smoking bowls and watching movies. Was it time to move on? He had a hundred thousand dollars in cash that he kept hidden in a safe under his bed. Money certainly wasn't the issue. And if he sold off the rest of his stash and paid off his supplier, there wouldn't be any problems there, either. So what was keeping him from going? Certainly not his buyers. And as much as he'd miss Curtis, life would ultimately go on just fine without him. Was he really leaving because he had gotten careless and opened up too much to a woman he'd likely fuck a few times and then lose interest in? Women had never been a distraction. What was so special about this one? Sure, she was a ten here but she'd only be in a seven in New York (not that he had any desire to go back there). Was the humiliating experience with her the straw that finally broke the camel's back? Mario sometimes fantasized about picking up and leaving but he had no idea where he would go or what he would do. There were a lot of places where the money he had would take him a long way but it wouldn't last forever. And even if he got into the drug trade in another small town, how safe would it be? He went back years with his suppliers and while his buyers were mostly idiots; they were at least trustworthy idiots. Unable to pull the trigger on a decision, Mario reached for his phone and dialed familiarity: Curtis.

"I can't come over today, dude," Curtis said. He sounded excited and even a little scared.

"What do you mean? What else do you have to do?" Mario asked.

"There was another murder last night," Curtis said in a hushed tone. "Just like the other one."

"Another homeless guy?"

"No, it was Miles Potter. Remember him?"

Mario did but only vaguely.

"He had a fight with his wife last night and went on a bender," Curtis explained. "He was gone all night, which is a frequent occurrence with him so his wife didn't think anything of it. Garbage men found him in an alley, completely torn to shreds."

"Shit," Mario said, though as gruesome as it was, he didn't really care. Miles being dead meant one less drunken wife-beating redneck.

"Chief's got us all working double shifts until we find a lead."

"So that's it? You're bailing on me?" Mario said. It came out a little harsher than he intended.

"I'm not bailing, I have to work!" Curtis whined.

"Fuck that, man, you should have gotten on the ground level with me. Then you wouldn't have to worry about shit like this."

"Yeah, well, not all of us have parents who were as doting and forgiving as Tom and Maria," Curtis replied.

"Fine, have fun."

"Wait, want me to call you when…" Curtis began but Mario hung up on him.

"Friends like these," Mario said aloud to nobody in particular. "Time to get the fuck out of this shit hole town."

He sat back and turned on Pee Wee's Big Adventure. As the movie started, he sparked a new bowl and took a big drag from it.

At least Pee Wee wouldn't let him down.

The movie was almost over and Mario was half asleep when he heard somebody knocking on his door in short, frantic bursts. Groggy, he sat up and listened. The knocking came again but Mario stayed on the couch. If it was a buyer, they could wait until tomorrow or find another dealer altogether. Unfortunately, his visitor didn't take the hint and the knocking persisted. Annoyed, he got up and was ready to yell for them to fuck off when an unexpected voice came through the door.

"Mario? Are you home?"

It was her!

A sudden rush of adrenaline hit Mario and he went to the door, stopping to check himself in the mirror. Aside from red eyes, he looked presentable. He opened the door to reveal Holly, dressed in a sheer blouse and a wine-colored skirt. She gave him a sexy smile.

"I didn't wake you, did I?"

"Not at all, I was just watching a movie."

"Anything I've seen?"

Mario thought fast.

"Oh, nothing special. Just The English Patient. Seen that one?"

"It's one of my favorites," she said. "I'll even tell you a secret."

She leaned in close and Mario could smell her perfume. It was subtle but alluring.

"Daisy's dad looked a bit like Ralph Fiennes. I think that's why I married him."

Mario was unsure how to respond to this. Ralph Fiennes was a suave motherfucker. Did he really compare to him?

"Anyway, I just wanted to come over and apologize. I was rude yesterday," she said.

"That's okay, I can come on a little strong sometimes."

"No, you were fine, I was just in a bad mood. I was thinking if you weren't busy, maybe you could come over and join me for a drink."

Mario couldn't believe it. Was this real? How high was he?

"Sure thing. Can you give me a few minutes?" he said, trying not to sound too eager, though he doubted he was succeeding. Still, her interest didn't seem to waver.

"Of course. Take your time and come over when you're ready. I'll be waiting," she said, shooting him another sexy smile.

"Do you want me to bring anything?"

"Just yourself. See you in a few minutes," she said walking away, her ass twitching seductively beneath her skirt.

Mario shut the door and stared at himself in the mirror in disbelief. Staying in town suddenly didn't seem so terrible.

Ten minutes later, Mario was wearing a new shirt and walking over to Holly's house. He had a dime bag and a gram of coke in his pocket just in case she wanted to let her hair down. Mario reached the front door and cupped his hands to his mouth to check his breath one last time. All was well. He rang the bell and waited. There was no answer. Had she changed her mind? Just as the nervousness began to transition into anger, she opened the door. She had freshened up her makeup and changed into a halter-top and tight jeans. She looked ten years younger. Mario generally preferred younger women and her tacit understanding of this made her irresistible to him.

"Come on in," she said, giving him a grin that exposed her straight, white teeth.

Mario entered and looked around. He was slightly taken aback. He had been in this house once years ago and it well decorated with modern furniture. His mother called it cozy. Now it looked abandoned. There was one couch against the wall and it looked like she had picked it up from the curb. The coffee table, if you could call it that, was a piece of plywood propped up on cinder blocks. It reminded Mario of the ghetto apartments he used to deliver to in his early days. None of it remotely agreed with this classy, well-dressed woman.

"The moving van got into an accident on its way here," she explained. "It went off a bridge and into the water. Luckily the movers got out but all my furniture is at the bottom of the Mississippi. Can you believe that?"

"For real?" Mario asked. It sounded pretty unbelievable.

"Yeah, it was all insured of course but it took the moving company forever to get me the check to cover it. I finally ordered replacement furniture today but it won't be here until tomorrow."

"Damn," Mario replied. He didn't know what else to say.

"Is this okay?" she asked but it was merely a formality. She knew it was okay. She was a beautiful woman. Most guys (Mario included) would sit on a bed of nails to get one-on-one time with somebody who looked like her.

"Yeah, it's fine. Let's sit down," Mario said.

"You sit down. I'll be back with drinks. Gin and tonic okay?"

"That sounds great."

Mario hated gin and tonic. She went into the kitchen and he sat down on the ratty-looking couch. To his relief, she had sprayed it with Febreze but it only partly masked the dense smell of mildew and body odor. She had definitely gotten this couch from a curb and it wasn't in a nice neighborhood. Mario wondered if it had belonged to one his buyers.

He looked toward the kitchen, wondering what was taking her so long. When he turned back around, the daughter was standing in front of him. She wore childish pajamas again, only these were baby blue instead of pink. A grinning Care Bear was on the front holding a cloud that was spouting a rainbow. Mario couldn't put his finger on it but there was something vaguely sinister about it. He did his best to dismiss it. This girl was thirteen and harmless. He wished his instincts would take a night off for once.

"Hi," Mario said. "You must be Daisy."

Daisy stared at him and the resemblance to Holly was uncanny. She was definitely going to be a heartbreaker someday.

"Your mom's told me a lot about you."

"But you've only met her twice," Daisy replied, a knowing look on her face.

"And both times she did nothing but talk about you!" Mario said, trying to give her his best disarming grin.

Holly returned with the drinks in two tall, sweating glasses.

"Go back to bed, baby," she said. "I'll be up in a few minutes."

"Like an actual few minutes or a grown-up few minutes?" Daisy asked.

"Now you see the who the boss is," Holly said to Mario before turning back to Daisy. "I mean an actual few minutes. Go on." She kissed Daisy on the forehead and that did the trick. The girl went upstairs, taking each step with a loud, insolent thud.

"She's a sweetie," he said as Holly handed him his glass.

"She's my whole world," Holly said with a firmness that signified she wasn't totally for sale. Mario started to realize just how much of a fluke this was. He needed to take full advantage of it.

"So how do you like our town so far?" he asked. Keep it simple. That was his first rule with women.

"It's a town," she said with an indifferent shrug. "How do you like living here?"

"Spent my whole life here," he answered. "It's home."

"Wow, you're a real man of adventure!" she said, her tone becoming teasing.

"Hey, I spent six months in New York!"

"Why'd you leave?"

"Too busy. I'm a small town boy."

"With big city ambitions," she said in that same teasing tone.

"What's that supposed to mean?"

"Small town boys generally become insurance agents. You're a drug dealer."

"Small towns need my services, too. Maybe even more than big cities," he replied, taking a big sip of the gin and tonic. God, it tasted like dog piss.

"Well, I didn't call you over here to talk shop," she said.

"No?"

"No."

She suddenly threw herself on top of him and began kissing his face and neck. Mario grunted in surprise. He hadn't seen this coming at all. She continued kissing and pawing him in an aggressive fashion. Her breath was coming in short, fast bursts. It smelled of toothpaste but the unmistakable stench of fermented grapes was lingering beneath it. She had definitely been going at the bottle for a while. Mario regained his bearings and started returning her affections, kissing her gently in hopes she'd subside a little but her animal-like behavior only got more assertive as she continued kissing and groping him. Her teeth raked his neck sharply and her right hand reached into his pants and found his stiff penis. She began yanking it with painful, urgent tugs. Mario stopped kissing her and grabbed both of her arms.

"Take it easy!" he whispered.

"I'm sorry, it's just been a long time," she said, out of breath.

"And it's been awhile for me but I'm still going to treat you right."

Without another word, Holly resumed kissing and stroking him in a manner that was still hungry but much more pleasurable. His hands found her perfect breasts, squeezing them slightly and running his fingers over her firm, erect nipples.

She let out a soft moan and he continued kissing her and fondling her breasts. She began to pull at his belt and he reached down and undid his pants. His penis flopped out and fell back against his belly. She slid down her jeans and guided him inside her. The effect was electric. Mario's entire body jolted as she began to rock back and forth on top of him. He generally liked doing most of the work but he knew he'd never be able to top this. She was majestic and Mario had no qualms turning over complete control to her. The experience was his best by far but it was also short-lived. He came inside of her and she arched her back and gave one last protracted moan. She rolled away and planted herself at an awkward angle against the back of the couch but also still somewhat on top of him. She rested her head against his and he could feel her cool skin and hot breath against his cheek. It was wonderful.

"That was perfect," she said, still somewhat out of breath. "Thank you."

Mario had never been thanked before. It was a little odd but after that performance, she could dress like a clown and speak Klingon and he would be okay with it.

"How about another drink?" she asked him.

Mario shifted around and managed to get his arm around her. The couch was disgusting and there really wasn't enough room for them to properly lie together but he had no intention of letting her go, at least for the next few minutes.

"Can't we just sit here for a little while?"

"Sure, but I really need a drink first. What do you want?"

Mario intended to protest a little more but she had already shoved his arm away and was sitting up. He decided to let this one go.

Maybe another drink would mean round two. Or even rounds three and four.

"Anything but a gin and tonic," he said, giving her a wink.

"Red wine?" she asked, pulling up her jeans.

Red wine wasn't really his favorite, either but it beat the alternative.

"Sounds good."

She went into the kitchen and Mario exhaled loudly. He stared up at the ceiling. A dark stain that reminded him of a Rorschach test was directly above him. He stared at it, trying to assign a shape or object to it but nothing came. Holly had depleted just about everything from him. His postcoital moments usually consisted of him thinking about a video game he wanted to play or what fast food joint he wanted to eat at. In this case, there was nothing and only time and sleep would properly restore him. He hoped she'd let him stay over, not just because he yearned for more time with her but also because he didn't think he had the energy to walk home, even if it was only twenty feet away.

She came back with two water-spotted wine glasses, both half full. With a Herculean effort, Mario sat up and took one of the glasses from her. She sat down next to him and they clinked the glasses together without saying a word. Mario downed the wine in one big gulp. He didn't know if the wine was expensive or not. It had always tasted the same to him. It did have an odd flavor, though. There was the slightest hint of something that reminded him of aspirin. Whatever it was, it was gone now. Holly watched him with an amused expression on her face.

"Somebody was thirsty."

"After that, I'm a lot more than thirsty. Do you want to continue this upstairs?"

Holly gave him an apologetic look.

"I don't think so."

"What, you're kicking me to the curb already?" he said. The words had a slight slur and he felt dizzy. What the fuck was going on? He looked at Holly, who didn't answer him. Her face suggested she was a boss who was about to tell him he was going to be laid off despite years of loyal service. The room began to blur and spin. Mario dropped his glass and fell back on the couch. Forget round two, Mario just wanted the room to stop spinning.

Within ten seconds, his wish was granted. Mario was out.

When he woke up, he was on a dirt floor, his arms and legs bound with duct tape. The musty, wet smell in the room confirmed he was in a basement. A dingy light bulb enveloped him in a muted yellow glow, barely cutting through the darkness of the rest of the space. His throat was dry and constricted.

"What the fuck?" he finally managed, feeling needles in his throat as the taste of copper filled his mouth.

He heard footsteps coming toward him and eventually Holly stepped into the light. She wore sweats and a long-sleeved top

"Sorry about this," she said. And her face confirmed she meant it.

"Sorry for what?" he croaked. "Fucking untie me!"

"I can't do that," Holly explained. "I promised her this."

Mario didn't understand.

"What are you talking about?"

Holly dragged over a water-swollen box and sat down on it.

"I mean she's been waiting all night for this. I can't take it back now. She's my whole world, remember?"

Mario's brain was still foggy but that sounded familiar. Did she mean...

Someone else emerged from the darkness and Mario recognized the light blue pajama-clad legs that stepped into the light. However, the face that had looked so sweet just a few minutes ago was no more. What was standing in front of him was a monster. An honest-to-God, dyed-in-the-wool monster, just like you'd see in a horror movie. It had wide demonic eyes that rested above two thin slits that used to be a cute button nose. The mouth below that was three feet wide and had six-inch fangs coated with thick, mucus-like saliva.

Mario tried to scream but a choked, rusty sound came out instead. The thing that was introduced to him as Daisy moved closer to him and an unearthly growl emitted from its stomach.

"Normally I can keep her at bay with steaks and chicken but she still requires fresh meat," Holly said. Her casual tone suggested she was explaining a fascination with shoes and not an appetite for human flesh. "Lately, though, she's required fresh meat almost every night. I usually try to put it off as long as I can but she hasn't given me much of a choice. She's been a handful lately!"

Holly sat up and began to stroke the thing's head, which still had the dark ponytail of a little girl.

"We've obviously drawn too much attention to ourselves to stay here, so we're moving on. Again. That'll be six towns in two years but what are you going to do?"

"Please don't do this!" Mario rasped, tears starting to spill down his cheeks.

"It's too late now," Holly said shortly. "We're leaving tonight and I wanted to make sure she wasn't traveling on an empty stomach. I ordinarily avoid using the neighbors but I figured who's really going to give a shit about a drug dealer?"

Mario sobbed in response.

You got it all wrong, he thought. I'm not a bad guy! I just didn't know how to do anything else!

The thing began to make a strange purring sound as it continued to move closer to him. The end was coming. There was a faint glimmer of hope as Holly put a hand on the creature and gently guided it back. She knelt down next to him.

"She needs to eat but I needed something else tonight," she whispered in his ear. "I wasn't kidding when I told you it had been awhile. And you were wonderful. Thank you."

She kissed him on the cheek and stood up.

"All yours," she told it. "Just wait until I get upstairs."

She disappeared into the darkness and Mario could hear her footsteps going up the stairs.

"Holly!" he croaked at her but it was too late. She was gone.

The thing began to purr again. Its huge mouth opened and Mario gagged at the gangrenous odor that emanated from it. He tried to scream again but he was unable to produce a sound this time. As the thing got closer, Mario could see how much it relished the fear that was radiating from him in shaky droves. This wasn't just an act of survival but one of pleasure.

The thing lashed forward and took a huge chunk out of his neck; prompting pain that was brutal and intense but also mercifully short-lived.

As death fell over him, he was allowed one final memory. He was eight years old and had fallen off his bike and skinned both knees. He had screamed bloody murder as his mother tended to him. At the time, it was the most blood he had ever seen but she had fixed him and made him feel better. He was outside again with his friends in no time. It was like the skinned knees had never happened. It was a minor blight on an otherwise perfect summer.

He took solace in knowing his last memory was a pleasant one. Seconds later, he died facedown choking on his own blood.

And then Daisy fed.

A short time later, the house burned down and what was left of Mario went with it.

As Holly and Daisy drove the on the darkened and almost-empty highway, Holly looked at her daughter in the rearview mirror. She was an angel again. Their nomadic life had taken its toll on her but Holly remained determined to make the best possible life for them. To say her little girl wasn't perfect was an understatement but she was still everything to Holly.

"Mom?" Daisy called out from the backseat.

"What is it, sweetie?"

"Did you have sex with him?" she asked. Holly could hear how awkward it was for her to ask that. It has only been a few months since Holly explained sex to her. She figured even if her daughter would never have a normal life, she at least deserved some semblance of one.

"Excuse me?" Holly said, feigning anger. She hoped that would be enough for her to let it go.

"You heard me," Daisy said, unwilling to move past it.

"That really isn't something you ask your mother," Holly said, her tone firm.

"But did you?"

Holly squeezed the steering wheel.

"Let's just say Mommies have needs."

Her little girl went silent and Holly decided to change the subject.

"How about we talk names? What's your new one going to be?"

"I don't know. What do you think?"

"Do you like Abigail?"

"Yuck!" Daisy exclaimed, making a face.

"What about Abby?"

"That's better. I can live with Abby."

Holly felt relieved. That was one less thing to worry about it.

"What about you?" asked the little girl now known as Abby.

"I was thinking Maria."

"Maria's pretty."

"I think so, too," she said, giving Abby a warm smile.

It was a fitting tribute to the only friend she had made in that town, especially since he had given both of them so much. She hoped his sacrifice was as satisfying for Abby as it was for her. Deciding to test the waters, Maria turned on the radio and began singing along with Meghan Trainor. Normally Abby hated when she sang along to the radio but in this instance, she joined in.

Maria decided this meant they were both satisfied and continued driving, eager for a fresh start.

She just hoped it lasted longer than the others.

The Grand Finish

"Ready, Winston?"

The question from inside the engineer's booth was innocuous enough but the increasingly sharp pain shooting through Winston Davis' hands was anything but.

"Actually, do you think we could take five?" he asked Stu, offering him a sheepish grin.

"No problem, Winston. Take all the time you need," Stu said, spinning around in his chair to inspect the elaborate controls on the mixing board. Winston liked Stu. Of the two engineers at Electric Sonata Studios, he was the best. He was patient and sympathetic with Winston. A piece that would have taken Winston three hours to record two years ago now took eight but Stu didn't mind. He was a welcomed alternative to the other engineer, who Winston had dubbed "Nahtu," as in "Nahtu rush you but I have dinner plans" or Winston's all-time favorite: "Nahtu be a pain but I have LCD Soundsystem tickets tonight."

That one was the kicker. They had been working on a recording of Chopin's Nocturnes and this character had the nerve to mention LCD Soundsystem? They didn't even belong on the same planet as Chopin as far as Winston was concerned. That had been the last time he had worked with Nahtu. He had insisted on Stu from that point on and so far, the studio had accommodated him.

As Stu continued tinkering with the mixing board, Winston left the stuffy soundproof room and found his way to the drinking fountain down the hall. He popped three Tylenol and washed them down with the lukewarm, mineral-tasting water the fountain produced. He figured the Tylenol was a placebo at this point but it was at least an effective one, as the pain in his hands subsided a little.

Winston took a minute to examine his surroundings. He inhaled deeply, allowing the stale and familiar metallic odor of the building to invade his nostrils. It took him back to music school when he was a chubby undergrad scurrying from lecture halls to practice rooms and ending each day with a brisk three hours of sleep. He thought of the endless bowls of Ramen he consumed, as well as the pages of sheet music that turned into indecipherable code after poring over them for hours on end.

Those moments often brought about an existential crisis for Winston. Just what was he doing and why was he doing it? He was at one of the top music schools in the world, yet he lived like a rat and would likely have high blood pressure before turning thirty (if he didn't already have it). And what if the hours and hundreds of thousands of dollars amounted to him becoming a music teacher while his classmates went on to be the best in the world, earning the acclaim and respect they all viciously desired? Was that a life?

These musings were brief, however, as Winston only needed to remind himself that was very lucky just to be there in the first place. His audition was not perfect and anything less than perfect meant you were not Vickman School of Music material. Despite that, the school had placed Winston on their waiting list. If something changed with one of the students who hadn't botched their audition, Winston would earn a seat in the incoming class. Although his father had been disappointed, his doting mother noted how proud she was of Winston. Out of two thousand applicants, a mere two hundred would be admitted, so his place on the waiting list still placed him well above the majority of the other applicants. That did little to comfort Winston and he spent the next two weeks in a funk until lightning inexplicably struck.

One of the incoming students had fallen into some kind of legal trouble and that definitely didn't make you Vickman material. The student's admission was revoked and Winston was allowed in on a probationary basis.

He worked harder than he ever thought possible and by the end of his senior year, he was one of the school's best students with a brilliant future ahead of him. And the subsequent years had been brilliant, at least until tendonitis struck two years ago.

Playing this ancient history in his head had prompted Winston to stare blankly at the gold records that covered the walls in the hallway. He had yet to earn one of those (classical musicians rarely garnered such certifications) but working exclusively as a recording artist and not a performer was something Winston was still coming to terms with. He had spent time in the studio of course but the idea that this was what the rest of his career would consist of seemed premature and anti-climactic. He was only forty-three. Worst of all, he felt weak. Jia Yang, an insanely talented Chinese girl, was making huge waves as a concert pianist and she was born blind. Would tendonitis slow her down? Winston decided it was best not to think about it.

He continued to stare at the gold records and realized if Stu saw him at this moment, he'd think Winston was on the verge of a seizure or an out-of-body experience. As a result of this trance-like trip down memory lane, Winston's body felt like it was filled with cement. He finally mustered the initiative and strength to start moving again. He had kept Stu waiting long enough. Once they finished this final piece, they would be done for the weekend. Winston (and his hands) were extremely grateful for that.

He went back inside the room and sat down at the shiny black baby grand (a vast improvement over the relics he played in music school). The pain in his fingers was slight but still very much in the equation. These days, that was as good as it got.

He turned to Stu and nodded at him. Stu began to roll and as soon Winston saw the red light turn on, he began to play. It was his best performance of the night.

Forty-five minutes later, they were wrapped and headed for the parking lot. The chatter was pleasant but it confirmed what Winston already knew: Stu was a great engineer but hardly a friend. Stu worked with the best musicians in the world and Winston was merely a drop in that bucket. It was humbling and a little sad. In his performing days, finding someone to have dinner or a drink with was no problem. Now that he had been put out to pasture, Winston found that people didn't really seek him out anymore and aside from the Stu the engineer, there weren't a lot of people in his life anyway. Miriam had left him three years ago and save for a Christmas card and a dutiful phone call on his birthday, he barely heard from her.

After a polite farewell, Stu had jumped in his sporty little two-door and disappeared into the night. Winston imagined the company of a lovely lady was in his future. Good for Stu. Winston was embarrassed to admit he hadn't enjoyed the company of a lady since Miriam's departure. Of course that was nothing a fast broadband connection couldn't fix. Or so he told himself.

As Winston reached his silver BMW, he thought a glass of wine (or a bottle) and a good cigar would be the perfect way to cap off a productive recording session. It would also help him sleep, which was proving to be quite difficult these days. However, before he had time to think about which bottle he'd be opening, he heard quick footsteps shuffling behind him and then felt the briefest pinprick in his neck. Seconds later, everything went dark.

Winston wasn't so lonely after all.

Steinway. The word started out blurry but slowly came into focus as Winston regained consciousness. It took him a few moments to get his bearings and when he did, he realized he was seated at a grand piano. A Steinway. The same type of piano that had been delivered to his house when he was five years old. His father has grumbled about the cost and the space it took up but his mother couldn't stop smiling. She even had tears in her eyes the first time Winston sat down at it. The Steinway didn't just become a part of it his childhood, it consumed it. While other children dedicated themselves to Little League and all things Star Wars, Winston Davis spent his days with the same 88 friends until he left for Vickman. And they were loyal, unlike the other friends that had come and gone in the years since.

His current situation still made no sense, though. Why was he seated at a Steinway? That was when he noticed his ankles felt especially heavy. He didn't have to look down to know he wasn't just seated at a Steinway but chained to it. Although still weak, he dragged his feet slightly and it only took about four inches for the chains to become taut. He wasn't going anywhere.

"Welcome back, Winston," a voice from behind him said. "I was beginning to grow impatient with you."

As Winston slowly craned his neck to see who was speaking, footsteps echoed on the concrete floor. The owner of the voice was now in front of him, leaning on the Steinway with a strange look of admiration of their face. Said face was narrow and pallid with a stubby nose. Whatever hair had been on top of his head was long gone, replaced by patchy and sporadic wisps. Winston thought he looked like a strange hybrid of Humphrey Bogart and Michael Stipe.

"I've been wanting to meet you for a long time," Humphrey Stipe said, his blood red lips forming a grotesque grin. "You've had quite a career. One could say there wasn't much else for you to accomplish but we both know that's not true."

Winston could only gape at him in response. None of this seemed real.

"You see, I like a good underdog story," Humphrey Stipe continued. "Waitlisted at Vickman after, shall we say, a rocky audition, only to gain admittance later, where you became one of the top pupils in the music program. My hat is off to you."

"Thanks," Winston finally managed. It wasn't much but he wanted to say something, especially since Humphrey Stipe's calm and laudatory demeanor was obviously a razor-thin cover for something much more dangerous.

"It defies logic, you know," Humphrey Stipe said, the color rising in his cheeks. The pleasant demeanor was already starting to crack. "How does a third-rate talent luck into a first-rate school and go on to have a career that rivals Moravec?"

"I don't know. Just lots of practice," Winston said.

"No!" Humphrey Stipe shouted, slamming his hand on the top of the Steinway. "Lots of people practice! Most of them are practicing right now and they will never come close to what you've achieved!"

Whatever fatigue remained from Winston's unconscious state was long gone. His heart rate had increased and he could feel large beads of sticky sweat collecting on his forehead.

His captor seemed to take pleasure in Winston's fear and discomfort. He eased down and moved away from the piano.

"Another thing I'll credit you with is that when you were performing, you took to the stage almost to the minute of concert's stated start time. That is rare in any arena and in the interest of maintaining such a stellar record, let's get down to brass tacks," Humphrey Stipe said rubbing his hands together eagerly. "Inside this beautiful Steinway is a very large bomb…"

Winston interrupted him with a gasp and abandoned all restraint by struggling and screaming for help.

"Somebody get me out of here!" Winston bellowed and his voiced echoed in the vast space. It was likely a warehouse and one that had been long abandoned.

"Go ahead and scream, Winston!" Humphrey Stipe yelled, matching his volume. "I promise no one can hear you!"

Winston struggled with the chains at his feet but that proved equally useless. Humphrey Stripe watched him, a look of weary disgust on his face.

"Have some dignity, Winston," he said. "You haven't even heard me out yet."

Already tired from this brief outburst and feeling the all-too familiar throbbing sensation starting up in his hands and wrists, Winston relented.

"Now as I was saying. There's a large bomb in that piano and it's a very special bomb. One I've customized myself. I'm going to give you three pieces to play. They happen to be three of the most difficult ones in the world. Play them flawlessly and you go home. Make one mistake and..."

With an apologetic look on his face, Humphrey Stipe mimed an explosion with their hands.

"This can't be," Winston stammered. "Why are you doing this?"

Humphrey Stipe's expression turned sour.

"Because I'm the man fate shit on to give you the career that rightfully belonged to me, Winston."

The next few minutes were a blur. Winston pleaded with Humphrey to keep talking with him but Humphrey didn't respond. He merely hummed a song Winston recognized but couldn't exactly place. After another agonizing moment of Humphrey pacing around the room and humming, he set out pieces of sheet music on the piano's rack. He started with the last sheet. It was a flurry of notes so complicated Winston thought he was going to pass out at the mere sight of it. As Humphrey continued to set the sheets down as if preparing an elegant place setting, Winston found himself growing woozy. His entire body was coated with sweat and despite his best efforts to keep them relaxed; his hands were warming up to sing a song of intense pain and unprecedented stiffness.

Humphrey Stipe finally laid the last sheet down and Winston saw it was Liszt's Feux Follets. Winston had attempted it once and fumbled through it somewhat successfully. Given the duress he was currently under, was perfection even in the cards?

Humphrey sensed his trepidation and smiled at him.

"I've been preparing this for a long time, Winston," he said. "If you need a few extra minutes to gather yourself, I completely understand. I'm not a total monster, you know."

"You said I stole your career," Winston said. "I've never stolen anything from anybody. And I worked my ass off to get this far. Why would you say I stole it from you?"

Humphrey reached into the frayed blazer he was wearing and pulled out a small black box.

"Because you did. I understand the confusion because I don't think you realized it but you did," Humphrey said as he examined the black box. "And truth be told, I was just going to let it go because like you said, you had earned it."

"So why am I here?" Winston asked him.

"Easy, Winston," Humphrey answered. "You got weak. Tendonitis? Come on!"

That touched a nerve. Winston could feel anger stirring inside him. Of course he thought that about himself just about every minute of every day but to hear this asshole say it?

"Weak?" Winston asked, his voice developing a slight edge. "You think a condition that's hindered my greatest passion is a sign of weakness?"

"Maybe not consciously, Winston," Humphrey said, looking away from the black box to make eye contact with him. His eyes were watery and his pupils had dilated. Winston wondered what he was under the influence of. "Now, I'm not a doctor but you know what I think the real cause of tendonitis is?"

Winston had spent hours Googling his affliction, not to mention the six different doctors he had visited. He had read numerous theories on the various causes of tendonitis. None of them mattered. He had it and it had driven a stake in the heart of his greatest achievement. That's what mattered.

"Well, Winston?" Humphrey pressed him, maintaining eye contact.

"What difference does it make?" Winston responded. "Is there an answer I can give where you'll let me go?"

"No, the arrangement is that you play these three pieces and then I let you go." Humphrey stated matter-of-factly. "But in terms of your tendonitis, I think the real cause is tension. You were so tense and nervous when you played that it finally caught up to you and your body said no more."

Winston didn't reply. He had heard tension could be a contributing factor but aside from the normal jitters before any big concert, he was never tense when he played. He doubted revealing that would make any different with this nutcase.

"That's when I knew what a fraud you were, Winston," Humphrey said. "Guys almost twice your age are still playing and you cop out in your early forties? That's unacceptable. That's the thing about frauds. At some point, they're always revealed and it usually doesn't take that long but somehow you managed to pull a long con. Kudos."

"So what does this prove then?" Winston asked. "What does tying me to a piano and making me play these pieces possibly achieve?"

"Call it peace of mind, Winston," Humphrey said. "Or don't. I don't really give a shit. Either way, this shouldn't be that much of a challenge for one of the world's most renowned pianists. This should just be another day at the office. Begging me to stop and sweating like the pig you are only confirm you were never cut out for any of it."

"So if you did the same thing to Mozart, he'd take it in stride and play flawlessly?"

"He'd at least play flawlessly, Winston" Humphrey said. "And he'd never be in this position because he wasn't weak to begin with."

Humphrey paused to let this sink in. Winston could only stare down at the piano keys while sweat poured off him in buckets and the dull throbbing in his hands increased.

"Do you want to get started now, Winston? The longer you wait, the harder it's going to get for you to play."

Winston gave Humphrey an answer but it was too low for him to hear at first. He leaned in closer.

"What was that Winston?"

"I said prove it," Winston replied. "A bomb that's programmed to go off if I make a mistake? I don't buy it."

Humphrey stared at him, his rheumy eyes wide and determined. He lifted open the top of the Steinway to reveal a complicated electronic device. It had been Frankensteined together with numerous wires and store-bought electronic parts. Most damning were the brown clay bars that Winston recognized as C-4. He had seen enough action movies to know that.

Humphrey held up the small black box in front of Winston's face.

"Now, I could give you a demonstration but that would be pretty messy and pointless, wouldn't it, Winston?" he said waving it in a taunting manner. "Are you that desperate not to play that you'll allow yourself to be stuccoed all over this building?"

Winston's breath was coming in short gasps now.

"Still not convinced?" Humphrey said, his finger over a red button on the box. "Okay then."

He pressed the button and the device strapped to the inside of the piano immediately came to life with a series of beeping sounds and blinking lights.

"One more press of the button and you'll know I'm really not fucking around. Is that what you want, Winston?" Humphrey asked, his forefinger shaking over the button.

"No, I believe you!" Winston said. "Please make it stop!"

"I can't, Winston!" Humphrey answered like Winston was a clueless five-year-old. "It's been activated!"

He slammed the top of the piano closed, causing Winston to jump.

"Now play!" Humphrey spat at him. "I've been patient enough!"

He walked away from the piano, his worn dress shoes clacking on the cement in short, impatient bursts.

Winston stared at the sheet music. Could he do this? Whether he could or couldn't, Humphrey's patience was gone. Taking a deep breath, Winston placed his hands over the keys and steadied them as best he could. Giving himself a silent count off to three, Winston brought his hands down and began to play.

He nailed it. He was so good that Humphrey had set the remote down to applaud him. Winston expected it to be mocking but it was genuine and appreciative. Having been on both ends of the applause spectrum throughout his career, Winston recognized when somebody truly loved what he had done and Humphrey had loved it. Was he off the hook?

"Outstanding, Winston," Humphrey said, his clapping echoing loudly in the large space. "Only two more to go and you're free."

The sweetness of his victory immediately drain from Winston's body, which Humphrey picked up on.

"What, did you think I'd let you go?" he asked Winston with a smirk. "No fucking way, Winston. I didn't get any breaks. Why should you?"

"Don't you think it's time I knew your name?" Winston asked. He wondered what his chances were of actually making it out alive. He supposed they weren't good, so why not ask Humphrey's real name and try and reason with him? He had already seen his face and as it was, Winston was exhausted from playing. He needed time to recover.

"Why do you want to know my name, Winston?" Humphrey asked. "To establish a connection with me?"

"For better or worse, I think we've already got a connection. Why not tell me your name?"

Humphrey dwelled on this before answering him.

"Fine. My name is Norman Sherwood. Does that mean anything to you?" he asked Winston.

"No, it doesn't," answered Winston. And he was being honest. He had never heard that name in his entire life.

"Well, who do you think you stepped on to get yourself removed from waiting list limbo at Vickman?"

"I didn't step on anybody," Winston answered. "They called me to tell me I was off the waiting list. I heard something later about a candidate having legal troubles…"

"No!" Norman said, cutting him off. "It wasn't legal problems, it was a bogus witch hunt!"

Winston didn't know how to reply to this. He knew crazy people had a tendency to disconnect from reality and he could only imagine what Norman had done to get his admission revoked.

"After I received word I was admitted to Vickman, my older brother and his friends took me out to celebrate. I had two glasses of wine at his friend's house and rode home on my motorized scooter. I was pulled over and charged with a DUI. Apparently anything with a motor is illegal to drive impaired under," Norman continued, the color in his cheeks rising again.

"Prior to that evening, I had never touched a drop of alcohol. Never had a sip of Daddy's beer, didn't take of nip of vodka from the water bottles people smuggled onto to the bus during class trips. Two glasses of cheap red wine and my future is flushed down the toilet. Does that seem fair to you?"

"No," Winston answered. And it really didn't.

"It was all downhill from there. Twenty-five years of imposed mediocrity, Winston," Norman shouted bitterly. "And you hang it all up because your fingers hurt. If it were me, you would have needed to physically cut my hands off to stop me from playing!"

Another wave of defensive anger rush over Winston.

"My fingers hurt? Is that what you fucking reduce it to?"

"I didn't reduce it, Winston, I've summed it up."

"Fuck you!" Winston yelled back at him. "If you think spending the remainder of my career recording sonatas for the easy listening crowd is what I had in mind, then guess again! What took three hours to do now takes an entire day. You may have lost your ride but if you've got full use of your hands, you're still doing better than me!"

"And how do your hands feel, Winston?"

"Like they're on fucking fire."

"And yet you still played beautifully. Shall we move on?" Norman queried.

"Just a few more minutes."

"Nonsense!" Norman said, striding over with a fresh stack of papers. "Beethoven's father made him practice night and day with no respite. I think as you're finding out, we do our best work under great duress!"

"I found that out at Vickman," Winston responded. "I was admitted on a probationary basis."

"And you rose to the challenge wonderfully. Now you get to do it again."

Feeling defeated, Winston inspected the sheets Norman was putting in front of him.

"Which one is this?"

"Prokofiev's Eighth Sonata," Norman announced. "Familiar with it?"

"Yes, I'm familiar with it," Winston responded. This was another ball breaker. The throbbing in his hands flared. He began to wonder if it really was all in his head but that concept did him no good now, as the pain grew more intense.

"It's what I played to get into Vickman," Norman said. "I played it to perfection. Let's see if you can do the same."

"Are you really going to let me go?" Winston asked. It seemed like a fair question, though it probably wouldn't get a fair answer.

"Why do you ask? Because you know my name and you've seen my face?" Norman asked. "Keep in mind if you fuck up, we both die. And if you make it out of here and tell the police who I am, which I suspect you will, then let them arrest me. My life ended twenty-five years ago."

"So what kept you going?" Winston asked him, eager to delay things further. His hands felt like they were being crushed inside a vice.

"Good question, Winston," Norman responded. "The best answer I can give you is that fate was grooming me for this very moment and regardless of how it ends, I'm destined for infamy now. You already have your legacy and this will give me mine. And isn't that what it's all about?"

"You could have kept playing," Winston said. "There are plenty of other music schools. And plenty of musicians who did well without a formal education."

"You can spare me the Tony Robbins nonsense, Winston," Norman said, sounding tired and bored. "I've heard all it before."

He held up the remote.

"Now play!" he commanded.

Winston sighed deeply before arranging his hands over the keyboard. He stared intently at the sheet music, allowing it blur and distort for a few seconds but Norman wasn't having it.

"Come on, Winston," he said. "The White Album was written and recorded in less time than you're taking to play this piece."

"I'm more a Rolling Stones guy," Winston said, allowing his vision to refocus on the sheet music.

Norman laughed.

"I guess as far as classical pianists are concerned, you are a bit rough around the edges and unorthodox. So how about you consider this your Altamont and fucking play?"

More sweat had formed on Winston's already-marinating body. And in addition to his throbbing hands, he began to feel nauseous. He feared this wasn't going to be a flawless performance. He kept his eyes on the sheet music but let his thoughts drift to Miriam, the way the sun had shown through her curly brown hair the day he asked her to marry him. He missed the cool touch of her creamy skin in countless hotel rooms in the rare and wonderful instances when she accompanied him on tour. He wanted to feel that touch again, as well as the rush and applause of an adoring crowd after he wowed them with a riveting performance. Norman was proving to be a poor substitute for all of that.

"Ten seconds, Winston," Norman said. "And there's one less washed-up, whiny asshole in the world."

He placed his finger over the trigger on the remote for effect.

No longer able to comfort and torture himself with good memories, Winston brought his hands down and began to play.

He had a made a mistake at the end. He was sure of it. It was slight and unnoticeable to the untrained ear but he recognized it, which meant Norman likely did as well. However, Norman's subsequent applause and the fact he wasn't in pieces suggested otherwise. Winston allowed himself a glimmer of hope. The bomb was a dud after all.

"Pretty good, Winston," Norman said, still clapping. "I don't even think some of the admission officers at Vickman would have caught that little gaffe at the end."

Winston froze. He did know. But what about the...

"I disarmed the bomb," Norman revealed with quickness and an ease that chilled Winston to the bone.

"I thought you couldn't do that once it was activated," Winston said.

"So I lied. I've decided if this going to end in flames, let's save it for the finale."

"What's the finale?" Winston asked.

241

Norman's face lit up.

"Oh, Winston, you're really going to love this. Or not. Either way, what I've got planned for you Is something really special. Call it a blend of something old and something new!"

And with that, Norman disappeared into the darkness of the vast space. Winston could hear his footsteps fading into the distance. He allowed himself a few weak and delusional tugs on the chains binding his ankles but it was still fruitless. Winston wasn't going anywhere.

Norman returned a short time later rolling a cart with a large monitor on top of it. The grin he was sporting made him look like a hybrid of the Joker and Louie Armstrong.

"What are you doing, Norman?" Winston asked.

Without a word, Norman pressed a button on the keyboard next to the monitor and a video began to play on screen. It was a concert. Winston's heart sank when he saw whose concert it was. Jia Yang. The blind pianist. Of course. If nothing else, musicians' insecurities were universal and Norman had tapped into one of the major ones. It was the nagging fear and resentment of somebody who's younger than you, more talented, and who had to overcome bigger obstacles to make their mark.

"Beautiful, isn't it, Winston?" Norman asked, his voice dripping with derision. "Sixteen years old and already one of the most renowned players in the world. And the darling little thing is blind, to boot. Doesn't it just make you sick?"

"No, I admire her," Winston said, more in the interest of getting under Norman's skin than saving face.

"Good for you, Winston," Norman said, his expression souring again. "Because it pisses me off!"

He pressed another button and suddenly Jia's piano playing could be heard with perfectly clarity all through the warehouse. Winston looked up and saw speakers were wired to the support beams and rafters.

"Recognize the piece, Winston?"

It took Winston a minute but then he did recognize it. It was the same one Norman was humming earlier. He suddenly understood Norman's plan for the finale perfectly.

It meant Winston was going to die.

Norman allowed the piece to finish, allowing Winston to soak in every eloquently played note. Winston focused on the screen at times, watching as Jia dipped and bobbed with the music like some obscene animatronic on a ride at Disneyland.

Once it had ended, Norman wheeled the computer away and emerged from the darkness, wiping sweat from his brow.

"What did you notice about the piece, Winston? Aside from the fact she actually played it to perfection?" he asked.

Winston thought of the year he had been spent mastering that very piece (or so he thought). It didn't take him long to come up with an answer.

"She played it at a faster tempo."

Norman's eyes light up and he pointed at Winston.

"Exactly! So here's your final challenge. You play that piece, the very one you used to audition at Vickman and failed at, and you play it perfectly at a faster tempo."

He stared at Winston, hoping for some reaction but Winston gave him nothing.

"Since you couldn't play it right at its normal tempo, playing it faster should present quite the challenge. Am I right in assuming you haven't touched it since that painfully blundered audition?" Norman continued.

The fucking prick was right. Winston hadn't touched it since.

"It's funny, it's the easiest of the three pieces we've played but I'm willing to bet it gives you the most trouble. And that's what I want Winston, to remind you of your greatest failure. That despite everything you've accomplished in the past twenty years, you will always be second-rate and a loser."

Winston could taste bile in his throat. And that's when he knew he was going to die. Fumbling through the third movement of Beethoven's Moonlight Sonata. It seemed perversely fitting.

"Ready when you are, Winston."

Although only a couple of minutes had passed, it seemed like a lifetime. Winston was on the verge of breaking down completely.

"Whatever energy you're going to exert, save it for the music," Norman said. "Because you're going to play. I'm not going to detonate the bomb if you don't."

"Then fuck you," Winston shot back.

"Oh, I didn't say there wouldn't be penalties. I'll start by making short, paper cut-like incisions on your abdomen with this." Norman said, holding up a utility knife. "Then comes the lemon juice. You refuse to play after that, I leave you here, tied up like an animal and I find that pretty ex-wife of yours. When that happens, I am going to rape and murder her. I'll cut off her tits and bring them back here as proof. And it won't take long because I know she's still in town."

"Wrong, you bastard! Miriam left months ago..."

"5645 Lone Green Terrace," Norman said while picking at a hangnail. Now this son of a bitch was bringing Miriam into the equation.

Winston had met her a full ten years after Vickman. She didn't belong in this equation at all.

"It's all about this moment, Winston, and you're not getting off easily," Norman said, his voice wavering. "Play the fucking song and or I am going to fuck you up in ways you've never dreamed of."

Winston knew he had no choice.

"Two minutes."

"You've got thirty seconds."

With no other recourse, Winston's placed his hands over the piano key. They were screaming in agony from the wrists down but he'd have to power through. It didn't feel possible but he at least owed Miriam the effort.

"Mind the tempo, Winston," Norman reminded him.

As Winston stared at Norman's hateful eyes, he didn't just feel like he had a chance now. He suddenly felt like he was holding all the cards.

He began to play, his touch light and crisp. The faster tempo came to him so naturally it was like the song had been composed that way. This was going to be the greatest performance of Winston Davis' life.

"I want to thank you, Norman!" Winston shouted over the music. Norman looked surprised. Winston was playing beautifully without even looking at the keys.

"You see, I've been really down on myself these last couple of years but I can look back on a life of accomplishment," Winston continued. "Sold out shows around the world, collaborating with some of the greatest musicians who ever lived, accolades beyond anything I could hope for..."

He stopped to concentrate on a particular difficult passage but as expected, he sailed through it with ease.

"Let's pretend for a minute you hadn't sucked down cheap wine and gotten busted riding your little scooter," he said, taunting Norman and taking a great amount of pleasure when Norman's face filled with rage.

"You were never cut out for this. If that's what one setback does to you, then you were never destined for greatness. What I do takes talent but it also takes guts. And you lack that in spades, you fucking little worm."

Norman ran up to the piano but Winston didn't miss a beat.

"Watch your fucking mouth, you pathetic hack!" Norman screamed, spraying Winston with thick, white spit but Winston played on.

"I was going to be the best!" Norman continued, his eyes bugging out of his head cartoonishly.

"You would have been a mid-level studio musician at best, Norman," Winston said. "Greatness is something you never would have been acquainted with."

"Oh yeah? Well, look at you!" Norman cried. "Who's got the upper hand now, asshole?"

Winston continued playing, allowing the richness and intricacy of the piece envelope him. Even if it was going to be cut short, he had lived a good life. Playing just one more show would have been nice but mostly he thought of Miriam. He would have given anything at that moment for one last perfect kiss. Scratch that. He'd take one last look into her striking jade green eyes. That would be the perfect capper but nobody gets everything they want. Ready for his grand finish, Winston turned his focus over to Norman, who's lips were moving soundlessly as his head bobbed erratically and impulsively.

"You think you're going to get the pleasure of taking me out on your terms, Norman?" Winston asked him while shaking his head. "I'd never let a dipshit like you get that opportunity. You know we had a saying at Vickman, right?"

"Of course I know Vickman's motto! I had it memorized before I was ten!" Norman said, snot and spit shooting from his mouth and nose.

"No, not the motto, what the students who actually attended the school used to say," Winston proclaimed, his fingers effortlessly sweeping the keyboard.

Norman stared at him intently, waiting for Winston's dénouement.

"We would say 'Alas for those who never sing, but die with their music in them.' Tough break for you, Norman," Winston said before purposefully and loudly playing a wrong note, letting the sour and atonal chord carry loudly through the warehouse.

Norman let out a sound that fell somewhere between a shriek and a busted car horn.

And then there was nothing.

When Winston came to, he was on a stretcher surrounded by emergency vehicles. Two EMTs were attending to him while a police detective stood next to them.

"Welcome back, Mr. Davis," the detective said. "How are you feeling?"

Winston didn't know what to say. He was still alive? But how?

"The bomb," he finally managed.

"Inside the piano?" the detective asked. "It was a dud. Homemade C4 generally is. Count yourself lucky."

The rest of the evening came flooding back to him. Norman's crazed face was the most vivid image of all. Recalling it caused Winston to bolt upright, prompting the detective and EMTs to gently guide him back down to the stretcher.

"Easy, Mr. Davis," the detective said in a soothing voice. "You need to rest."

"Where is he?" Winston asked, his voice high and panicky.

"Norman Sherwood is dead, Mr. Davis," the detective stated.

"Dead?" Winston whispered.

"Self-inflicted gunshot wound. Count yourself lucky again some kids were walking by, probably looking for a place to smoke dope or drink. They heard it, looked in the window, and called 9-1-1."

Now it was the EMT's turn to speak.

"We're going to get you to the hospital now. Is there anybody you'd like us to call?"

"Miriam," Winston said without hesitation. "My wife, well, my ex-wife but…"

The detective nodded.

"We'll track her down and talk more at the hospital," he said. I'll see you there."

He nodded at the EMTs, who lifted Winston into an ambulance. With a whir of the siren, they were off. Winston let out a huge sigh. It was over. He thought back to those final moments. He couldn't believe he had done any of that. And in addition to the bomb and knife (more than enough to do the job), Norman also had a gun, meaning he could have ended Winston's life in a number of colorful ways.

As Winston sat back and enjoyed the ride, he knew why the gunshot had been self-inflicted. The bomb had failed. After everything else in his life, poor Norman couldn't stand to face another failure. Winston actually mustered up some sympathy for him. Some people truly had no luck, as well as an inability (or a refusal) to turn things around. Yes, Winston could definitely feel sorry for somebody who lived like that but he also relished the second chance he just been given.

And his hands felt fine.

Incident at the Lowell House

Before the incident at the Lowell house, Peter Murphy didn't believe in ghosts. That was surprising, especially considering he had spent the six months leading up to that event being haunted by one. It wasn't a malicious ghost or a particularly intrusive one but its presence lingered over every aspect of his life just the same. He had wondered what it would take for this ghost to move on. Better yet, did he really want it to move on?

Said ghost was his mother, who had passed on after a three-year battle with cancer. Peter had put his career on hold to be with her during those last years. Seeing as how she had spent her own life doing everything for him, Peter knew he owed her at least that. His father had left when Peter was two and his mother, with no college education, was left to pick up the slack. She worked as a waitress during the week, a housekeeper on the weekends, and still managed to get her degree in child psychology. Despite her exhausting and overwhelming schedule, she was a prominent presence in Peter's life. They had time to discuss each other's days and figure out what movie they were going to see in the rare instance she had a Sunday off. It wasn't an easy time for them but they made it work. By the time Peter was fifteen, she had finished her doctorate and Peter knew their ship had come in. She had warned him that it might take her awhile to find a job but Peter knew one would find its way to her in no time. As it would turn out, he was right. The ink was barely dry on her diploma when she got a job at Peter's old elementary school. She came highly recommended by the retiring counselor and her interview was nothing more than a formality. She began that fall, trading in drab uniforms and stained aprons for smart pantsuits and her own office.

While Peter couldn't complain about the subsequent years (they were wonderful), he had to admit that he missed the strife and struggle of their lean times. Life was a battle back then. It gave them strength and resolve when they went out the door each morning. Now that things hummed along at a pleasant and stable pace, Peter could tell that resolve was steadily dissipating. In its place was a complacency that wasn't bad but still lacking.

When it came time for college, Peter spent four years at the state university up the road, majoring in criminal justice. Although he spent most of his time at school, he made sure to call his mother three times a week and have dinner with her once a month. When school ended, Peter enrolled in the police academy. His mother was hoping he'd continue his schooling and become a professor but Peter remembered the papers and piles of books his mother had to wade through when she was getting her degrees. It seemed tedious to him and something he'd knew quit doing halfway through.

"Let's just save us both some time and grief," he said to his disappointed mother. "I can really help people as a police officer."

"But the way they treat black people," she said shaking her head.

"It needs to change," he agreed. "And what better to do it than from the inside?"

"Do you really think they're going to care what you think? I was pulled over one night after working a fifteen-hour shift," she said. "Did I ever tell you about this?"

She hadn't.

"That cop treated me like a criminal. He didn't even give me a good reason for pulling me over. Something about my tail light not working, which was completely bogus."

"There're some bad ones, all right," Peter said with an apologetic smile.

"There was another cop with him. And he was black. Do you know what he did?"

"Offered to take you to dinner?"

"Very funny. He sat in the car and didn't say a word," his mother said, her tone stiff and admonishing.

Okay, she wasn't wrong but Peter didn't see any other options. He was done with school and without an advanced degree; criminal justice wouldn't get him very far. His mother eventually accepted his decision and proudly proclaimed it on Facebook. It was mostly met with a positive response from family and friends, save for his uncle, who referred to him a "fascist-in-training."

"That's coming from a man who looked for all his answers at the bottom of a bottle," his mother said with a dismissive wave.

Things appeared under control after that but then the diagnosis came three days after Peter graduated from the police academy. Ovarian cancer. The doctors gave her six months if she was lucky. Peter didn't buy it. His mother was strong. She'd get through six months standing on her head. She insisted Peter join the police force to get his career underway but that could wait. His mother had been in her forties before she started her career. If he had to wait a few years, so what? There were more important things in life than a badge and a gun he'd likely never fire.

The next three years were trying. His mother's spirits remained intact, at least until she had to walk away from her job. That was when Peter saw her spirit break. The entire school had a special assembly for her and her office and the house were flooded with cards and gifts from friends and students. Peter tried to tell her that she'd be able to return to her job once she got better but it was no use. His mother slowly withered away to nothing and after being in a coma for two weeks, she was gone.

The loss had devastated Peter. She was his whole world. Living in the house was too much for him and he immediately put it on the market. As he would drive around town running errands, he realized it wasn't just the house; he'd need to leave town. Everything here was a reminder of his old life.

He managed to secure a job as a police officer in Jackson, a small town in upstate New York. The force was small, with only twenty-five officers total. Based on the research he did, the department appeared to be unblemished from any scandals, so it seemed like a good fit. The only catch was that he would be the only black officer but he didn't think that would be a problem.

It wouldn't take long for him to find out just how wrong he was in that assumption.

Before the notes started showing up, he was thinking he had just become another face in the department and that was fine with him. His co-workers were mostly friendly and accommodating. A few were distant but then Peter noted they were kind of distant with everybody. He hadn't held an abundance of jobs but he had never seen them as a place to make friends, either. He obviously had no desire to make enemies but that appeared to be out of his control when he found the first note in his locker.

"We may actually have a good basketball team this year" was scribbled across the paper in blue, blocky letters. It was a tad problematic but Peter dismissed it as a misguided joke. And he actually did laugh at it because the joke was on them. Peter was a terrible basketball player. He threw the note out and mostly forgot about it until the next one arrived a week later. It was a tad more hostile.

"I know it's not welfare but working's not so bad, is it?"

Peter's face grew hot as he stared at the note. This one was tucked inside his running shoes, which he had left out while he showered. He tried to make sense of it but it just seemed so random. He couldn't even really think of a proper suspect. He didn't know any of them well enough to draw such a conclusion. He resolved to keep all his stuff locked up and if it happened again, he'd go to the Chief.

Obvious reasons aside, he was hoping it would stop. He hadn't been in town that long but he liked living there and he feared shaking things up would mean resigning or bringing a lawsuit against the town that would span years and bring about unwanted publicity. He went home that day and dwelled on his situation over a six-pack of Shock Top. But mostly he just missed his mom. She wouldn't tell him that she had told him so; she'd offer him guidance and a solution. And that's what he was lacking. She wasn't just his mother; she was his mentor. Since he was new to this town, he didn't even have any friends yet; let alone someone to tell him how to handle a situation like this. While he still felt his mother's presence at every step, it wasn't the same. He needed to hear her voice.

He hoped his admirer would take some time off but it was only two days before the next note arrived. And this one was a doozy.

"I liked working here when it didn't have niggers" was scribbled across the page in those all-too-familiar blocky letters. Peter suddenly hated everything. The last three years had been bad enough and now he had this to deal with this?

Jesus fucking please us.

Chief Shale was a barrel-chested man in his early 60s. He seemed genuinely angered and took immediate action. He reviewed all the security tapes, looking for anything suspicious but instead found the usual workplace doldrums. People coming in and out with about as much excitement as being a small-town cop can elicit. He held several staff meetings and did his best to put the fear of God in his men but nobody came forward. He remained convinced that this was the work of one person and he asked his men to keep their eyes open.

Since that time, there hadn't been any more notes. The only thing Chief Shale requested of Peter was to keep it out of the papers and off social media until they could find the guilty party. Peter agreed but they both knew it was a small town. Word would get around sooner or later (and probably already had).

Halloween came a week after Chief Shale's request and Peter was working the second shift. He was ready for an exciting evening. Yes, it would mainly be chasing off vandals and hauling in costumed drunks but it beat sitting at a speed trap for hours on end, which is what his days mainly consisted of.

It was nine o'clock when the phone call came in about the Lowell house. Peter had no idea what the Lowell house was but judging by his co-workers' reactions, it was a big deal.

"So who wants it?" the Chief asked.

To Peter's surprise, the handful of officers in the room didn't reply. He could see Chief Shale wasn't happy, so he volunteered.

"I'll go," Peter offered. Everyone turned to him, some of them looking amused, others looking somewhat fearful. It was hard for Peter to believe he was in a room full of cops. What could possibly be so terrible about one house?

"All right, Murphy," the Chief agreed. "Who's going with him?"

None of them raised their hands.

"Fine," the Chief said, scanning the room. "You're up, Mickey."

Mickey Dole was in his thirties with glasses and close-cropped dark hair. He was one of the quiet ones but he seemed okay. Peter could tell he wasn't happy about being drafted but he stood up.

"Sure thing, Chief," he said heading for the door. Peter started to follow after him but Doug Jameson, another officer, called out to them.

"Make sure you tell him the whole story, Dole," Doug said. "He's a newbie. Otherwise he wouldn't have volunteered!"

"Yeah, Dole, and make sure to hold his hand if he gets scared," John Sanders added. "Better yet, make sure you have permission to hold his hand if you get scared!"

That prompted some laughter from the other men but Peter couldn't deny how forced and nervous some of it sounded. As he went out the door with Mickey, he gave his co-workers one last look. What he saw wasn't hate or contempt but relief. After all, it was Peter going to investigate the Lowell house and not them. Based purely on their reactions, it was a decision he was already regretting. In fact, he was beginning to wish he hadn't even moved to Jackson in the first place, which was a shame.

It had seemed like such a nice place.

Peter and Mickey drove in silence for the first leg of the trip before Peter finally spoke up.

"So what's the deal with the Lowell house?" he asked.

"Some dipshit high school kids broke in and we have to flush them out," Mickey responded.

"Yeah, I know that but why did everybody freak out when it came up?" Peter asked. "Is it haunted or something?"

He laughed but Mickey didn't seem amused. He finally turned to Peter with his lips pursed so tightly they were almost white.

"It just might be, new guy."

Peter didn't know how to respond to that. When he joined the force, he figured he was going to be subjected to a lot of pranks and bullshit but he could tell Mickey was serious.

"And you believe that?" he asked Mickey.

"I don't know what I believe," Mickey answered. "But I've never gone within a hundred feet of that place and I've lived here almost my whole life."

"So what happened?" Peter asked. Even if he didn't believe in ghosts, it wouldn't hurt to learn about the history of the town.

Mickey looked over at him. Peter could tell he was appraising him. He knew to most of the people in this town, he wasn't one of them yet (and if the notes were any indicator, he might never be) but Mickey must have decided under the circumstances, an exception could be made. And so he began.

"Back in the 1950s, the Lowells were the wealthiest family in town," Mickey said. "Do you know that old building at the end of the Water Street?"

Peter nodded. He had driven past it several times. It wasn't so much a building but a shell. Peter thought it was an eyesore but if it had a history, letting it stand made sense.

"That was a factory and Jackson's main employer until it closed in the early 70s."

"What did they make?" Peter asked.

"Appliances. Refrigerators mostly. If you lived in America in the 1950s and the 1960s, chances were good your fridge was built right here in Jackson."

Interesting tidbit. Peter nodded for Mickey to go on.

"Vincent Lowell and his wife Eunice owned that factory but don't go thinking that they were these Dickensian tyrants," Mickey said.

Dickensian. Peter was impressed.

"They paid well and they were well-regarded by just about everybody in town. They organized the tree-lighting ceremony every Christmas, put on a Halloween party for the children at the old rec hall," Mickey continued. "Jackson was a thriving, pleasant little place, thanks in no small part to the Lowell family."

Mickey paused.

"Then they had Toby."

"Ah ha!" Peter exclaimed. "The plot thickens!"

"Toby was the apple of their eye. Beautiful kid, pleasant, did well in school, had a lot of friends," Mickey explained. "That kid had every possible advantage and it seemed like the Lowell family could do no wrong."

"Until…" Peter said, ready for him to cut to the chase.

"Toby got meningitis. And being the early 1960s, medicine was good but not quite as good as it is now and little Toby went to that great refrigerator plant in the sky," Mickey said. "As you would expect, it was a big blow to the entire town but the Lowells were devastated. The parties ceased and while the factory continued operating, they disappeared from the public eye for two years."

Peter thought it was a pretty interesting story so far, albeit a tragic one. And Mickey hadn't even gotten to the really good stuff yet.

"When they finally re-emerged, the Lowells revealed they adopted two special needs children. The oldest, Brady, was around sixteen and Nigel was ten. The townspeople were touched when they found out. Here was this couple that had been dealt just about the nastiest hand you can get and they were making the most of it and helping children who might not get a chance otherwise. Nice, right?"

"Very," Peter answered. "But that's not the whole story, is it?"

"It wouldn't be a very exciting one if it was," Mickey said with a cynical smile. "It turns out Toby's death took a bigger toll on Vincent and Eunice than most people realized. It seems they deemed it unfair that their perfect child should die so young and these two abnormal children were allowed to live. See where this is going?"

A lump formed in Peter's throat. He was afraid he did.

"They physically and mentally abused those kids for years, all under the noses of the trusting townspeople who couldn't imagine them doing anything wrong, let alone evil. As you might expect, everyone has a breaking point, even the feeble-minded. The kids got together one night and let Vincent and Eunice know just how much they appreciated their unique brand of love."

Mickey went silent for a minute, allowing Peter to formulate his own conclusions about the gruesome fates of Vincent and Eunice Lowell.

"They slit Vincent from dick to chin. Police found him in the bathtub floating in his own blood and innards," Mickey stated matter-of-factly. "As for Eunice…"

Another pause. Peter wished he would just finish at this point.

"They gouged out her eyes and took turns raping her before slitting her throat. She was found naked and strung up by her ankles in the very parlor she used to host afternoon tea in."

"Jesus."

"That's most people's reaction," Mickey said. "Do you want to know the really sad part?"

"It gets worse?"

"It does. While that woman performed unspeakable acts of evil on those kids, she was still their mother, so unable to cope with their own heinous deeds; they hung themselves in the forest behind the house," Mickey said. "It was closed up and nobody went inside it for years."

"And since then?"

"The usual. Lights, strange noises."

"So why is everybody so scared of it then?" Peter asked.

"Probably because four Cub Scouts disappeared in the woods near the house about twenty years ago. And then there was the psychic who went inside, lost her mind after ten minutes, and committed suicide the next day. And do you want to hear all the dead birds they found on the property five years ago?" Mickey asked.

"No," Peter said. "I think I get it."

"Good," Mickey said. "Because we're almost there."

He pointed to a crumbling Victorian-style mansion looming on the horizon up ahead.

"Why hasn't the place been torn down?" Peter asked. "And who even owns it?"

"It's been through a few different owners but every time somebody bought it, something horrible would happen," Mickey answered.

"Like disappearing Cub Scouts," Peter said reflexively. "It's almost like…"

"Like the house doesn't want anybody messing with it?" Mickey finished. "I guess you could say that. The last guy to own it ran a Ripley's Believe it Or Not Museum down south. He wanted to turn the house into some kind of tacky tourist trap, which the town wasn't crazy about," Mickey said.

"So what happened to him?"

"He was wandering around the house taking pictures. He stepped on a rusty nail and despite getting a tetanus shot, his foot became so infected they had to amputate it. He ended up donating the house to the Jackson Historical Society and left town. They've been twiddling their thumbs with it ever since," Mickey finished.

At that moment, twiddling his thumbs sounded like an ideal alternative to Peter but there was no turning back now. They were at the Lowell House.

Peter got out of the car and took in the crisp fall air. He looked over at the Lowell house, which loomed against the night sky like an oversized prop taken from a Tim Burton film. The road it was on was mostly empty, save for a small, shabby-looking residence down the road about a hundred feet. The place wasn't so much a home but a glorified shed. Peter couldn't imagine anybody living in it but as they approached the Lowell house, a man (likely the shed's sole resident) was waiting for them at the end of the long, cracked driveway. He wore a wrinkled plaid shirt over tattered khakis that hung from his emaciated frame. His face was ancient and wrinkled, with yellow teeth and thinning white hair messily held in place with what Peter assumed to be Brylcreem. The man eyed Peter suspiciously before turning to Mickey.

"Howdy, Officer Dole," he said in a voice that reminded Peter of Burgess Meredith.

"How's it going, Ralph?"

"Got a prostate the size of a grapefruit and a rash on my keister that's managed to outlast my second wife," Ralph answered turning his gaze to the clear, starry sky. "But I can't complain."

Peter smiled but Mickey remained all business.

"So we've got some high school kids breaking in?" he asked Ralph.

"Three of them. I was walking Brutus when I seen them all running up the driveway, laughing like they was on that funny gas they give you at the dentist," Ralph said.

Based on Ralph's teeth, Peter decided his last trip to the dentist occurred when Reagan was still in office. Maybe even Carter.

"Had paper bags, probably filled with booze, drugs, and God knows what else," Ralph continued. "They was in costume, too."

"Costume?" Mickey asked.

"Yeah. It's Halloween, ain't it?" Ralph said, spitting on the ground.

"What were they dressed like?" Peter asked and Ralph turned to him with the same suspicious gaze he had greeted him with. Mickey was quick to step in.

"Ralph, this is Officer Peter Murphy," Mickey said. "He recently joined the force."

Ralph continued to eyeball Peter, a strange smile forming at the corners of his mouth.

"He's okay, Ralph."

"I'm sure he is, Officer Dole," Ralph finally said, averting his untrusting gaze away from Peter. "Anyway, as for what they were wearing, it wasn't nothin' special. Boys had on hoodies and their faces was painted like skeletons…"

Probably paying tribute to you, Peter thought.

"And the girl had on some goddamn Elvira wig, 'cept it had streaks of purple in it," Ralph continued. "Dressed like a whore, too.

What the fuck is wrong with kids these days? And you know what else, I'll bet that girl wasn't always a girl, she was probably a boy at one time and…"

"Seen or heard anything since they went in, Ralph?" Mickey interrupted. Peter could sense the slight irritation creeping in his voice. Patience didn't appear to be one of Officer Dole's virtues.

"Not a peep," Ralph said. "Think they may have left through the woods?"

"If we're lucky but we'll take a look anyway," Mickey replied. "Thanks, Ralph!"

"You got it and if you need anything, I'll be home," Ralph said, pointing to his shed. He started to walk away when Peter called out to him. He couldn't help it.

"Based on the stories I've heard, I didn't think anybody would want to even live near this place."

Ralph turned back to Peter, appraising him again with his watery eyes.

"Someone needs to keep watch," he said. "And I ain't necessarily happy it's me. You best watch yourself, Officer Murphy. There are sinister things at play in there."

And with that, Ralph was headed back to his shed. Based on how lethargically he was moving, Peter expected to be at the police station and filling out his report before Ralph reached his front door.

"Come on, Officer Murphy, " Mickey said. "The bell tolls for thee."

Mickey began walking up the driveway, his flashlight bobbing on the cracked pavement.

Just remember, asshole, you don't believe in ghosts, Peter thought as he followed Mickey. His mind went to the bottle of ten-year-old Scotch he had waiting at home (a gift from his cousin Shawna). It was meant to be savored but where was the fun in that? Peter intended to get good and drunk tonight. He had a feeling he was going to earn it.

As they got closer to the Lowell House, Mickey pointed his flashlight at the front of the house.

"We have to go around back," he said.

"Why?" Peter asked.

"A tree fell on the front patio a few years ago," Mickey said. "The historical society hired a landscaper to clear it away and guess what happened?"

"The tree attacked him," Peter replied half-jokingly.

"No, he had the tree cleared away in five minutes. But he said he could hear people laughing inside the house."

"People laughing?"

"Yeah. He said it sounded like two boys," Mickey said, keeping his flashlight trained on the collapsed front patio.

"Did he think to call the police or go in and investigate?" Peter asked, some long-overdue skepticism creeping into his voice.

"I guess he didn't want to tempt fate," Mickey answered. "Still up for this or should we call for back-up?"

Peter could tell him he was smiling. It made him feel stupid for being scared of this place. He was the new guy and Mickey had taken advantage of it. There was no such thing as ghosts. This was just a rickety old house that had some bad history but it was hardly a place of evil. Houses couldn't be evil. They were just structures made of wood, plaster, and concrete. Peter wasn't sure how much he liked Mickey at this point but he was stuck with him for the evening. Best to get it over with.

"Well, let's go," he said, waving Mickey on with his flashlight.

"Lead the way, new guy," Mickey said, sounding amused.

Peter walked to the back of the house, his feet squishing in thick, sticky mud that had the same consistency as wet cement. It hadn't rained today. Why was the ground so wet? He pointed his flashlight at the expansive house until he found the chipped and swollen back door. When

Peter opened it, the door made a drawn-out creaking sound that reminded him of the old William Castle movies he used to watch on Friday nights when he was a kid. He started to go inside when he felt Mickey's hand on his shoulder, causing him to jump.

"Easy, new guy, I just wanted to show you something," Mickey said, clearly enjoying how much he startled Peter.

Peter turned around and Mickey shined his flashlight into the dense forest that seemed to sprawl infinitely into the distance. The same forest that had gotten hungry for Cub Scouts years ago (assuming Mickey wasn't full of shit).

"See that big-ass oak?" he asked, pointing his beam at an overgrown tree with branches that had likely stopped producing leaves when Peter was still in diapers.

"What about it?"

"That's where Brady and Nigel hung themselves. Supposedly if you get close enough you can still see where the ropes dug into the branch."

"How about we just get this over with?" Peter asked. It came out a little sharper than he intended but he had enough of this nonsense. He could practically taste that fine scotch already.

"All right, Pete, let's go inside," Mickey said.

"What's with this Pete shit?"

"Nothing. Just a little humor between co-workers," Mickey said, his amused tone suggesting there was definitely a joke at play but Peter wasn't in on it. He was already anticipating Mickey laying it on thick with the other guys at the station.

"You guys should have seen him," Mickey would say. "Scared shitless. Got all agitated with me for the stupidest things."

And the guys would laugh. Peter would smile politely and if he was really lucky, he'd find another one of those lovely notes in his locker. Just another night with the Jackson Police Department, please and thank you.

"I'd prefer Peter or Officer Murphy if you don't mind," he said, applying the same tone he used for speeders and underage drinkers.

He didn't need to see Mickey's face to know his jovial mood had dissolved. He could feel him seething from three feet away. Nobody talked to Mickey like that. Especially not some...

Peter stopped. It couldn't be. Could it? He looked back at Mickey, who regarded him with roughly the same affection he might have for a cockroach he found scurrying across the floor.

"See anything you like, Officer Murphy?" he asked, putting a patronizing emphasis on the last part.

Peter turned around and pointed his flashlight around the kitchen. It wasn't especially big but this wasn't a room the Lowells would have spent much time in, anyway.

"How about we split up and each take a section of the house," Mickey suggested. "The sooner we get out of here, the better."

"Fine," Peter said. "You want upstairs or down?"

"I'll take the upstairs," Mickey said. "You okay staying down here?"

"Works for me."

"All right then," Mickey replied. "Just don't forget about the basement."

"Basement?"

Mickey walked across the kitchen and opened a door next to the stove, revealing a staircase.

"I thought you'd never been here before," Peter said.

"I haven't but I've seen the crime scene photos."

Peter looked at him incredulously.

"Don't worry. Nothing bad ever happened down there," Mickey said. "That I know of, anyway."

Peter could detect the mocking tone in Mickey's voice when he said this last part and decided not to indulge it any further.

"See you in a few minutes, Officer Dole," he said. He started to go down the stairs and when noticed Mickey was watching him.

"See anything you like, Officer Dole?" Peter asked. Mickey stared at him for a few seconds before finally speaking.

"Keep your radio and give me a holler if you see anything," he said before disappearing into the next room. Thank God. It hadn't taken long for things to get tense with him and if they had spent any more time together, Peter was guessing it would have turned nasty.

He continued down the stairs but stopped when he heard one of them give a nasty groan. He pointed his flashlight down and wondered how safe they were to walk on. Probably not very, so he took the remaining ones as light as he could. When he reached the bottom, he was relieved to see that the basement was a lot like the one in the townhouse he and his mother had lived in while she was still getting her degree. This place was much bigger but it had the same wooden shelves and dirt floor as their old place. He had been scared of it when they first moved in but it was where the landlord had put the washer and dryer. His mother always asked him to retrieve the clothes out of the dryer, citing her own fatigue from going up and down stairs for her housecleaning job. These trips to the dryer had gradually diminished his fear of the mildew-smelling space until it was virtually nonexistent. As Peter checked the various rooms in the Lowell basement, he wondered how Mickey was doing. Likely on his phone with another officer, laughing at how he had the new guy shitting his pants. Peter did his best to put this out of his mind. He still had a job to do.

As he headed for the last section of the basement, he decided the kids had likely split into the woods not long before he and Mickey had arrived. This was a waste of time but at least Peter managed to get a decent ghost story out of it. Even it had come from an asshole.

Peter entered the last room and found a half-empty bottle of Popov vodka on the floor, along with a bong and several crushed cans of PBR. Kids these days had no taste.

Peter knelt down and touched the side of the bong. It was still warm. They had been here relatively recently. For the first time that evening, he almost laughed at the absurdity of the whole thing. He pictured himself filling out the report later that night.

I came across a marijuana water pipe and was able to ascertain that the suspects had been in the room recently, as it was still warm, suggesting recent use, he would type (not with a straight face of course). He was tempted to take a sip of the Popov but decided against it. The last thing he wanted was somebody smelling booze on him.

He took his radio off his belt and called for Mickey.

"Officer Dole, do you copy?"

There was dead silence.

"Officer Dole?"

More silence. Peter decided the copper pipes were screwing up the reception. He'd have to find Mickey and bring him back here. He started to leave but stopped dead in his tracks when he heard the moan.

It was so quiet Peter wondered if it was just his imagination acting up but then he heard it again, slightly louder this time. He pointed his flashlight around the room but didn't see anything. Nervousness crept up his spine and Peter started to exit the room again when he heard another noise. It wasn't a moan this time but a creak. He stopped and looked around again and to his surprise; there was a partially open door at the far corner of the room. How had he missed that? Peter put his hand on Glock and cautiously approached the door.

"This is the Jackson police," he called out, doing his best to muster authority. "If you're in there, come out with your hands up!"

Silence.

Peter continued toward the door and as he got closer, it opened a little further and another moan came from inside, this one longer and louder than the previous ones.

"Police!" he called out again. "Show yourself!"

"Help me," a meek voice finally answered.

Peter opened the door the rest of the way and pointed his flashlight inside. It was a small closet. Sitting on the floor was a boy of about sixteen. His face was painted up to look like a skull but the make-up was badly smeared. Had he been crying?

"Are you all right?" Peter asked the boy, who looked up at him with shell-shocked expression on his face.

"They attacked us," he said in a husky whisper.

"Who attacked you?"

Fresh tears formed in the boy's eyes.

"Monsters."

"Do you need medical attention?" Peter asked him.

"It wasn't just them, either," the boy continued, completely oblivious to Peter's question. "My grandpa was here. And he's been dead for years."

The boy let out a gasping sob.

"Do you know where your friends went?" Peter asked as he helped the boy up and walked him toward the door. He didn't answer but when they reached the doorway, the boy stopped and planted his feet.

"What are you doing?" Peter asked.

"No," the boy said.

"What?"

"No!" he said again, his voice rising. "No!"

"Hold on!" Peter said but the boy was hysterical.

"No!" he continued screaming. "No!"

Peter stepped away from him and grabbed his radio.

"Dole!" he hollered into it. "I need you down here! I've got a situation!"

Still nothing. Frustrated, Peter replaced his radio on his belt and walked back to the boy, who was still screaming. Peter readied himself to slap him but something reached in and yanked the boy into the hallway. Peter drew his pistol and pointed it in the direction the boy disappeared in. Peter could hear him screaming but he sounded far away now. The screaming continued until Peter heard a sickening crunch. He held his flashlight and pistol with shaking hands, unsure how to proceed.

"This is the Jackson police!" he called out, his voice high and uncertain. "Come out with your hands up!"

His answer came in the form of ominous footsteps dragging on the dirt floor outside the door. As they got closer, he could hear giggling. It sounded like two boys but there was an inhuman element to the laughter that made Peter's blood freeze.

"I said this is the police! Show yourself with your hands up!"

The footsteps and giggling stopped and was replaced with an agonizing silence, save for some water dripping nearby. Something popped out of the shadows and struck Peter in the chest, knocking the wind out of him. When he pointed his flashlight down at the object, he was horrified to see it was the severed head of the boy.

He screamed and two figures stepped into the doorway. He shined his flashlight at them and saw the bloated, purple faces of two children leering at him, their cracked lips receding over blackened teeth. Peter didn't need them to introduce themselves to know he was looking at Brady and Nigel Lowell.

"Stay where you are!" he screamed, pointing his gun at them. They laughed boorishly and began to advance on him. Peter opened fire and the bullets struck their bodies, with each impact producing a hideous squelching sound. They continued to come at him and Peter stumbled back and fell to the ground, dropping his pistol and his flashlight. Although he could no longer see them, they had a rancid odor that was so powerful he could taste it. With no idea where he was going, Peter stood up and ran. He could feel their jagged fingernails at the back of his neck as the blindly moved forward. He cracked his left shoulder against the doorframe but managed to enter the hallway. He pulled out his phone and turned on the flashlight as he ran with Brady and Nigel behind him. He had no clue how close they were and didn't care to find out. Despite how fast he was running, the hallway seemed endless. He feared he had taken a wrong turn and would end up cornered but was relieved to finally see the stairs up ahead.

His feet struck the rickety wood with loud thuds as he made his way up the stairs. He was almost at the top when two of them broke, causing him to almost fall through the staircase. He managed to grab hold

of the last stair, which fortunately proved sturdier than the others. He

could hear footsteps behind him and knew Brady and Nigel were getting

close. Peter pulled himself up, ripping his pants and his legs on the

splintered wood. He managed to get through the door and close it just as

something crashed into it. The impact was so hard it almost knocked

Peter to the ground. He pressed his weight against the door as Brady and

Nigel struggled to open it. After a few seconds, the pressure finally

subsided. Peter looked across the room and saw an old table. He dragged

it over and propped it against the door just to be safe.

"Dole!" he screamed into the living room but there was no

response. He reached for his radio.

"Dispatch, this is Unit 13, over!"

There was a light crackling sound but dispatch didn't respond. He

checked his phone but saw he didn't have any service. How was that

possible?

"Dole!" he yelled again but there was more silence. Peter had the

grim realization that Mickey was likely dead. He started to head for the

back door but was interrupted by a scream. It was a girl. Peter hesitated.

Was there anything he could do? He had already lost his pistol and was

unable to call for backup. The screaming resumed, louder and more

insistent this time. If the other kids were still alive, they wouldn't be for very long. Determined to save at least one life, Peter drew his nightstick and went into the living room. He saw a young girl standing at the front door, sporting the same catatonic look as the unfortunate boy in the basement. The black and purple wig on her head confirmed it was the girl Ralph had seen enter the house earlier that evening.

Peter approached her with his nightstick at the ready.

"Are you okay, miss?"

The girl stood frozen in place and let out another scream. As Peter got closer to her, he suddenly understood why. An old woman stood at the top of the stairs leading up to the second floor. She was naked and had a hideous laceration across her throat. The girl screamed again and the old woman laughed. It was a dusty, rattling sound. The thing that used to be Eunice Lowell floated down the stairs and came at the girl with her hands out. As Eunice got closer, Peter noticed she didn't have any eyes, just empty black sockets.

The girl continued to scream but seemed incapable of moving. Peter ran over to her and tried to drag her away but the old woman grabbed her. To Peter's horror, Eunice ripped out the girl's eyes and stuck them in her empty sockets. She blinked several times and as the eyes came to life, the girl collapsed to the floor dead. Eunice stared at Peter at with a contemptible glee for what was to come next. She blocked his path to the front door and Peter ran for the kitchen again but found Brady and Nigel standing in the doorway. Peter was trapped. The young girl had been bait and he had taken it. Brady and Nigel giggled and began to advance on Peter. With no other option, Peter ran up the stairs to the second floor.

"Dole!" he screamed as he ran down the long hallway. There were numerous rooms on both sides and Peter had no idea where he was going. As he reached the end of the hallway, one of the doors opened and a figure stepped out. Peter shrieked at the top of his lungs.

"Murphy?"

It was Mickey. He pointed his flashlight in Peter's face.

"What the hell are you doing?"

Peter was dumbfounded.

"Are you fucking kidding me?" he shouted at Mickey. "You didn't hear anything? I fired my gun for fuck's sake! I thought you were dead!"

"What are you talking about?" Mickey asked.

Peter pushed Mickey back into the room and shut the door. He looked around and saw they were in a bathroom, complete with a broken toilet and a bathtub against the far wall.

"What the fuck, Murphy?" Mickey asked, bewildered.

"This place is fucking haunted!" Peter screamed at him.

Mickey stared at him.

"Look at me!" Peter continued, motioning to his ripped and bloodstained clothes. "Do you think I did this to myself?"

"I don't know, Murphy," Mickey said. "But I haven't seen or heard anything. Any sign of those kids?"

"They're fucking dead!"

Even in the dim moonlight, he could see Mickey blanch.

"Where are they?" Mickey asked, his voice low and controlled.

"Fuck that, we need to get out of here!" Peter said, striding across the room to the small window at the end of it. He began to strike the window with his nightstick.

"Murphy!"

Peter continued to hit the nightstick against the glass but it didn't even crack. Was it Plexiglas?

Mickey came over and grabbed Peter's arm.

"Enough!" he said. "Now sit down and get your head straight!"

"I'm not spending another fucking minute in this place!" Peter roared at him. "If you want to stay here and die, that's your business!"

He resumed striking the window with his nightstick and Mickey reached for his radio.

"Already tried that," Peter said, shaking his head.

Mickey ignored him and talked into it.

"Dispatch, this is Unit 6. Over."

No response.

"Your phone isn't going to have any service, either," Peter told him.

Mickey replaced his radio and checked his phone.

"All right. So reception's bad in here."

"And does that make any fucking sense?" Peter asked him.

"It makes more sense than fucking ghosts!" Martin yelled back. "Just what the fuck happened, Murphy?"

"I already told you," Peter said, his voice weary. "This place is actually haunted..."

"Bull shit!" Mickey interrupted. "They're just stories, Murphy. Some cop you are. My niece has more balls than you do."

Peter ignored his insults and resumed trying to break the window when an unearthly and nauseating gurgling sound came from across the room.

They looked over to see an old man standing up in the bathtub. The deep gash running down the full length of his torso confirmed it was Vincent Lowell. As he got to his feet, the gash opened up and his rotted insides poured out and hit the ground with a sickening plop. He opened his mouth to speak but the only sound to come out was the vile gurgling sound that had gotten their attention in the first place. He lumbered toward Mickey and Peter, stepping on his insides and squishing them.

Mickey drew his pistol but the old man grabbed him and the gun went flying. Peter ran over and picked it up. He pointed it at Vincent, who now had Mickey's head between his hands. He was squeezing it. Mickey screamed as blood began to pour from his scalp.

"Let him go!" Peter yelled but Vincent squeezed Mickey's head even harder. He was going to crush his skull. Peter began to pepper the old man with bullets, prompting a thick and foul-smelling fluid to pour out of Vincent's body. He turned around and to Peter's horror; one of the bullets had hit Mickey dead center in the forehead. He was dead. Vincent dropped him and began to laugh. Peter let out an anguished cry and ran out of the room. He looked down the hallway and saw Eunice Lowell standing in front of the stairway with Brady and Nigel at her side. With nowhere to go, Peter entered the door that sat at the very end of the hallway. As he went inside, he was hit with a bright yellow light.

His first thought was that he had died and was (hopefully) in heaven. Even if it was hell, he couldn't imagine it being worse than the Lowell house but when his eyes adjusted, he found himself in a clean and well-decorated bedroom. A Mickey Mantle poster hung on the far wall and there were toys spread across the floor. It was all stuff Peter had seen when he used to go to flea markets with his mother. These toys were at least fifty years old but unlike the rusted and worn-out versions at the flea market, these were pristine and new. A metal fire truck with a bright red paint job sat two feet away from him. There was a twin bed next to the window with "Toby" etched neatly into the headboard.

"Hello," a happy voice called out to him.

Peter turned around to see a handsome and healthy-looking boy of about eleven rummaging through the closet.

"Want to play catch?" the boy asked.

"I don't have a glove," Peter heard himself say.

"It's okay, I've got another. My parents buy me two of everything cause they're real rich," the boy said. "They tell me to not let it go to my head."

"That's smart of them," Peter continued. "Money isn't everything."

"I suppose not," the boy agreed. "But it's nice to have."

"I think I need to go," Peter managed. "Can you show me how to get out of here?"

"You can't get out," the boy stated matter-of-factly. "If you've come this far, you're going to die. My parents and brothers will see to it. They don't like people coming in here."

"Please!" Peter begged. "I'm one of the good guys. I came here to help people."

"That doesn't matter," the boy said, his tone growing sad. "This is a bad place. This is what happened to the last person they sent to play with me."

Toby walked across the room and opened a large, bright blue toy box. Inside was the folded-up body of a teenager wearing similar skull make-up to the boy in the basement. His face was locked in a permanent look of terror.

"This is a bad place," the boy repeated. "A bad place."

As continued this chant, his face began to melt, with chunks of bloody flesh falling to the carpet.

"Bad place," the boy said as his face fell apart, his nose sliding down his stripped shirt and bouncing off his black Converse sneakers.

"Bad…" the boy repeated, only this time his lower jaw fell off and he was no longer able to speak. He raised a baseball gloved-hand to Peter before collapsing into a pile of dusty bones.

As if on cue, the door opened and a figure stepped in, only this time it wasn't anyone from the Lowell family.

It was his mother.

She looked as she did when she died, her body thin and ravaged by the cancer that had slowly destroyed her. He stared at the person who had given him everything and wanted to weep but couldn't. This thing wasn't his mother. She was dead, as was the thing standing in front of him. The only signs of life were her formerly loving eyes, now filled with evil and hatred.

"Peter," she croaked at him. "You should have listened to me."

Had she not have spoken, Peter maybe could have held it together but it was too late. He started screaming and wasn't sure he'd ever be able to stop.

"You should have listened to me!" her voice boomed, piercing his eardrums. With no hope left, Peter turned and ran full-speed into the paneled window on the far wall. He jumped and dove out headfirst, easily breaking through the glass this time. He was immediately met by a blast of cold air that whistled past his head as he fell onto the concrete below. He landed mostly on his right side, breaking his ribs and his leg. He lost most of his teeth and fractured his cheekbone when his face hit the pavement. The pain was agonizing but he was able to stand up using his left leg. The house itself was alive now, screeching and moaning behind him.

Peter hobbled into the woods, passing Mickey's body on his way. It was hanging from the tree Mickey had pointed out to Peter when they entered the house an hour ago. Or was it two hours? Peter honestly didn't know or care; he just wanted to get as far away from that awful place as he could. He pushed through the seemingly nonstop blockade of trees and bushes, his hands and face getting scratched by the razor-sharp twigs and branches. He only made it fifty feet before stepping inside a patch of thick mud. He tried to wade through it but each step seemed to drag him down even further. He tried to scream again but could only produce the remnants of his teeth and mouthfuls of blood. Within seconds, he had sunk into the thick and putrid-smelling muck up to his neck. He managed to free one of his arms to reach for solid ground, finally grabbing hold of a stick. He pulled on it and found it wasn't a stick at all but a human bone. He was holding the skeleton of a small child. A torn and faded neckerchief was wrapped around its neck, confirming it was one of the missing Cub Scouts.

Peter attempted one final cry for help before disappearing into the wet ground altogether. Before he lost consciousness, he was strangely grateful that he hadn't met his end inside that house.

That evil fucking house.

He awoke later to find himself in a hospital bed. Chief Shale and a man Peter had seen around town but didn't recognize were standing at the foot of his bed talking to a doctor. Groggy, Peter did his best to sit up but immediately fell back on the bed. His entire body was throbbing with pain. He doubted he'd ever feel right again.

The doctor came over and shined a light in both of Peter's eyes. He asked Peter questions. Peter answered them. Satisfied, the doctor stepped away and Chief Shale and the other man walked over and stood to his left. It was at that point Peter noticed he was handcuffed to the rails of the bed. He gave the cuffs a weak tug, causing more pain to shoot through his body.

"You're not going anywhere, Officer Murphy," Shale said. He sounded authoritative but also sad.

"What happened?" Peter finally said. Just getting those two words out was a chore. It was like his throat was full of gravel and thumbtacks.

"We were hoping you could tell us," Shale replied. "We found you wandering in the woods about a mile from the Lowell house. You were covered in blood and dirt and going on about your mother and ghosts. Do you remember any of that?"

"I wasn't wandering anywhere," Peter said, coming out of his disoriented state. "I escape from that terrible fucking place and ran into the woods. I sank into some mud. One of the bodies of the Cub Scouts was in there with me!"

Chief Shale and the man exchanged a quick glance before turning back to Peter.

"Peter, this is Sam Baldwin. He's the city attorney." Shale said.

"So what?"

"So maybe you need to think about getting your own attorney."

"What the hell are you talking about?" Peter asked. None of this made sense. He was the victim.

"After you and Office Dole left the station tonight, one of the other officers brought something to my attention," Shale said, looking at Peter as if expecting some kind of response.

"What was it?" Peter asked.

Shale paused briefly before going on.

"It seems Dole was the one leaving you those notes. This officer knew but was afraid of what might happen if he came forward."

So his harasser was Mickey. That made sense, though it did little to alleviate the other horrors Peter had experienced that evening.

"Just as I was going to radio both of you, Ralph Loomis called and reported gunshots. We dispatched all units and although it took us some time, we eventually found you," Shale said.

"Did you go in the house and find the other bodies?" Peter asked.

Another pause.

"We went inside the house, Officer Murphy, but we didn't find any bodies. The only body we found was Officer Dole's and he was outside."

"Bull shit!" Peter yelled, despite the immense pain in his throat. "The ghosts killed all of them!"

Shale looked away at this last part. Peter could see he had tears in his eyes.

"Was it the ghost that shot Officer Dole in the head?" he asked.

Peter's breathing grew rapid.

"He was being attacked! That thing had him and I didn't know what to do so I shot at them! I was trying to save him!"

He could tell neither Sam nor Shale believed him. This was madness.

Shale wiped his tears away before looking at him.

"Here's what I think happened, Officer Murphy. You knew Dole was behind the notes but instead of coming to me, you decided to take matters into your own hands…"

"No!" Peter shouted but Shale continued.

"You took this opportunity to kill him and those kids just happened to be at the wrong place at the wrong time. I understand you've been under a lot of stress with your mother dying and with Dole's harassment but that doesn't mean…"

"I didn't kill anyone! It was the fucking ghosts!"

"You'll need some time in here to recover. Once that happens, we're going to move you to a jail up north. You're not safe here anymore."

"Chief, you have to believe me, I didn't hurt anybody and I didn't know about Dole until you told me just now! You were the one who sent me out with him!"

"And I'll regret that decision for the rest of my life," Shale said, more tears forming in his eyes. "You should probably rest but once you feel up to it, make sure you find yourself a good lawyer. And think about telling us where those kids are. That'll go long way in soothing some wounds and helping your case."

He stood up and left the room with Sam following behind him.

"Chief!" Peter called out to him. "Chief! I didn't do anything wrong!"

They were gone.

Until that moment, Peter couldn't have imagined things getting worse. How wrong he was. With no possible hope for justice, he began to sob.

The doctor came in and looked him over one last time. A nurse brought him some pills for his pain and to help him sleep. Two officers were stationed outside his door and based on the looks they gave him; Peter knew they'd rather being contending with a nasty case of herpes than guarding him. He heard occasional taunts and angry shouts from outside his window but the drugs were beginning to numb him. Peter knew he had a hard and unforgiving road ahead of him but he would take a few hours of respite in the meantime. He still didn't understand why his mother had been there. Couldn't those bastards at least let her rest in peace? Unable to process the horrors of the evening, Peter let the drugs take hold. He was almost asleep when he heard his mother call out to him.

"Peter," she whispered.

He slowly opened his eyes. His mother was standing at the foot of his bed.

"Peter," she whispered again. "Nobody escapes."

He looked over and saw his door was closed. Through the small window, he could see the officer stationed outside lazily checking his phone, completely unaware of what was going on fifteen away from him.

Peter turned back to his mother and saw she was no longer alone. The entire Lowell family was standing with her. They grinned grotesquely at him and began to close in. Peter tried to call out for help but was unable to make a sound. He sat paralyzed as they continued to converge on him, laughing and leering as they went in for the kill.

Luckily for Peter, it was over quickly.

Swipe Left

Snowboarding and fedoras were out. If Jillian saw either in a profile pic (and to her horror she had seen both in more than a few), she would immediately swipe left. She wondered what aspects of her own profile acted as instant turn-offs. Could it be her age? That was likely. Thirty-seven seemed ancient in her twenties but less so in her thirties, at least until she started online dating. She had to contend with the fact that men her age wanted women ten years younger, which left her options pretty scarce. She had been on three dates since activating her profile and each one was slightly less enjoyable than downing a container of Ben & Jerry's and watching old episodes of The Gilmore Girls for the umpteenth time.

Most of her girlfriends from college and high school were either married or in long-term relationships. There were times when she was relieved her days consisted of Netflix and Happy Hours and not dirty diapers and playgrounds but those moments were fleeting. Even if her friends had almost no time to themselves, she could sense their satisfaction and stability. Jillian wasn't acquainted with either of those things. She worked a soul-sucking day job and her true passion (writing) had fallen by the wayside. She had attempted to write a poem but the end result was so embarrassing she deleted it and reformatted her entire hard drive. She loathed social media posts on Valentine's Day that consisted of lonely young women professing their contentment with being single and embracing a "date" that was likely alcohol or a beleaguered pet. As her thirties continued its painful trudge into her forties, Jillian realized she was in no position to judge these women. She was one of them; she just didn't advertise it on Twitter. Her six-year relationship with Adam ended last fall and although she had tried to resuscitate it, Adam had made up his mind. It was over. Once she was through the necessary mourning period, Jillian knew she wasn't going to miss Adam; she was going to miss the comfort of having a companion as she neared middle age.

She signed up with a dating site at the urging of her friends and mother, all of them people who never had to bother with something so demeaning. She wondered how much her mother would actually approve of a service that was mainly looks based. While Jillian wasn't unattractive, she knew she lacked the flourish and youth of the most desirable candidates (who didn't need the service at all). Despite those obstacles, Jillian had accumulated a decent number of likes, a few crude PMs, and a relatively small number of dick pics. The best candidates were average-looking men with steady jobs and bland personalities. She wasn't asking for Channing Tatum but a little excitement wouldn't hurt, either. The last date consisted of a well-meaning but misguided man who spent the entire dinner discussing his screenplay. He had connected with Jillian because she was a fellow "wordsmith" (his phrasing) and it was a relief for him to meet somebody else who was serious about the craft. Jillian didn't have the heart to tell him that if one horrendous poem in the last year meant she was serious about the craft, then the written word was truly doomed. Still, she smiled and nodded politely as he explained how his script defied the traditional three-act structure and switched genres in a way that wouldn't just challenge the audience but the entire medium as well. It would be unfair to completely judge his script without reading it but it was safe to say it was about as compelling and marketable as edible toilet paper.

The evening ended with a hug and a polite "Yes" when he asked her if he could call her again sometime. He had called twice and texted three times over the next week. Jillian didn't respond and he mercifully took the hint. Now it was back to the drawing board. Jillian stared at her phone. The guy looking back at her flashed a mouth full of white teeth as he posed on the summit of Griffith Park. Jillian swiped left. Hiking was boring. The next lucky guy was at The Wizarding World of Harry Potter and he was proudly hoisting a mug of butterbeer in the air. Jillian swiped left. Theme parks were Adam's thing and that was one aspect of the relationship she definitely didn't miss. She spent her weekdays stuck in traffic, so standing in line on her days off wasn't exactly what she had in mind as a fun alternative.

Three more left swipes followed and Jillian was ready to forget the whole thing until she found Kevin. She was drawn to him almost immediately. His profile pic wasn't an attempt to show success or physical prowess. It was a simple pic of him sitting on a couch and sporting a smile that emphasized his adorable dimples. He was a year older than she was and resided in West Hollywood. Not exactly close to her but still within a reasonable distance. She scrolled through his other pics and found that Kevin seemed uncomplicated but still interesting. He had traveled to a number of countries and seemed to live well without appearing ostentatious. Even the mole on his neck looked cute. Jillian swiped right and to her surprise, it was a match. Five minutes later he sent her a message that read "Finally, somebody who hates this thing as much as I do!"

It was as perceptive as it was perfect. Jillian didn't believe in love at first sight (or PM in this case) but Kevin was certainly making a compelling case for it.

"What's wrong with your face?" Shannon asked a few days later. Shannon was her closest work friend. Jillian didn't make a point to hang out with her co-workers but she made an exception for Shannon. She shared Jillian's cynical sense of humor and had no real interest in her job, meaning they were practically soul mates. Shannon was an aspiring actress but unlike all the other actresses Jillian came across, Shannon (mostly) managed to stay grounded. She had done some commercials and a few guest spots on some network television shows but none of it went to her head. She had also written and directed her own web series and while it wasn't very good, Jillian admired the effort. If she couldn't give her own chosen medium the time of day, it was inspiring to see someone else do it.

"What do you mean?" Jillian replied. She was confused. Hadn't she covered the honker of a pimple on her face with foundation before she left the house that morning?

"I mean you're smiling," Shannon exclaimed. "You almost never smile!"

"I guess I'm just in a good mood," Jillian said, returning to her computer screen.

"Did you meet somebody?"

"Haven't you ever heard of the Bechdel Test?" Jillian asked. "We're supposed to talk about things besides men!"

"Did you meet somebody or not?" Shannon pressed, unabated.

"Sort of," Jillian said, smiling again as she thought of Kevin.

"Who is he?"

Shannon had a report due before lunch but that was clearly on the backburner now.

"It's just a guy I met online," Jillian replied. She didn't want to go into too much detail. The messages she exchanged with Kevin were great (they were even Facebook friends now) but they hadn't met face-to-face yet. She was still in a fragile place with him and she didn't want to jinx it.

"What's his name?" Shannon asked. "What does he do for a living? Is he cute?"

"His name is Kevin, he's a day trader, and if you think Steve Buscemi's cute, then you'd love this guy!"

"I love Steve Buscemi!" Shannon said. "So he's older then?"

Okay, so Shannon had her faults.

"Shannon, I'm kidding, he doesn't look like Steve Buscemi but I like where it's going so far. I think we're meeting up soon."

"If he wants to meet a bar, walk away."

"Why?" Jillian asked. "I like meeting in bars. I'm in the perfect place if it doesn't go well."

"Because meeting in bars is fine in your twenties but if he wants to do that in his thirties, he's deluding himself into thinking he's still young and hip. And once he sees how old you are, he might lose interest!"

"He knows how old I am, Shannon," Jillian said. "He's actually a year older than me."

"All the more reason for him to want somebody even younger," Shannon said. "He'll realize if he can land a chick in her late thirties, then why not a chick in her early thirties or better yet, her late twenties!"

"Wasn't your last boyfriend twenty-five?" Jillian asked, raising an eyebrow at Shannon.

"Yes, but he's shacked up with a fifty-year-old producer now!" Shannon said.

"Kind of throws your theory out the window, doesn't it?"

"The producer's a guy. Different set of rules when it comes to same-sex relationships," Shannon said, turning back to her report.

Shannon's absurd theories on life and dating were one of the things Jillian loved about her but there was the slightest tinge of uncertainty now. What if Shannon was right? Jillian tended to stay guarded, especially when it came to men but she had really let her defenses down with Kevin. Was that a mistake? Jillian hated the non-stop speculating that came with dating. If Kevin was going to pull the plug on her, she just hoped it was before their first date.

Regardless of how it turned out, there was a bottle of cheap wine waiting for her in the fridge. Cracking it open when she got home sounded wonderful.

Jillian was halfway through the bottle when Kevin messaged her. Her phone buzzed and she didn't pay it any mind. Usually a message this time of night was work informing her of some project that needed to be done before lunch tomorrow. As she polished off another glass, she decided it was time to see what couldn't wait until the next morning. To her surprise, it was a message from Kevin.

"I think it's time to meet up. What do you say?" it read.

Jillian poured herself another slug of wine and gulped it done before answering "Sure. When and where?"

There was a two-minute gap before he responded, suggesting a bar in West Hollywood. Shannon's warning lingered in her mind but her lowered inhibitions dismissed it. She agreed and they were set for Saturday night at nine. Jillian set her phone down with shaking hands. She had a date.

Please don't let this one be an asshole, she thought as she poured herself one final glass of liquid assurance. She wanted to end the night on a hopeful note, so she finished her wine and went to bed. She'd deal with the doubt and second-guessing in the morning.

She had two days left in the workweek and decided not to tell Shannon until they were going out the door on Friday.

"I'm meeting Kevin Saturday night," she said, trying to sound as casual as possible.

"Bar or restaurant?"

"Gastropub," Jillian answered. It was sort of the truth, too. The place served food but she wasn't sure if it really qualified as a gastropub. The menu was mostly appetizers and side dishes. She just wasn't in the mood to listen to Shannon analyze every minor detail of a first date that hadn't even happened yet.

"Watch your drinking and don't order the most expensive thing on the menu!" Shannon warned her.

"Can I order the most expensive drink on the menu?"

"Of course! You're a classy lady!"

"Do classy ladies use Magic Marker to fill in the holes in their stockings?" Jillian asked. "Because I totally did that yesterday."

"And he hasn't changed his underwear all week."

"You don't know that!" Jillian said.

"Go in there thinking that anyway. You're more than this guy deserves and don't be afraid to show that!" Shannon replied.

"Good advice. I'll picture his dirty underwear. That makes for an appetizing evening."

"I'll want details on Monday!" Shannon said, giving her a coy smile as she climbed in her powder blue Volkswagen.

"If it goes well, you probably won't even see me on Monday!"

"I'm holding you to that!" Shannon said before driving off, leaving Jillian alone to ponder her first date with a guy she actually liked. How long had it been since that had happened?

Too fucking long, Jillian thought as she started up her aging Honda. The radio was playing Adele's "Give My Love To Your New Lover." The song sounded foreboding to Jillian, so she changed the dial until she found an obnoxious country song. It was going to be a long drive home but anything was better than riding in silence with just her thoughts to keep her company.

They had proven to be a pretty shitty companion as of late.

Jillian spent the evening watching old music videos on YouTube. She opened up Word at one point in an attempt to write something but nothing came to her. The upcoming date was just too distracting. It seemed in the rare instances she opened up Word, she always had an excuse as to why she didn't write anything. Being nervous before a big date at was at least somewhat legitimate, so she closed the program mostly guilt free and went to bed a little before midnight. As she tried to fall asleep, she thought about how predictable life had become since her break-up with Adam. While their relationship wasn't exactly adventurous, having another person in her life at least provided some variety. Adam wasn't the most thrilling guy but he knew how to surprise her from time to time. There was the night he screamed like a girl and went under the covers when a bat had gotten inside their bedroom. She was finally able to chase it out with a broom but it was difficult, not just because the poor creature was in full-on panic mode but also because she couldn't stop laughing at her boyfriend's cowardice. Adam wasn't a macho guy but seeing him scared of such a tiny little animal was as humorous as it was off-putting. She doubted Kevin was scared of bats and she likely wouldn't ever find out but the thought of getting close to someone new and seeing what surprises they held was enticing. With renewed assurance, Jillian fell into a calm and dreamless sleep.

She spent her Saturday getting an early jump on next week's work. Her boss was clueless but her assignments were always done on time, which meant he didn't hassle her very often. Finishing up her work early meant downtime in the office but mostly it was an excuse to pass the time until her date. She allotted herself an hour to get ready, plus another half an hour to get to the bar. It had been a few years since she needed to dress to impress and her dated wardrobe made that difficult. She eventually settled on a black skirt and a short-sleeved peach blouse. Comfortable but dressy. It was the kind of outfit she wore when she went to church with her mother, which suddenly gave her pause. Was a church outfit proper attire for a first date at a hip bar in West Hollywood? She

gave herself one final look in the mirror and decided if her outfit doomed

her, it wasn't meant to be. She had worn jeans to her other dates and two

of those guys had expressed continued interest. With a final sweep of her

hair and a quick application of lip-gloss, she was out the door.

She arrived at the bar ten minutes early. It wasn't very crowded

and the music was playing at a reasonable volume, which meant they'd

actually be able to have a conversation. She ordered a white wine and

resisted every urge to check her phone. Nothing looked sadder and more

desperate to Jillian than a person alone at a bar that constantly checked

their phone like they had business or friends to attend to. The ten

minutes became fifteen minutes and the desire to check her phone itched

liked a phantom limb. Just as she was about to cave, he came in.

He did a quick scan of the bar before spotting her and walking

over. He wore slim gray slacks and a maroon V-neck sweater. He was a

little late but not enough that it seemed rude or dismissive. Still, there was

something off. She knew everybody cheated a little with their photos but

Kevin, while as blandly handsome in person as he was in his photos,

looked a little different. Was he taller than she had initially thought? His

mole and adorable dimples appeared to be intact, so she decided it must

be his height. He had at least six inches on her and she assumed he'd be much shorter. With that nagging qualm out of the way, Jillian allowed herself to return the smile and give him a hug.

"Good to finally meet you!" Kevin said as the bartender walked over. He looked down at her wine glass.

"Preparing for disappointment?" he asked her with a wink.

"Just a little liquid courage," she said. "I thought about ordering you a Vodka tonic…"

"You remembered!" Kevin exclaimed. "I'm impressed!"

"But I didn't know if you wanted to mix things up."

"As a matter of fact, that's exactly what I had in mind," he said, turning his attention to the bartender. "Two shots of tequila!"

"Tequila? Aren't we moving a little fast?" Jillian asked, only half-joking when she said it. It was a strange way to start a date.

"I look at it this way," he said. "We've had some really nice chats but this may be our only drink together. Wouldn't you regret it if we didn't cut loose at least once?"

The bartender set the tequila shots in front of them and Jillian's thoughts went back to her utterly banal and predictable existence since Adam had left.

Fuck it, she thought as she raised her shot to Kevin, who reciprocated the gesture. They clinked the glasses together and Jillian downed her shot. Her throat closed and she shuddered, which was why she generally avoided tequila shots. At that moment, however, it felt great.

Jillian was ready for an adventure.

Unfortunately, the first half-hour of the date was a disaster. The warm and funny personality that radiated so clearly from the messages he had sent her was almost completely absent here. Kevin was awkward and had nothing interesting to say. He got her hometown wrong (St. Louis) and he didn't seem to remember the embarrassing story about the time her skirt fell down at the Getty (maybe that was a good thing).

"Sorry if I seem a little out of it tonight," he said with an apologetic grin. "It was a long week at work."

"That's okay, I'm usually out of it most nights," she replied, hoping some lame humor would break some of the strange tension.

Kevin laughed. It was an odd, reedy sound.

Jesus, if I had to listen to that all the time, I'd lose my fucking mind, she thought. She silently admonished herself. She had built this guy up too much and all over a few pleasant conversations on a dating site. She knew better than that. Or so she thought.

"I have to go to the bathroom. Do you mind watching my purse?" she asked him.

Kevin nodded, a strange a look on his face she couldn't quite place. Was he bummed out the date wasn't going well? Was he indifferent? Oblivious? She decided it didn't really matter. She began planning her exit strategy as she walked toward the bathroom.

"Now there's a friend I'd like to get to know!" a nearby voice bellowed out. Jillian looked up to see a beefy red-faced man leering at her.

"Not you, sweetheart," he said, his leer transforming into a lopsided grin. Relieved the pig wasn't talking to her, Jillian continued walking.

"I meant your ass," he called out. "That thing is choice!"

Jillian clenched her jaw. It had been awhile since she had heard such a lewd catcall. In the rare instances it happened, she always assumed she had time traveled back to the 70s. Who the hell still talked like that?

Just as she was about to enter the bathroom, she saw Kevin approach the man, a disarming smile on his face. Jillian moved away from the door and watched as Kevin engaged the man in a seemingly friendly manner. The man laughed and nodded at what Kevin was saying. Jillian was confused. Was Kevin in league with this asshole? Just as she was about to walk back to him and call it a night, he leaned in and whispered something to the man. His formerly cheerful demeanor darkened and he lashed out at Kevin who effortlessly grabbed his arm and twisted it at an unnatural angle. The man cried out in pain and Kevin guided him to his knees. The handful of other patrons watched in stunned silence as the scene unfolded. Kevin made eye contact with Jillian and motioned for her to come back with his free hand.

She walked over and looked down at the man. Thick beads of sweat were forming on his face and forehead.

"Tell her," Kevin commanded, giving the man's arm another twist.

The man howled in pain.

"I said tell her," Kevin repeated, his tone growing menacing.

The man exhaled and a thick runner of snot flew out of his nose.

"I'm sorry," he said, the words barely audible.

"Again!" Kevin said. "Louder!"

"I said I'm sorry!" the man said in a choked sputter.

"Good," Kevin answered, finally letting him go.

The man stayed on the ground and he immediately grabbed his wounded arm. Kevin looked at the bartender, a nervous little blonde (likely an actress) who clearly wasn't fit to deal with a situation like this.

"He's settling his bill and leaving," Kevin told her, his tone calm but authoritative. The man stood up and reached into his wallet, pulling out a small wad of bills. He pulled a twenty off the top and tossed it on the bar before walking out without another word.

Kevin turned to Jillian.

"Do you want another glass of wine?"

Jillian thought about the time a man had crudely hit on her in front of Adam. He hadn't said a word and finally went to the bouncer when the man wouldn't let up. She was disappointed with Adam that evening. She was more than capable of handling herself of course but sometimes you needed a little backup. And the kind of backup Kevin had just provided was a bit of a turn-on. She smiled at him in appreciation of the interesting turn the night had just taken.

"How about another shot of tequila instead?" she asked.

A few drinks later, Jillian found herself drunk on a first date. She never got drunk on a first date. Not only was it careless, it made her feel cheap but the damage was already done. She'd have to take an Uber home and then retrieve her car in the morning. And she was sure to find a fat parking ticket planted on her windshield. L.A. doled those things out like Halloween candy. Worse yet, she'd have to handle everything with a nasty hangover and then go to work on Monday. That meant dealing with Shannon, who would spend the entire day bugging her for details so she could tell Jillian exactly what she did wrong. That wouldn't get old at all.

And what if Jillian never heard from Kevin again? She would spend the rest of the week pondering what had gone wrong before finally convincing herself that Kevin was just a flake and there was (maybe) still hope for her. Yes, the next few days were definitely going to suck but as Jillian sucked down another tequila shot while an amused and significantly looser Kevin looked on, she knew none of that mattered.

She was having a great time.

"Catch!"

It was several shots later and they were headed to the next bar. Jillian saw something arc through the air and she reflexively put her hands up to catch it. Whatever it was pricked her right palm but the tequila helped dull the sensation. When she saw what it was, she laughed. It was a grinning purple octopus holding a cocktail umbrella. "Kitschy" would be the euphemism for it but Jillian knew it was tacky and ugly. That didn't stop her from immediately falling in love with it when she saw at the bar a few minutes ago. It was exactly the kind of thing her grandparents had shamelessly kept on top of the bar at their house in Florida. Both grandparents were dead now and that wonderful junk was long gone. She had conveyed this to Kevin but he didn't seem especially interested in hearing about it. Now she was holding evidence of his attentiveness in her hand. Maybe he was a keeper.

"Did you steal this?" she asked.

"No, I offered the bartender a thousand dollars for it but she refused," Kevin said. "So I upped it to five grand and she begrudgingly accepted. I have to go back and wash dishes tomorrow, though."

"Well, I appreciate your sacrifice," Jillian said, resting her head on his shoulder. Jesus Christ. What was she doing? It seemed to be the right move, as he put his arm around her. She could smell the spice of his deodorant but lurking not far below that was the sour smell of sweat. It wasn't necessarily a bad thing, though. The bar had been hot and she was guessing she probably didn't smell too fresh herself. Given how disastrous the date had started, some minor B.O. was a trifling complaint at best.

"Where are we going now?" she asked him.

He didn't answer her right away; the only sounds were the slow and methodical scraping of his dress shoes on the sidewalk.

"Do you really want to go another bar?" he finally responded.

"Yeah, why not?"

"Because a classy lady deserves a classy destination," he answered. He stopped and gently swung her around. A garish Pinkberry sign looked down on them.

"I hear the flavor this month is raspberry white chocolate," he said, his face bathed in the red and white light of the sign.

Pinkberry actually did sound good. She normally preferred heavy grease after a lot of alcohol but she suddenly found herself craving mango froyo. As they walked inside the restaurant, a blast of cool air prompted gooseflesh to spring up on her arms and legs. They approached the counter and Jillian could see her reflection on the shiny wall behind it. It showed a drunk and disheveled-looking woman who was about to eat froyo with a guy she barely knew. Under normal circumstances, that would seem odd but she didn't let any strange or suspicious feelings invade her thoughts.

There would be plenty of those later on.

As they ate their frozen yogurt, Jillian could feel herself sobering up. The excitement and adrenaline from the events at the bar were also starting to diminish. A headache was starting to form above her right eye. It wasn't too bad yet but she knew it was going to be a doozy before the night was over. As thrilling and unexpected as the date had turned out, she was ready to call it a night.

"Penny for your thoughts," Kevin said, picking up on her waning interest.

"That tequila's starting to get to me," she replied. "I think I need to head home after this."

"Fair enough," he said, his tone even and relaxed. "Can I suggest one thing?"

"Sure," she said, hoping it wasn't a cheap ploy for a kiss.

"Can we go to one more place for a nightcap?" he asked. "We'll have one last drink and then I'll get you an Uber. How's that sound?"

Jillian almost said no but then she felt the pointy tentacles of the octopus in her purse. It was a perfect keepsake and one that would proudly sit atop her work computer for the foreseeable future. Didn't that earn him just a little bit more of her time?

She scooped the remainder of the froyo from the bottom of the container and that's when she noticed his hands. They were shaking. Badly. After everything that had happened, was he really still nervous? As she swallowed the rest of her yogurt, she decided the gesture was actually somewhat endearing. He was bold but still vulnerable. Despite her aversion of a good night kiss just a few seconds ago, she suddenly pictured his warm lips pressing against hers with a nervous, schoolboy-like hesitancy. It was an awkward thought but not an entirely unpleasant one, either.

She looked past his shaking hands and at a small, dark splotch on the sleeve of his sweater. That was okay, too. It actually provided a nice complement to the bleach stains on her underwear. With these minor chinks in his armor starting to show, she thought about her current options. She could go home now and immediately fall asleep or she could open herself up to one more mini-adventure. Even with a headache staking its claim on her physical well-being, it was an easy decision.

"Where to?" she asked, gathering up her purse.

"A nice little out-of-the-way place. You're going to love it," he said, gently grabbing her elbow and guiding her out of the restaurant.

Three years with Adam and he was almost always wrong when he said she was going to love something. As she followed Kevin, she hoped his track record would prove better.

The bar he chose was loud, dimly lit, and skeezy. If this was his way of writing her off, a polite hug and a promise to call would have been much more bearable. The miserable people filing in and out stank of cigarettes and their clothing hung off their emaciated bodies in near-tatters. Jillian wondered how many of them had hit the coast in hopes of becoming the next Brad Pitt or Jennifer Lawrence.

Jillian decided long ago she'd settle for being the next Sarah Vowell but right now she'd settled for making it out of this place alive.

"So why this bar?" she asked Kevin as he patiently waited for the surly-looking bartender to serve them.

"I've only ever seen it from the outside," he said with a somewhat sheepish grin. "I thought it was going to be nicer."

"So you've never been here?"

"Hey, L.A.'s a big place. I've only been here three years!"

"I thought it was four," Jillian yelled over the loud classic rock piping through the ancient and sticky-looking speakers.

"Three, four, it all kind of blurs together once you hit your thirties!" he responded as the bartender finally came over.

Jillian couldn't really debate him on that one. She watched as Kevin leaned in and placed his order with the bartender, who nodded and began pouring their drinks.

"I had a really good time tonight!" he said, turning back to her.

"Me too."

And it was mostly true, save for the beginning of the date and their current location. The bartender came back with their drinks and Kevin pulled out his wallet, accidentally dropping his keys in the process.

"Oh, shit, do you mind?" he asked her as he handed the bartender two twenties.

The drinks were sixteen dollars each. That was a little steeper than she had expected. Picking up his keys from a floor that likely had its last mopping somewhere in the late 80s seemed like a fair trade. She bent down and retrieved the keys, making sure no part of her hand touched the ground. When she came back up, her drink was on the bar in front of her.

Kevin raised his glass to Jillian.

"To the gross end of a great date!"

Jillian clinked glasses with him and took a sip. She didn't know what it was but it tasted a little salty. It wasn't great but it at least provided a nice contrast to the sweet-tasting drinks Adam had favored. Jillian used to love teasing Adam about his love of "girly drinks." Still, her headache was growing worse and it was now coupled with nausea churning inside her stomach. She knew she wouldn't be able to finish the drink. Kevin kept his eyes trained on her as he continued sipping from his own glass. Even if there wasn't another date, she didn't want it to end on an awkward note. She was holding a rather expensive drink and refusing to finish it or pawning it off on him would sour the evening. She decided to utilize an old trick she learned in college.

"Are they watching Seinfeld?" she asked, pointing at the grimy television on the wall. He turned his attention to the television and she dumped most of the contents of the glass onto the floor. When he turned back, he saw her polishing off the remaining drops.

"Damn, you really downed that thing!" he said, impressed. He finished his own drink and set it on the bar.

"And they're watching Friends. Your nineties television knowledge is a little lacking," he told her in a playfully mocking tone.

"Yeah, well, they kind of blur together once you hit your thirties," she replied.

"Touché. Now let's call you an Uber."

Ten minutes later they were making out in the back of a late-model Prius. Jillian wasn't sure how it had happened but her headache and nausea had somewhat settled and were replaced with a euphoric feeling that was foreign to her but fantastic nonetheless.

"Scenic route?" the driver asked Kevin.

"I think we're ready to call it a night," Kevin said as he resumed kissing her. He wasn't hesitant like she'd thought he'd be but he wasn't pushy or assertive, either. The last guy she had made out with was too eager. He practically smashed his teeth against hers. Kevin's gentle but firm approach was a pleasurable alternative.

"Want to go back to my place?" he asked, slightly out of breath.

She did. She definitely did.

Once they were in his apartment, she was relieved to see it had been well represented in the photos posted on his profile. Although he kept the lights off, she could see it was decorated nice but not in an especially showy way. The biggest relief was the smell. A lot of guys, even the successful ones, hadn't quite mastered the art of making their living domiciles not smell like burnt food and old socks. Not that she spent a lot of time in strange men's apartments but a lot of Adam's friends had just that problem with their places. And they were single. Go figure.

They continued making out on his couch and his hands found their way to her breasts. He massaged them gently, occasionally squeezing her nipples between his fingers. The euphoric feeling was starting to wear off a little and she suddenly found herself wondering what the hell she was doing here. Adam didn't even get this kind of action until the third date and her connection with him was more immediate than the one she had with Kevin. Was she this starved for affection? The kissing continued, so she decided she was. It went on for a few more seconds and then she finally pushed him away.

"I think this is going too fast," she said, her face apologetic.

"Really?"

"Yeah. I like you but maybe we should take it a little slower," she continued.

She could tell he wasn't happy.

"Well, okay, but you made the first move. I wasn't planning on trying anything," he said.

Had she made the first move? She honestly didn't remember and it had only been half an hour.

"Sorry, but I should really go," she told him.

"Okay," he said, sounding agreeable enough. "Want me to call you another Uber?"

"Do you mind?" she said. She appreciated how understanding he was.

"Not at all," he said. "Wait here."

"Do you mind if I use your bathroom?" she asked.

"Sure. First door on the left," he said, standing up and walking out of the room.

Jillian walked into the bathroom and flipped on the light. She looked in the mirror and was startled when she saw a dark streak next to her mouth. She wiped it off with a tissue and examined it. Whatever the substance was, it was crumbly and had a paste-like texture. Had she gone around the whole night with that on her face? Before she could think about it any further, she let out an unexpected burp. Her mouth was suddenly filled with the salty taste of that last drink Kevin had bought for her.

It was at that moment a horrible realization fell over her. Everything made sense now. Making out and coming back to his place, that strange euphoric sensation that still lingered inside her like the remnants of a bad head cold. Kevin had put something in her drink. How could she have been so stupid and careless? She had dropped her most rudimentary defenses for a guy she had never even met before tonight. Talk about desperate. Deciding she'd dwell on her own foolishness later, she grabbed her phone out of her purse and left the bathroom. As soon as she stepped into the hallway, she was met with a fist that traveled at a vicious and blinding velocity. Her nose was immediately pulverized and she hit the ground with streams of hot blood pouring out of both her nostrils.

Kevin was standing over her, a wild look in his eyes. In the full light of the bathroom, she could see a smear on his neck. It was the same substance she had away from her face. His adorable mole was makeup. Why would anybody fake such a random thing?

"So that's how you finished the drink so fast!" he exclaimed. "You didn't drink it at all! You fucking lied! And I hate bitches that lie!"

She tried to scream but he planted his foot on her throat, choking her. She gasped but the intense pressure he was applying didn't waver.

"You should have drank the entire thing," he said. "Because this is going to hurt a hell of a lot fucking worse now!"

He took his foot off her throat and kicked her in the chin, using enough force to knock her teeth together, chipping three of them. The newly exposed nerves shrieked with an agony so intense she almost passed out.

He grabbed her hair and proceeded to drag her down the hallway. Jillian tried to struggle and break away but it was useless. He pulled her to her feet before shoving her into the darkened bedroom at the end of the hallway.

The small of her back cracked against hard wood and she slid to the ground, too dazed and terrified to move.

He stood over her, the darkness of the room transforming him into a silhouette that looked impossibly large and imposing.

He took out a box cutter and bent down next to her.

"The other ones had open casket funerals. You aren't going to be so lucky," he whispered, hot spittle spraying her ear. He placed one hand over her mouth and dragged the box cutter across her right cheek. She let out a muffled scream as the sharp metal ravaged her flesh. Fresh blood poured onto her blouse as he lackadaisically ran the blade down her face. He reminded her of an elementary school child completing a maze. He finished with a gash across her chin and drew the blade away.

She realized she was still gripping her purse and she reached inside it, hoping to grab anything that could act as a weapon. He noticed and brought his foot down. Hard. There was a muffled crunch as several bones in her hand broke. She screamed again but it was a hoarse, choked sound. Her mouth was filled with blood and she was starting to lose consciousness. As she dragged her broken hand out of her purse, the octopus he stole came with it, shattered into a million jagged pieces. In her dazed and somewhat intoxicated state, the jagged pieces gave her a shred a hope.

He smiled down at her, enjoying his handiwork. She was a bloody, disfigured mess.

"Having fun?" he asked. "Maybe it's time to call it a night for real this time. I'm getting tired."

He retracted the box cutter and put it inside his pocket.

"I'll be right back."

He left the room and Jillian used her good hand to grope for one of the jagged octopus tentacles. It was her only shot.

When he came back, he was carrying a plastic grocery bag and some duct tape.

"Time to go sleep," he stated matter-of-factly. "I realize this ended up being a pretty grueling night but you'll sleep now. And it'll feel good. I had a nice enough time to allow you that. In fact, out of all the women I've met off that site, you're probably my favorite."

He paused as he prepared to lower the bag over her head.

"Oh, fuck it, I say that to all of them," he said, laughing as he brought the bag down, her vision obscured by a sheath of white plastic. She knew she didn't have much time. She gripped the ceramic tentacle and swung it around, her hand connecting with the flesh and bone of his face. She had mustered enough strength to swing it so hard she felt the impact all the way up to her shoulder.

He screamed in pain and fell to the ground. She pulled the bag from her head and looked over at him. The tentacle was jutting out of the corner of his right eye. The sight was so gruesome it was almost comical.

"You fucking bitch!" he gasped. The box cutter had fallen out of his pocket and was on the floor a few feet away from him. Jillian fell to the floor and used her good hand to reach for the box cutter. She kept expecting him to attack her again but he remained motionless. It was almost like he was unable to move. She thought of everything he had done to her but unlike him, she was still going. She realized that underneath his sadistic and vile personae was a weak and inefficient coward. She didn't expect to make it out of this alive but she wasn't going down alone.

She reached the box cutter and just as she wrapped her good hand around it, he grabbed her and began to pummel the small of her back with his fists. Even if he was weak in spirit, he was certainly strong in body. She struggled to turn over as he continued to bring his fists down but she could hear him getting winded. If she could stay conscious for just a few more seconds, she'd be able to turn over. His punches gradually weakened and his weight shifted. Knowing this would be her only chance, Jillian managed to roll over on her back and stare up at him, the ceramic tentacle still jammed in his eye and his crazed face glazed with sweat.

"It's fucking over for you!" he said, struggling to get the words out. "I'm going to cut you into fucking pieces and mail them home to your mommy in St. Louis! How's that sound?"

Before he knew what was happening, Jillian took the box cutter and slit his throat. And unlike the night she came across his profile, she made sure to go left this time. His throat opened up and a geyser of blood sprayed her ruined face. A nauseating and prolonged gurgling sound came from Kevin as he made a feeble attempt to grab at his throat but it was too late. The blood continued to pour from the jagged gash at an obscene and rapid rate. Jillian wanted it to end, oh God, how she wanted it to end. Just when it seemed like it was going to go on forever, he finally fell back, hitting his head against the dresser with a sharp thud. He let out one final gurgle and died, his eyes transfixed in a look of shock and hatred.

I can't wait to hear Shannon analyze this date, Jillian thought as she finally lost consciousness. It wasn't exactly how she planned to end the evening but under the present circumstances, it'd do.

If the single life had taught her anything, it was to be adaptable.

A year later she was back home in St. Louis. She had gone through two bouts of plastic surgery to deal with scars on her face and save for faint traces on her cheek and chin they were mostly gone. Jillian couldn't deny the decision was partly out of vanity but given the events of that night would haunt her for the rest of her life, it was hard to pass up an opportunity to eliminate any visual reminders of it. Her broken teeth had been capped and her nose, save for looking a little crooked, had also healed up nicely.

She was in counseling three times a week with a lovely woman named Patty and while she knew she was making progress, the nightmares still came without fail every evening. Some nights she'd wake up and see him standing at the foot of her bed. She had learned to stifle her screams when that happened but the rush of terror that came with it never subsided. It was another burden she'd have to spend the rest of her life with.

On the good side, the press had mercifully died down after about three weeks. She had numerous offers from publishing companies to tell her story but living it had been more than enough. She asked Patty and her mother if she had an obligation to other women to tell her story but they both said the same thing: Her only obligation was to heal herself. She had started writing an unrelated novel under a nom de plume and that was helping her immensely. She doubted it was very good but she was at least writing every day and she could actually see herself improving with each chapter. She sometimes laughed at the absurdity of the whole thing. She had gotten so lazy with her writing that it took getting disfigured and almost murdered for her to get her ass in gear again.

In terms of her old life, she occasionally emailed with Shannon but now that she was away from Los Angeles, she could tell the bond was gradually weakening and that was to be expected. Los Angeles was its own world and once you removed yourself from it, you were nothing more than an ephemeral vapor to the people who had known you.

As for Kevin (the real Kevin), she didn't think much about him anymore. There wasn't much to think about. The messages they had exchanged were lovely and the connection, however indirect, felt genuine but they had never met in person. They were never given that chance, as a monster had murdered him the same day they were supposed to have their first date. Said monster's real name was David Victor Josephs, a serial killer blessed with considerable hacking skills. Josephs' MO was to hack dating sites, find the profile of a man he vaguely resembled, murder them, and then take their place on the first meet-up with whatever lucky lady they had chosen. Besides Kevin, he had killed four people. Two were in New York and two more were in Austin. Jillian wondered how much longer it would have gone on before somebody connected the dots. Better yet, why hadn't someone already connected them?

As Jillian learned that evening, Josephs loved to prolong the date as long as he could. "Romancing them" was how he put it in the journals the police discovered afterward. Jillian couldn't deny he was smooth but the clues were still there. Why had she ignored them? The information he had gotten wrong was stuff Kevin and Jillian had exchanged over Facebook, which he hadn't bothered to hack. As for the salty taste in her drink, he had spiked it with liquid ecstasy. An unusual taste should have been an immediate red flag but it wasn't. She had only stopped drinking it because she had already consumed too much alcohol around a man who was a complete stranger (and a fucking psychopath to boot).

The mole was a nice touch but she supposed the biggest factor was when he roughed up the big guy who had hit on her. That was kismet. No way he could have planned that. She was getting ready to leave before that went down. And if she had come back and said she wanted to leave, what would he have done then? Spiked the rest of her wine with the liquid ecstasy? Followed her to back her place? It was best not to think about it. That evening was not her finest hour by any stretch of the imagination.

Family, friends and well-wishers always made a point to remind her that none of it was her fault and part of her knew that was true. But mostly she continued to blame herself. No amount of support and counseling would ever be able to fix that.

At the very least, there were moments where she could escape. Working on her novel provided most of them, though she had also taken up jogging. On this particular day, she was deep into a new chapter as she waited for her mother to get home with dinner. Tonight they were having vegetable lasagna with carrot cake for dessert.

These moments didn't completely halt the self-loathing and nightmares but they definitely beat the alternative.

And maybe that was enough for the time being.

Just You Wait

Maddy stared at the giant Grim Reaper that forebodingly loomed above her. She half-expected it to bring its scythe down and cut her in half or perhaps scoop her up and devour her like a handful of potato chips. As Maddy continued to take in the Reaper's sinister gaze, she decided both of those options were preferable to what waited just beyond the long, bony finger that seemed to be pointed directly at her.

"Turn back, Maddy! You'll only find humiliation and pain in there!" she imagined the Reaper saying, its voice a dusty rasp from an eternity of misery and death.

"Move it!"

Maddy was elbowed from behind and looked around to see Tina, her brown eyes twinkling beneath her white eye shadow.

"I'm going!" Maddy insisted as she took a small step forward.

"Well, can you do it before we graduate?" Tina asked, a smirk forming on her glossy pink lips.

Maddy took a deep breath and walked below the Reaper, her final hopes of being cut into pieces or eaten dashed as she passed through its ragged black cloak. She turned back to see Tina strutting through the cloth and plastic façade with Amy following behind her like a faithful hound dog. Although Maddy found Amy's slavish loyalty to Tina to be mostly pathetic, she was also a little jealous. Amy was no ball of fire and she had been mostly drafted into their tiny group after she and Tina had played soccer together during their junior year. At first, Maddy didn't mind her but it quickly became apparent there was a new dynamic at work and she wasn't going to be a part of it. She couldn't help but feel a little lonely as she watched Amy practically cling to Tina as they entered the main queue for The Death Rattle. Maddy and Tina had been friends since second grade but their friendship had cooled somewhat in the last year, as in addition to Amy, Tina had also developed a newfound interest in boys and drinking (not necessarily in that order). While Maddy wasn't morally opposed to drinking, she also didn't have the stomach for it. She had snuck some champagne at her cousin's wedding in sixth grade and wound up puking down the front of her brand-new dress.

As for the boys Tina hung around with, Maddy found them to be gross and immature. She had attended a party with Tina right after Christmas and one of them had pinned her up against the wall and began roughly groping her. While the act was bad enough, what scared her most was the look on his face when he did it. He looked like he was in a trance; the edges of his mouth wet with drool as he carelessly squeezed and rolled her breasts around. She had tried to push him away but as a football player with a hundred pounds on her; that was easier said than done. She cried for help until Tina finally came over.

"Hands off, animal!" she said, her tone as light and playful as the slap on the back she gave him. Said animal let go of Maddy's breasts, which were now throbbing with pain.

"Sorry," he slurred without looking at her.

"Go!" Tina said as she gave him a friendly shove. The animal disappeared down the hallway without further protest, likely already forgetting Maddy and his vile treatment of her. Tina, somewhat intoxicated herself, leaned in and squinted at Maddy.

"Are you crying?" she asked. "He was just goofing around."

That was the last party Maddy went to with Tina.

While the memory of that horrible evening was forever burned in Maddy's brain, it was taking a backseat to another traumatic memory, this one going all the way back to the summer before sixth grade. She was at Six Flags with her family and it had been a wonderful day, at least until they decided to ride The Annihilator. Maddy had only been tall enough to ride rollercoasters for a year by that point and The Annihilator would be her first one. Despite all that, Maddy wasn't scared. There was no reason to be. Everybody exiting the ride looked like they just had the time of their lives.

She boarded the ride with her brother and found it pretty underwhelming at first. It did a slow, steep climb up a long length of track that seemed to stretch on endlessly. When did it get good? She watched as the people below grew smaller and smaller as the car continued its arduous march toward the sky, making a chunky and rhythmic clicking sound as it went. They finally reached the top and there was the briefest pause as both the car and the people inside it seemed to prepare for the short and exhilarating journey that was set to follow. Maddy gripped the metal handlebar as the car dove back toward the earth at what felt like an impossibly fast rate. Her long blonde hair billowed behind her as she let out an excited sound that was more of a squawk than a scream but it still perfectly represented her feelings at that moment. The ride was invigorating but its high velocity and tight turns prevented her from expressing herself in a coherent manner. It was almost as if the ride had put her in a mild state of shock. It was a feeling she continued to enjoy until the ride got stuck upside down, mid-loop. Maddy, already somewhat disoriented, couldn't comprehend what was going on at first. She glanced over at her brother, two years her senior, who was similarly red-faced and confused-looking. Within a few seconds, the other riders understood what had happened. Some of them laughed but a few of them let out frightened screams. Maddy felt the blood rushing to her head as they sat suspended in that terrifying state. She looked to her brother for comfort but saw he was just as scared as she was, if not more so. And although the ordeal couldn't have lasted more than ten minutes, Maddy hastily exited the ride with urine in her pants and a vow never to get on a roller coaster ever again.

The expected wait for the Death Rattle was only fifteen minutes, which was maybe the biggest advantage of Senior Night. The park was full of seniors from a handful of high schools and no one else. Since the Death Rattle was a new ride, it would normally have a line that went well past the Grim Reaper façade and last anywhere from forty-five minutes to two hours on a busy day.

"One hundred and twenty miles an hour! You won't just defy death, you'll laugh in its face!" a voice that sounded like a hybrid of Vincent Price and Michael Buffer boomed over the loudspeakers hanging above the queue. "The most exhilarating experience of your life is minutes away! Just you wait!"

Maddy knew the voice was designed to get people excited (and based on the eager looks of the other seniors standing in line, it was successful) but it sounded ominous to her and she didn't like it. And not just because her last ride on a rollercoaster left her suspended two hundred feet above the earth with pee in her pants.

Tina reached into her jacket and pulled out a flask, offering it first to Maddy, who shook her head and then to Amy, who subserviently took it and snuck a small sip. Maddy guessed it was less a sip than a drop on the tip of her tongue but she didn't bother to let on. What was the point? She did have to smile at Tina's flask, though. The stainless steel was covered in sparkly star stickers and Tina had also used pink paint to scribble her initials on one side. It was a childish and tacky gesture that provided the perfect contrast between the contents of the flask (a cheap booze likely cribbed from her parents' liquor cabinet) and the actual maturity and readiness of its owner to drink from it.

Tina brought the flask to her own lips and made a show of tipping her head back in the interest of drawing attention to herself. It was successful.

"Yeah!" a deep voice called out from behind them. Maddy looked back and saw two boys watching Tina with smiles that managed to look both vacant and predatory.

"Think we can get some of that?" the one asked.

"Definitely!" Tina said with a flirtatious grin as she held the flask out.

The boys cautiously looked around before accepting it, which almost made Maddy laugh. Tina was a hundred pounds soaking wet with a pixie haircut and yet she had more balls than these two. The boys each took a quick sip (likely drops on the tongue) and discreetly handed it back to Tina before striking up a conversation with her, which Tina gladly partook in.

Maddy ignored it and turned her attention to the black and purple track that snaked above her head. Rollercoaster cars blurred by, their inhabitants screaming at the top of the lungs from adrenaline and the knowledge they were forever free from the shackles of the public school system.

Maddy thought back to when they first announced the plans for Senior Night. When she heard it was being held at a theme park, she immediately decided she wasn't going to go. That decision would have stood firm had her mother not gotten wind of it.

"You have to go!" she had told Maddy on their way to dinner at Panera Bread. "All your friends are going. It's the last time you'll ever see some of those people!"

"Not really," Maddy responded. "There's still graduation and there's going to plenty of parties in the summer. I'd just be missing a boring night at a dumb theme park."

"Is this about what happened at Six Flags?" her mother asked.

Maddy hesitated before speaking again, which of course answered her mother's question for her.

"No…" Maddy began but her mother interrupted her.

"That was a long time ago. Nothing bad ever happens on those rides anymore. Plus you have much a stronger bladder now!"

"Mom!"

"So don't go. You can always stay home and watch Frasier re-runs with your father and me," her mother said with a knowing grin on her face.

Maddy thought about this. Frasier re-runs with her parents meant sitting on the couch listening to her mother talk a mile a minute about God knows what while her father stared glassy-eyed at the television and offered the occasional noncommittal grunt as a response. It was pretty grim but it was how they had spent their Friday nights for as far back as Maddy could remember. She imagined it was a routine that would last well into the future. Senior Night, however, was a one-time event that Maddy would never get to revisit, even if it meant risking further trauma or possibly death.

"I'll go if Tina's going," she finally offered.

And of course Tina was going. It's where the boys would be.

"At one hundred and twenty miles per hour, you'll be leaving Death in the dust! The most exciting ride of your life is almost here! Just you wait!" the voice bellowed over the loudspeaker.

"We're already fucking waiting!" Tina hollered, eliciting laughter from some of other people in the queue but also earning a dirty look from a mother with two small children, which Tina took note of.

"Oh, relax," Tina yelled at her. "Those kids aren't even big enough to go on this ride. And besides, you've obviously been out of high school for a really long time. I thought this was Senior Night, not Senior Citizen Night!"

The mother gave Tina the stink eye before turning her attention back to her children.

"Yeah, look away," Tina said, though it was only loud enough to be heard by Maddy and Amy.

Maddy stared at her, suddenly realizing she didn't know this girl at all anymore. When they first met, Tina was a shy and awkward girl whose mother dressed her like an American Girl doll on just about every day of the week (Saturdays included). She had long, beautiful hair that Maddy spent hours brushing at their frequent sleepovers and they had no secrets. When Maddy accidentally spilled her mother's favorite perfume from Paris, the first person she told was Tina. When Tina shoplifted a top from American Apparel sophomore year (the beginning of her transition into the crude party girl currently swigging from a flask and flirting with strange boys), the first person she told was Maddy.

She was Maddy's oldest friend and while it made Maddy a little sad to know they had drifted apart, she was also ready for a fresh start.

So what am I even doing here? she thought as the Death Rattle launched another car onto its serpent-like track.

Her heartbeat started to increase and dear God, did she have to pee? Although it was torture, she continued to think about the day she had gotten stuck on the roller coaster at Six Flags. Once they had gotten down, her brother didn't say a word and his face was the color of cottage cheese. Maddy was much more vocal, sobbing and yelling as her parents did their best to calm her down. Once they had done that, they left the park, despite the fact it was still early in the day. Maddy's face with sticky with tears and she had the worst headache of her life. She walked slightly bow-legged to deal with the pee in her pants. Several kids and even a couple of adults had laughed at her as she walked by with dark streaks running down both legs of her pants. What made it more humiliating was that she just turned twelve two months ago. That was way too old to throw a tantrum and certainly too old to have an accident. The family rode home in silence and until Maddy's mother convinced her to attend Senior Night, none of them ever mentioned that day again.

"Maddy?" a timid voice said, interrupting her from replaying that horrible day in her head. She looked around to see Amy standing to her right. Tina was still busy with her new friends, which meant she had no time for Amy. Usually Amy clung to Tina no matter what but aside from lacking Tina's boisterous personality, she also had a plain face and was slightly overweight, which meant boys (at least the ones Tina liked) had no interest in her. Perhaps Amy was starting to finally realize this.

"How's it going, Amy?" Maddy responded, hoping her tone sounded nonchalant.

Amy looked at Maddy inquisitively for a few seconds.

"Are you okay?" she finally asked.

The queue moved forward and Maddy used it as a distraction, turning away from Amy and walking ahead, which prompted her stomach to flutter. They were almost to the front of the line.

"Maddy?" Amy asked again. So she wasn't going to let it go. Yay.

"I'm fine," Maddy said, though she knew it sounded like bullshit.

Tina let out a piercing laugh at something one of the boys said and Maddy saw Amy wince. She was a man without a country right now. And Maddy's mom always said talking things out helped.

"I had a bad experience on a rollercoaster a long time ago," she said.

Maddy had Amy's full attention now. Not only was Maddy opening up to her for the first time since they had met over a year ago, she actually had something interesting to say. Not even Tina could tear her away from this.

"I was on a roller coaster that got stuck upside down," Maddy continued and Amy's eyes (which bore a strong resemblance to a basset hound's) widened.

"That must have been so scary!" she exclaimed.

"Yeah, and of course it was at like, the highest point in the ride!"

Maddy didn't know if this part was true but it had seemed close enough at the time.

"I kind of freaked out," Maddy said. "And made a vow never to ride one of these stupid things ever again."

"No wonder!" Amy said, her hand instinctively going to her mouth. "Does Tina know?"

"Yeah, she knows," Maddy answered. "She also promised never to tell anyone."

And as far as Maddy knew, she hadn't. Tina even knew that she peed her pants. Realizing this stirred a wave of sadness inside Maddy. The two really had been best friends. And a few months from now, it was likely going to be over for good.

"You can't run, you can't hide, you won't even be able to scream! Just you wait!" the voice over the loudspeaker promised. They were directly below one of the speakers now and the voice was so loud it actually caused the guardrail Maddy was holding to vibrate. Already nervous from her proximity to the ride, the sensation startled her and caused her to jump back.

"The exit's right over there," Amy said, her face full of genuine concern. "If you want to wait for us, that'd be okay."

Maddy smiled at Amy's kindness and somewhat regretted her indifference toward the girl since they had met. She made a mental note to spend more time with her over the summer (as long as she could be torn away from Tina).

The group ahead of them got on the car, which meant they were next. Maddy could hear her heart thundering in her ears, even over the loud people in the queue and the obnoxious heavy metal they played on the ride. It was now or never. The car ahead of them jerked forward and disappeared around the corner. Maddy watched it reappear as it began its slow voyage to the top of the track.

That's going to be the worst part, Maddy thought. Thirty seconds or so of that and then the thing will be moving so fast it'll be over before I know it.

A hand fell on her shoulder and Maddy turned around to see Amy giving her an encouraging smile. Their car came into the station, its current occupants slightly dazed and windblown from their adrenaline-filled brush with death. The safety locks clicked free and the riders departed, laughing and recounting their experience.

In two more minutes, that's going to be me, Maddy thought as she stepped forward. She took a deep breath and started toward the car when she was suddenly struck by a dizzying sensation. The world began to swirl around her and she stumbled back, momentarily terrified she was going to fall over. Luckily Amy caught her.

"And she hasn't even had anything to drink!" she heard Tina say to the boys, who laughed like boorish trolls in response.

You bitch, Maddy thought, her anger allowing her to somewhat regain her bearings.

"Go ahead and get on!" the pimple-faced ride operator called out. That did little to boost Maddy's confidence. He didn't look much older than they did and he was in charge of their safety.

Maddy was ready to make her escape when she was shoved from behind. She looked back to see Tina and the boys pushing her and Amy forward with lupine smiles on their faces.

"Hey!" the ride operator called out in a feeble attempt to maintain control but it was too late. Maddy banged her shins on the roller coaster car and almost fell over again. She grabbed the back of the car and managed to balance herself. One of Tina's new friends stepped over her and got into the seat closest to the exit.

"Have a seat!" the boy said, his lupine grin growing even wider.

With other people pushing to get on, Maddy officially had no way out. She sat down next to the obnoxious boy, a cold sweat breaking out on her face and torso. Amy gave her another concerned glance before taking the seat in front of her. Tina flopped down next to Amy and let out an excited whoop as she brought her safety bar down over her head. Her other potential suitor looked disappointed as he took a seat toward the front of the car. Maddy smiled slightly as he sat down next to a fat kid with bad acne. At least the night wasn't a total loss.

Maddy scanned the rest of the car and saw it was completely full and ready to go. She was ready to jump out but the ride operator came by and brought her safety bar down. It clicked in place and he gave it one hard yank to ensure it was locked. He walked past the other riders, pulling on their safety bars before taking his seat at the console and pressing a large glowing green button, which sounded an abrasive alarm.

The car hissed like a sleepy dragon and lurched forward. Maddy closed her eyes and gripped the handles on her safety bar, ready for this entire evening to be over. They still had a lot of rides to go on but Maddy was content to get back on the bus and sleep until everyone else came back.

As the car started its protracted climb to the top of the track, the boy next to her let out a shrill "Whooo", which hurt Maddy's ears. Her eyes remained closed and the wind grew sharp and frigid, making the sweat on her face feel like tiny particles of ice. The obnoxious heavy metal music was being played at full volume now and the other riders let out shrieks of anticipation as the car finally reached the top. There was a microscopic pause before the cars shot out like a bullet and roared down the track like a rabid lion. The screams of the other riders were almost as loud as the awful music and Maddy gripped the handles even tighter. The car spun easily through three short loops and that was when Maddy smelled burning oil. It was a thick, pungent odor and as if to further live up to its name, The Death Rattle began to vibrate in an unstable manner that Maddy did not like at all. The shaking was so bad it caused Maddy's teeth to clack together like a jackhammer.

Oh, God, something is wrong, she thought. Something is wrong, something is wrong, something is wrong.

Cables began to groan and snap below her and Maddy screamed. She had no idea if anybody else knew what was going on. It didn't matter; in a few minutes they'd be splattered across the kiddie rides and concession stands below. Maddy could see the pictures on the web already, the students nothing more than blood and chunks of meat that hung off the cheerful signs and billboards advertising games and popcorn. The smell of burning oil was starting to make Maddy feel nauseous. Forget peeing herself, she'd end up coating herself with the McDonald's she had for dinner before the roller coaster car crashed to the earth in a flaming mess of twisted metal and broken plastic. Just as Maddy expected the entire ride to collapse, it smoothed out and slowed down as they gently re-entered the queue. Maddy couldn't believe it. Had it all been a part of the ride? It was as confusing as it was impressive. Some ride engineer certainly had a sick sense of humor. The cars stopped at the landing and the safety bars clicked free. Maddy took a few seconds to compose herself before standing up and following Amy and Tina to the exit. The two boys had mysteriously vanished but that was no loss. Maybe it meant the three of them would actually have fun together.

As they exited the ride, the voice boomed over the loudspeakers one last time: "The ride of your life and possibly your death…"

"Just you wait!" Maddy bellowed in a very passable impression of the Michael Bumper and Vincent Price hybrid. Tina and Amy turned to her with startled expressions on their faces and laughed.

"Is somebody ready to finally have a good time?" Tina asked as she held out her flask to Maddy.

"Fuck yeah!" Maddy said, grabbing the flask and taking a huge sip. She had no idea what it was but it tasted delicious, stinging her throat and creating a pleasant, warm sensation that flowed all the way to her stomach. Maddy was ready to have a good time. Not only had she conquered her fear; she did it on the scariest ride imaginable.

As they walked past the main entrance of the ride with its massive and looming Grim Reaper pointing its bony finger at the hapless souls foolish enough to enter its domain, Maddy gave it a finger of her own, prompting more laughter from Amy and Tina. She took their hands and began to lead them toward the bumper cars. She suddenly had no shortage of energy and ramming a bunch of assholes she'd never see again after graduation seemed like the perfect way to use it.

They were halfway there when Maddy heard the terrified screams of teenagers and the strained shrieks of twisting metal. The smell of burning oil entered her nostrils again and she turned around to see that the car had flown off the rails of the Death Rattle and was headed directly for her and her friends. It was a surreal sight and Maddy found herself unable to move, transfixed by the oversized purple and black bullet flying at her. The people inside looked insane with fear, their eyes the size of dinner plates and their mouths all locked in a gaping and crooked "O" shape. It was almost funny.

Maddy's final thought before being crushed by the roller coaster car was how much better it would have been to stay at home and watch Frasier re-runs with her parents.

Even with pee in her pants.

There Was a Knock at Her Door

Della Morgan was on her way to the kitchen when she first heard the knocking. She needed a drink (or several) very badly. There was a part of her that knew drinking was irresponsible, especially since she had sole custody of Chelsea and Bryce. Unfortunately it was the only way she knew how to fall asleep as of late.

The first knock jolted her, which wasn't surprising considering the clock on the stove read 12:15. Her first instinct wasn't fear but anger. Chelsea and Bryce had been sleeping soundly for hours. Della wasn't in the mood to go through the bedtime routine again. She intended to enjoy her drink and pass out to reruns of Friends on Netflix. It was a tradition that had suited her well since bringing the kids out to her parents' cabin a month ago.

Della waited and listened. Maybe it was all in her head. Another moment passed and the knocking came again in short, impatient bursts. She definitely had a visitor.

The anger was now giving way to fear. Who could it possibly be? The closest neighbors were a mile away and Della hadn't seen them for weeks. The knocking continued and with two kids asleep and a drink to make, Della decided it was now or never. She crept into the main hallway and made her way to the front door, her bare feet whispering across the hardwood floor. It was at this moment Della expected the wood to creak at a volume that would rival a jet engine starting up but the floor took mercy and stayed silent.

Della reached the front door and looked through the peephole. What was standing at her door wasn't a person at all. It was a shadow. Della tried to peer closer but the figure standing in front of her had no detail at all. She was convinced her eyes were playing tricks on her until the figure raised its arm and knocked on the door again.

The fear that began as a fluttery knot in Della's stomach rose all the way to her throat and brought with it the bitter taste of bile. She tiptoed away from the door, only this time the wood floor was far less merciful. The creak it produced pierced the comforting shield of silence Della had managed to maintain. The figure knocked in response. It was slower and more drawn out, suggesting they were willing to wait for Della now that she had revealed herself. She knew it was only a matter of time before their patience ran out and they made their way inside. Della ran down the hallway and entered her bedroom.

She went for her phone, which was charging on the nightstand. Or so she thought. It's where she had placed it earlier. Why wasn't it here now? As she walked around the room to trying to find it, she kicked something that skittered across the floor. It was her phone.

Curious, Della bent down to pick it up and a fresh wave of terror gripped her chest. Someone (or something) had smashed the screen. She tried turning the phone on but it was dead. Della was holding an overpriced paperweight.

She knelt down to check the router but the blinking red light confirmed she had no Internet, either.

As if confirming their role in these terrible deeds, the figure knocked again at a faster rhythm.

"Just open up, bitch," the knocks seemed to say. "It's getting cold out here."

Della left her bedroom. She poked her head in Chelsea and Bryce's rooms and found they were still asleep. Grateful for this small miracle, Della crept out back into the hallway to figure out her next move when a realization hit her. The landline. God bless old people. Regardless of how fast technology moved there were some things old people would never part ways with and a landline was one of them. Feeling profoundly grateful for this archaic fluke, Della found herself running to the kitchen, where a puke green phone waited on the wall. Della remembered growing up and expressing disdain for the ugly color but her father always smiled in response and said it helped maintain the cabin's outdoors-themed feng shui.

Della decided the phone could be the color of shit (or even made of it) as long as it allowed her to call for help. Her relief was short-lived as she grabbed the phone off its cradle and placed it to her ear. There was nothing. Della pressed the receiver down a few times but it was no use. She had no way of communicating with the outside world.

The figure waiting outside her cabin knocked again in acknowledgment of Della's progressively hopeless situation. It knew she wasn't going anywhere. Her cobalt blue BMW station wagon sat a good fifty feet away from the cabin. Given her present circumstances, it may as well have been a mile.

As Della contemplated her next move, a blast of static interrupted her, causing her to cry out. It was her father's old radio. She walked across the kitchen to investigate it and as she got closer, the radio squealed and let out staccato bursts of more static. When she reached it, the abrasive noise gave way to a voice that chilled her blood.

"Della," the radio hissed at her. "Open the door."

A dumbfounded Della could only gawk at it.

"Della," it hissed again. "We're coming in!"

She swatted at the off switch and breathed a sigh of relief when the radio went silent. The knocking persisted but Della knew the danger was inside now as well as outside. Somebody had gotten inside the cabin. She racked her brain trying to think of when that would have been. She usually took Chelsea and Bryce for a walk after dinner but had that happened tonight? Della honestly couldn't remember.

She did her best to relax and think of a game plan when the TV switched on in her bedroom. It startled her and the understanding that she wasn't alone was far more frightening than whoever (or whatever) lurked outside. She grabbed a knife off the counter and worked her way back to her bedroom.

When she entered, she saw the television was displaying the start-up screen for Netflix. As she walked over to shut it off, the screen switched to the view through her peephole, where the mysterious figure looked distorted but still imposing. To Della's horror, the figure stepped away from the door and went toward her bedroom. The television shut off and she could hear the rustling of plastic, followed by the crunching of leaves and gravel as the figure worked its way toward her. It stopped right outside her window. She held her breath as a cold drop of sweat ran down her back.

The figure remained silent and Della found the tension unbearable. She almost preferred the knocking. At least that was consistent. Della's stomach and chest began to tighten and just as she was about to call out, the television switched back on, enveloping Della in a monochromatic glow. When she looked over at it, she saw the view was now of her, staring awkwardly at the television screen. Della looked across the room and through her peripheral vision; she caught her onscreen doppelganger doing the same thing. Della tiptoed across the room and stopped at the wall, where a fist-sized hole was cut cleanly into the wood. Della couldn't believe it. How had that gotten there and when? Della looked back at the television screen. The image confirmed she was at the right spot. She bent down to peer inside and saw only black in front of her. As Della backed away to leave the room, an eye suddenly appeared in the hole and stared back at her.

Della screamed. The pupil looking at her was a deep, vicious red. There was no way it could be human. Whatever it was, it was too hideous to look at. Della turned away and looked back at the television screen, which immediately shut off.

She heard footsteps move away from her window and the knocking at the front door resumed. Della ran out of her bedroom and checked on Chelsea and Bryce again. The two were still asleep. Not even Della's scream had stirred them. She would likely need to wake them before long but for the moment, she was grateful they were being spared this terrifying ordeal.

Della went back to the front door and looked through the peephole where the shadowy figure waited.

"You should know I have a gun," she warned. "And I'm not afraid to use it."

She knocked the on the door with the handle of the knife for effect.

It worked. She heard the figure walk away and when she looked through the peephole, she saw it was gone.

Relieved, Della went into the kitchen and prepared herself a vodka tonic. She took it into the hallway and leaned against the wall between Chelsea and Bryce's rooms. She slid down to the floor and set the knife next to her, taking a big sip of her drink. It tasted like heaven and Della could feel some of her fear and anxiety melting away. Not even her meds had that effect anymore.

She intended to stay here all night. She would be close to the children if the figure decided to come back. And as for the thing in the wall…

Della stopped and shuddered at the thought of the inhuman eye that had stared back at her when she peered through the hole in her wall. Even if the inside of the cabin was compromised, it was still safer than going outside. She at least had some form of control in here.

She poked her head in both kids' rooms and saw they remained unmoved. What was she going to tell them when they woke up? And where would they go? There was the apartment in the city but Della knew that meant seeing Justin and even after the divorce had been finalized six months ago, she still wasn't ready to see his smug, doughy face.

She went back to her days as a mousy undergrad, cutting herself and spending far too much time on the web reading Buffy the Vampire Slayer fan fiction.

Friends weren't common and boys were mostly non-existent, at least until she met Justin Morgan. His attraction to her seemed inexplicable, though not due to looks. Justin wasn't especially handsome but he was cute and Della was immediately smitten with his dimples. Though Della didn't have much going for her in those days, she had her striking green eyes. The rare attention she got from boys stemmed mostly from her eyes and Justin was no exception. Despite her withdrawn nature and general aversion to people, Justin pressed her for a date and after asking her three times, she finally relented. His insistence didn't make sense then and it definitely didn't make sense now. While Della's family was well off, Justin came from what her father called "stratosphere wealth". He was destined to marry other stratosphere wealth and her name would likely be Blair or Miranda. However, Justin decided to fight fate and stick with Della. They became engaged that next year. At the time, Della thought happiness was a distinct possibility. She had mostly stopped cutting herself and she even considered giving up her meds but her parents and Justin insisted she continued to take them. Della was fine with that. If things were going to get better, sticking with her meds seemed more than fair.

They married three months after graduation and Justin took a position at his father's investment firm. The money flowed freely and though Justin didn't like his job, things were okay. It wasn't the happiness Della had hoped for but it was a step in the right direction.

Things stayed okay through the births of Chelsea and Bryce but something went sour about two years ago. Della didn't exactly know what it was but they grew short with each other, often arguing over trivial matters like the reality shows Della recorded on the DVR, as well as Justin's increasingly long work days.

As the arguments grew more intense, Della found herself drinking frequently, as well as cutting herself on a more routine basis. Justin's formerly warm smile had given way to a petulant sneer and worse yet, he began to direct his anger at the children.

He gained weight and his lush, blonde hair receded into thin fuzz that he refused to shave. The anger and bad vibes came to a head one night when Della was on her second bottle of wine. Justin had tried to get her to stop but she refused. After that...

Della stopped and rubbed her wrist. It still hadn't healed properly.

The following day, she had taken the kids and left him. Justin made no attempt to stop her and within two months, the divorced was finalized. Della and the kids stayed in New York, living well off of the alimony and child support Justin provided but it didn't take long for Della

to grow weary of the busy city as a single mother. They only reason they

lived in New York in the first place was because Justin's job required it.

Della was a small town girl at heart and when she asked her parents to use

the cabin for the summer until she could find a place upstate, they happily

agreed. Della knew her parents worried about her. They always had, even

after she married Justin.

If only they could see me now, she thought as she finished her

drink. The intruders inside and outside her home had allowed her peace as

she took this bitter trip down memory lane. She supposed that warranted

another drink. Her head was already starting to swim from the first one.

She picked up the knife and went back into the kitchen.

The gnawing in the walls began as she was pouring the tonic

water into the glass. She set the bottle down and reached for the knife.

The gnawing was starting to sound harried and desperate. That red-eyed

thing in the wall wanted out.

With the knife in hand, she entered her bedroom again, half

expecting the television to turn on but it stayed off. Just in case, Della

bent down and yanked the power cord out before working her way to the

hole in her wall.

The gnawing continued. It had sounded like it was in the hallway before but it seemed to sense Della's presence, as it got louder and closer to the hole as she approached it. With the business end of the knife pointed at the wall, Della bent down to look in the hole. It wasn't a red eye that greeted her this time; it was a row of crooked brown fangs. They bit down on the edge of the hole and began to chew, leaving ragged gashes in the wood.

Della cried out and jumped back but the biting continued unabated. It finally subsided and a mangled, gangrenous claw with a ragged nail on the end poked through and started scratching at the wood, leaving even deeper gashes.

An odor accompanied whatever was behind the wall. It invaded Della's nostrils, triggering her gag reflex. It smelled like a skunk had died in an old outhouse. The scratching continued and Della lunged forward with the knife. She jammed it into the claw, causing dark, viscous blood to squirt out. The owner of the claw let out an unearthly squeal and pulled itself free of the knife, leaving a ragged streak of blood on the wood.

The creature retreated but the noxious odor still hung thickly in the air. Unable to stomach it anymore, Della ran into the bathroom, where her feet sloshed through cold water. Her toilet had backed up and was spilling water on the floor. Della didn't understand this. She had just used the bathroom. It was where she was coming from when she first heard the knocking. The toilet worked fine then. However, the creature's foul odor was still trapped in her nose. Unable to hold it in any longer, Della ran to the sink and vomited. It was mostly her vodka tonic but she also saw the remnants of her dinner. Della wasn't much of a cook. It stood to reason that the food looked better now than when it had gone down. Feeling exhausted but also somewhat relieved, Della wiped her mouth off with a hand towel and went back into the hallway. She left the toilet alone. At this point, she was too tired and afraid to wonder what was causing it to back up in the fist place.

As soon as Della stepped out of the bathroom, the knocking resumed at the front door. It was a pounding this time as if the shadowy figure did not approve of Della's treatment of its friend inside the wall.

With the bloodstained knife ready, Della went to the front door and looked outside. The shadowy figure had resumed its place. It gave the door three more drawn-out knocks.

"What the fuck do you want?" she hollered through the door.

The knocking came again, coupled with the gnawing of the intruder in the walls.

"Go away!" she called through the door. "I told you I have a gun, remember?"

She hit the door several times with the handle of the knife, causing flecks of dried blood to fly off the blade.

The gnawing in the walls grew louder.

"And you!" she said to the creature. "I stabbed you once! Do you think I'd hesitate to do it again?"

The wall groaned and pulsated in response and Della stepped back with the knife pointed out.

Let it come through the wall, she thought. I'd take care of it and that would mean one down, one to go!

That was when she heard footsteps moving around outside. The shadowy figure was on the go again. Della looked back at the wall, which had ceased all sound and movement. The creature was at rest, at least for now. As she went into the living room to investigate the shadowy figure's latest move, the pounding resumed. Della stopped halfway between the front hallway and the living room. The pounding at the front door continued, as did the footsteps.

There were two of them outside.

Or at least two, Della thought.

She listened as the figure moved toward the side of the house. She tried to keep track of where it was going but the gnawing started up again in her bedroom. Tears spilled down her cheeks. She was helpless against the madness converging on her. She thought back to when this cabin was a simple and inviting place. Della didn't have many positive memories from her childhood but the cabin was a place for her to escape from the bullying and hatred she received at school on a near-daily basis. A place where she could read on the patio without kids walking by and mocking her for her oversized glasses and buck teeth (both of which were fixed by the time she reached high school, not that it made much difference).

The cabin made sense. It was the one constant in her life and now forces were conspiring to take that away from her, too. On top of the all the other injustices she faced, this one was the worst.

Della decided it was time to take it back.

Her first step was to gently scoop up Bryce and put him in Chelsea's bed. She didn't know what was going to happen but she knew it would be safer if both children were together. Once that was done, her next step was to rid her walls of Rattykins. It was the name of her favorite stuffed toy as a child and reducing the strange and vicious creature in her walls to an innocent piece of fluff was comforting to her. She went to the recycling bin and gathered up all the empty two-liter soda bottles. When she was living in New York, the other mothers frowned on her for giving Chelsea and Bryce soda but Della had drunk plenty of it growing up and she turned out fine (more or less).

Despite the fact there were at least two figures circling the cabin, Della put all her concentration into ridding herself of Rattykins, who was back to chewing his way through the wall. Della loaded up the soda bottles with strips of napkins and paper towels. Once they were sufficiently filled, she grabbed a pack of matches and went inside her bedroom with the bottles.

The shadowy figures seemed to sense what she was doing, as the pounding was growing faster and more impatient with each passing minute. She went to the hole that was still streaked with Rattykins' blood. She lit a match and dropped it into one of the soda bottles.

The strips of napkin and paper towel lit up and once there was enough smoke built up inside, Della stuck the mouth of the bottle to the hole and began squeezing the smoke into the wall. Rattykins was chewing somewhere near the living room but he stopped as soon as Della started the filling the inside of the wall with smoke. She could hear him scurrying his way towards her and Della continued pumping smoke through the hole as fast as she could.

The shadowy figures continued to feverishly knock at her front door but the sound no longer frightened Della. It made her more determined. She needed peace. She deserved peace.

A phlegmatic coughing came from inside the wall as the smoke became too much for Rattykins. He began to claw and chew desperately at the small hole in the wall, sending out small puffs of smoke with each bite.

Della raised the knife and readied herself for his arrival. She had merely injured him before but Rattykins wouldn't be so lucky this time. She moved closer to the wall as Rattykins tried to make his way out. She looked down at the knife and was disturbed by the site of dried red blood covering most of the blade. When did that get there? She had only gotten Rattykins with the tip of the knife and the color of his blood was black.

Before she could give it any more thought, Rattykins splintered through the wall and a wave of smoke blasted out and hit Della in the face, burning her eyes and throat.

Through the smoke, she could see Rattykins' upper torso struggling to get through the wall. He was roughly the size of Bryce, who at three feet tall was about as terrifying as a Chihuahua but Rattykins may as well have been the size of an elephant.

He swiped his misshapen claw at Della, catching the knife and knocking it to the ground. She heard it slide across the floor, probably well out of her reach. She backed away and Rattykins lunged forward again, still caught in the wall but making progress.

Della screamed and fell to the ground, smoke billowing around her. She looked under her bed and saw her red stiletto heels, which she hadn't worn in the better part of a year. They were her date night shoes. In fact, the last person to wear them was Bryce, who had put them on shortly after they had arrived at the cabin. He strutted around as best he could, prompting gales of laughter from Della and Chelsea.

That was the last time I had a good laugh, Della thought as she reached for the shoe. She heard the wood groan and splinter some more as Rattykins continued to work his way out. Della gripped the shoe tightly and stood up. The smoke was still billowing out from the compromised wall but Della could see his ugly red eyes staring at her. She raised the shoe and swung at it Rattykins as hard as she could, planting the heel directly into his left eye.

He let out an ungodly scream as his dark blood splattered all over Della. Rattykins retreated into the wall and Della's shoe hit the ground with a weak thud. The smoke had dissipated and there was only the splintered wall in front of her. Her father would have to call Mr. Lyman, the local handyman, to fix it.

"I wonder if Mr. Lyman's even still alive," Della said aloud as she dropped back to the floor. Her work wasn't done yet but she needed to rest. As if to remind her that rest wasn't an option, the shadowy figure knocked on her door again. Della didn't want to think about where the others were or how many had joined them.

She gathered up her strength and went into the hallway, surprised at how winded she was. Heavy drinking and not exercising had taken its toll on her. If she made it out of this alive, Della decided it was time for a lifestyle change.

She crawled over to Chelsea's bedroom and opened the door and looked inside. Both kids were still out. Della started to shut the door when she heard footsteps approaching from the outside. One of the figures was by her children's window.

"No! Go away!" Della screamed but she didn't hear any footsteps move away. The figure was standing its ground. Enraged, Della went into her bedroom to look for the knife. Her stamina was back in full force. As she looked around the room, the TV switched on again. That was impossible. She had unplugged it.

The glow that bathed the entire room suggested otherwise and the image on screen explained everything. It was Justin. He was standing in a black room staring straight ahead. No, not straight ahead, he was staring at her.

"Is this your idea of a joke, you bastard?" she spat at the screen. "Is this what you want? To scare me to death and endanger your children? What kind of man are you?"

Justin simply stared at her in response. Unable to look at him, Della grabbed the TV and pushed it to the ground, where it shattered in a violent eruption of sparks and broken glass. The knife sat about two feet away from her. Della picked it up and went for the front door, where her uninvited guests continued to knock. Squeezing the knife so hard her hand hurt, Della unlocked the door and gripped the cold metal knob, ready for anything.

She waited for one last knock before swinging the door open. She ran outside at full speed and wasn't greeted by any of the shadowy figures, but with a blinding blast of light instead. Della screamed as numerous hands dragged her to the ground. It was over.

I'm sorry, babies, she thought as hot tears spilled down her cheeks. I tried.

Detective Rob Snyder was his name and although he was fifty-eight, he was not close to retirement. Putting three kids through college had that effect. He was finishing his lunch when he got the phone call. It was grim. Even after thirty years of being a cop, it never ceased to amaze him how much this shit still made his stomach turn. He had seen guys become numb to the gruesome horrors cops are often subjected to but not him. As he started up his Dodge Charger, he yearned for the days where could finally tell everybody he was close to retirement. Days of golf and fishing sounded just fine to him.

Back at the cabin, Della was being subjected to a cacophony of noise and a swarm people she didn't recognize. The shadowy figures were gone, replaced by cops and EMTs. She wanted to tell them about the shadowy figures and Rattykins but she found herself unable to speak. She still didn't understand how it was daylight outside. Her battle couldn't have lasted more than an hour and she remembered it being dark right before she braved the outside. How had all this happened? And where were her children?

It was 1:30 when Rob arrived at the scene. His timing could have been better. Some EMTs were wheeling out two small body bags. Rob felt the turkey bacon club he had eaten for lunch flop around in his stomach. As he watched the body bags get loaded into the meat wagon, he realized he could just as easily be watching his own children getting loaded up. That horrible thought did little to settle his stomach. Gary Pullman, the responding officer, walked up to him.

"All right, let's have it," Rob said.

"Two victims, ages nine and six," Gary responded. "Likely perpetrator is the mother."

"Jesus Christ," Rob said. "Where is she now?"

"Getting checked out by the EMTs," Gary said. "Hasn't said a word since she stumbled out of the house covered in blood and armed with a knife."

"What do we know about her?" Rob asked.

"Della Morgan, age 36, recently divorced," Gary said, flipping through his notes. "Cabin belongs to her parents, they hadn't heard from her in a few days, so they asked a neighbor to check on her. When the neighbor knocked, she claimed she had a gun, so he called us."

Rob looked closer at the cabin.

"What's that shit she has hanging everywhere?"

"She blocked out all the windows and doors with black garbage bags," Gary replied.

"Why?" Rob asked, trying to wrap his head around this scene. He had seen some crazy shit but a woman murdering her children and blocking her doors and windows with garbage bags was a new one for him.

"Turns out Ms. Morgan is bipolar. Probably off her meds," Gary answered.

"What the fuck was she doing out her alone with two kids?"

"The husband was supposedly abusive. Fractured her wrist a few months back."

"Hells fucking bells," Rob said. It wasn't much of a response but it was the only one he could muster.

Della sat in the back of the police car trying to make sense of everything that had happened. The detective she talked to was a very nice man named Rich or Rob. He listened (unlike Justin) as she told him about the figures knocking on the door, the cameras planted around her house, the radio, the television, and of course Rattykins. His kind eyes never wavered as she told him all this and more than anything; she wanted to warn him about Rattykins. He was still in the cabin somewhere but the most frustrating part was that Rich or Rob wouldn't give her a straight answer about her children. They had to be safe. She kept them locked in the bedroom, away from the shadowy figures and Rattykins. She had about killed herself trying to ensure their safety, which is something Justin would never do. Still, as she sat in the car, she was getting slivers of memories of what happened before the attack. It was a normal evening. She had fed Chelsea and Bryce dinner. They watched a little television and then it was bedtime. There were protests, mainly from Bryce, but she had won out in the end. She always did.

Didn't she?

Another memory suddenly came to her. In this one, the kids were crying and she was screaming. Why was she screaming?

Next she remembered putting black garbage bags over all the windows and doors. And had she smashed her own phone? Jesus.

Now she remembered getting the knife to protect herself from the intruders that had invaded her cabin. But that wasn't the first time she had used that knife, was it? She suddenly saw the sharp blade piercing pajamas and pale flesh. There was blood. What had she--

Oh, God.

Rob and Gary watched as the squad car with Della pulled away. As it drove up the road, they saw her lash out and start screaming. One of the officers turned around and did his best to calm her down but it was no use. She was hysterical.

"Shit," Gary said, his tone solemn. "I think what she did finally came back to her."

"Looks like it," Rob said, spitting on the ground. His mouth suddenly tasted bitter.

"Did any of that shit make sense? Cameras around the cabin, that creature in the walls?" Gary asked.

"Not a word. But like you said, she's probably off her meds, so that's to be expected," Rob replied. "Let's go inside and check it out."

At first glance, the inside looked neat and homey (save for the garbage bags hanging on the windows and in front of the doors) but the dense odors of sweat, blood, and vomit emanated through the cabin.

"Jesus," Gary said, covering his nose.

"If you like that, you're going to love the bedroom," a patrolman passing by called out to them.

Rob and Gary went down the hall but stopped at the bathroom. The floor was soaking wet and a grim-faced rookie had a gloved hand in the toilet while his older partner looked on.

"What's going on?" Rob asked them.

"Looks like she shoved a towel in there or something," the older officer said.

The rookie finally succeeded in loosening whatever was clogging the toilet. He pulled out a wadded up washcloth and opened it up, revealing three orange pill bottles. They looked full.

"I guess that's one way to ensure you'll stay off your meds," Gary said.

Rob stared at the pill bottles before motioning for Gary to follow him into the bedroom.

When they entered, they found the room in a state of chaos. While Rob could still smell sweat and blood, there was also a distinct smoky odor. There was a shattered television on the ground and blackened soda bottles were scattered around the room. Strangest yet, part of the wall had been ripped away.

"I guess that's where she fought Rattycakes," Gary suggested.

"Rattykins," Rob said. It was a trivial mistake but he still felt the need to correct it.

Gary took another look around the room and whistled.

"This was one hell of a manic state," he said. "Isn't that what they call it?"

"Yeah," Rob answered. His concentration was on the ripped wall, which had a small hole in it about the size of a fist. Rob snapped on a pair of gloves and ran his finger along the edge of the hole. It was jagged and splintered, with splatters of dark blood on it. He could almost buy something had chewed through this wall. Almost.

As Rob continued to examine the wall and the space behind it, a voice called out from the front hallway.

"Detective!"

"What is it?" Rob yelled.

"The husband's here!"

"Oh, shit!" Rob said, casting a frustrated glance at Gary. "Is the shrink here yet?"

"Still en route!" the officer called back.

Rob and Gary went outside to find a balding, paunchy man trying to push his way through the officers holding him back. His eyes were wet and desperate.

"Please let me through! That's my family in there!" he screamed at them.

Rob walked up to the man.

"Mr. Morgan, I'm Detective Snyder."

"Are my children..." Justin sputtered at him, unable to finish.

Rob didn't answer him but it didn't matter. His eyes told Justin everything and he immediately collapsed, letting out thick, hoarse sobs.

Rob looked back at the cabin.

Seven days until retirement, he thought. Wasn't that the cliché in movies and TV shows?

Rob spit on the ground again. He never wanted anything so badly in his entire life.

Della couldn't decide how she felt about her new home. The assortment of pills she was on kept her from feeling much of anything and that was all right by her. She spent most of her days staring out the window at the institution's sparse back yard. Mostly she just saw leaves blowing across the patchy grass. One time she had seen a squirrel run by. It surfaced memories of Bryce attempting to chase them through Central Park but she was quick to push that one away. The only time she felt anything was when she felt pain. And the only time she felt pain was when she thought of her children.

Della had relatively peaceful nights for the first two weeks. Then the knocking at her door started. A few nights later, a familiar and unmistakable chewing sound came from within the walls. Rattykins was back and that made sense. He owed her one.

On most nights, Della was able to sleep through it. Sleep was what Della craved most these days. She had group therapy sessions three days a week and one-on-one sessions with a nice doctor on the other days. She didn't say much during these sessions and she certainly didn't mention the knocking and Rattykins. What good would that do? As it was, there was part of her that wanted to see Rattykins. Would seeing him help her make sense of that terrible day? Della doubted it but she supposed it was worth a shot.

After a month of the knocking and Rattykins' chewing, he finally made his out of the wall and over to Della's bed. Silver moonlight shined through her barred windows. She finally had a clear look at him. Leathery skin had formed over his left eye but otherwise; he looked rather gentle.

As he stood over her, darkness began to consume her. In her final moments, she realized naming Rattykins after her favorite stuffed toy was no accident. He looked just like it (although he was much bigger of course) and that brought her back to memories of her childhood. She thought of the summers she had spent at the cabin and the simple but perfect pleasures she found there. Days where he father took her swimming in the lake. When they came back, dripping wet and laughing, her mother always had a freshly baked pie waiting for them. Della also remembered evenings on the back patio, where the only sounds were the content chirping of crickets and the gentle creaking of the old rocking chair she loved to sit in. As Della fell further into darkness, there wasn't any fear or guilt. There was just gratitude for being able to experience those moments of joy one last time.

And then she was gone.

It was business as usual for Mitch Harkins. As he made his way around the institution, he thought about the other jobs he had held and decided this one wasn't bad at all. He had worked at an ice cream plant, spent some time doing construction, and had even been a chef for a brief period but none of those jobs had suited him. He had quit most of them (quit, fired, same difference) but he decided he could probably do the orderly thing for at least a few years. Sure, the nuts got riled up on occasion but restraining them wasn't too difficult (and it was kind of fun).

The most action the place had seen lately was the death of the lady who murdered her children. They found her face down and suffocated in her bed. A death like that might seem strange to people outside this place but Mitch had once seen a guy rip his own balls off with his bare hands. Suffocating to death in your bed was pretty bland by comparison.

It was a real shame about that woman. Mitch really dug her green eyes and her tits weren't half bad, either. Had she been of sounder mind, Mitch could have pictured the two of them having some fun. And as it was, he did have some fun. Did he knock on her cell door every time he walked past it? Sure. It never got the reaction he hoped for but it still provided a minor thrill.

As Mitch walked past her room tonight, he knocked on it again for old times' sake. It was still empty and probably would be for the foreseeable future. On this particular night, however, something made Mitch stop. It was a faint sound. Mitch could have been mistaken but it almost sounded like chewing. Hadn't the crazy bitch said something about a giant creature chewing through her walls when they had arrested her?

Mitch leaned in and pressed his ear against the wall. There was a moment of silence and then he heard it again. Something was chewing inside the wall and it sounded big. Mitch thought back to the shithole apartment he grew up in. There were rats in those walls, so he knew the sounds they made but there was something different about this. The chewing continued and it sounded like it was moving even closer to him. Mitch quickly shied away from the wall and walked away at a much brisker pace.

As he exited the wing, he decided he'd keep it to himself and avoid this part of the hospital from now on. Mitch didn't want to seem crazy.

There was already more than enough of that going around.

Weekend at Nana's

The trip to Nana's was mostly unremarkable. The boy's parents were talking about their weekend trip to some place called wine country. They traveled frequently and usually brought the boy along but they had decided this particular destination wasn't for kids. That was all right with him. Wine country sounded boring and he hadn't been to Nana's in a long time.

His eyelids grew heavy as his parents continued to drone on about wine country and how they'd be drinking reds and whites all weekend. Drinking colors sounded somewhat intriguing but little else about their trip did. Just as he was about to fall asleep, his father called out to him.

"Take a look at that sky!"

The boy opened his eyes and glanced out the window. The sky was gray and gloomy looking. It had been that way when they had left the house. His mother was predicting rain but the air remained still and the ground stayed dry. The boy didn't understand why his father had woken him up until he saw the unusual formation of thick clouds in the distance. Stranger yet, there was a vivid orange light pulsing inside them.

"It's beautiful!" his mother exclaimed.

"What is it, Dad?" the boy asked.

"Good question, pal," his father answered. "Looks like some kind of electrical storm."

"Why is it orange then?"

"I don't know," his father said. "The sun doesn't go down for another half an hour, so maybe it's sunlight reflecting through the clouds."

The boy didn't think that made sense. He wished he could be as impressed as his parents. Something about the glowing orange light made him nervous.

"Let's see what they're saying on the radio," his father said, pressing a button on the steering wheel. The radio came on but there was silence. "Acquiring signal" flashed on the display in bright blue letters.

"Those weather must be causing some kind of interference," his father suggested. "What does your phone say?"

His mother held up her phone and swiped the screen a couple of times.

"No signal," she said, sounding concerned.

"That's okay. It's usually a little dodgy out here in the sticks," his father replied.

"Honey, I haven't had trouble getting a signal out here in five years," his mother said.

"I'm sure it's fine. We're almost at your mother's house, anyway."

Ten minutes later, they pulled into Nana's driveway. The tires crunched on the gravel as his father slowly rolled up to the house. Despite his father's assured claims that nothing was wrong, they watched as the cluster of clouds and orange light expanded, swallowing up most of the sky. The only additional commentary his father offered was a reserved "Isn't that something?"

The boy looked at his mother, who was staring at the strange phenomenon with wide, unblinking eyes. Her hand was pressed against her mouth, turning her knuckles a bloodless white. She was scared, which did little to alleviate the boy's own fears. He looked away from her and concentrated on Nana's house. He wondered what she thought about the weird weather when he saw her standing in her yard staring up at the sky. Her hand was shielding her eyes from the persistent flashes of orange light that were growing stronger as the cloud formation continued to expand. It was almost directly overhead now. His parents were the first to get out of the car, their eyes fixated on the sky. Panic fell over the boy as his parents walked away from the car in a trance. It was like they had forgotten he had existed altogether. Nana hadn't even turned around and acknowledged their presence until they were standing on both sides of her. He saw her turn her head slightly to speak to his mother and that was when his father turned around and realized they had indeed forgotten about him. Relief fell over the boy as the father walked back to the car but he still wasn't sure how comfortable he was going outside. He envisioned a bolt of lightning firing down with enough power to shake the entire earth to its core and instantly fry them until they were nothing more than blackened skeletons. The boy shuddered at that gruesome thought as his father swung the door open and motioned for him to get out.

"Join the party," his father said with a goofy lopsided grin that indicated his mood was one of good humor. It was a grin that usually improved the boy's own mood, no matter how dire it was. Today was different. The boy's stomach was doing queasy lurches as he slowly got out of the car. The air remained still but it had a frigid quality that stung the boy's nose and throat. His father picked him up and carried him over to his mother and Nana.

"Look who's here!" his father announced as his feet whooshed through the overgrown crabgrass. Lawn care was not one of Nana's specialties. She took him out of his father's arms and held him, giving him a big kiss on the forehead. She smelled faintly of peppermint and lavender. The boy noticed old people usually either smelled bad or tried too hard to smell good. Nana didn't have that problem. In fact, Nana didn't seem to have any of the problems that generally afflicted old people.

"Oh, my!" she said. "You're getting so big! I'm having a hard time holding on to you!"

The boy smiled at this. He knew she was being silly. Her grip was as strong and confident as his father's and he had played football in college. It was funny to think about, especially considering Nana was a foot shorter than his dad and at least a hundred pounds lighter. As she talked to the boy and asked him about school and everything going on his life, his fear and trepidation about the strange clouds and lights slowly dissipated. She carried him over to the car to get his bag and then brought him to her front door. She called out to his parents to come inside but they didn't seem to hear her; their eyes were still glued to the sky. Nana rolled her eyes at them and brought the boy into the house.

Nana was fixing hot chocolate when his parents finally came inside, his mother furiously swiping at her phone.

"Is your little toy acting up?" Nana asked.

The boy wanted to laugh but he knew his mother didn't appreciate Nana's sarcasm.

"I don't like the look of that sky and I still don't have a signal!" his mother exclaimed.

"Those newfangled electronics never work right out here," Nana said, pouring the boy's hot chocolate into a mug with a smiling Snoopy on the side of it. She brought it over to him and he immediately took a sip. It tasted wonderful. Nana knew how to make it at just the right temperature. Not even his mother had that skill.

"I told her the same thing," his father said with a helpless shrug.

"And like I told you, I haven't had a problem getting a signal out here in years," his mother shot back. "Cell towers are everywhere now."

"Sit down and have some hot chocolate," Nana told her. "You'll feel better."

His mother didn't sit down but she at least put away her phone.

"You know, Mom, if you had the Internet we could just check that and then I wouldn't have to worry about my phone not having a signal," she told Nana.

"I've told you before; I've survived sixty-eight years without that nonsense," Nana responded. "And I'm doing just fine."

"Yes, but…" his mother began but she was interrupted by a sudden roar of rain and wind. It was so strong the boy feared Nana's house would be blown clean away. It was built right after Nana and Grandpa were married, meaning it was really old. And just because Nana was strong didn't mean her house was.

The rain that pelted the windows had a milky quality that left whitish streaks as it ran down the glass in frantic zigzags. The wind continued to roar as jagged bolts of lightning struck the earth with a ground-shaking ferocity. The lights in Nana's house flickered and the house gave a series of strained groans as the vicious storm pushed the aging domicile to its limits. His mother let out a frightened yelp and his father had a look of grim intensity on his face. The boy shook until Nana held his hand. Her grip was steady and unwavering. She was the only one not fazed by the apocalypse that was unfolding outside. A few moments later, the storm was over as quickly as it began. The rain ceased and the wind died down to a gentle breeze. The boy's father went over to the picture window in Nana's living room and looked out.

"Take a look at the sky now," he called out.

Nana and the boy joined him at the window and saw the strange cloud formations and orange light were already retreating over the horizon. In their place was a clear night sky that was filled with vivid, twinkling stars. The sky suddenly looked clean to the boy. He never imagined he'd refer to it in such a way but he could think of no other way to put it. The sky simply looked cleaner than it had earlier that day. Most importantly, it looked safer.

"We're all clear, honey," his father said, offering the boy's mother his goofy grin. "Come and take a look."

"I'll take your word for it," she said, looking down at her phone. Even from across the room, the boy could see she was on her Facebook page. Order had been restored.

His parents headed home not long after that. His mother left Nana with a long list of phone numbers. She had written down every place in wine country they'd be stopping at. Nana made a joke about how much they'd be drinking but only the boy's father laughed. His mother muttered about Nana not having the Internet or a cell phone again but Nana just ignored her. Once that minor bit of unpleasantness had passed, the boy's father gave him a firm hug and his mother kissed him goodbye. Two minutes later, their car was disappearing down the road. The boy watched it go, mostly out of obligation. He loved his parents but he was with Nana now.

He had nothing to worry about.

The boy had another hot chocolate and some Oreos (which Nana always had an endless supply of). After that, they watched Monsters, Inc. for the umpteenth time. Nana had a very limited selection of DVDs but the movies she had never seemed to get old. After the movie ended, she sent the boy to the bathroom to brush his teeth and change into his pajamas. He protested at first but the huge yawn he gave mid-sentence confirmed he wasn't going to win this battle. Nana gave him a playful swat on the bottom and he went into the bathroom to brush the teeth that had been steadily falling out for the last six months. It seemed pointless to him but he supposed leaving clean teeth for the Tooth Fairy was probably the polite thing to do.

He had finished spitting the mint-colored toothpaste into the sink when a string of police cars zoomed past Nana's house with their sirens blaring. The boy ran to the window but the cars were already disappearing down the road. He found it unsettling. Nana hardly ever got any traffic on her road, let alone police cars going full speed with the sirens on. Nana must have sensed his trepidation because there was a soft knock on the door.

"You didn't fall in, did you?"

It was one of Nana's old standbys but the boy smiled in spite of his nervousness. Even if the world were ending, Nana would still find a way to cheer him up. The boy rinsed off his toothbrush and left the bathroom, the police cars already a distant memory.

As Nana put him to bed that night, they talked about what they were going to do the next day. She had a new box of his favorite cereal ready to go for breakfast and after they had eaten, they were going to take a walk through the nearby meadow (as long as it wasn't too muddy). Once they came back from that, she'd let him pick out his favorite fast food restaurant for lunch (his mother loathed fast food restaurants, so this was a rare treat) and then it was off to the toy store to pick out a new action figure. The boy asked her what they were going to have for dinner and she told him spaghetti. That sounded just fine to the boy, even if Nana bought her sauce at the store and didn't make it like his Dad did.

She kissed him on the cheek with her dry lips and the boy closed his eyes, ready for a long night of sleep. The odd occurrences had taken a quite toll on him but he was ready to put that behind him. A perfect Saturday was just hours away.

It was after eleven when the boy was awoken by frantic knocking at Nana's front door. He immediately sat up, his heart racing. Somebody knocking this late at night couldn't be a good sign and given how far out of the way Nana lived, it was definitely unusual. Still, given how the rest of the evening had unfolded, the boy couldn't help but think this was a fairly natural turn of events. He got out of bed and tiptoed to the door and opened it a crack. He saw Nana walking downstairs in her robe. Although it was dark, he could tell she wasn't happy but he also knew she wasn't scared. He listened as she reached the bottom of the stairs and opened the front door. He could hear a man's voice and while the boy couldn't make out what he was saying, he knew the man was frightened. The boy was tempted to jump back into bed and pull the covers over his head. He even thought about hiding in the closet but he knew that was cowardly and he couldn't do that to Nana. He quietly left the room, his feet stepping onto the cold linoleum of the hallway. He walked to the stairwell, catching brief snippets of the conversation.

"...knew you didn't have Internet or cable, thought you should know..."

Nana's response was too quiet to make out and the boy crept down a few more steps to try and hear what she was saying.

"They're evacuatin' the cities! Best to get to one of these safe zones now!" the man continued. "I printed information off the computer for you."

The boy could hear the shuffle of papers as he continued down the stairs.

"You was always real kind to me, so I thought I owed you at least this," the man said.

"Have you been drinking, Rich?" the boy heard Nana ask. She was speaking in the same tone she used on the boy when he was throwing a temper tantrum. Not that he did that anymore. That was baby stuff.

"Yes!" the man bleated. "But it's only cause I'm scared! This is for real!"

The boy reached the bottom of the stairs and poked his head around. The man talking to Nana was red-eyed and wearing a camouflage jacket. He looked desperate.

"Go home and get some sleep, Rich," Nana told him. "We can talk tomorrow."

"I ain't goin' home!" the man said, growing indignant. "I'm gettin' out right now! You need to do the same!"

"Do you want me to give you a ride?" Nana asked him.

The man slammed a grimy fist against Nana's doorway, causing the boy to jump slightly.

"Get out!" he said. "Follow that map and stay alive!"

He gave Nana a quick hug and stumbled out of the house.

"I'll pray for you!" he called back to her.

Nana waved and closed the door. She locked it and looked out the window as the man's rickety pick-up truck started up with a strained growl. It took off down the road jettisoning a cloud of blue smoke as it went. She turned around and noticed the boy standing at the bottom of the stairs.

"Nana?" he asked.

"It's okay, sweetie," Nana said. "That was just my neighbor."

"Was he okay?" the boy asked.

"He was fine," Nana replied, walking over to him and tousling his hair. "He just had a little too much drink. It happens sometimes and…"

A brilliant red light suddenly came out of the sky and vaporized the man's truck just up the road from Nana's house. The force of the blast blew out the windows as a wave of blistering hot air filled the room. Nana grabbed the boy and quickly guided him into the downstairs bathroom, where she slammed the door behind them.

"What's going on, Nana?" the boy shrieked.

"I don't know, my angel," Nana said. "Are you okay?"

The boy was suddenly too panic-stricken to respond. It had been such a strange day and things were starting to make less and less sense. The world that had seemed so warm and safe suddenly seemed angry and unpredictable.

Nana saw how scared he was and looked him over to make sure he wasn't hurt. Outside the door, there was only silence. She bent down so she was eye-level with the boy.

"I want you to stay right here. I'm going to open the door and see if it's safe to go outside. Do you understand?"

The boy nodded and Nana cautiously opened the bathroom door. Her house was in shambles. The formerly cozy living room was strewn with shards of glass and chunks of jagged wood. The furniture had been torched and the walls that were immaculate and white just minutes ago were now black. The few remaining pictures hanging were burnt beyond recognition. Nana walked over to the blown-out picture window with bits of broken glass crunching under her slippered feet. She looked around but found only the calm of her country surroundings. The boy took a step out of the bathroom and Nana immediately spun around.

"Stay back!" she commanded. "There's glass everywhere!"

"Is everything okay, Nana?" the boy asked.

"Just stay there," she said. "I need to call the police."

Nana walked over to her phone and picked it up to dial but there was dead air. She pressed the receiver down several times but it was useless. She hung up and turned to face the boy.

"Go upstairs and get dressed," she told him. "We're leaving."

"Where are we going?"

"To the Sheriff's station," Nana said. "Now hurry up!"

The boy went up the stairs, mindful of the broken glass that was spread all over Nana's floor. He entered his bedroom and pulled his clothes on in the dark. It was hard to see but he was afraid to turn the lights on. As much as the boy loved coming to Nana's house, he wanted to leave. Going to a place where there were lots of people with guns suddenly seemed like a good idea.

The boy was tying his shoes when he heard something moving around in the grass below his window. He badly wanted to call for Nana but he knew staying quiet was the best course of action at that particular moment. Whatever it was continued to walk around right under his window. The boy couldn't tell if it was a man or an animal. It was moving like it either didn't know where it was or it was trying to stay quiet. Whatever it was, the boy doubted it was up to anything good. He stood up and worked his way over to the window, terrified of what he might find but also curious. If he could find out what it was, maybe Nana would know what to do.

As the boy got closer to the window, the floor creaked and the creature below stopped moving. It had heard him. The boy's heart was pulsing in his ears and throat as he finally reached the window. He looked down and saw a pair of softball-sized yellow eyes staring up at him. The boy backed away from the window and ran out of the room as fast as he could.

"Nana! Nana!" he screamed as he ran downstairs. The creature already knew he was there, so why bother hiding? He finally reached the bottom of the stairs but Nana was nowhere to be found. Had the horrible creature taken her? Where was she?

"Nana!" he screamed again but she didn't respond. The boy heard the creature moving through the grass again; only its steps sounded much faster and louder now. It was coming inside! The boy knew he was helpless against whatever it was. He was small for his age and had nothing to defend himself with. He wouldn't last long. The footsteps were close now; it would only be a matter of seconds before he saw those horrible yellow eyes staring at him. The footsteps grew even louder and they were now accompanied by a guttural snarl. The boy wanted to run but he didn't where he would go. Just as he saw the outline of something huge moving past the window, someone grabbed him from behind and pulled him out of sight. The boy nearly screamed but was immediately shushed by the familiar and soothing voice of Nana.

"It's just me!" she whispered to him. "This way."

The boy followed Nana through the kitchen and into the basement, where Nana closed and bolted the door. They went down the stairs quietly and listened as the creature with the yellow eyes walked around Nana's house.

"What is that thing, Nana?" the boy whispered.

Nana shushed him again.

The creature paused directly above them before moving around again. Its immense weight caused the floor to groan and dip and the boy once again wondered how well Nana's house could withstand all this chaos. Nana held him close as the creature went into the kitchen, putting it right next to the basement door. The boy wondered if it knew how doors worked or if it could smell them or something equally terrifying.

The creature began to scratch at the door, prompting a nervous gasp from the boy. Nana placed her hand over his mouth as the scratching suddenly stopped. Hot tears squirted out of the boy's eyes as he waited for it to break the door down so it could hurt him and Nana.

And if that did happen, it would be his fault. He had given away their hiding place. Fortunately, the creature lost interest in the door and moved on. They listened as it went back out the front window. Nana walked over to an ancient toolbox that sat on an equally ancient table. She dug around in it before removing a large wrench. The boy figured it belong to his Grandpa but he knew Nana was more than capable of using it, whether it was to fix a pipe or knock some sense into a creature that was foolish enough to cross her path.

Nana gripped the wrench tightly and climbed the stairs. She reached the door and took a deep breath before opening it. Although it looked like they were alone again, Nana motioned for the boy to wait as she went around and checked the rest of the house. He listened as her soft footsteps moved around the living room, causing the occasional floorboard to creak. After a minute, she came back and gave the boy thumbs up. He quickly joined her at the top of the stairs, somewhat relieved but also aware they probably weren't out of danger yet.

"We're getting in the car," Nana said. "And we're going to get help."

The boy remembered what happened to the man's truck and shook his head at Nana.

"We can't do that!" he cried. "They'll blow us up!"

"I know you're scared, my angel, but we can't stay here. It's not safe. We'll make sure the coast is clear and don't forget, I'm a fast driver!"

She said this last part with a wink but the boy was still scared.

"What about my mom and dad?" he asked. "Are they okay?"

It was unfair to ask Nana this but he needed some kind of assurance and she was the best possible person possible for that.

"Of course they are," she said with a confident smile. "Your mom and dad are strong, just like you and me. It runs in the family."

That gave the boy a little peace because Nana was right, they were strong. His dad had pushed a huge couch into their house all by himself last summer. His mom had complained he was going to throw out his back but he had responded with his usual lopsided grin and finished getting it into the house like it was nothing. If one of those creatures had made the mistake of trying to get inside his parents' house, his dad would take care of it. His mom, too, if need be.

"I just have to get one thing," Nana whispered. She walked over to the front closet and opened it. Leaning against the wall with a bunch of old umbrellas was his Grandpa's shotgun. Nana picked it up and grabbed a small box of extra shells before returning to the boy.

"And to think your mom wanted me to get rid of this," she said with a smirk.

They reached the front door and Nana cautiously looked around outside but there was no sign of the creatures. She took the boy's hand and led him toward her car that was parked at the end of the driveway. It used to belong to the boy's uncle but he gave it to Nana after her old car had broken down the previous year. It was pretty nice, though not as the nice as the car his dad drove to work. The boy doubted that sort of thing really mattered to Nana, so he didn't let it bother him, either. As he was quickly learning, there were much more important things going on than what car you drove.

"So why do you still have that gun?" he asked Nana.

"Target practice," she said. "It's a great stress reliever."

"Stress reliever?"

"Sometimes you just need to…"

Before she could finish, another red light shot out of the sky and vaporized Nana's house into a cloud of ash and black smoke. The boy and Nana were thrown to the ground like wads of tissue paper. The boy struggled to breathe and his entire body felt like it was on fire. He was finally able to catch his breath and crawl over to Nana. To his horror, she wasn't moving.

"Nana!" the boy screamed, shaking her. "Nana!"

Suddenly, a bright beam of blue light was shining down on both of them. The boy looked up and saw a triangular-shaped craft hovering above them. It began to emit a strange humming sound and the boy immediately became dizzy and nauseous. He collapsed next to Nana as the world spun around him at an impossibly fast rate. Unable to deal with this disorienting sight, the boy closed his eyes. He knew it was going to be over soon.

He just prayed his parents were okay.

The boy awoke later to find himself in a place he didn't recognize. Is this where the attackers had taken him? It smelled bad and looked like it hadn't been inhabited in years.

"Nana?" the boy called out, his voice high and shaky.

"Right here, my angel."

He looked over and saw Nana standing in front of a grimy window. She was holding the shotgun with the barrel pointed at the ceiling.

"Where are we?" the boy asked, relaxing a little. Even if he didn't know where he was, at least Nana was here.

Nana rested the shotgun against the wall and sat down next to him, pressing her warm hand against his forehead.

"How are you feeling?" she whispered, ignoring his question.

"Still a little sick," he answered. "What happened?"

Nana looked out the window briefly and turned to the boy and shook her head.

"I honestly don't know, my angel. When I came to, I saw something flying around above us and you looked so sick. You scared me!"

"I keep hearing this weird sound and then I felt dizzy!" the boy said. "Didn't you hear it?"

"I did when I first woke up," Nana replied. "But then I remove these and it was no longer a problem."

Nana reached into her ears and removed a pill-shaped object from each one. It took the boy a moment to realize they were her hearing aids.

"If they are aliens, they aren't very smart," she said with a cocky grin.

The boy laughed and gave her a big hug before taking another look around at the strange place they were in.

"So what is this place?" he asked.

"Milton Ambrose's gambling shack," Nana answered as if it were the most obvious thing in the world.

"Who's that?" the boy asked.

"Milton Ambrose was my old neighbor. He liked to play cards but his wife Abby didn't approve of it. She was very religious. So he built this in the woods behind his house and hosted card games."

"That couldn't have been very much fun," the boy said. "This place looks dirty."

"Milton died about fifteen years ago and everybody stopped using it after that," Nana replied. "It was much nicer then."

"Did his wife not know about it?"

"She knew," Nana said. "But she let it go. As long as he wasn't bringing sin into their house, she was okay with it."

"Did you ever play cards?"

"It was boys only," Nana answered. "So I wasn't invited. I also think they were afraid of losing to me."

The boy imagined that was probably true but unfortunately, they had more pressing matters to deal with.

"Your house is gone," the boy said, the memory of its destruction still playing vividly in his head.

A look of sadness fell over Nana's face and she didn't reply right away.

"I'm just grateful I was able to get you out of there and someplace safe," she finally finished.

The boy didn't let on but he saw Nana wipe a tear away.

"Can we find Mom and Dad now?" the boy asked.

"Not until daylight. We'll have to find a car," Nana answered.

"What about your car?"

"I'm not sure it survived the attack. Plus I dropped my keys getting you out of there. And there's one other thing."

She frowned at this next part.

"More of those creatures are out there."

The boy froze with dread.

"How many?"

"Three," Nana replied. "They're just creeping around outside right now but it's only a matter of time before they come in. But we'll be ready."

She motioned to the shotgun and while the boy knew guns were dangerous, he was also extremely grateful Nana had one. He wanted to ask her what time it was but something big crashed against the door of the shack, causing Nana to jump to her feet.

"Get under the table and stay there," she commanded, grabbing the shotgun.

"Nana!" the boy cried out as tears formed in his eyes.

"It'll be okay, my angel," she said as she pointed the business end of the shotgun at the door. There was another crash and the door broke apart completely. One of the creatures came in and growled at

Nana. She fired, striking the creature in the head. It let out a squeal that was so loud and high-pitched it caused the boy to cover his ears. The shotgun had sheared away part of its head and purple fluid splattered the wall behind it with an acidic hiss. The creature hit the ground with a loud thud, flopping around and sending spatters of its purple blood everywhere. Some of it struck Nana's arm and she cried out in pain.

"Nana!" the boy screamed but there was no time to rest. Another one crashed through the window and Nana spun around, racking the shotgun and killing it with one clean blast to the face. The buckshot shredded its horrible yellow eyes like newspaper. It was a ghastly sight but the boy couldn't help but take some joy in its demise. His ears rang from the loud blasts but save for the hissing of the blood that had come out of the creatures, there was silence.

"Are they gone?" he whispered.

Nana shook her head.

"There were three!" she insisted as she racked the shotgun again.

"Maybe the other one ran away!" the boy suggested.

Suddenly, the other creature burst through the wall behind him and flipped the table over. The boy shrieked and tried to crawl away but the thing grabbed him with its slimy, spade-shaped claw.

Nana ran over and swung the shotgun at it like a baseball bat. It caught the thing square in the chest but its grip on the boy remained firm.

Nana began to repeatedly strike creature's bullet-shaped skull with the butt of the shotgun. The room was a cacophony of the boy's screams, the creature's roars, and the meaty thud of the shotgun against its head. It finally relinquished its grip and backed away. The boy scurried away to safety and Nana pointed the barrel of the shotgun at the creature and fired. There was a squeal of pain and hiss of acidic blood as it was knocked back by the blast. It was over. All three of the creatures were dead.

An out-of-breath Nana dropped the shotgun and flopped down, the misshapen wound on her arm glistening in the moonlight. The sobbing boy went over to Nana and hugged her as tightly as he could. After a few moments, he finally calmed down and looked at Nana's sweaty face.

"What's going to happen now, Nana?"

Nana took another minute to catch her breath.

"We're going stay here until daylight," she answered, sounding almost like herself again. "Nothing's changed."

"But what if more of them come back?"

Nana held up the shotgun.

"Then we'll greet them the same way we greeted their friends."

The boy smiled. He had always thought Nana could do anything and she had just proven it. He sat back and looked at her arm.

"Are you hurt?"

"I'm fine," she said, pulling away from him.

The boy knew she was lying. As tough as Nana was, she was hurt and probably needed help. He knew he'd have to be firm with her.

"Let me see it, Nana!"

"I told you I'm fine," she said, her tone clipped and impatient.

"Remember when I skinned my knee on the gravel last summer and you took care of it right away because you said it's bad to let cuts go?"

"I think this is a little different," she said.

The boy reached for her arm and after a moment she slowly held it out to him. The boy finally got a good look at her wound. It stretched across her forearm like an ugly stain.

"We have to run it under cold water!" the boy exclaimed. "Mom says you have to run burns under cold water!"

"Warm water, actually," Nana said. "Your mother must not have been paying attention to me that day. And I'm pretty sure this place doesn't have running water."

"So what are we going to do about it?"

"Tough it out and wait until morning. Art and Sue will have medical supplies at their house."

"What if their house is gone, though?" the boy asked, thinking again of Nana's house and how easily it had been destroyed.

"Then we'll move on until we find a house that does have medical supplies," she answered confidently. "Now get some sleep. We've got a long day tomorrow."

"I don't think I can sleep!" the boy protested.

"Try," Nana said with a smile. "You'll need your rest."

"What about you?" the boy asked, his eyes falling to the gash on her arm that was still weeping blood.

"I'll catch a wink here and there," Nana said. "Old people need less sleep than kids."

"Are we going to find my mom and dad tomorrow?"

"Of course," Nana answered, loading fresh shells into the shotgun. "Now go to sleep."

The boy thought about saying something else but Nana's eyes were trained on the door. She was done talking. The boy closed his eyes.

Sleep came easier than he expected.

He awoke to find Nana looking out the window. He could see the light from the triangular-shaped crafts shining through the trees that surrounded the long-forgotten gambling shack. The boy feared they were going to make that strange humming sound that made him feel sick and dizzy. He looked over to see Nana staring at him.

"Go back to sleep," she said.

The boy stared back at her but her expression remained stern. One of the crafts flew directly overhead and her face was briefly illuminated by the bright light emanating from it but she didn't even blink. The boy sat back and closed his eyes. Something about her look let him know they'd be safe. And that was enough for him.

Nana woke the boy up at first light. She slung the shotgun over her shoulder and held her hand out. The boy took it and they set out on foot, hoping the day was more welcoming than the previous night had been. As they emerged from the woods, they saw the sky was an ugly gray that stretched endlessly in every direction. The lush green of the trees and grass also seemed strangely muted. It was as the attack had made everything in the world ill. They walked down the road and passed an open field filled with dead deer. Although they were hard to look at, the boy noticed there weren't any marks on them. It was as if they had died of fright mid-stride.

The boy pointed this out to Nana but she simply nodded and began to walk faster. They finally reached a ranch-style home with a yellow Jeep parked in the driveway. This gave the boy hope. Not only was the house still standing but they also had a car. Nana and the boy walked up to the front door and Nana gave it three loud knocks.

"Art?" she called out. "Sue? Are you home?"

Nana knocked again but there was no answer. She checked the front doorknob but it was locked.

"That's not good, is it?" the boy asked.

"It's not necessarily bad," Nana replied. "If they ran out of here in a hurry or were chased, they wouldn't have taken the time to lock the door."

She and the boy walked around to the back, which was a much more discouraging sight. The back door looked like it had been torn off its hinges. The doorframe was a mess of twisted metal and splintered wood. The boy had no desire to go inside so he planted his feet and refused to move any further.

Nana let go of his hand and looked down at him.

"I know you're scared but if we're going to get out of here, this could be our only way," she said. "It might be fine. Art's a big guy like your dad."

Although Nana intended this to be comforting, it actually caused the boy to suddenly fear the worst. There was a point last night where he was sure his parents were okay but what if those horrible things had taken him and his mom by surprise like they had done with Art and his wife? What if...

"Until we know for sure there's bad news, let's just assume everything's okay," Nana said as if reading his thoughts. "Now wait here."

She raised the shotgun and gave him a brave smile before disappearing into the house.

Nana didn't come out for a long time. The boy wasn't sure how long it had been but it seemed like forever. He couldn't hear anything, either. Somehow that made him more nervous than hearing gunshots or that awful humming sound. Suddenly, there was a loud explosion in the distance, startling the boy and prompting him to run inside the house.

He found himself in a kitchen that wasn't unlike Nana's. Everything looked old but still clean and cared for. A plate of oatmeal cookies was visible on the counter. The boy watched with distaste as a fat black fly crawled across them. A kid in the boy's class had told him that when flies crawled on your food, they tracked germs and even puked on it. Later that spring, the boy had thrown away a plate of chicken after he saw several flies crawling around on it. His father wasn't happy but the boy couldn't imagine eating fly puke.

"Nana?" he called out. He walked toward the hallway when a horrible smell filled his nostrils. It made his eyes water and caused him to gag as he stopped dead in his tracks.

"Nana?" he said, struggling not to throw up.

The only sound was the buzzing of the fat black fly staking its claim on the oatmeal cookies. For what seemed like the millionth time in the last couple of days, the boy started to cry but Nana finally answered him.

"In here," she replied, her voice a dull monotone.

"Where?" the boy asked.

"The living room," Nana said. "Turn left when you enter the hallway."

"It smells so bad, though!" the boy cried, covering his nose with his hands.

"It's better in the living room," Nana answered, her tone still strange and flat. The boy wondered if Nana's wounded arm had made her sick. He went into the living room and found Nana sitting in an easy chair. The shotgun was resting on a couch that was covered in clear, shiny plastic. Nana was staring at the photographs on the wall, most of them showing a happy older couple. The man was fat and had a big mustache that reminded the boy of Mario and Luigi. The woman was much thinner with oversized glasses and curly blonde hair. They looked nice.

"They're dead," Nana said.

The boy didn't know how to respond.

"They were upstairs on their bed," Nana continued. "Holding hands."

As she said this last part, a tear spilled down her cheek. That was the second time the boy had seen Nana cry and both times had been within the last day.

"Art and Sue were the two of the nicest people I've ever met," Nana said. "They didn't deserve that. And then these things also got poor Rich last night. And my house."

She paused as if trying to decide if all this was real or not.

"I'm afraid of what we might found out there, my angel."

The boy couldn't believe what he was hearing. Was Nana giving up?

She sat and wept for the next hour. The boy wanted to talk to her but he still didn't know what to say. He wanted to find his parents and for this nightmare to finally be over. That wouldn't be possible without Nana. He didn't know how to drive and he wouldn't know where to go even if he did. Unable to look at Nana at any longer, the boy went outside.

The sky still looked like it was made of aged pewter. The boy wondered if they would ever see the sun again. He walked further into the backyard when he saw something in the distance. It looked like the triangular-shaped crafts they had seen last night; only this one was much bigger. The boy could see smaller crafts being dispatched from it and he knew it was only a matter of time before they came back to finish the job they had begun the previous evening.

It was time for him and Nana to go.

The boy found Nana seated in the same chair with the same vacuous look on her face. The only signs of life were the tears slowly dripping down her cheeks. The boy went up to her and gently put his hand on her shoulder.

"Nana, we have to leave," he said.

Nana looked at him.

"Go where?" she asked. "There's nothing but death out there."

"We have to find Mom and Dad!" the boy responded, trying to mimic the same commanding tone Nana had used on him the night before. "They're probably already looking for us!"

"I wish that were true, my angel, but I honestly don't know anymore," Nana said without looking at the boy.

"I'm scared something bad might have happened to them, too," the boy replied. "But we have to try. Mom said when she stayed out all night one time you went looking for her. She said she was in big trouble when you found her!"

Nana's eyes finally came to life.

"Oh my, I had forgotten about that," she said. "She was at a bonfire with her friends and ended up falling asleep in her friend Debbie's car. And she was in big trouble! I grounded her for the rest of the summer. She didn't speak to me for months. She actually told you about that?"

"I heard her telling my dad about it," the boy answered. "And he said he could see you doing that because you never give up!"

"My job now is to keep you safe," Nana said. "It's what your parents would want."

"But you've already done that," the boy insisted. "Now we can find Mom and Dad and you can keep them safe, too. So come on!"

He did an exaggerated wave to get her moving while doing his best impression of his dad's lopsided grin. To the boy's relief, Nana laughed.

"Is being a ham what you do to get your way now?" she said, playfully raising her eyebrows at him.

"Is it working?" the boy asked.

Nana's hopeful smile was the only answered he needed.

Thirty minutes later they were on the road in Art and Sue's Jeep. The boy liked it. It wasn't a big car but it sounded powerful and had a full

413

tank of gas. The shotgun and some food Nana had taken from the kitchen were piled neatly in the backseat.

Nana turned on the radio and found a station that was broadcasting instructions on where to go and how to stay safe. It didn't seem like anyone knew exactly what was going on or where the attackers had come from but it seemed like everybody was regrouping and most importantly, surviving.

A lot had happened since the prior day but things were already improving. Even Nana's wound looked better. They had finally dressed and disinfected it before leaving and the boy was pleased to see it wasn't even bleeding through the bandage.

The road was mostly empty, save for the occasional burnt-out car or truck. It looked like they had suffered the same fate as Rich but the boy didn't let that faze him. As the man on the radio somberly read off the locations of safe zones, the boy found himself falling into a deep and dreamless sleep. It was okay because he knew things were going to be just fine.

He was with Nana.

He had nothing to worry about.

Acknowledgments

Special thanks go to Mom, Dad, and Jeanne for a lifetime of support and encouragement. To Joyce, Mike, Chris, David, and Eric for the years of memories and laughter (unintentional and otherwise). To Patty and Greg for your support of these stories from the get-go.

To Liz Von Notias for designing the awesome cover to the original edition of Stone Canyon. To Sionnan Wood for her assistance with the cover to this collection. To Jennie Harland for her feedback and insight on Rerouted. To Olaolu, Brian, Alex, Micah, Will, Nick Seibel, Nick Campbell, and Justin for your friendship (and shelter when I needed it). To Arlene, Renee, Dixie and the rest of the "Circle of Love" for the support, as well as the delicious drinks and food. To Hani, Bridgette, and Harrison for your kindness and friendship since my arrival on the West Coast. To Paul Frederick and Henry Danielson for your encouragement in high school. To Mac Nelson, Pam Kirst, and John Stinson for your encouragement in college. To Doug Eboch and Victoria Hochberg for your encouragement in grad school. To Eric Sherman for your guidance and invaluable teachings. To John Hartzog for the proofreading job that gave me much-needed income and helped keep my editing skills sharp. To Ross LaManna and Paul Guay for your encouragement and help with getting my work out there. And to all of you for purchasing this collection and for reading the acknowledgments. Thank you! Here's a bonus story:

Sullivan was on his second whiskey and Coke when he noticed the strange man seated at the end of the bar. The man certainly wasn't a regular at Billy's Tavern and Sullivan (Sully to his friends) would know. He had been a regular at Billy's for going on ten years now.

As he looked closer at the man, he realized he probably wasn't even from their town. He was dressed in all black and had skin so pale it was almost translucent. The only sign of color on him was a ruby ring he wore on his left pinky. That was what really got Sully's attention. If it weren't for the ring, he'd probably make a few cracks about the guy to Dale the bartender and be done with it. No, this strange man was somebody Sully wanted to get to know a little better. And as it was, it had been a couple of weeks since his last mark and he didn't want to risk getting rusty.

Sully grabbed his drink and strode confidently toward the man. As he got closer, he realized this guy wasn't just from out of town; he might not even be from the same fucking planet. He seemed to be almost floating in his sickly pale skin and his hound dog eyes looked black in the dim overhead lighting. Nonetheless, Sully had the man's attention. There was no turning back now.

"Howdy!" Sully said, giving him a friendly clap on the back.

The man nodded and continued to nurse the beer he had in front of him. Sully noticed he had peeled the label clean off.

"What are you drinking?" Sully asked him.

The man set the beer down and finally made eye contact.

"I'm not much of a talker," he said.

"Well, lucky for you, I am," Sully said, his grin becoming wide and lupine. "I know everybody that comes into this bar. I'm practically the owner. As such, it's up to me to welcome you!"

"That's really not necessary," the man replied as he began to fidget with the ruby ring that would soon belong to Sully.

"Dale!" Sully bellowed. "Two shots of Cuervo!"

"You really don't have to…" the man started to say but it was too late. Dale was already pouring the shots. He brought them over and set them down in front of Sully and the strange man.

Sully raised his shot.

"To new friends!"

The man looked around and realized he was now the center of everyone's attention. He obediently picked up his shot and clinked his glass against Sully's. They both drank and Sully slammed his glass down on the bar.

"That's the stuff!" he proclaimed. "One more!"

"I really can't..." the man started to say but Dale had already poured the shots. Sully and the strange man raised their glasses and drank again.

"Hat trick!" he yelled at Dale, knowing full well that the third one was going to be the charm. It almost always was. Dale poured the shots and they drank. Sully looked into the man's charcoal-colored eyes and was pleased to note they were already getting bloodshot.

This was going to be his easiest mark yet.

They downed two more before Sully went in for the kill.

"Drinking contest!" he announced to the cheers of the other patrons. "Winner picks up the loser's tab plus..."

He drew this last part out, as if he were a game show host announcing an amazing prize. Which was true. It just wasn't going to the other guy. It never did.

"If you win, you get my car," he said, holding up a set of keys. "A brand-new Dodge Charger parked right out back!"

And there was a brand-new Dodge Charger parked right out back. It just didn't belong to Sully, who was quite the fan of hat tricks. In fact, he had scored his third DUI a mere six months ago. That particular hat-trick had cost him his driver's license. He had been on foot ever since then. But did this guy need to know that?

"And what happens if you win?" the man asked, his eyes bloodshot but still knowing.

"Your ring!" Sully said, holding up the man's hand so everybody could see it.

The man quickly pulled his hand away and tucked it under his other arm.

"Do we have a deal?" Sully asked him.

The man stared back at him and for a second, Sully thought he was going to refuse. That meant Phase 2, which involved Sarah, another upstanding regular at Billy's. She'd sweet-talk the guy and talk about all the rides they could take in a new car. Sarah wasn't much to look at but she knew what men liked to hear and after a few shots of tequila, any woman looked fine enough. Sully had learned that lesson the hard way on more than a few occasions.

Just as Sully was about to nod at Sarah to do her thing, the man smiled.

"You've got a deal."

The bar erupted in applause. The spider had caught himself another fly.

The contest began like usual, with Dale pouring the first two shots and Sully trading his for the one in front of his mark. While it seemed like a meaningless gesture on the surface, it actually proved quite effective for what came next. Sully would down the first shot with his mark and then Dale would pour another round for each of them, only Sully's was pure water. All his shots after the first one were but his marks were oblivious to this. It was a perfect system that had yet to fail him.

This particular night was shaping up to the exception, though. They were four shots in when Sully began to grow concerned. Usually his opponents were showing fatigue by now and while the man's eyes were bloodshot, they still retained that odd knowing look.

For one delirious moment, Sully wondered if Dale wasn't accidentally serving the man shots of water as well. He almost said something but stopped himself. That was ridiculous. Dale would probably clear a hundred bucks after Sully sold the ring. Why sabotage that?

They drank five more and Sully was baffled. The man didn't appear affected at all. How was that possible?

"Give up?" the strange man asked Sully, his black eyes twinkling.

"Are you kidding?" Sully responded. "I'm in my prime!"

He said this last part in his best impression of Val Kilmer in Tombstone but he couldn't deny he was getting more nervous. How much longer could this go before they were dragging this poor bastard out on a stretcher?

"How about two more?" his new friend suggested and that's when Sully knew he had him. The guy was mortal but Christ, what a poker face.

"And then what?" Sully asked. "You give up?"

"I guess I do," the man replied with a helpless shrug.

"Line 'em up, Dale!" Sully said, already thinking about how he was going to spend the money he'd get from selling the man's ring.

As Dale started to pour the shots, Sully knocked on the bar three times. Dale understood. He was to switch back to booze for Sully. There were only two shots to go and what the hell, he had earned it. He was looking at a thousand easy for that ring.

The strange man held up his glass and Sully knocked his against it and drank. One more and the ring was his. The man smiled at Sully and slid the final shot over to him. Sully almost admired the man's attitude. Most of his marks were either too drunk to function by now or they became morose, sometimes even belligerent. This guy was downright cheerful. It was enough to arouse suspicion in Sully but he was too close to the finish line now to start second-guessing.

"You put up a hell of a fight, my friend. I salute you!" Sully exclaimed as he raised the glass to his lips and drank.

The tequila went down bitter but there was something else. It was hard and sharp and blocked Sully's windpipe. He began to gasp and choke but whatever it was had lodged itself deep inside his throat. It wasn't going anywhere.

Amused, the strange man finished his last shot and stood up.

"Thank you for the entertainment, good sir. It was truly a memorable evening."

He walked toward the exit as Dale and a few of the other patrons surrounded Sully to try and help him.

As Sully struggled to breathe, he watched the man exit the bar and noticed that he looked exactly as he did when Sully had first noticed him.

Only his ring was missing.

www.ingramcontent.com/pod-product-compliance
Lightning Source LLC
Chambersburg PA
CBHW072106250626
47159CB00007B/2319